ACROSS THE STREAM

BY

E. F. BENSON

British Library Cataloguing-in-Publication Data
A catalogue record for this book is available from the
British Library

E. F. Benson

Edward Frederic Benson was born at Wellington College (where his father was headmaster) in Berkshire, England in 1867. He was educated at Marlborough College, where he proved himself as an excellent athlete, representing England at figure skating, and published his first novel, *Dodo* (1893), when he was 26. The novel was quite popular, and Benson eventually expanded it into a trilogy (*Dodo the Second*, in 1914, and *Dodo Wonders*, in 1921). Nowadays, Benson is principally known for his 'Mapp and Lucia' series about Emmeline "Lucia" Lucas and Elizabeth Mapp. The series consists of six novels and two short stories, and remains popular to this day, being serialized for Radio 4 as recently as 2008. Benson was also a respected writer of ghost stories – indeed, H. P. Lovecraft spoke very highly of him, especially his story 'The Man Who Went Too Far'. Benson died of throat cancer in 1940, aged 72.

INTRODUCTION

There is a very large class of persons alive to-day who believe that not only is communication with the dead possible, but that they themselves have had actual experience of it. Many of these are eminent in scientific research, and on any other subject the world in general would accept their evidence.

There is possibly a larger class of persons who hold that all such communications, if genuine, come not from the dead but from the devil. This is the taught opinion of the Roman Catholic Church.

A third class, far more numerous than both of these, is sure that any one who holds either of these beliefs is a dupe of conjurers, or the victim of his own disordered brain. This type of robust intellect has, during the last ten decades, affirmed that hypnotism, aviation in machines heavier than air, telepathy, wireless telegraphy, and other non-proved phenomena, are superstitious and unscientific balderdash. In an earlier century it was equally certain that the earth did not go round the sun. It is, happily, never disconcerted by the frequency with which the superstitions and impossibilities of one generation become the science of the next.

The first part of this book may be accepted by the first of these three classes, the second by the second, and none of it by the third. Its aim is to state rather than solve the subject with which it deals, and to suggest that the dead and the devil alike may be able to communicate with the living.

E. F. BENSON.

BOOK I

CHAPTER I

Certain scenes, certain pictures of his very early years of childhood, stood out for Archie like clear sunlit peaks above the dim clouds that shrouded the time when the power of memory was only beginning to germinate. He had no doubt (and was probably right about it) as to which the earliest of those was: it was the face of his nurse Blessington, leaning over his crib. She held a candle in her hand which a little dazzled him, but the sight of her face, tender and anxious, and divinely reassuring, was the point of that memory. He had been asleep, and had awoke with a start, and, finding himself alone in the midst of the immense desolation of the dark that pressed on him like an invader from all sides, he had lifted up his voice and yelled. Then, as by a conjuring-trick, Blessington had appeared with her comforting presence that quite robbed the dark of its terrors. It must still have been early in the night, for she had not yet gone to bed, and had on above her smooth grey hair her cap with its adorable blue ribands in it. At her throat was the brooch made of the same stuff as the shining shillings with which a year or two later she bought the buns and sponge-cakes for tea. He remembered no more than that; he knew nothing of what she had said: the whole of that memory consisted in the fact of the secure comfort and relief which her face brought. It was just a vignette of memory, the earliest of all; there was nothing whatever before it, and nothing for some time after.

Gradually the horizon widened; scenes and situations in which Archie was still a detached observer, as if looking through a telescope, made themselves visible. He remembered gazing through the bars of the high nursery fire-guard at the joyful glow of the fuel. At the corner of the grate (he remembered this with extreme distinctness), there was a black coal, the edge of which was soft and bubbly. A thin streamer of smoke blew out of it, and from time to time this smoke caught light and flared very satisfactorily. But all that, the joyfulness and the satisfaction, was external to him; it was the coals and the streams of burning gas that were in themselves joyful and satisfactory. That must have been in the winter, and it was in the same winter perhaps that he came home with Blessington and two other children—girls, and larger than himself—whom he grew to believe were his sisters, through a wood of fir-trees between the trunks of which shone a round red ball that resembled the coals in the nursery-grate. He knew—perhaps Blessington, perhaps a sister, perhaps his mother had told him—that it was Christmas Eve, and he saw that when Blessington spoke to him she steamed delightfully at the mouth, as if there had been a hot bath just inside her lips. At her suggestion he found he could do it, too, and his sisters also; whereafter they played hot-baths all the way home. But of the Christmas Day that followed he had no recollection whatever.

His observation became a little less detached; he began to form in his mind an explorer's map of the places where these phenomena occurred, to be dimly aware that he was taking some sort of part in them, and was not a mere spectator, and one summer evening he definitely knew that the day-nursery and the night-nursery and the room beyond where his sisters slept were all part of the red-brick house which he and others inhabited, just as, according to Blessington, the rabbit which he had seen pop into its hole in the wood beyond the lawn, had a home within it. He had already had his bath, on a patch of sunlight that lay across the nursery-floor, and escaping, slippery as a trout, from Blessington's towelling hands, had run with a squeal of delight across to the window. Outside was the lawn, which hitherto he had thought of as a thing apart, a picture by itself, and beyond was the wood where the rabbit had a house. On the lawn was his mother, playing croquet with his two sisters, and of a sudden it flashed upon him that the wood and the rabbit, the lawn and the croquet-players, the night-nursery, Blessington, the shine of the sun low in the west, and his own wet self were all in some queer manner part of the same thing, and made up that to which he and Blessington went back when, at the limit of their walk, she said it was time to go home.

"Oh, there's mummy," he cried. "Mummy!" And he danced naked at the window.

Blessington caught him in the towel again.

"Well, I never!" she said. "That's not the way for a young gentleman to behave. There, let me dry you, dear, and put your night-shirt on, and you shall say good-night to your mamma out of the window."

This was duly done, and it struck Archie as a very novel and delightful discovery that he could say good-night to his mother when she was on the croquet-lawn and he up in the night-nursery. It shed a new light on existence generally, and coloured with a new interest the few drowsy moments which intervened between his being put into bed and falling asleep. Blessington still moved quietly about the room, emptying his bath, and putting his clothes tidy, and he just remembered her kissing him when she had finished. He was already too suffused with drowsiness to make any response, and he slid softly out over the tides of sleep.

That night he became acquainted with a new sort of experience, something hitherto quite foreign to him. Once again he woke in the night and found himself surrounded by the vast dark, save where, in a corner of the nursery, there burned the shaded night-light. But now there was no sense of terror; he did not want to call for Blessington, but lay open-eyed and absorbed in the amazing thing that was happening. The night-nursery (where he knew he was), and he with it, were expanding and extending, till they comprised the lawn and the wood beyond the lawn, and all else that he had ever known. His sisters and his mother and father were all there, though he could not see them; Blessington was there, and Graves the butler, and Walter and William, the two footmen. He could not see them, any more than he could see the moon and the sun, which were there also, but they were there as part of an unusual presence that filled the place. He could not see that unusual presence either, but it was tremendously real and filled him not in the least with awe, but with the feeling with which Blessington's face and his mother's face inspired him… And the next thing that he was aware of was the rattle of the blind, and Blessington's voice saying, "Eh, what a time of morning to have slept to. I know a sleepy-head!"

He recounted this remarkable experience to Blessington at breakfast, who was quite sure that it was all a dream; a nice dream, but a dream.

"Wasn't a dream," said Archie firmly.

"And where did Mr. Contradiction go?" asked Blessington.

Archie knew where Mr. Contradiction went, for Mr. Contradiction lived in a very dull corner of the nursery with his face to the wall for five minutes.

"Well, it didn't seem like a dream," he said. "May I get down?"

"Yes, and say your grace."

"Thank God for my good dinner," said Archie, who was not attending.

"Say it again, dear," said Blessington; "and think."

"I meant breakfast," said Archie. "Amen."

The discovery of the connection, made last night, between himself in the night-nursery and his mother on the lawn, which proved that the lawn and the house were part of the same thing, produced further results that day. Instead of memory consisting of different and severed pictures, it began to flow into one coherent whole. He knew, of course, already that at the end of the nursery passage was a wooden wicket-gate, and that outside that was the long gallery that skirted round three sides of the hall, while on the fourth ran a broad staircase each step of which had to be surmounted and descended either by a series of jumps, or, if the feet were tired, by the extension of one foot on to the next stair where it was joined by the other; but he began now to put these isolated facts together, and form them into the conception of a house. When the staircase was negotiated you found yourself in a large oak-floored hall, where you were not allowed to slide on purpose, though both Blessington and his mother had the sense to distinguish between deliberate and unintentional slidings. There were bright rugs spread here and there over the hall, forming islands in a glassy sea. Archie knew it was not made of glass really, but he chose to think that it was, for it had the qualities of a looking-glass in that it reflected his own bare-legged form above it, and the slipperiness of glass as exhibited in the window-panes of the nursery, and he chose also to think that it was to the hall-floor that the hymn alluded which was sung last Sunday morning in a dazzling and populous place to which his mother had taken him. The people who sang loudest were two rows of boys dressed in crinkly white night-shirts, in company with some grown-up men who were attired in the same curious manner. But none of them went to bed, and at a pause in the proceedings Archie had suddenly asked his mother, in a piercing voice, why they didn't go to bed. Evidently that had puzzled her too, for she had no reply to give him except "Hush, darling!" which wasn't an answer at all. Then another man had begun talking all by himself. He had a quantity of hair on his chin which wagged in so delightful a manner when he spoke that Archie watched him entranced for a little, and then, afraid that his mother was missing this lovely sight, said:

"O mummy, *isn't* that a funny man?"

Upon which Blessington, magically communicated with, appeared by his side and whispered that they were going for a walk, and towed him down the aisle, still rapturously looking back at the funny man. Archie had thought it all very entertaining, but he was told afterwards by his father that he had disgraced himself and should not go to church again for many Sundays to come.

Archie was frightened of his father, and always went warily by the door of the room at the dark corner of the hall where this tremendous person lived. There were other dangers about that corner, for on the floor were two tiger-skins which looked as if the animal in question had, with the exception of its head, been squashed out flat, like as when he and Blessington sometimes put a flower they had gathered on their walks between two sheets of blotting-paper, and piled books on the top, so that it ceased to be a flower, and became the map of a flower. Archie wished the tigers' heads had been pressed in the same way; as it was, they were disconcertingly solid and life-like, with long teeth and snarling mouths and glaring eyes. He had always made Blessington come right up to his father's door with him when he went in to say good-night, so that she should pilot him safely past the tigers on his entry and escort him by them again on his return. But one night his father had come out with him, and, finding Blessington waiting there, had divined, as by some awful black magic, why the nurse was waiting, and had decreed that Archie should in future make his way across the danger zone unattended. But, next evening, the trembling Archie, hurrying away in the dusk, had fallen down on the glassy sea between the awful Scylla and Charybdis, and, convinced that his last hour had come, when these two cruel heads beheld him prostrate on the floor, had cried himself to sleep from terror of that awful ending. But next day his mother, who understood about things in general better than anybody, had caused the tigers to make friends with him, and in token of their amity they had each of them presented him with a whisker-hair. That assured their friendship, and they wished it to be understood that their snarlings and glarings were directed, not at Archie, but at Archie's enemies. This naturally changed their whole aspect, and Archie, after he had wished his father good-night, kissed the hairy heads that had once been so terrifying, and thanked them for successfully keeping his enemies from molesting him.

But though now the presence of the tigers, ceasing to be a terror by night, had become a protection to Archie, their corner of the hall still constituted a danger zone to be gone by swiftly and silently, lest a raised voice or an incautious noise should cause him to be called from within the closed door of his father's room. There were risks in that room; you never quite knew whether you were not going to be blamed for doing something which you had no idea was blame-worthy. One day Archie had found a lovely wax match with a blue head to it on the floor, and had put it in his pocket, where he fingered it delightedly, for he knew it to be the sort which flamed when you rubbed it against your boot or the bricks of the house, as he had seen his father do. But then, when a little later he had come to sit on his father's knee and be shown pictures in a book of natural history, it was detected that his small fingers smelled of phosphorus, and when the reason was discovered, he was told by his father that he had stolen that match. To Archie's mind there was something inexplicably unfair and unjust about this; he knew quite well that the match was not his, but he had no idea that it was stealing if you appropriated something that was dropped on the floor. A thing dropped on the floor was nobody's, and anybody, so he supposed, might take it. It had been quite another affair when he had taken eight lumps of sugar out of the basin on the tea-table in the drawing-room and hidden them in his domino-box. He had been perfectly well aware that he was stealing them, and had no sense of injustice when his mother had promptly and soundly smacked him for it. But he intensely resented being told by his father that he had stolen (even though he was not smacked) when he had not the least idea that a match dropped on the floor was a stealable article at all, and he felt it far more bitter to be unjustly blamed than justly punished.

"But I didn't know it was stealing, daddy," said he.

"But didn't you know it wasn't yours?"

"Yes."

"And didn't you know that to take what isn't yours is stealing?"

Archie couldn't explain, but he was still quite sure he had not been stealing…

His father's room then, at least when that potentate was in it, was a place where extreme caution was necessary, and, however cautious you were (he had not felt guilty of the smallest temerity in picking up that match), you could never be quite sure that Fate, like some great concealed cat, would not pounce upon you from the most unexpected quarter. But, considered in itself, the room had a tremendous attraction for him. There was a delicious smell about it, subtly compounded of the leather backs of books and the aroma of tobacco, which to Archie's dawning perception had something virile and masculine about it. He could understand the manliness of the place, it answered to something that was shared by him, and not shared by his mother or Blessington or his sisters, and belonged to a man. The furniture and the appurtenances of the room conveyed the same message; they were strong and solid, without frillings or frippery, and had a decisive air and a purpose about them which somehow concerned that mysterious difference between boys and girls and between men and women. His mother's sitting-room, it is true, seemed to Archie a fairy-palace of loveliness, with its spindle-legged tables, its lace-edged curtains, its soft, silky cushions, its china, its glittering silver toys on a particular black lacquer table, its nameless feminine fragrance. But this room, with its solid leather chairs, which held small limbs as in a tender male embrace, its gun-case in the corner, its whip-rack, its few solid, sober pictures which hung above the book-shelves, struck a different and more intimate and more intelligible note. Archie felt that he knew what it was all about... it was about a man, to which *genus* he himself belonged. This particular specimen, his father, might be unjust to him, and severe to him, but in some secret inexplicable manner Archie understood him, though fearing him, better than he understood either his mother or Blessington, both of whom he loved. His two sisters, in the same way, had a quality of enigma about them.

These floating impressions, the untranslatable instincts of early childhood, began to thicken, when Archie was getting on for six years old, into thoughts capable of being solidified into language. He could not have solidified them himself, but if any one capable of presenting them to him in actual words had asked him, "Is it this you mean?" he would have assented. And his solidified thoughts would have taken the following mould:

There was something odd about females, and it was a mystery into which he did not at all want to enquire. They wore skirts, which perhaps concealed some abnormality, which would be fearful to contemplate. They had soft faces and soft bodies; when his mother took him on her knee—she already said that he was getting too big a boy to sit on her knee, which to Archie sounded very grand and delightful—she was soft to his shoulder, and her cheek was soft to his. But when he sat on his father's knee he felt a hard, firm substance behind him, and the contrast was similar to the contrast between his mother's soft cushions and his father's leather-clad chairs. And his father had a hard, bristly cheek on which to receive Archie's good-night kiss. Judged by the standards of pleasure and luxury, it was not nearly as nice as his mother's, but it gave him, however great need there was for caution, a sense of identity with himself.

He was of that species... And this conception of abnormality in women was strongly confirmed when, one morning, he went as usual to his mother's bedroom to see her before she went down to breakfast. She had been late in getting up that day, and, not finding her in her bedroom, Archie's attention had been arrested by hearing sounds from her bathroom next door, and very naturally had turned the handle in order to enter. But a voice from inside had said:

"Is that you, darling? Wait just a minute."

"But I want to come in now," said Archie. "I'm coming in."

"Archie, I shall be very angry if you come in before I give you leave," said the voice. Then there were rustlings. "Come in now."

And there was his mother standing by her bath, which smelt deliciously fragrant, in a lovely blue bath-towel dressing-gown.

"Good-morning, darling," said she. "But you must never come into a lady's bathroom unless she gives you leave."

"Why not?" said Archie. "You come to see me in my bath without my saying 'Yes.'"

She gave that delicious bubble of laughter that reminded Archie of the sound of cool lemonade being poured out of the bottle.

"I shan't when you're as old as me," she said. "I shall always ask your leave. And probably you won't give it me."

"Why not? It's only me," said Archie.

"You'll know when you're older," said she.

Archie rather despised that argument: it seemed to apply to so many situations in life. But he had already formed the very excellent habit of crediting his mother with the gift of common sense, for was it not she who had discovered that the snarl of the tiger-heads was a snarl not at Archie, but at his enemies? But on this occasion it merely confirmed his conviction that women were somehow deformed. They wore skirts instead of breeches, and though, judging by his younger sister, they were normal up to about the level of the knee, it seemed likely that their legs extended no farther, but that they became like peg-tops, swelling out in one round piece till their bodies were reached. What confirmed this impression was that they seemed to run from their knees instead of striding with a swung leg. Blessington always ran like that: her feet twinkled in ridiculously short steps, and after a moment or two she said:

"Eh, I can't run any more. I've got a bone in my leg."

"And haven't I?" asked Archie.

"No, dear: you're just made of gristle and quicksilver," said Blessington, with a sudden lyrical spasm as she looked at the shining face of her most beloved.

"What's quicksilver?" asked Archie. "And why haven't I got a bone in my leg? O-o-oh!" and a sudden thought struck him. "Have women got bones in their legs and not boys? Is that why they can't run properly? Mummy can't run, nor can you; but William can, damn him."

"Master Archie!" said Blessington in her most severe voice.

"What for?" asked Archie.

"You must never say that, Master Archie," said Blessington, who only called him Master Archie on impressive occasions. "You must never say what you said after 'William can.'"

"But daddy said it to William this morning," said Archie.

Blessington still wore the iron mask on her face. It was lucky for her that Archie did not know how puzzled she was as to the correct answer.

"Your papa says what he thinks fit," she said, "and that is right for him. But young gentlemen never say it."

"How old shall I have to be——" began Archie.

"And look at your shoe-lace all untied," said Blessington with extreme promptitude. "Do it up at once, or you'll be treading on it. And then it will be time for you to go in, and you can write your letter to Miss Marjorie before your dinner."

Miss Marjorie was the elder of Archie's two sisters. She was ten years older than he, and at the present time was staying with her grandmother, whom Archie strongly suspected of being either a witch or a man. She was large and rustling, and had a bass voice and a small moustache and a small husband, who was an earl, to whom, when he came to stay with Archie's father, who appeared to be his son, every one paid a great deal of unnecessary attention. Both of them, Archie's father, and Archie's father's father, were lords, and Archie distinctly thought he ought to be a lord too, considering that both his father and his grandfather were. Blessington had hinted that he would be a lord too, some day, if he were good, but when pressed she couldn't say when. In fact, there was a ridiculous reticence about the whole matter, for when he had asked his mother, in the presence of his grandfather, when he was going to be a lord, his grandfather, quite inexplicably, had giggled with laughter, and said:

"I've got one foot in the grave already, Archie, and you want me to have both."

That was a very cryptic remark, and when Archie asked William the footman what grandpapa Tintagel had meant, William had said that he couldn't say, sir. On which Archie, looking hastily round, and feeling sure that Blessington was not present, had repeated "Damn you, William," as daddy said.

Then William, after endeavouring not to show two rows of jolly white teeth, had said:

"You must never say that to me, Master Archie."

In fact, there was clearly a league. Blessington and William, who didn't love each other, as Archie had ascertained by direct questions to each, were at one over the question of him not saying that. Under the stress of independent evidence, Archie decided not to say it any more, without further experiments as to the effect "it" would have on his mother. If William and Blessington were both agreed about it, it had clearly better not be done, any more than it was wise to walk about among the flowers of the big, herbaceous border. The gardener and the gardener's boy and his mother were all of one mind about that, and the gardener's boy had threatened to turn the hose on to him if he caught him at it. The gardener's boy was quite grown up, and so for Archie he had a weight of authority that befitted his years.

It was a lovely, disconnected life. There were all sorts of delightful and highly coloured strands that contributed to it, and others of a more sombre hue, and others again quite secret, which concerned Archie alone, and of which he never spoke to anybody. Of the delightful and highly coloured strands there were many. Waking in the morning, and knowing that there was going to be another day was one of them, and perhaps that was the most delightful of all except when, rarely, it was clouded with some trouble of the evening before, as when Archie had broken a window in his father's study in the laudable attempt to kill a wasp with a fire-shovel, and had been told by Blessington that his father wished to see him the moment he was dressed in the morning. But usually the wakings were ecstatic; and often he used to return to consciousness in those summer months long before Blessington came in to call him. The window was always open—all the windows in the night-nursery were opened as soon as he got into bed—and the blinds were up, and on the ceiling was the most delicious green light, for the early sun shone through the branches of the beeches outside, and painted Archie's ceiling with a pale, milky green which was adorable to contemplate. He would pull up his night-shirt, and with his bare arms clasp his bare knees, and, lying on his back, rather unsteadily anchored, would roll backwards and forwards looking at the green light, and rehearsing all the delightful probabilities of the day. Sometimes his mother had promised him that he should go out fishing on the lake when his lessons were done, and this implied the wonderful experience of seeing Walter or William come out on to the lawn, and pour out of a tin gardening can a mixture of mustard and water. When the footman did that it was certain that in a short time the grass would be covered with worms, which William put in a tin box lined with moss. Then Archie and William, sometimes with a sister, whose presence, Archie thought, was not wholly desirable, since she impeded the free flow of talk between him and William, would go down to the lake, and William, who could do everything, put worms on hooks (they did not seem to mind, for they said no word of protest), and sculled across to the sluice above which was deep water, where the fish fed, and away from the reeds, where the line got entangled, so that it was impossible to know whether you were engaged with a fish or a vegetable. The fishing-rod came out of his father's study—that was another delightful male attribute about the room—and when Archie went in to ask for it, William came too, not in his livery, but in ordinary clothes, and his father said, "Take good care of Master Archie, William. Good sport, Archie." Sometimes again, if he was not busy, Lord Davidstow came out with Archie instead of William. That was somehow an honour, but Archie did not like it so much.

Once there was a great happening. William produced a curious object that looked like the bowl of a spoon with hooks set all round it. He said there were going to be no worms this time, and, instead of drifting about, he rowed up and down, while Archie, with his rod over the stern, saw the spoon flashing through the water. Then a great shadow came over it, and Archie felt the rod bend in his hands. He was so excited that he stepped on to the seat of the boat, in order to see better, and promptly fell overboard.

He was not the least frightened, and rather enjoyed the splash and the sense of soda-water round him. With both hands he held on to the fishing-rod, which seemed an absolutely essential thing to do, and sank down, down in the deep water, seeing it green and yellow above his head. And then instantly he knew he was going to be drowned, and a feeling precisely identical to that which he had experienced one night when he woke, of a universal presence round about him, took complete possession of him. Then, even before he was conscious of the least sense of choking or discomfort, but was still only aware of coolness and depth and greenness, a great dark splaying object came right down upon him from above, and he found himself tucked underneath a human arm, coatless and in shirt-sleeves which he took to be William's. But still Archie did not let go of the fishing-rod, and mistakenly trying to speak, bidding William take care of it, his mouth and apparently his whole interior filled with water, and drowning suddenly seemed to be a disagreeable process. Next moment, however, his head emerged from the water again, and William caught hold of the boat.

"Let go the rod, Master Archie," said he, "and catch hold of the boat."

"But there's a fish on it," spluttered Archie.

"Do as I tell you, sir," said William quite crossly.

Archie had been told that, when he went out in the boat with William, he had to do precisely as William told him. He was not, it is true, in the boat at the moment, but the injunction probably applied. So he let go of the rod, and the moment afterwards found himself violently propelled over the side of the boat, and tumbled all abroad on the floor of it. They were but a dozen yards from land, and William having once got Archie into the boat, grabbed hold of the rod with his spare hand, and swam, shoving the boat in front of him.

"Oh, well done, William. Oh, William, I love you," screamed Archie when, having righted himself, he observed this brilliant manoeuvre. "Is the fish there still?"

William scrambled up the bank, still holding the rod.

"Run indoors at once, Master Archie," he said. "Don't wait a moment."

"But William, is the fish—" began Archie.

"Do as I tell you, sir," said William again. "I'll bring the fish for you, if I get him."

Archie ran with backward glances across the lawn, where he was met by Blessington who had observed the accident out of the window, and, before he could explain half the thrilling things that had happened, was undressed and rubbed down and put between blankets. And then, after a few minutes, in came William, having also changed his clothes, with a great pike, and his father followed and shook hands with William, and his mother did the same, saying things that made William blush and stand first on one foot and then on the other, murmuring: "It was nothing at all, my lady," and Archie asked if he and William might go out again that afternoon, and catch another pike. Then in came his younger sister, Jeannie, who was only two years his senior. She appeared to be on the point of crying, and she flung her arms round Archie's neck in an uncomfortable sort of way, and Archie told her she was messing him. After that, in reaction from those thrilling affairs, he felt suddenly tired, and, being encouraged to go to sleep, nestled down in the blankets and woke up to find that there was his fish stuffed for dinner, and for himself and William an era of unexampled popularity.

Archie did not understand at the time why he had suddenly blossomed into such favouritism, unless it was for having clung tight to his father's fishing-rod but he enjoyed it immensely. It was pleasant, too, not long afterwards, to be given a gold watch by his father, to present to William, with a gold chain provided by his mother. And William permitted him to put the gold watch into one waistcoat pocket, and the end of the gold chain into the other, and his father and mother and Jeannie all shook hands with William again (every one seemed to be spending their time in shaking hands with William). So Archie, since William was his friend more than anybody else's, kissed him, in order to mark the difference between himself and other people with regard to him. He was surprised to find that William had got a soft cheek like his mother's, and supposed that men's faces grew hard as they grew older. He instantly mentioned this surprising fact, and William appeared rather glad to leave the room. But in all Archie's life no event ever occurred which approached the splendour and public magnificence of this whole experience.

Every day the world widened, and, lying looking at the green light on the ceiling in the cool still mornings of that summer which seemed to last for years and years, Archie found himself not only speculating on what fresh joys the day would bring, but joining together in his mind the happenings that at the time seemed disconnected, but which proved to be part of a continuous thread of existence. Just as the nursery passage, and the steep stairs, and his father's room, and the lawn, and the lake passed from being isolated phenomena into pieces of a whole, so things that happened proved to be the experiences of the person who was known to others as Archie Morris, and to Archie as himself. Sometimes he so tingled with vigour when he woke that, contrary to orders, he stepped out of bed and leaned out of the window, to look at the bright dewy world, with one ear alert to hear Blessington's foot along the passage, in order to leap back into bed again, for now he had the night-nursery to himself, and Blessington slept next door. At that hour the lawn would be covered with a shimmering grey mantle, pearl-coloured, and here and there a few diamonds had got in by mistake which shone with just the brilliance of his mother's necklace. Perhaps these were the bed-clothes of the lawn, and when day came, they were covered over by the green bed-spread like that which lay on his own bed. The lake away to the right had different bed-clothes, thicker ones, but of the same colour. No doubt they were thicker because the lake was colder, for on some mornings he could not see through them at all. To the left, out of the window, rose the wood where the rabbits lived; sometimes one of them, an early riser like Archie, would have found a gap in the netting and was out on the lawn nibbling the grass. The gardener did not approve of that, for the lawn, it appeared, belonged to the people who lived in Archie's house, and not to the folk in the wood, and this was a trespass on the part of the rabbits, for which the punishment, rather a severe one, was death by shooting. This had added a new terror to the notice in another wood where he and Blessington sometimes walked, which announced that trespassers would be prosecuted. Blessington was foolhardy enough to disregard that notice altogether, saying that it was his daddy's notice, and didn't apply to them; but for some time Archie never chose that walk for fear that Blessington might be wrong about it, and that they would meet somebody in the wood who would instantly shoot them both for trespassing. But in childish fashion he kept those terrors to himself, sooner than enquire about them, till one day they actually did meet in that wood a man with a gun. Then in a sudden wild terror Archie clung to Blessington, crying out, "Oh, ask him not to shoot us this time!"

"Eh, darling," said Blessington. "Who's going to shoot us? It's only one of your daddy's keepers."

"No, but he will shoot us," screamed Archie. "We're trespassers, and he'll shoot us like the rabbits."

Matters being thereupon explained, and Archie convinced that he and Blessington were not going to be shot for trespassing, he found that he could make up for himself an entrancing story of how Master Rabbit and his nurse (who were good) never trespassed on the lawn, and that the rabbits he saw there corresponded to Grandmamma Tintagel, and so he did not care whether they were shot or not.

These stories which he told himself in the early morning, looking out on to the lawn, or lying curled up on his back in bed, looking at the green ceiling, were not vague, dream-like imaginings, but were endowed with a vividness that made Blessington's entry with his bath and his clothes seem less real than they. It became impossible indeed for him to disentangle reality (as judged by people like his father and the gardener) from imagination. He told himself so strongly that there was Grandmamma Tintagel sitting on the lawn, trespassing and nibbling grass for her breakfast, that her presence there, or her absence when there was no trespassing rabbit, became things as vivid as his subsequent dressing and breakfast. Had he been definitely asked if he believed it was Grandmamma Tintagel, he would have said "No"; but in his imaginative life, so hard for a child to dissociate from his real life, there was no question as to her identity. It happened also that at this time his mother was reading to him the realest of all books, namely, *Alice in Wonderland*. No imaginative boy of five could possibly doubt the actual existence of the White Rabbit in that convincing history, and Archie would not have been surprised if, one morning, there had proved to be a white rabbit sitting by the fence, who looked at his watch and put on his gloves. Yet he never spoke of this possibility even to Blessington or William; it did not belong to the sphere of things about which it was reasonable to converse to grown-up people, simply because they were stupid about certain matters and would not understand him. The fact that Grandmamma Tintagel sometimes sat on the lawn in the early morning was among the topics which he kept quite completely to himself.

There were other such topics. Sometimes, when he lay in bed, waiting for Blessington to call him, and did not choose to get up and look out of the window, it was because these other secret affairs engaged him. If he lay still, and stared at the green-hued ceiling, curious waves of shadow appeared to pass over it, and it seemed like that sunny floor of water that had closed above his head on the morning when he fell out of the boat. There was he lying in bed deep below some surface of liquid light that cut him off from the outer world, and he wondered if in a moment a splayed starfish of arms and legs which turned out to be William would dive down for him, and bring him up among the common things again. But William never made this impressive entry through the ceiling, and if he stared long enough, Archie only seemed to himself to slip down and down, gently and rapturously, through deep water, and another world, the world of hidden things that dwelt below the surface, came slowly into existence, like as when, on mounting a slope, fresh valleys and hillsides arise and unfurl themselves. Only, in this case, you had to go down somewhere inside yourself to become aware of them. And something, some inner consciousness, recognized and hailed them. It was not that he was getting sleepy, and sinking into the waters of dreams; rather the experience was the result of a more vivid life and awakened perceptions. But he never got further than that, and during the day he was far too busy with the affairs of normal life to trouble about those perceptions that dawned on him on still quiet mornings when he lay a-bed and stared at the ceiling with its flickering green lights and moving shadows.

CHAPTER II

Archie's birthday was in November, and for a day or two before that tremendous annual event there was always a certain atmosphere of mystery abroad, which he was conscious of at odd minutes. He met Marjorie on the morning of the day before he would be six, walking down the nursery passage with a parcel in her hand, the contents of which she would not divulge. That afternoon, too, his mother drove into the neighbouring town in the motor, and would not take him with her, on the excuse that she had some shopping to do, though it was the commonest thing in the world for her to take him with her when she went shopping. This year he vaguely connected these odd happenings with his birthday, as he did also the fact that a week ago Blessington had brought a total stranger into the nursery, who had very politely asked him to take off his coat. The stranger had then knelt down on the floor in front of him, and had produced a tape, with which he proceeded to measure Archie all over, from his hip to his knee and his knee to his ankle, and round his waist, and round his chest, and all along his arms, making notes of those things in a book. Blessington had told him that Mr. Johnson wanted to see how much he had grown, which was certainly a very gratifying attention, especially since Archie had grown a good deal, and was extremely proud of the fact. Mr. Johnson congratulated him too, and said that he himself hadn't grown as much as that for many a year, and tried to account for his visit on general grounds of interest in Archie. But in spite of that Archie connected this call with his birthday, though he did not arrive at the deduction that it meant clothes.

His mother came up to tea in the nursery on her return from her mysterious drive, and said that she had just caught sight of the fairy Abracadabra as she drove down the High Street; she had not known that Abracadabra was in the neighbourhood. She asked Archie if Abracadabra had called while she was out, and Archie, after a moment's pause, said that he hadn't seen her... but in that pause something of the glory faded out of the bright trailing clouds. When he was asked that directly he did not feel sure whether he believed in Abracadabra in the same way in which he believed in Blessington or Jeannie. So short a time ago—last summer only—Alice in Wonderland and the identity of Grandmamma Tintagel had been so much realler than the paltry happenings that took place in the light of common day. Now, quite suddenly and unexpectedly, at the mere question as to whether he had seen Abracadabra they all began to fade; indeed, it was more than fading: it was as if they passed out of sight behind a corner.

Archie had been told that he must never, if he could help it, hurt people's feelings. The particular occasion when that had been brought home to him was when his sister Jeannie had to wear a rather delightful sort of band round her front teeth, which showed a tendency to grow crooked. She was shy about it and hoped nobody saw it, and when Archie called the attention of the public to it, she turned very red. He had not had the least intention of embarrassing her, for he thought the band rather nice himself, and would have liked to have had one had his teeth been sufficiently advanced for such a decoration. But on this occasion he saw instantly and clearly that he must not hurt his mother's feelings by expressing scepticism about Abracadabra. Perhaps his mother still believed in her herself (though there were difficulties about supposing that, seeing that if Abracadabra was not Abracadabra she was certainly his mother); but, in any case, she thought Archie believed in Abracadabra, which made quite sufficient reason for his appearing to do so. If Abracadabra was an invention designed to awe, delight, and mystify him, the most elementary obligation of not embarrassing other people enjoined on him that he must be awed, delighted, and mystified. Perhaps by next year something would have happened to Abracadabra, for nowadays she only made her appearance on his birthday, whereas he could remember when she paid Jeannie also a birthday visit. But this year she had not come on Jeannie's birthday, and the various members of the family had given her birthday presents themselves, which did not happen when Abracadabra came, for she was the chief dispenser of offerings.

So Archie replied that Abracadabra had not been during his mother's absence, and, in order to spare his mother the mortification of knowing that he had doubts about that benevolent fairy, laid himself out to ask intelligent questions.

"Why didn't you speak to her, mummy?" he said, "when you saw her in the High Street?"

"Because she was in a hurry; she went by like a flash of lightning, in her pearl chariot."

"Was there any thunder?" asked he.

"Yes, just one clap; but that might have been the wheels of the chariot. What do you think she'll bring you?"

Archie was holding his mother's hand, and slipping her rings up and down her fingers. As he held it, he suddenly became aware what one of these presents would be.

"A clock-work train," he said quickly.

He knew more than that about the clock-work train. He felt perfectly certain that it was in his mother's bedroom at this moment, reposing in the big cupboard where she kept her dresses.

"Do you want a clock-work train?" she asked.

"Yes, mummy, frightfully," said he, feeling that he was playing a part, for he knew his mother knew that he wanted a clock-work train.

"What else?"

"Oh, thousands of things. Particularly a pen that writes without your dipping it in the ink."

"Well, if I were you I should write down all the things you want, and leave the paper lying on your counterpane when you go to sleep."

"What'll that do?" asked Archie.

"It's the fairy-post. Instead of putting letters into boxes to be posted when you want them to reach the fairies, you have always to put them on your bed. Mind you address it to Her Fairy Majesty the Empress Abracadabra. Then, when the fairies come round to collect the post, they will find it there, and take it to Abracadabra. And perhaps if she comes to-morrow—let me see, it must be a year since she was here—she will bring a few things for your birthday. I can't tell; but I think that is the best chance of getting them."

Certainly this seemed a very pleasant sort of plan; Archie had never heard of it before, and the extremely matter-of-fact tone in which his mother spoke lit again a dawning hope in his mind that perhaps it was all true. Why shouldn't be a fairy Abracadabra, and a fairy-post, just as there had been, and now was no longer, a glassy sea between the rugs in the hall, and snarling tigers to keep off his enemies? If you believed a thing enough, it became real, with a few trifling exceptions—as, for instance, when, on one of the days last summer, a day crammed full of the most delightful events, Archie had found himself firmly believing that that particular day was never coming to an end. True, it had come to an end, but that perhaps was because he hadn't believed strongly enough… There was a lovely story which his mother had read him about a man called Joshua, who wanted a day to remain until he had killed all his enemies, and sure enough the sun stood still until he had accomplished that emphatic task. He never doubted that, because it came out of the Bible, and in the spirit of Joshua he set himself now to believe in Abracadabra and the fairy-post. And, with that in his mind, he kept his eyes firmly away from the cupboard where his mother kept her dresses that evening, when her maid opened it, lest he should see there the parcel which he felt secretly convinced was there, and contained the clock-work train which his mother had bought, and which Abracadabra would to-morrow assuredly bring out of the basket of pure gold with which she habitually travelled.

Archie put the letter for the fairy-post on his bed, and determined to keep awake so that he should see the fairy postman come for it. It was a very cold night, and a big fire burned in his grate, so that, though the windows as usual were all open, there was a clear, brisk warmth about the room and a frosty and soapy smell, for his bright brown hair had been washed that night—this was a special evening bath-night, for by now baths had been promoted to the morning—and stuck up all over his head in a novel and independent manner. Blessington had dried it by the fire for him with hot towels, and a very extraordinary thing had happened, for when she brushed it afterwards it gave forth little cracklings, which she told him was electricity which was the thing that made the lamps burn. She had allowed him to take a brush to bed with him, and make more cracklings for five minutes until she returned to put his light out, and Archie made a wonderful story to himself as he looked at the fire, that he would get an electric lamp and paste it to his head, so that he should be able to read by the light of his hair. All at once this seemed so feasible, so easy of belief that he pictured to himself everybody walking about the house in the evening lit by themselves... And then William came round the corner (he did not know what corner), carrying an electric pike for a birthday present to himself, and when Blessington stole in five minutes afterwards, Archie's brush had slipped from his fingers and his breath came evenly between his parted lips. There was a gap in his front teeth because a tooth had come out only to-day, embedded in a piece of toffy he was eating, which had made Archie squeal with laughter, for here was a new substance called tooth-toffee... And Blessington softly lifted his arm and laid it under the bedclothes without awaking him, and looked at him a moment with her old face beaming with love, and put down on his chair out of sight at the bottom of his bed the new sailor-suit, and took away the note to her Fairy Majesty the Empress Abracadabra.

* * * * *

Archie woke next morning and instantly remembered that he had attained the magnificent age of six. Six had long seemed to him one of the most delightful ages to be. Eighteen was another, mainly because William was eighteen, but six was the best of all, for at eighteen you must inevitably feel that you have lived your life, and that there is nothing much left to live for; for the rest would be but a slow descent into the vale of years. But to-day he was six, and it was his birthday, and... and there was no sign of the letter he had written to Abracadabra on his counterpane. But it might have slipped on to the floor, and not have been taken away by fairies after all. Or it might have slipped over the bottom of the bed; and Archie got up to see. No: there was no note there, but on the chair at the foot of his bed was a suit of sailor-clothes...

Archie gave a gasp: certainly their presence there constituted a possibility that they were for him; but he hardly dared let himself contemplate so dazzling a prospect, for fear it should be whisked out of sight. Yet who could they be for, if not for him? They couldn't be Blessington's, for she was a female, and wore mystery-cloaking skirts. Sailor-suits were boys' clothes: Harry Travers, the son of a neighbouring squire, aged eight, had a sailor-suit—it was the thing that Archie most envied about that young man. Harry had taken the coat and trousers off one day in the summer when the two boys were playing in the copse by the lower end of the lake, and had let Archie put them on for three minutes. That had been a thrilling adventure; it implied undressing out of doors, which was a very unusual thing to do, and he loved the feeling of the rough serge down his bare calves.

He had, of course, offered Harry the privilege of putting on his knickerbockers and jacket, if he could get into them without splitting them, but Harry, from that Pisgah-summit of eight years, had no desire to go back to the childish things of the land of bondage, but had danced about bare-legged while Archie enjoyed his three minutes in these voluminous and grown-up lendings. And now perhaps for him, too, not for three minutes only, but for every day… and he took a leap back into bed again as Blessington's tread sounded on the boards outside.

Archie pretended to be asleep, for he wanted to be awakened by Blessington and hear his birthday greetings. He loved the return of consciousness in the morning— when he had not already been awake, and speculating about Grandmamma Tintagel on the lawn—to find Blessington, with her hand on his shoulder, gently stirring him, and her face close to his, whispering to him, "Eh, it's time to get up." So this morning, not for the first time, he simulated sleep in order to recapture that lovely sense of being awakened by love. (You must understand that he did not put it to himself like that, for Archie, just at the age of six, was not a mature and self-conscious prig, but he wanted to know what Blessington's greeting to him would be, when she thought she woke him up on the morning of his sixth birthday.)

From the narrow chink of his eyelids not quite closed, he could see some of her movements. She took

the exciting suit of sailor-clothes from the bottom of his
bed, and laid it on the chair where she always put his
clothes with a flannel shirt of a quite unusual shape, and
his socks on top. Already Archie had heart-burnings at
the knowledge of his knowledge of the sailor-suit.
Blessington meant it to be a surprise to him, and a
surprise he determined it should be. In the interval there
was another surprise: how would Blessington wake him?
She would be sure to rise to the immense importance of
the occasion. She moved quietly about; she shut the
windows, and brought in his bath. And then she came
close up to his bed. He felt her hand stealing underneath
the bedclothes to his shoulder and she shook it gently—
"Eh, Master Six," she said.

Oh, she had done exactly the right thing! She had
divined Archie, as he had divined himself, knowing
himself. That was just the only thing to think about this
morning. He ceased to imagine: Blessington, out of her
simplicity of love, had given the real birthday greeting.

He rolled a little sideways, and there was her face
close to his, and her hand still underneath his bed-
clothes. He put up both of his hands and caught it.

"Many happy returns," said Blessington. "Wake up,
my darling: it's your birthday. Happy returns," she
repeated.

Archie released her hand and flung his arm round
her neck.

"Oh, Blessington, isn't it fun?" he said. "What did you do when you were six?"

"I got up directly," said Blessington, kissing him, "and had my bath and put my clothes on. Now, will you do the same, for I'm going downstairs for ten minutes, and then I shall be back."

"All right," said Archie.

She went out, and Archie again, as with the question of Abracadabra last night, felt he must make it a surprise that there were sailor-clothes on his chair. It was quite likely that he would not be supposed to notice them at once, and so he stripped off his night-shirt, and took his bath in the prescribed manner. He had to lie down on the floor first of all, and wave his legs about; then he had to stand upright, still with no clothes on, and put his hands each side of his waist, and wave his body about eight times in each direction. Then he was allowed to pour out the hot water into his bath, in order to encourage himself, but before he stepped into that delicious steamy warmth he had to bend down eight times with a long frosty expulsion of breath, and stand up eight times with a great draught of cold air in his lungs. All this had been explained to him by a stranger—not Mr. Johnson—who, a year ago, had come into his nursery and had been very much interested in his anatomy. Archie understood that this was a doctor, though he didn't give him any medicine, but had merely showed him how to do these things, after first putting a sort of plug on Archie's chest which communicated with two other plugs that the stranger put in his ears. Then Archie had to say "ninety-nine" several times, which seemed to be a sort of game, though it didn't lead any further (the doctor, for instance, didn't say "a hundred"), and then he had to promise to practise those contortions every morning.

All this was done, and Archie fled from the cold of the morning to his bath. The water was of that divinest temperature so that when he stopped still it was lovely, but when he moved he almost screamed with the rapturous heat of it. It cooled a little as he sat in it, and, still remembering that he was six, he poured a sponge-full down his spine. That over, he might wash his face and his neck, and well behind his ears with soap. Up till a few months ago Blessington had always superintended the bath, and done these things for him; but now he did them for himself as agent, with Blessington as inspector-general in the background, who might always make the strictest scrutiny into the place behind the ears and the toe-nails to see that the effects of the bath were perfectly satisfactory. If not, Blessington superintended again for the next three mornings; so Archie was very careful, since it was so much grander to wash oneself than to be washed by anybody else.

Then came the most exciting part of the bath, for close at the side of it was a big tin full of the coldest possible water. He had then to stand up in his bath, and, after washing his face in the cold water, to put cold water everywhere within reach of him on one arm and then the other, on a chest, on a stomach, on one leg and on another right down to the foot, and finally (a vocal piece) to squeeze a full sponge down his back. Archie squealed at this, and flew for a towel.

He flung himself into his new clothes and was already half-dressed when Blessington returned.

"Oh, Blessington," he said, "look at me, and they're just as easy to manage as the old ones, and may I go to see Harry after breakfast and show him?"

"Master Harry will be here for tea," said Blessington.

"Yes, but I want him to know sooner than that. Did they come just ordinarily, like other clothes? Or are they a birthday present?"

"Well, I should say they were a birthday present," said Blessington.

"Who from?" demanded Archie.

And then suddenly he guessed.

"Oh, Blessington," he said. "I like them better than anything!" he said.

"Well, dear, and I wish you health to wear them and strength to tear them," she said. "Eh, but how you're disarranging my cap!"

Archie promptly handselled his clothes by spilling egg on the coat, and bread-and-butter upside down on the trousers, and, when the time came for him to make his public entry into the world, was seized with a sudden fit of shyness at the thought of anybody seeing him. The housemaid would stare, and William would laugh, and Marjorie would pretend not to know him, and for the moment of leaving the day-nursery (which from this morning was to be known as Archie's sitting-room) he would almost have wished himself back in his knickerbockers. But the remembered rough touch of the serge on his legs provided encouragement, and soon the new glories burst upon a sympathetic and not a mocking world. They were at breakfast downstairs, and Archie, though he had already had his, was bidden by his father to have a cup of coffee, which he poured out himself at the side-table, and to drink it slowly, and at the bottom of it, among the melted sugar, there came to his astonished eyes the gleam of silver, and there was a new half-crown with his father's happy returns. Thereafter came a hurried visit to Harry, a motor drive with his mother and Jeannie, Archie sitting on the box-seat and permitted to blow the bugle practically as often as he wanted, and the return to dinner, to find that the two things he liked best, namely boiled rabbit and spotted dog pudding, formed that memorable repast.

Up till now he had received only two birthday presents, the clothes and the half-crown, and he could not help feeling that a visit from Abracadabra was more than likely, since no one else had made the slightest allusion to clock-work trains or pens that wrote without being dipped. But in the afternoon, as he returned home from his walk with Blessington and Jeannie in the early dusk, he received an impression which was to be more inextricably connected with his sixth birthday than even the sailor suit. They were within a few yards of the front-door when there ran out of the bushes Cyrus, the great blue Persian cat. He held something in his mouth, which Archie saw to be a bird. There he stood for a moment with the gleaming eyes of the successful hunter, and twitching tail, and then trotted in front of them towards the porch. Simultaneously Jeannie called out:

"Oh, Blessington, Cyrus has caught a thrush. We must get it from him; it may be still alive."

Till then Archie had only thought about the cleverness of Cyrus in catching a bird, which was clearly a very remarkable feat, since Cyrus could only run and climb, and a bird could fly. But, as Jeannie spoke, he suddenly thought of himself in the jaws of a tiger, of the clutch of the long white teeth, of the fear, and the helplessness; and a queer tremor made him catch his breath, as there smote upon him an emotion that had never yet been awakened by the passage of his sunny days. Pity took hold of him for the bright-eyed bird. It suffered; his imagination told him that, and never yet had the fact of suffering come home to him.

They hemmed Cyrus in, and Blessington took the thrush out of his mouth, while Cyrus growled and struck at her with his paws, and then, greatly incensed, bounded out into the garden again, so as not to lose the chance, at this cat-hour of dusk, of a further stalk and capture. They carried the bird into the hall, where they looked at it, but it lay quite still in Blessington's hand, with its helpless little claws relaxed, and with its eyes fast glazing in death. Its beak was open, and on its speckled breast were two oozing drops of blood, that stained the feathers.

"Eh, poor thing, it's dead," said Blessington.

Archie felt all the desolation of an unavailing pity.

"No, it can't be dead, Blessington," he said. "It'll get all right, won't it?" and his lip quivered.

"No, dear, it's quite dead," said Blessington; "but if you like we'll bury it. There'll be just time before tea. Shall I run upstairs and get a box to bury it in?"

Without doubt this was a consoling and attractive proposal, and while Blessington went to get a suitable coffin, Archie held the "small slain body" in reverent hands. It was warm and soft and still; by now the bright eyes had grown quite dull, and the blood on the speckled breast was beginning to coagulate, and once again, even with the novel prospect of a bird-funeral in front of him, Archie's heart melted in pity.

"Why did Cyrus kill it, Jeannie?" he said. "The thrush hadn't done any harm."

"Cats do kill birds," said Jeannie. "Same as birds kill worms, or you and William kill worms when you go out fishing."

"Yes, but worms aren't birds," said Archie. "Worms aren't nice; they don't fly and sing. It's an awful shame."

Blessington returned with a suitable cardboard box which had held chocolates, and into this fragrant coffin the little limp body was inserted. This certainly distracted Archie from his new-found emotion.

"Oh, that will be nice for it," he said. "It will smell the chocolate."

"It can't; it's dead," said hopeless Jeannie.

But Blessington understood better.

"Yes, dear, the chocolate will be nice for it," she said, "and then we'll cover it up with leaves and put the lid on."

"Oh, and may it have a cris—a crisantepum?" said Archie. "May I pick one?"

"Yes, just one."

Archie laid this above the bird's head, and the lid was put on.

"Oh, and let's have a procession to the tool-shed to get a trowel," said Jeannie.

"Yes!" squealed Archie, now thoroughly immersed in the fascinating ritual. "And I'll carry the coffin and go first, and you and Blessington shall walk behind and sing."

"Well, we must be quick," said Blessington.

"No, not quick," said Jeannie. "It's a funeral. What shall we sing?"

"Oh, anything. 'The Walrus and the Carpenter.' That's sad, because the oysters were dead."

So, to the moving strains, the procession headed across the lawn, and found a trowel in the tool-shed, and excavated a grave underneath the laurestinus. The coffin was once more opened to see that the thrush was quite comfortable, and then deposited in its sepulchre, and the earth filled in above it. But Archie felt that the ceremony was still incomplete.

"Ought we to say a prayer, Jeannie?" he said.

"No, it's only a thrush."

Archie considered a moment.

"I don't care," he said. "I shall all the same."

He took off his sailor cap and knelt down, closing his eyes.

"God bless the poor thrush," he said. "Good-night, thrush. I can't think of anything more. Amen. Say Amen, Jeannie."

"Amen," said Jeannie.

"And do get up from that damp earth, dear," said Blessington. "And let's see who can run the fastest back to the house."

Blessington ran the least fast, and Archie tripped over a croquet-hoop, and so Jeannie won, and very nearly began telling her mother about it all before Archie arrived. But, though breathless, he shrilly chipped in.

"And then I picked a crisantepum, and we had a procession across the lawn, and made a lovely grave by the tool-house, and I said prayers, though Jeannie told me you didn't have prayers for thrushes. Mummy, when I grow up, may I be a clergyman?"

"Why, dear?"

"Don't they have lots of funerals?"

"Pooh; that's the undertaker," said Jeannie. "Besides, I did say Amen, Archie."

"I know. But mummy, why did Cyrus kill the thrush? Why did he want to hurt it and kill it? That was the part I didn't like, and I expect the thrush hated it. Wasn't it cruel of him? But if he kills another, may we have another funeral?"

He stood still a moment, cudgelling his small brain in order to grasp exactly what he felt.

"The poor thrush!" he said. "I wish Cyrus hadn't killed it. But, if it's got to be dead, I like funerals."

* * * * *

Tea, on such solemn occasions as birthday feasts, took place for Archie, not in the nursery, but in the drawing-room, as better providing the proper pomp. He appreciated that, and secretly was pleased that Harry Travers should be ushered by William into the drawing-room, and have the door held open for him, and be announced as Mr. Travers. With that streak of snobbishness common to almost all small boys Archie thought it rather jolly, without swaggering at all, to be able to greet his friend in the midst of these glories, so that he could see their splendour for himself. In other ways, he would have perhaps preferred the nursery, and certainly would have done so when the moment came for him to cut his birthday-cake, for the sugar on the side of it cracked and exploded, as such confectionery will do, when Archie hewed his way down that white perpendicular cliff, and (a number of fragments falling on the floor), he had to stand quite still, knife in hand, till William got a housemaid's brush and scoop and removed the debris, for fear it should be trodden into the carpet.

Marjorie had not appeared at tea at all, and when this sumptuous affair was over, Jeannie and Harry and Archie gathered round Lady Davidstow on the hearthrug with a box of chocolates planted at a fair and equal distance between them, and she told them the most delicious story about a boy whose mother had lost his birthdays, so that year after year went by without his having a birthday at all. The lights had been put out, and only the magic of leaping fire-light guided their hands to the chocolate-box, and every moment the phantasy of the story got more and more interwoven with the reality of the chocolates. Eventually, while the birthday-less boy's mother was clearing out the big cupboard underneath the stairs, she came across all his birthdays put away in a purple box with a gold lock on it.

"Was it the cupboard underneath the stairs in the hall here?" asked Archie, for questions were permitted.

"Yes. There they all were: eight birthdays in all, so he had one every day for more than a week. My dears! What's that?"

It certainly was very startling. A noise like a mixture between the Chinese gong and the bell for the servants' dinner broke in upon the quiet, with the most appalling clamour. Archie swallowed a chocolate whole, and Harry, with great prudence, took two more in a damp hand to sustain him in these rather alarming occurrences.

"It sounds as if it was in the hall," said Lady Davidstow. "Harry, will you open the door and see what it is?"

"Yes, I'll go," he said firmly. "But—but shan't Archie come too?"

The noise ceased as suddenly as it had begun, and with a pleasing sense of terror the two boys went to the drawing-room door and opened it.

"But it's quite dark," said Archie. "Oh, mummy, what *is* happening?"

"I can't think. I only know one person who makes a noise the least like that."

"Oh, is it Abracadabra?" asked Archie excitedly, finding that his scepticism of the day before had vanished like smoke. It had occurred to him that

Abracadabra was his mother, but here was his mother telling them stories.

"Well, the only time I ever heard her sneeze it was just like that," said Lady Davidstow.

Archie came running back, shrieking with laughter.

"And what does she do when she blows her nose?" he asked.

The words were hardly out of his mouth when a piercing trumpet-blast sounded, and his mother got up.

"She did it then," she whispered. "What had we better do? Shall we go into the hall? She would like us to be there to meet her, perhaps, if she's coming."

She went to the door, followed by the children, and they all looked out into the black hall. The wood-fire in the hearth there had died down to a mere smoulder of red, which sent its illumination hardly farther than the stone fender-curb.

"But there's something there," said Lady Davidstow in an awe-struck whisper. "There's something sitting in the chair."

"Oh, mummy," said Archie, coming close to her. "I don't think I like it."

"I'm sure there's nothing to be frightened at, Archie," said she. "Which of us shall go and see what it is?"

There was no volunteer for this hazardous job, for now, with eyes more accustomed to the faint light, they could all see that it was not Something there, but Somebody. The outlines of a head, of a body, of legs all clothed in black, could be seen, and Somebody sat there perfectly still...

Then all of a sudden the gong and the bell and the trumpet broke out into a clamour fit to wake the dead, the great chandelier in the hall flared into light, and the black figure sprang up, throwing its darkness behind it, and there, glittering with silks and gems and gold and the flowers of fairyland, stood Abracadabra. She had on a huge poke-bonnet which cast a shadow over her face, and left it terrifyingly vague. Her bonnet was trimmed with sunflowers and lilies of the valley, and round the edge of it went a row of diamonds which were quite as big as the drops in a glass chandelier. Another necklace of the same brilliance went round her throat and rested on a crimson satin bodice covered with gold. From her shoulders sprang spangled wings, and from below her skirt, with its garlands of roses, were silver shoes with diamond buckles. In her hand she carried a blue wand hung with bells, and by her side was a clothes-basket (such was its shape) made of gold.

She stamped her foot with rage.

"Here's a nice welcome, Lady Davidstow," she said in a thin, cracked voice. "I sneezed to show I was coming, and, when I got through the keyhole, I found the hall dark, and no one to receive me. How dare you?"

Lady Davidstow advanced with faltering steps and fell on her knees.

"Oh, your majesty, forgive me," she said.

"Why should I forgive you?" squeaked the infuriated fairy. "Why shouldn't I take you away in my basket and put you in the Tower of Toads?"

Archie gasped. He would have given much for a touch of yesterday's scepticism, but he couldn't find an atom of it. The thought of his mother being whisked off to the Tower of Toads was insupportable.

"Oh, please don't," he said.

"And who is that?" asked Abracadabra.

Archie almost wished he hadn't spoken, and took hold of Jeannie on one side and Harry on the other.

"It's me; it's Archie," he said.

"And you don't want me to take your ridiculous mother away?" she asked.

"No, please don't," said Archie.

"Very well, as it's your birthday, I won't. Instead I'll make her extra lady-in-waiting on my peacock-staircase, and mistress of my tortoise-shell robes."

"Oh, mummy, that will be lovely for you," said Archie, remembering that his mother was something of the kind to somebody already.

Then there came the giving of presents, with the surprises that occurred during such processes. Archie was told to advance and put his hand in the left far corner of the golden basket, and, as he prepared to do so, Abracadabra sneezed so loudly that he fled back to the bottom stair of the staircase where they had been all commanded to sit. There was a tennis racquet for Harry, but the lights all went out when he had just reached the clothes-basket, and Abracadabra blew her nose so preposterously that his ear sang with it afterwards. There was a great parcel for Lady Davidstow, as big as a football, which was found to contain, when all the paper was stripped off, nothing more than a single acid drop, in order to teach the mistress of the tortoise-shell robes better manners when her mistress came to pay a visit, and Blessington, summoned from the nursery, was presented with a new cap. But the bulk of the gifts, as was proper, was for Archie, a clock-work train, and a pen that needed no dipping, and a fishing-rod, and a second suit of sailor-clothes. And then the light went out again, and Abracadabra began sneezing and blowing her nose with such deafening violence that the screen which stood just behind her rocked with the concussion, and the children, at the suggestion of the mistress of the tortoise-shell robes, groped their way back into the drawing-room with their presents, and shut the door till Abracadabra was better. And when, from the cessation of these awful noises, they conjectured she might be better, and ventured out into the hall again, that audience-chamber was just as usual, and Archie's father came out of his room, looking vexed, and asking what that beastly noise was about. But when he heard it was Abracadabra, who had gone away again, he was greatly upset and said that it wasn't a beastly noise at all, but the loveliest music he had ever heard.

Then came bed-time, and Archie, still excited, said his prayers with a special impromptu clause for Abracadabra, and another for the thrush, which he suddenly remembered again, and then lay staring at the fire with his hands clasped round his knees, as his custom was. Certainly Abracadabra had been wonderfully real to-day, and certainly she was not his mother. Then he recollected that Marjorie had not appeared at all, and wondered if Marjorie perhaps was Abracadabra, or if the thrush was Abracadabra, of Cyrus... And his hands relaxed their hold on his knees, and when Blessington came in he did not know that she kissed him and tucked the bed-clothes up under his chin.

CHAPTER III

Archie did not often come into contact with Miss Schwarz, his sisters' governess; she was not a person to be lightly encountered. Sometimes, if Blessington was busy, he and Jeannie went out for their walk with his eldest sister and Miss Schwarz, and on these occasions Miss Schwarz and Marjorie would talk together in an unknown guttural tongue, very ugly to hear, which Archie vaguely understood was German, and the sort of thing that everybody spoke in the country to which Miss Schwarz went for her holiday at Midsummer and Christmas. That uncouth jargon, full of such noises as you made when you cleared your throat, was quite unintelligible, and it seemed odd that Marjorie should converse in it when she could speak ordinary English; but it somehow seemed to suit Miss Schwarz, who had a sallow face, prominent teeth, and cold grey eyes. Otherwise he did not often meet her, for she led an odd secret existence in his sisters' school-room, breakfasting and having lunch downstairs in the dining-room, but eating her evening meal all by herself in the school-room. She had a black, unrustling dress for the day, and a black rustling dress for the evening, and a necklace of onyx beads which she used to finger with her dry thin hands, which reminded Archie of the claws of a bird. His mother had told him that, after Christmas, he would do his lessons with Miss Schwarz, and this prospect rather terrified him. He supposed that Miss Schwarz would probably teach him in the guttural language that Jeannie was beginning to understand too, and he had moments

57

of secret terror when he pictured Miss Schwarz, enraged at his not comprehending her, striking at him with those claw-like hands.

He was coming upstairs one evening, rather later than usual, for his father had been showing him the contents of a cabinet of butterflies, and Archie, enraptured with the gorgeous, brilliant creatures, had begged to be allowed to wait till the gong rang for dinner. On his way upstairs he remembered that he had lent Jeannie the pen that wrote without being dipped, with which to write her German exercise. She had gone to bed early that night with a bad cold, and Archie, recognizing the impossibility of going to sleep without the precious pen in his possession again, ran along the passage to the school-room, where he was likely to find it. This might entail a momentary encounter with Miss Schwarz, but the recovery of the pen was essential, and he entered.

Miss Schwarz had finished her dinner, and was sitting by the fire on which steamed a kettle. She held a big glass in her hand, and was pouring something into it from a bottle. There was a high colour in her usually sallow face, and as she saw Archie she made one of those guttural exclamations.

"What do you want?" she said, and though she spoke English, Archie noticed that she spoke it in the same thick, guttural manner as German.

Archie froze with terror. This was quite a new Miss Schwarz, a gleaming, eager Miss Schwarz.

"Oh, I lent Jeannie my pen," he stammered. "I came to look for it, but it doesn't matter."

"Nonsense! That is not why!" said Miss Schwarz angrily. Then she suddenly seemed to take hold of herself. "*Ach*, that sweet little pen. You will find it on the table, my dear. Luke, and find it. And then say goodnight to poor Miss Schwarz. *Ach*, I am so ill this evening. Such a heartburn, and I was just about to take the medicine vat makes it better. Do not tell any one, dear Archie, that poor Miss Schwarz is ill. I wish to troble nobody. Poor Miss Schwarz naiver geeve troble if she can 'elp. *Ach*, you have your pen! Good-night, my deear."

Archie fled down the passage to the nursery with terror giving wings to his heels. This Miss Schwarz angry one moment, and affectionate and effusive the next, was a new and a more awful person than the one he was acquainted with, and he felt sure she must be very ill indeed. It would be a terrible affair if Miss Schwarz was found dead in her bed, in spite of her medicine, just because he had not told anybody that she was ill, and so a doctor had not been fetched. There would be a burden on his conscience for ever if he did not tell somebody. He burst into the nursery with a wild look behind him, to make sure that Miss Schwarz was not following him in her evening rustling dress.

"Oh Blessington," he cried, "Miss Schwarz is ill; do go and see what is the matter. I went to the school-room for my pen, and she was sitting by the fire, all red, and angry, and then polite, mixing her medicine."

Blessington got up from her rocking-chair.

"Eh, I'll go and see," she said.

"Don't tell her I told you," said Archie.

"Nay, of course I won't. Now you begin your undressing, and I'll be back very soon."

Excited and frightened and yet hugely interested, Archie stood at the door of his room listening. Suddenly he heard the sound of Miss Schwarz's voice raised almost to a scream. Then there came the crash of a glass, and the ringing of a bell, while still Miss Schwarz's voice gabbled on, shrill and guttural. Trembling, and yet unable to resist the call of his curiosity, he stole to the corner of the nursery passage, and saw William come upstairs and go along to the school-room. Then Blessington came out, and, instead of coming back to the nursery, she went downstairs, and presently his father came up again with her. He, too, went along the school-room passage, and suddenly, as if a tap had been turned off, the shrill voice ceased. Once, for a moment, it broke out again, and as suddenly stopped, and then came the very odd sight of Miss Schwarz being led along the landing to her room by his father and Blessington. Blessington and Miss Schwarz entered together, his father went downstairs after a moment's conversation with William, and presently William came along the landing towards the nursery.

"Oh, William, what's happened?" said Archie. "Is Miss Schwarz very ill?"

"Well, she ain't very well," said William. "Lumme!"

"What does that mean?" asked Archie.

"It don't mean anything particular, Master Archie."

"Will Miss Schwarz be better in the morning?" asked Archie.

"Lord, yes. They're always better in the morning, though they don't feel so. Now Blessington won't be back yet awhile, so I'm to look after you, and see you safe to bed."

Suddenly the thought of lying helpless in bed, with no Blessington next door, and the possibility of Miss Schwarz guessing that Archie had told of her illness, filled him with awful apprehension. She might come screaming down the passage, with her claw-like hands starving for Archie's face.

"Oh, William, don't leave me till Blessington comes back," he entreated.

"No, sir, of course I won't. There, let me undo your shoes for you. You've got the laces in a knot."

"And she won't hurt Blessington either?" asked Archie.

"Bless you, no sir," said William. "And there's your night-shirt. Now jump into bed, and I'll open the windows."

William put out the light, and Archie, with a delicious sense of security seeing him seated by the fire, dozed off. Once, just before he got fairly to sleep, an awful vision of Miss Schwarz's red face came across the field of his closed eyelids, and he started up. But in a moment William was by him.

"It's all right, sir," he said. "I'm on the look out."

* * * * *

There was a decided air of mystery concerning Miss Schwarz next morning. She was better, but she remained unseen, and nobody would answer any questions about her. But in the afternoon Archie met Walter and the odd man carrying her luggage downstairs, and he gleaned the information that she was going away, and again, later in the day, Archie saw a housemaid coming out of her bedroom with a basket full of her medicine-bottles, and he drew the conclusion that she must have been ill a long time without anybody knowing. Not a syllable of news could he obtain from anybody, and, as the image of Miss Schwarz faded now that her dark, ill-omened presence was withdrawn, there was left in Archie's mind no more than a general sense of some connection between screaming voices, red faces, indistinct utterance, and the drinking of yellow medicine out of a large glass, instead of the usual small one.

There was a pleasant holiday sense for a few days after the departure of Miss Schwarz, for Marjorie took Jeannie's and Archie's lessons, which made a perfect festival of learning; but immediately almost came the ominous news that a new governess was coming next day. Archie believed that Miss Schwarz was a typical specimen of the genus governess, who were all probably in league together, and that some colleague of Miss Schwarz's, bent on avenging her, would render his own security a very precarious matter. It was, indeed, some consolation to know that Miss Bampton was a personal friend of his mother's and was not a "regular" governess at all but was just going to stay at Lacebury and teach lessons; yet Archie wondered, when he went downstairs on the morning after her arrival, whether he would not detect, under the guise of his mother's friend, some secret agent of Miss Schwarz.

Jeannie had lately been promoted to have breakfast with the rest of the family, and as Archie opened the door he heard a burst of laughter. There was Miss Schwarz's secret agent sitting next his father, and she it must have been who had made them all laugh, for she was not laughing herself, and Archie already knew that a joke was laughed at most by the people who hadn't made it. She was a little roundabout person, with blue eyes and a short nose and pincenez, and she got up as he entered.

"And is this Archie?" she said. "Why, I always thought of Archie as a baby. And here's an able-bodied seaman! How are you, Archie?"

Archie stared a moment. He reviewed his suspicion about governesses in general, but certainly if this plump, genial female was a secret colleague of Miss Schwarz her disguise was of the most ingenious kind. But it was as well to be careful.

"I'm quite well, thank you," he said, and, perceiving that a kiss had been intended, presented a sideways cheek. Miss Bampton made a sucking sound against it, and sat down again.

"Well, as I was saying," she went on, "the only plan of teaching is the co-operative principle. There are such heaps of jolly things to learn, that if the girls and I have a meeting, as I suggested, after breakfast, I'm sure we can find plenty of subjects between us. So I summon the meeting for a quarter past ten in the school-room."

Archie suddenly felt he was being left out. A meeting to discuss what you were going to learn sounded most promising in the way of lessons. He ran round to his mother's side.

"Oh, mummy, may I go to the meeting?" he said.

"You must ask Miss Bampton," said she.

Archie stifled his sense of distrust, for he wanted tremendously to go to a meeting where you settled what you were going to learn. He hated lessons, in the ordinary acceptation of that term, with their tiresome copy-books, in which he had to write the same moral maxim all down the page, and the stupid exercise—called French lesson—in which he had to address himself to a cat, and say in French "of a cat," "to a cat," "with the female cat," "with the male cat," and a thing called geography, which was a brown book with lists of countries and capital towns in it. But co-operative lessons, though he had no idea what co-operation meant, sounded far more attractive.

"May I come to the meeting, Miss Bampton?" he said.

"Yes, my dear, of course," said Miss Bampton, "if your mother will let you."

Thereupon there dawned for Archie a great light. Hitherto his lessons had been conducted by his mother, with occasional tuition from his father, and they had always made the impression that they were tasks, not difficult in themselves, but dull. He had learned the various modes of access in French to male and female cats, he had grasped the fact that Rome and not Berlin was the capital of Italy, and Paris not Vienna the capital of France. But these pieces of information were mere disconnected formulae, lessons, in other words, which had to be learned, and which, if imperfectly learned, caused him to be called lazy or inattentive. In the same way, the fact that he had to write in a laborious round hand all down the page "To be good is to be happy" meant nothing more than the necessity of filling the page without a plethora of blots or erasures. But from the date of this exciting meeting on co-operative learning, a whole new horizon dawned on him. It was settled at once that he was to do his lessons with Miss Bampton, and from that moment they ceased to be lessons at all. Instead of the lists of countries and capitals to be learned by heart, there was provided a jig-saw puzzle of the map of Europe, and Italy became a leg and foot, perpetually kicking Sicily, and Rome the button through which Italy's bootlace passed. And, instead of the dreary copybook maxims heading each page, Miss Bampton, in a hand quite as perfect as Mr. Darnell's, wrote the most stimulating sentiments on the top of each blank leaf. "He would not sit down, so we bit him" was one, and Archie, with the tip of his tongue at the corner of his mouth, an attitude which is almost indispensable to round-hand orthography, was filled with delightful conjectures as to who the person was who would not sit down, and who were those tigerish people who bit him in consequence. And then Miss Bampton had the most delightful plans of where lessons might be done. One day, when it was snowing hard, she conceived the brilliant plan of doing lessons in the motor in the garage, which gave the most extraordinary stimulus to the proceedings, for early English history was the lesson that morning, and so she and Archie and Jeannie were royal Anglo-Saxons, specially invited to come in their coach to the coronation of William the Conqueror (1066), and it would never do if, at the Coronation banquet afterwards, he asked them questions about their ancestors and they didn't know. Another day, when the sun shone frostily, and the lawn was covered with hoar-frost they wrapped themselves up in furs, and worked at geography, as Laplanders, in the summer-house. Marjorie was too old to need such spurs to industry, but Miss Bampton had enticing schemes for her also, giving her verse translations of Heine and Goethe, and encouraging her to see how near she got to the original when she translated them back into their native tongue.

The Christmas holidays, looked forward to with such eager expectation in the baleful reign of Miss Schwarz, drew near; but now, instead of counting the hours till the moment when Miss Schwarz, safe in the motor, would blow claw-fingered kisses to them, the children got up a Round Robin (or rather, a triangular Robin, which Marjorie translated into German), begging Miss Bampton to stop with them for the holidays. For she was as admirable in play-time as she was over their lessons: she told them enchanting stories on their walks, and painted for them in real smelly oil-paints the most lovely snow-scenes, pine-woods laden with whiteness, and cottages with red blinds lit from within. Never had any one such a repertory of games to be played in the long dark hours between tea and bed-time, and it was during one of these that Archie made a curious discovery.

The game in question was "Animal, Vegetable, or Mineral?" One of them thought of anything in heaven or earth or in the waters under the earth, and the rest, by questions answered only by "Yes" or "No," had to arrive at it. On this occasion Miss Bampton had thought: it was known to be Animal and not in the house.

Archie was sitting on the floor in the school-room leaning against Miss Bampton's knee. He had been staring at the coals, holding Miss Bampton's hand in his, when suddenly there came over him precisely the same sensation that he remembered feeling one night, years ago, when he woke and imagined himself and the night-nursery expanding and extending till they embraced all that existed. That sensation throbbed and thrilled through him now, and he said:

"Oh, Miss Bampton, how easy! Why, it's the longest tail-feather of the thrush that Cyrus killed."

"Oh, Archie, don't guess," said Jeannie. "It's no use just guessing."

"But it is!" said Archie. "I'm not guessing. I know. Isn't it, Miss Bampton?"

It certainly was, and so, by the rules of the game, since it had been guessed in under five minutes, Miss

Bampton had to think again. But now Archie tried in vain to recapture the mood that made Miss Bampton's mind so transparently clear to him. He knew what that mood felt like, that falling away of the limitations of consciousness, that expansion and extension of himself; but he could not feel it; it would not come by effort on his part; it came, he must suppose, as it chose, like a sneeze...

As Christmas drew near another amazing talent of Miss Bampton's showed itself. Marjorie had been up to London one day, to combine the pains of the dentist with the pleasure of a play, and came back with a comforted tooth and the strong desire to act. Instantly Miss Bampton rose to the occasion.

"Let's get up a play to act to your father and mother on New Year's night," she said.

"Oh, it would be fun," said Marjorie. "But what play could we act?"

"I'll write you one," said Miss Bampton. And write it she did, with a speed and a lavishness of plot that would have astonished more deliberate dramatists. There was a villain, a usurper king (Miss Bampton); there was a fairy (Marjorie); there was the rightful and youthful king (Archie); who lived (Act I) in painful squalor in a dungeon, attended only by the jailer's daughter (Jeannie) who knew his identity and loved him, whether he was in a dungeon or on a throne. Luckily, he loved her too, anywhere, and they were kind to a beggar-woman, who turned out to be the fairy, and did the rest. Miss Bampton was consigned to the lowest dungeon, and everybody else lived happily ever afterwards.

Then came the question of dresses, and Marjorie rather thoughtlessly exclaimed:

"I'm sure mother will let me have her Abracadabra clothes for the fairy. Oh—I forgot," she added, remembering that Archie was present.

There was an attempt (feeble, so Archie thought it) on the part of Miss Bampton to explain this away. She said that Abracadabra kept a suit of birthday clothes in every house she visited. Archie received the information quite politely, said, "Oh, I see," and remained wholly incredulous. His faith in the Abracadabra myth had tottered before; this was the blow that finally and completely compassed its ruin, and it disappeared in the limbo of discredited imaginings, like the glassy sea between the rugs in the hall, and the snarl of the tigers at his enemies. Never again would the combined crash of the servant's dinner-bell and the Chinese gong make him wonder at the magnificence of Abracadabra's sneezings, and when the play arrived at the stage of dress-rehearsal it was no shock to see Marjorie in Abracadabra's poke-bonnet and bediamonded bodice.

But it must not be supposed that, with the disappearance of those childish illusions, the world became in any way duller or less highly coloured to Archie; it grew, on the contrary, more and more fairy-like. The outburst of spring that year filled him with an ecstasy that could best be expressed by running fast and jumping in the air with shouts of joy. The unfolding of gummy buds on the horse-chestnut by the lake filled him with a rapture all the keener because he could not comprehend it; presently, the sight of pale green five-fingered leaves, weak as new-dropped lambs, made him race round and round Blessington till she got giddy. There was a smell of damp earth in the air, of young varnished grass-blades pushing up among the discoloured and faded foliage of the lawn, and, for the hard bright skies or the sullen clouds of winter, a new and tender blue was poured over the heavens, and clouds white as washed fleeces pursued one another aloft, even as their shadows bowled over the earth beneath. Birds began to sing again, and sparrows, chattering in the ivy, pulled straws and twigs about, practising for the nest-building time which would soon be upon them. A purplish mist hung over the birch-trees, and soon it changed to a mist of green as the buds expanded. Violets hidden behind their leaves bedecked the lane-sides, and one morning the first primrose appeared. Last year, no doubt, and in all preceding springs the same things had happened; but now for the first time they were significant, and penetrated further than the mere field of vision. They filled Archie with an unreasoning joy.

Anything in the shape of natural history received strong encouragement from Lord Davidstow, as well as anything (Archie did not fully grasp this) that tended to keep him out of doors when his short lessons were done, and he and Jeannie started this year a series of joint collections. Certain rules had to be observed: flowers that they picked must be duly pressed and mounted on sheets of cartridge paper, and their names must be ascertained. One bird's egg might be taken in the absence of the mother-bird from any nest which contained four, and must be blown and put in its labelled cell in the egg-cabinet; but when three specimens of any sort had been collected, no more must be acquired. That, perhaps, was the collection Archie liked best, though the joys of the aquarium ran it close. The aquarium was a big bread-bowl lined at the bottom with spa and crystals, and in it lived caddis-worms and water-snails and a dace—probably weak in the head, for he had allowed himself to be caught in the landing-net without the least effort to get out of the way. He had an inordinate passion for small bread-pills, in pursuit of which he was so violently active that he often hit his nose against the side of the aquarium so hard that you could positively hear the stunning blow. When satiated he would still continue to rush after bread-pills, but, after holding them in his mouth a moment, he would expel them again with such force that he resembled some submarine discharging torpedoes.

Then there was the butterfly and moth collection, which was of short duration, and was abandoned on account of a terrible happening. The insects were emptied into the killing-bottle, and when dead transfixed with a pin, and set. But one morning Archie, examining the setting-board to see if they were stiff and ready to be transferred into the cork-lined boxes, found, to his horror, that, so far from being stiff, two butterflies, a tortoiseshell and a brimstone, were alive still, with waving antennae and twitching bodies. That dreadful incident poisoned the joy of that collection; he felt himself guiltier of a worse outrage than Cyrus, and all Blessington's well-meant consolations that insects hardly felt anything at all would not induce him to run the risk of committing further atrocities. For a day and a night the two had writhed under their crucifixion, and that day the caterpillars were released from their breeding-cage (even including that piece of preciousness, the caterpillar of the convolvulus hawk with a horn on his tail), and the killing-bottle was relegated to the attic.

The Sunday church-goings for which an intermission had been ordained in consequence of Archie's infant remarks about the amusingness of the man with the wagging beard, had long ago been resumed again, and this year he had a sudden attack of spurious and sentimental religion that caused his mother some little anxiety. He developed a dreadful conscience, and came to her with a serious face and confessed trivial wrong-doings. (This phase, she comforted herself to think, occurred in the autumn of this year, at a time when there was nothing much to be done in the way of collecting.) One morning Archie came to her with a crime that sorely oppressed him. Nearly two years ago, somebody had sent her a painted Easter egg, an ostrich's egg, adorned with gilt designs of a cross and a crown and some rays, which Archie had been forbidden to touch.

"I touched it," he said. "I wetted my finger and rubbed it on the crown, and some of it came off."

"Well, dear, of course you shouldn't have done it, if I had told you not to," she said. "But don't bother about it any more. What made you come and tell me so long after?"

Archie grew more solemn still.

"I was leaning out of the nursery-window," he said, "and I heard Charles singing 'A few more years shall roll.' So I came and told you before I 'was asleep within the tomb.'"

His mother laughed, quite as if she was amused.

"We'll hope there'll be more than a few years before that, darling," she said.

"And shall I be forgiven now I've told you?" asked Archie.

"Yes, of course. Don't think anything more about it."

Archie would have preferred a more sentimental treatment of his offence, and rather wished his mother bore a stronger resemblance to Mrs. Montgomery, in the *Wide, Wide World*, whose edifying tears fell so fast and frequently, and after this he tended to keep his misdeeds more to himself and repent of them in secret. Simultaneously also the copy of the *Wide, Wide World*, which he had discovered in a passage book-case, mysteriously vanished, and no one appeared to have the slightest idea where it had gone. So, unable to stuff himself further with that brand of mawkishness, the desire that his mother should be more like Mrs. Montgomery faded somewhat, and there seemed but little pleasure in repentance at all, if your confessions were received in so unsentimental a manner, and it was no fun really keeping them to oneself. But for some weeks Sunday morning service in church (he had expressed a wish to go to evening church as well, but his mother had told him that once was as much as was good for him) became the emotional centre of his life, though his religion was strangely mixed up with a far more mundane attraction. There was a particular choir-boy there with blue eyes, pink cheeks, and a crop of yellow curls who sang solos, and thrilled Archie with a secret and perfectly sexless emotion. Only last Sunday he had sung "Oh, for the wings of a dove," and religion and childish adoration together had brought Archie to the verge of tears. He longed to be good, to live, until a few more years should roll (for he felt that he was going to die young), a noble and beautiful life; he longed also to fly away and be at rest with the choir-boy. He made up pathetic scenes in which he should be lying on his death-bed, with his weeping family round him, and the choir-

boy would sing to him as he died, and they would smile
at each other. When this vision proved almost too
painful for contemplation he would console himself by
picturing an alternative scheme, in which there were to
be no death-beds at all, but instead he would get into the
church choir, and sit next the choir-boy, and they would
sing duets together before a rapt congregation. But,
adorable though his idol was, he did not really want to
know him, or even find out who he was. The idol existed
for him in some remote sphere, becoming incarnate just
for an hour on Sunday morning, a golden-haired
surpliced voice, that suggested the vanished thrills of the
Wide, Wide World. He pronounced certain words rather
oddly, and had a slight lisp which Archie tried to copy,
until one day his father told him never to say "Yeth"
again, or he should write out "Yes" a hundred times.

Then came the most exciting discovery: this vocal
angel proved to be the son of the head-keeper, and it was
therefore perfectly easy to make his acquaintance. The
notion of meeting him face to face, of exchanging a
"good-morning" with him was almost overpowering, and
yet Archie instinctively shrank from bringing the idol
into contact with actual life. He began to choose for his
walk the rather dank and gloomy path that led past the
keeper's cottage, and yet, when that abode where the idol
lived came within sight, Archie, with beating heart
would avert his eyes, for fear he should see him. Then
one day, as they got opposite the gate, a small boy in
corduroy knickerbockers with a rather greasy scarf round
his neck and a snuffling nose came out, and touched his

cap. There could be no doubt about his identity, and
Archie suffered the first real disillusionment of his life.
The fading of Abracadabra was nothing to this: that had
been a gradual disillusionment, whereas this was sudden
as a lightning-stroke. He was a shattered idol, and from
that moment Archie could hardly recall what it had been
about, or recapture the faintest sense of the emotion
which had filled him before that encounter in the wood
which caused it to reel and totter and fall prone from its
unsubstantial pedestal. This blow, on the top of the
robust reception of his confession, did much to restore
Archie to the ways of normal boyhood, and it was really
rather a relief to his mother, when his expanding
experimenting nature took a very different turn, and he
became for a time obstreperously naughty. She thought,
quite rightly, that this evinced a greater vigour. That it
undoubtedly did, and the imagination contained in some
of Archie's exploits rivalled the more visionary power
that constructed death-bed scenes for himself and the
idealization (cruelly shattered) of the choir-boy.

One very dreary November afternoon, shortly after
his seventh birthday, he was sitting alone in his mother's
room. All day the sullen heavens had poured their
oblique deluge on the earth, and sheets of water were
being flung against the windows by the cold south-
easterly gale. Archie was suffering from a slight cold, and
had not been out of doors for a couple of days, and this
unusual detention in the house had caused him to be
very cross, and also had dammed up within him a store
of energy which could not disperse itself innocuously in

violent movement. Jeannie had gone for a motor-drive with his mother, Marjorie and Miss Bampton were closely engaged over their rotten German, and Archie that morning had been stingingly rebuked by his father for sliding down the banisters in the hall, a mode of progress strictly forbidden. Blessington had not been less stinging, for an hour ago Archie had been extremely rude to her, and, with a dignity that he both respected and resented, she had said, "Then I've nothing more to say to you, Master Archie, till you've remembered your manners again." And had thereupon continued her sewing.

Archie knew he had been rude, but his sense of that was not yet strong enough to enable him to apologize, though of sufficient energy to make him feel woebegone and neglected. He had been allowed by his mother to sit in her room that afternoon, when she went out with Jeannie, and to investigate what was known as her "work-box," which contained her "treasures." In earlier days these had been a source of deep delight: there was a minute china elephant with a silk palanquin on his back; there was a porcupine's quill, there was a set of dolls' tea-things, a pink umbrella, the ferrule of which was a pencil, a chain of amber. Once these had held magic for Archie: they were "mummy's treasures," and could only be seen on wet afternoons or in hours of toothache. But to-day they appeared to him perfectly rubbishy; not a gleam of glamour remained; they were as dull as the leaden skies of this interminable afternoon.

Archie lay in the window-seat, and wondered that his sailor-trousers only a year ago had given him so complete a sense of happiness. He rubbed one leg against the other, trying to recollect how it was that that rough serge against his bare calf felt so manly. He tried to interest himself in *Alice in Wonderland*, and marvelled that he could have cared about an adventure with a pack of cards. He longed to throw the book at the foolish Dresden shepherdess that stood on the mantelpiece. He supposed there would be trouble if he did, that his mother would be vexed, but trouble was better than this nothing-at-all. Probably it would rain again to-morrow, and he would have another day indoors, and the thought of Nothing Happening either to-day or to-morrow seemed the same as the thought of nothing happening for ever and ever.

There was a bright fire in the hearth and beyond the steel fender a thick hearthrug of long white sheep's wool. Suddenly Archie remembered the odour that diffused itself when, one day, a fragment of hot coal flew out of the fire, and lodged in this same hearthrug. There was a fatty, burning smell, most curious, and simultaneously the wild, irresistible desire of doing something positively wicked enthralled him. Instantly he knew what he was going to do, and with set, determined face, he took the fire-shovel in one hand and the tongs in the other, and heaped the shovel high with burning coals. He emptied them on the hearthrug.

The smoke of singeing, burning wool arose, and he took several more lumps of glowing coal from the fire-place and deposited them on the rug. Then a panic seized him, and he tried to stamp the conflagration out. But he only stamped the glowing coals more firmly in, and, though amazed at his audacity, he did not really want to extinguish it. He wanted something to happen. Quite deliberately, though with cheeks burning with excitement, he walked out of the room, leaving the door open, and simultaneously heard the crunch of the gravel under the wheels of his mother's returning motor. He did not wish to see her, and went straight to the night-nursery (now his exclusive bedroom) and locked himself in. But he was not in the least sorry for what he had done: if anything he wished he had put more coals there. Nor was he frightened at the thought of possible consequences. Merely, he did not care what happened, so long as something happened. That, he reflected, it was pretty certain to do. But he made no plans.

Before very long he heard some one turning the handle of his door, and he kept quite still. Then his father's voice said:

"Are you there, Archie?" And still he said nothing.

The voice grew louder and the handle rattled.

"Archie, open your door immediately," said his father.

Not in the least knowing why, Archie proceeded to do so. He still felt absolutely defiant and desperate, but for some instinctive reason he obeyed.

Enormous and terrible, his father stood before him.

"Did you put those coals on your mother's hearthrug?" asked Lord Davidstow.

"No," said Archie.

"Then how did you know they were there?" asked his father.

Archie had something of the joy of the desperate adventurer.

"Because I put them there," he said.

"Then you have lied to me as well."

"Yes," said Archie.

Lord Davidstow pointed to the door.

"Go downstairs at once," he said, "and wait in my study."

Archie obeyed, still not knowing why. At the top of the stairs was standing his mother, who took a step forward towards him.

"Archie, my darling—" she began.

"Leave the boy to me," said his father, who was following him. Archie marched downstairs, still without a tremor. It occurred to him that his father was going to kill him, as Cyrus killed the thrush. There was a whispered conversation between his mother and father and he heard his mother say, "No, don't, don't," and he felt sure that this referred to his being killed. But he was quite certain that, whatever happened, he was not going to say he was sorry.

He went into his father's study and shut the door. On the table he noticed that there was standing one of Miss Schwarz's medicine-bottles, and a syphon beside it, and wondered whether Miss Schwarz had come back. But there was no other sign of her.

In another moment his father entered.

"Now, you thoroughly deserve a good whipping, Archie," he said. "You might have burned the house down, and if you were a poor boy you'd have been put into prison for this. But your mother has been pleading for you, and, if you'll say you are sorry, and beg her pardon for burning her hearthrug, I'll let you off just this time."

Well, he was not going to be killed, but he was going to be whipped. Archie felt his heart beating small and fast with apprehension; but he was not sorry, and did not intend to say he was.

"Well?" said his father.

"I'm not sorry," said Archie.

"I'll give you one more chance," said his father, moving towards a cupboard above one of the bookcases.

"I'm not sorry," said Archie again.

His father opened the cupboard.

"Lock the door," he said.

But, before he could lock it, it was opened from without, and his mother entered. His father had already a cane in his hand, and he turned round as she came in. She looked at him and then at Miss Schwarz's medicine-bottle on the table.

"Go away, Marion," he said. "I'm going to give the boy a lesson."

She pointed at the bottle.

"You had better learn yours first," she said.

"Never mind that. Archie says he's not sorry. It is my duty to teach him."

Suddenly Archie felt tremendously interested. He had no idea what all this was about, or what his father's lesson was, but he felt he was in the presence of some drama apart from his own. It was with a sense of the interruption of this that he saw his mother turn to him.

"Archie, my dear," she said. "You have vexed and grieved me very much. Supposing I had felt wicked and had burned you stylograph pen, shouldn't I be sorry for having injured you? And aren't you sorry for having burned my hearthrug? What had I done to deserve that? Hadn't I given you leave to sit in my room, and look at my treasures? Why did you hurt me?"

Immediately the whole affair wore a different aspect. Instead of anger and justice, there was the sound of love. His heart melted, and he ran to her.

"Oh mummy, I didn't mean to vex you," he cried. "I didn't think of that. You hadn't done anything beastly to me."

He burst into tears.

"Oh, mummy, forgive me," he said. "I don't mind being whipped, at least not much; but I'm sorry; I beg your pardon. Please stop my allowance till I've paid for it."

"Yes, dear, it's only right that you should pay some of it. You shall have no more allowance for three weeks.

Now go straight upstairs, and go to bed till I come to you and tell you that you may get up. And Blessington tells me you have been rude to her. Go and beg her pardon first."

* * * * *

The effect of this episode on Archie's mind was that his mother understood, and his father didn't. The prospect of a whipping had not made him falter in his resolve not to say he was sorry, so long as he wasn't sorry, but the moment his mother had put his misdeeds in a sensible light he saw them sensibly, and would not have minded being whipped if by that drastic method he could have borne witness to the reality of his sorrow. But only three days later he received six smart cuts with that horrible cane for climbing on to the unparapetted roof of the house out of his bedroom window, which he had been expressly forbidden to do. But then there was no question of being sorry or not—as a matter of fact he was not—summary justice was executed for mere disobedience, and, before doing the same thing again, he added up the pleasure of going on the roof, and balanced it against the pain inflicted on the tight seat of his sailor-trousers as he bent over a chair, and found it wanting.

It was during this same month which saw his seven completed years that he did a very strange and unintelligible thing, though he suffered it rather than committed it. He did it, that is to say, quite involuntarily, and did not know he was doing it till it was done. This was the manner of it.

Miss Bampton had set him one of her delightful exercises in handwriting in his copy-book. "Never brush your teeth with the housemaid's broom" she had written in her beautiful copper-plate hand at the top of the page, and Archie was sitting with his tongue out copying this remarkable maxim, and amusing himself with conjectures as to what other strange habits such people as were likely to brush their teeth with the housemaid's broom might be supposed to have—perhaps they would lace their boots with the tongs, or write their letters with a poker... He had got about half-way down the page when suddenly there came over him that sensation with which he was beginning to become familiar, that feeling of extension and expansion within himself, that falling away of the limitations of consciousness which opened some new interior world to him.

His pen paused, and then in the wrist of his right hand and in the fingers that still held his pen he felt a curious imperative kind of twitching, and knew that they wanted to write of their own volition, as it were, though it was not his copy that they were concerned with. Under this sensation of absolute compulsion, he took a sheet of paper that lay at his elbow, and let his pen rest on it, watching with the intensest curiosity what it would do. He had no idea what would happen, but he felt that something had to be written. For a couple of minutes perhaps his pen traced random lines on the paper, moving from left to right with a much greater speed than it was wont to go, and the letters began to form themselves with a rapidity and certainty unknown to his careful, halting calligraphy, and in firm upright characters. He saw his own name traced on the paper followed by a sentence, and then his pen (still apparently obedient to some unknown impulse from his fingers) gave a great dash and stopped altogether. And this is what he read:

"Archie, do let me talk to you sometimes.

"MARTIN."

The queer sensation had ceased altogether, and Archie stared blankly at the words that he knew his hand had written. But what they meant, he had no notion, nor did he know who Martin was. The whole thing was quite unintelligible to him, both the impulse that made him write, and that which he had written.

Miss Bampton had left the room on some errand, when she had set Archie his copy, and came back at this moment expecting to find the copy finished. She looked over his shoulder to see how he was getting on.

"My dear, haven't you got further than that?" she said. "I thought you would have finished it by this time."

She saw the other piece of paper half-concealed by Archie's left hand.

"Why, you've been writing something else," she said. "That's why you haven't got on further. Let me look."

"Please not," said Archie. "It's private."

Miss Bampton remembered that, a week ago, Archie had been seized with a strong desire for literary composition, and had composed a very remarkable short story, which may be given in full.

"CHAPTER I

"There was once a merderer with yellow eyes, and his wife said to him,

"'If you merder me you will be hung.'

"And he was hung on Tuesday next.

"FINIS. "

When Archie had brought this yarn to her she had laughed so uncontrollably that he was hurt. So, in the hope of finding another such (though Archie had no business to write stories in lesson-time) she said:

"My dear, do show me; I won't laugh."

Archie hesitated; he felt shy about disclosing this sentence he had written, but, on the other hand, Miss Bampton, who appeared to know everything, might help him towards the interpretation.

"Well, it's not a story," he said. "It's just this. I wrote it without knowing. Oh, Miss Bampton, what does it mean, and who is Martin?"

If it was Archie who hesitated before, it was Miss Bampton who hesitated now. Suddenly she had a clever thought.

"My dear, you've been thinking about the Martins that built in the sandpit last spring," she said. "Don't you remember how you and Jeannie made up a story about them?"

This was true enough, but it failed to satisfy Archie. Also he had a notion that Miss Bampton had made a call on her ingenuity in offering this explanation.

"But isn't there any other Martin?" he asked.

"None that you ever knew, Archie," she said. "I think it's one of those in the sandpit. Now get on with your copy, and we'll walk there before your dinner."

The incident passed into the medley of impressions that were crowding so quickly into the storehouse of Archie's consciousness, but it did not lie there quite unconnected with others. He laid it on the same shelf, so to speak, as that which held the memory of his waking vision one night in remote days, and held also the fact of his knowing what Miss Bampton had thought of in the guessing game. But those were among the secret things of which he spoke to nobody. One more impression for secret pondering, though of different sort from those, he had lately added to his store, and that when a whipping seemed imminent, and he saw one of Miss Schwarz's medicine-bottles standing on his father's table.

CHAPTER IV

Lady Davidstow and Miss Bampton were sitting together that night in Lady Davidstow's bedroom. She had sent her maid away, saying that she would not want her again that night, and now she held in her hand the sheet of paper covered with lines of meaningless scribbles, with the one intelligible sentence at the end, which Archie had written that day when he should have been doing his copy. In the other hand she held a letter written in ink that was now rather faded, and she was comparing the two. She looked at them for some time in silence, then turned to Miss Bampton.

"Yes, you are quite right, Cathie," she said. "What Archie wrote might actually be in Martin's handwriting. Look for yourself: there's the last letter he ever wrote to me."

Miss Bampton took the two papers from her.

"There's absolutely no difference," she said. "The moment I saw what Archie had written, I thought of Martin's handwriting. And then it was signed 'Martin.' Are you sure he has never heard of him? Not that that would account for the handwriting."

Lady Davidstow shook her head.

"I think it's impossible," she said. "Jeannie assured me she had never spoken to him about Martin, nor has

Blessington. He may have heard his name. He probably has heard his name mentioned. I remember mentioning it in Archie's hearing the other day, but he didn't pay the slightest attention. And he can't possibly recollect him even in the vaguest way. It is five years now since Martin died, and Archie was then only just two, and for six months before that Martin was with me at Grives."

Cathie Bampton laid down the two papers.

"I can't think why you never told Archie about him," she said.

Lady Davidstow's great grey eyes grew dim.

"Ah, my dear, if you were Martin's mother and Archie's mother you would know," she said. "If you had seen your eldest son die of consumption and your second son threatened with it, you would understand how natural it was not to tell Archie yet of the brother he had never consciously seen. Jack agreed with me, too. I have long been prepared for Archie asking questions, which certainly I would answer truthfully, and let the knowledge come to him quietly by degrees. I may have done wrong; I don't know. But I think I did right. I couldn't begin saying to Archie, 'You had a brother, but he died.' More would have come out; that he died of consumption; that for fear of that Archie lives so much in the open air."

"But, my dear, how will Archie begin to know unless you tell him?"

"Oh, in many ways. There is Martin's picture, for instance, in my room. Archie may ask who it is. Or, when he hears Martin's name mentioned, he will ask some time who Martin was. Indeed, I have often thought it odd that he hasn't. Only the other day Jack was talking to me about it, suggesting that it was time that Archie knew. Indeed, he rather urged me to tell him. And now, all of a sudden, we find Archie writing in Martin's handwriting, and signing with Martin's name."

"Shall you tell Lord Davidstow?" asked Miss Bampton.

"No, I certainly shall not. Jack hates all that approaches the neighbourhood of anything that might be called occult or spiritualistic. He says 'Pshaw,' as you know, if even hypnotism is mentioned. I did tell him about Archie's intuition in that guessing game, and, as you again know, he asked you not to play it any more, though at the same time he insisted that it was a mere guess on Archie's part."

Cathie was silent a moment.

"And those scribbles of Archie's?" she asked. "Do they not make it more difficult for you to tell him about Martin now? A sensitive boy like that might get it into his head that his dead brother was writing to him."

"Certainly I don't want Archie to think that," said his mother. "No, I shall put off telling him now."

"And if he asks?" said Miss Bampton.

"I have an idea that he won't ask."

She got up and moved about the room for a moment in silence.

"My dear, all children have got a secret life of their own," she said, "and, oh, how their mothers want to be admitted! But every young thing has a walled-up place in his heart, to which he admits nobody, and, if you ask to be admitted, not only is the door shut, but locked. We all had our secret places, and I make a guess that this bit of paper—by the way, mind you put it back in the school-room where Archie left it—lives in Archie's secret place. How I long to get in, the darling! But all I can do is to wait outside, and take what he gives me. Archie doesn't tell me everything, why should he? He didn't tell me what it was that made him put the burning coals out of the fire on to my hearthrug."

"Probably he didn't know."

"Something inside him knew, or else he wouldn't have done it. All we do is accountable for by what is inside us. Impulses come from within."

"But they are suggested by what is without," said Miss Bampton.

"Yes; that's the box on which the match is struck, but the fire is in the match. All you can do for a child, even your own child, is to suggest, and hope he'll take your suggestions."

Miss Bampton got up.

"It's late; I must go," she said. "But I want to ask you one thing. Do you believe in the possibility of Martin's having made a communication to Archie?"

"Yes; I think I do. That's why this affair has upset me so. The idea is so strange and new, that I'm frightened about it, though why I should be so I can't tell. With my whole heart I believe that my darling is living somewhere in an existence as individual as ever, and even more vivid, because the weakness and the illness and the weariness are past. So why should I be frightened at the thought that he could communicate with Archie? Ah, my dear, if only he would communicate with me! Or with Jack! Poor Jack, how he would scout the idea! How shocked he would be! I suppose that's part of my secret garden which I keep from Jack!"

She held her friend a moment after kissing her.

"Jack never really got over Martin's death," she said. "He couldn't bring himself into line with it. It was then

that it became a settled habit with him to try to forget...
Just lately he has been very bad. There, good-night, my
dear; I can't talk about it."

* * * * *

The whole incident affected Archie far less than it
affected either his mother or his governess, and next day
when he found his scribbled paper lying where he had
left it the day before, it excited no further curiosity in his
mind. He put the thought of it away on his shelf of
secret things which had nothing to do with his ordinary
normal life. In certain moods, which, after all only lasted
for a moment or two, the things that shelf contained
became far more real to him than any other of his
experiences; but for weeks and months at a time its
contents remained out of his reach, and if he shared
them, as his mother had said, with nobody else, he had
no share in them himself except at these odd, queer
moments. So when, next day, he came across this curious
sentence again, caught by him, as by some process of
wireless telegraphy, he felt but little interest in it, though
he sat for a couple of minutes with his pen held idly in
his hand, just to see if anything else happened. But there
was no sensation that ever so faintly resembled the
twitching and yearning of his hand to write he knew not
what, and he crumpled the paper up, and put it into the
fire. Somewhere below the threshold of his conscious self
lay the perceptions that were concerned with it, those
perceptions that guessed what Miss Bampton had
thought of, that somehow swam up to the surface, as he

used to lie in bed of a morning, and sink into the depths that lay below the green-tinted ceiling of his room; and, while they lay dormant, it was as if they never existed.

But now for some weeks there had been no light whatever on his ceiling, and morning after morning he awoke with no sense of exhilaration at all in the coming of another day, but with a drowsy depression lying thick upon him, as he heard the rustle of the endless rain in the shrubs outside, and languidly went through those exercises that used to invigorate him but now only tired him. All through the month the damp chilly weather persisted, and day after day the same lowering heavens obscured the sun; never in this bright Sussex upland had there been so continuous a succession of rain-streaked hours. The wonder of seeing the lake slowly rising till it engulfed the lower end of the lawn, and made an island of the summer-house failed to stir him, and there was no magic in the unique experience of punting across the lawn to it. Then, one morning early in December, the deluge was stayed, once more the sun slid up a cloudless sky, and the whole nature of the world was changed.

Archie had again been indoors for a couple of days, with a return of the cold that really was responsible for the burning of his mother's hearthrug, and once more the ecstasy of living possessed him. As consolation for his imprisonment, he and Jeannie were both given a holiday, and, breakfast over, they scampered out, and once more saw their shadows racing in front of them. The game was to tread on somebody else's shadow. Blessington's shadow did not count because anybody could tread on that; but it required real agility to tread on Jeannie's, for it had the nippiest way of dodging before your foot could really descend on it. So they ran in circles round Blessington, and Marco, the collie, ran in circles round them; and though it counted two to tread on Marco's shadow (you must not hold Marco and then stamp on his shadow), no one had got nearer than a doubtful claim to have trod on his tail.

Quite suddenly Archie stopped; he had an odd, warm sensation in his mouth that required investigation. Two days ago Jeannie's nose had bled, which Archie thought rather grand. There had been rather a fuss about it: she was laid down on the floor, and Miss Bampton put the door-key down her back, and eventually some ice was brought, and it was all quite important. But now it was not his nose that was bleeding, but his mouth.

"Oh, I say, I'm bleeding in my mouth," he said. "That's just as good as Jeannie's nose."

Even while he spoke he felt rather giddy, and instantly Blessington's arm was round him.

"Eh, my dear," she said. "That'll never do. You lean against me, and we'll go home very quietly. You mustn't chase any more shadders this morning."

As a matter of fact, Archie did not want to. He felt a rather enjoyable lightness in his head, but he felt weak also, and disinclined to run.

"Oh, here it is again," he said, and once more, now with a sensation of choking, he coughed up blood.

He saw Blessington's tender, anxious face above him, exactly as it had appeared in the earliest of all his memories, and, as then, felt absolutely comfortable in the thought that she was there. Her arm was close round his neck now, and with her other hand she made a sign to Jeannie.

"Run straight back home, dear," she said, "and tell your mamma to come out here at once, and bring William. Master Archie and I are going to sit down quietly till she comes."

Archie rather enjoyed all this. He was completely in Blessington's hands, and utterly content to be so. Then Blessington did a very odd thing.

"Well, I'm so hot with seeing you and Miss Jeannie running about," she said, "that I'm going to sit down, and wait for a bit. And you'll wait with me, dear, won't you? There! Put your head on my knee and lie down. I know you're hot with running about."

As by a conjuring trick, Archie knew that Blessington's cloak with its collar of rabbit's fur was tucked round him. It was rather odd to be lying with his head on Blessington's knee out of doors in the winter, but he had no desire to question the propriety of all this, for it fitted in so well with his main desire, which was to stop still. A couple of minutes ago he had been running about at top-speed; now he had no wish except to do as he was told, to put himself into responsible hands. It was all rather dreamlike; his mother and William were coming here soon, but that seemed quite natural. And it was still rather grand to bleed at the mouth. Then came a gentle singing in his ears, a pleasant sense of complete indolence, that never quite passed into unconsciousness, and presently it was just as natural to find himself in William's arms. Out of a half-opened eye he saw William was in livery, for the blue and white stripes of his low waistcoat were close to him, and his cheek rested on William's shirt-front. And then he saw that there was a bright red stain there which certainly was not part of William's ordinary livery.

"Oh, William, I've messed you," he said. "I am sorry."

"That's all right, Master Archie," said William. "It wasn't a new shirt this morning."

Some dim reminiscence about something William had told him concerning beer-money and washing came into his head. William had beer-money or washing; he could not remember which.

"I shall pay for it anyhow," he said.

Still feeling rather dizzy, he had the impression of his own room with Blessington and his mother near him. Apparently he had been laid on the floor, for his bed looked tall beside him. Then he was not on the floor any more, but in his bed, and whether it was at once or later, he never knew, but presently there was in the room the stranger who once had made him play the pointless game of saying "ninety-nine!" Here he was again with a plug against Archie's chest, and two other plugs in his own ears. Archie remembered him quite distinctly: he was a doctor who didn't give any medicine.

"Shall I say 'ninety-nine'?" he asked.

"No, just think 'ninety-nine,' and don't talk. If you think 'ninety-nine' it will do just as well."

Archie had no desire to do anything beyond what he was told to do. He thought "ninety-nine," and the stranger smiled very kindly at him.

"That's capital," he said. "Now just go on thinking 'ninety-nine'..." and whether he floated out of the window, or vanished like the Cheshire cat, or walked away in the ordinary manner, Archie was quite unaware.

Then he was hungry, and, behold, there was Blessington with boiled rabbit, and he was sleepy and hungry again, and again sleepy. Sometimes his mother was there, and sometimes his father, who looked rather odd, and sometimes William brought coals, though the housemaid usually did that; and there was Blessington again, who washed his face, and then, uncovering him limb by limb, washed these also. Archie could not understand why he acquiesced in this odd state of things, or why he did not ask to get up and run about and play the shadow-game again. But merely he was quite content to lie still, and he hoped that when Jeannie came and talked to him she would not suggest the resumption of the game that had been so ecstatic but had been interrupted so suddenly. And Miss Bampton came in, and read to him something she had been writing. He noticed that she read from printed pages, not like the pages of an ordinary book, but long strips. It appeared that it was a story she had written which had got printed, and he asked whether his story about "the merderer" would ever get printed. They all came in, and talked gently and melted away again.

Then arrived a memorable morning when, instead of being gently awakened by Blessington, he awoke entirely of his own accord, and felt strong and cross. Cross he certainly proved to be, for when the morning washing began, which hitherto had been a pleasant and luxurious performance, he found that Blessington could do nothing right. She put soap into his eyes, she tickled his feet and scratched his shoulder with her disgusting flannel. Archie made firm complaints against each of these outrages, of a sort that would usually lead to rebuke on Blessington's part. Indeed, he had not been nearly so rude on the occasion when he had been told to apologize to her.

But now she merely beamed at each disagreeable remark, and, instead of scolding him, she made a most cryptic answer.

"Eh, my darling," she said. "Thank God you feel like blaming me again."

"What *do* you mean, Blessington?" said Archie angrily. "Oh, do take care of my little toe. You've nearly pulled it off once already."

"Well then, I'll kiss it," said Blessington. And did.

Archie looked at her.

"Why are you crying?" he asked, wriggling his foot away from her. He did not want it to be kissed.

"Crying? I'm just laughing," said Blessington. And that was true; she was laughing. But she was crying also.

An idea struck Archie which had not occurred to him before.

"Am I ill, Blessington?" he asked. "Am I going to die?"

At that there was no question of what Blessington was doing. Her laughing quite ceased, and she gave a great sob.

"No, my darling, you're not going to die," she said. "Get that out of your silly head. You're not…"

And then she broke down altogether, and hid her face in the towel with which she had been washing Archie's left foot. He saw her shoulders shaking; he knew that, for some reason, she could not speak. But she was crying, and was not cross with him for being cross. It behoved a man to administer consolation.

"Oh, don't cry, Blessington," he said. "What is there to cry about? Unless it's because I'm so cross."

"I don't mind your crossness," she said. "You let me finish wiping your foot. And then I'll go down and tell your mamma—"

"Oh, don't say I was cross," said Archie. "I'm sorry I was cross."

"Nay, I'll just tell her how much better you feel this morning. And I shouldn't wonder if there was a great treat coming, something you'll like ever so much."

"Is it another train?" asked Archie.

"Bless the boy!" said she. "How you think about trains!"

* * * * *

Archie ate his breakfast, and passed an entrancing morning. Everybody seemed desirous of congratulating him, as if he had done something particularly meritorious, as on the occasion of his not getting drowned when he jumped out of the boat after the pike. He held a sort of levee, the most remarkable incident of which was the appearance of Miss Bampton with a piece of white chalk, with which she drew on the green drugget by his bed, so that he could easily see it, a great map of England and Central Europe. There was the South of England, with London written large, and here was Lacebury also conspicuously marked. Then there was the English Channel with France below it, and Paris in the middle, and away to the right, some distance below, the Lake of Geneva. Then, still explaining, she made marks like caterpillars which were mountains, and said that now the mountains were covered with snow, even down to the tails of the caterpillars and below was the Lake of Geneva, quite blue. All the roads were covered with snow up by the caterpillars' tails, and there were no wheels on the carriages, but they slid over the frozen snow instead. There was skating up there, for they made lakes which were covered with ice. They just put water into flat places, and there was your lake, and it instantly froze. It never rained there, but if it wanted to do anything, it just snowed. Usually it didn't want to do anything, and there was the sun and the snow, and wouldn't it be jolly to go there?

This presented itself to Archie's mind as a purely abstract proposition. Of course it would be jolly to go to a place where you saw the real mountains and had a glimpse of the real Lake of Geneva, and slid instead of walking; but what next? Did any one ever go there?

Apparently. Right at the tail of the caterpillar was a place called Grives. There it was, written down: the railway only went as far as Bex, and there the sledges began. And always the sun shone, so that you sat out of doors with the snow all round you, and felt perfectly warm.

Suddenly Archie could stand it no longer. It was like talking to a starving man about roast beef. There was roast beef somewhere in the world, and he wanted it so badly. In the same way something inside Archie starved for sun and snow and thin air.

"Oh, shut up, Miss Bampton," he said. "I want it so frightfully."

His mother was sitting on the edge of his bed watching the map of Europe.

"Archie, we're going to Grives in a few days," she said. "You and Blessington and Jeannie and I."

* * * * *

It was memorable moment when the boat rose up and then curtsied to the big seas that were jostling each other up the Channel. Archie's only knowledge of the sea was culled from a single visit to Brighton two years ago, and the sea to him then appeared but one among an assembly of unusual bright objects: nigger-minstrels and tin buckets and piers and penny-in-the-slot machines. But on this bright winter day he hailed a new and glorious creature, when he saw the steep white-capped waves, grey in the bulk but lit with lovely green where they grew thin, come streaming up to the ship's side and fall away again in puffs of white smoke and squirts of high-flung foam. Warmly wrapped up in his new fur-coat, he sat on deck sheltered from the weather and watched with ecstatic wonder the rollicking, untamed creatures that sent the boat now over on one side, now on the other, and threw it up and caught it again within their firm, liquid embrace. Behind it lay a wake of white foam, like a long string still tying them to dazzling chalk cliffs and the wave-smothered pier, and overhead the masts, thrumming to the wind, struck right and left across a wide arc of the sky, and their shadows sped across the deck. These swervings and upliftings and descents of the ship as she whacked her way across the shifting mountains produced in him no physical discomfort, but only the sense that a new and glorious being had come into his life.

All too soon, even as the jig-saw puzzle of the map of Europe had warned him by the narrowness of the straits, the shores of France began to rear themselves up above the wave-moulded horizon, and presently another pier received them, and men spoke a strange tongue (probably French, though it might have been Hebrew) and made novel gestures, and wore blouses, and boots that turned up at the toes more than was usual in England. There were no platforms: you had to climb the sheer carriage side from ground-level, and the engines were altogether different, and the movement of the train was other than that he was accustomed to. Then, sure enough, they came after nightfall to a great town, and drove across it, keeping firmly to the wrong side of the road, though, as everybody else did the same, there were not so many collisions as might have been expected. Then came the novelty of eating dinner in a restaurant perched up in another station, from the windows of which you could romantically observe train after train sliding out into the winter night. Before long Archie's train did the same, and then came the glorious experience of undressing in a train, while it was going at full speed. There was never so remarkable a bedroom, all gold and looking-glass and stamped leather, and instead of his bed and Blessington's being put on the floor, one, which Archie begged to have, was put above the other. Close by him in the roof of the carriage was the electric light which, when you turned a small handle the requisite distance, dwindled to a mere speck. At some timeless hour he woke up, and found a very polite stranger in his bedroom, to whom Blessington explained that they had neither spirits nor lace nor tobacco in their luggage. And the total stranger then apparently guessed that he had been misinformed, for he went away again without another word.

The clever train found its way without any mistake through the darkness of the long winter's night, for next morning it was skimming along by the edge of a lake so large that no wonder it appeared on the jig-saw map of Europe. The lake at home, once an almost boundless sheet of water, was no more than a wayside puddle to this; the hills at home were no more than the tunnelled earth of moles compared with those slopes on which the rows of pines looked smaller than the edging of a table-cloth against the blue. Blue? Archie thought he had never known what blue was till now, not what sunshine was until he saw the dazzle of it on those sparkling slopes. And they, so his mother told him, were not mountains at all: they were only hills; but soon he should see what mountains meant. As they passed through the glittering towns that stood on the edge of the lake, he could see the sleighs sliding over the streets with jingle of bells crisply sounding in the alert air. Other smaller sleighs were drawn by pleased, smiling dogs. There was never such a morning of discoveries. The only drawback was that, though it ought only to have been ten o'clock, the Swiss chose that it should be eleven, and thus an hour of this immortal day was lost; but his mother told him that the French had taken care of it, and would give it back to them when they returned.

All this was romantic enough, but the romance grew more deep-hued yet when, in the early afternoon, Archie was packed into a sleigh and the journey up through the pine-woods began. White-capped and white-cloaked stood the red-trunked trees, and now and then, with a falling puff of snow, a laden branch, free of its burden, sprang upwards again. Then the pines were tired of climbing, and the sleigh left them and came out on to a plateau high above the valley. And could that have been sunshine down there? For the valley seemed choked with grey fog, and here above was real sunshine and air that refreshed you as with wine. The hills that had appeared so gigantic had sunk below them, but behind them rose the spears and precipices, remote and blue, of the real mountains, and, as they went upwards, these soared ever above them, and presently the blue on them was tinged with apricot and rose in the glow of the declining sun. And the driver cracked his whip, and the horses jingled their bells in response, and, pointing with it to a row of toy houses still far above them, he grinned at Archie and said "Grives."

The rose of sunset had faded and the snows were turned to ivory-crystal beneath the full moon when they entered the long, lit village street, with its old carved wooden houses, deep-balconied towards the south, and the modern hotels now just opening again for the winter season. These, too, they left behind them, and again mounting a steep slope, came to where, round a sudden corner, stood the big chalet which Archie's mother had taken.

"And here we are," she said.

Archie sat staring. Somehow he felt he knew the house; perhaps it was a house he had dreamed of. There were pines to right and left of it, just as there were in this picture of a house that existed somewhere in his mind; it had the same broad balconies, where you could lie all day in the sun, and look over the village roofs below and across the valley from which all afternoon they had climbed. He felt he knew it inside too: there would be rooms with wooden walls, and china stoves—where had he heard of china stoves?—and the smell of pine-wood haunting all the house. It was extraordinarily interesting...

A big, genial woman had turned up the electric light outside the door when she heard the crack of the driver's whip, and stood bareheaded, ready to welcome them. Archie felt that he knew something about her too.

"Ah, *miladi*," she said to his mother in very crisp good English, yet with a funny precision, as if she had learned it as a lesson, "I give you welcome back to Grives. And how is my dear Madame Blessington?"

Archie thought his mother interrupted these greetings rather suddenly.

"How are you madame Seiler?" she said. "And here is my daughter Jeannie and Archie"—and she added something in an undertone, which sounded like the language Miss Schwarz used to talk.

Madame Seiler whisked round with renewed cordiality.

"And such lovely weather you have come to," she said. "The sun all day and the frost all night. But we keep out the frost and let the sun in."

They passed into the entrance-hall, aromatic and warm, heated by a big china stove that roared pleasantly, and instantly, without any reason, there came into Archie's mind the remembrance of the words his hand had scribbled one morning with the signature "Martin." It came out of the darkness like a light seen distantly at night; it flashed like a signal and vanished again. But for one second it had been there, remote, but visible and luminous.

Lady Davidstow, for some obscure and grown-up reason, thought good at supper that night to explain incidentally that she had written to Madame Seiler that Blessington was coming, and that was how she had known Blessington's name. Archie had a very strong and wholesome confidence in his mother, but he knew that grown-up people sometimes made statements which have got (by the rules) to be accepted, but which do not always convince. Blessington's saying that she could not run any more because she had a bone in her leg was an instance of this class of statement, as also was the occasion when his mother spoke, a year ago, about Abracadabra's sneezings. This mode of accounting for Madame Seiler's knowing Blessington's name came under the same head: as far as it went it might be true, and though it did not particularly interest him whether it was true, so to speak, all the way, he felt that there was something mildly mysterious about it. And, having made this unconvincing statement, his mother at once passed on to more interesting topics.

It was a blow, when Blessington called him next morning, to be told that he was tired with the journey and must stop in bed for breakfast. That was a perfectly unfounded statement, but, like those others, had grumblingly to be accepted, though Archie knew quite well that he had never felt less tired.

"You mayn't feel it, dear," said Blessington, "but you are."

"I should think I ought to know best," said Archie.

"No, I know best," said Blessington firmly. "And your mamma says so, too."

Archie began to wonder they were not right. He did not feel tired, as he had told Blessington, but something inside him said that it did not want to run about, or even skate, but it was very well pleased that his body, well wrapped up, should sit up in bed, and bask in the sun which blazed in through the opened French window communicating with the big balcony outside his room. Then, after breakfast, there came in his mother with a big jovial man, whose name was Dr. Dobie.

"I never saw such a lazy fellow," exclaimed this rather attractive person. "Fancy not being up yet!"

"They wouldn't let me," said Archie.

"Well, as soon as I've had a look at you, up you shall get," said the doctor. "But I can't wait till you're dressed. Now, undo your coat a minute."

Once again the instrument with plugs was produced, and the ninety-nine game played.

"That's capital," said the doctor, "and now in a minute I'll have done with you. Just put that into your mouth with the end under your tongue. There, like that."

This was a very short process, and Dr. Dobie got up.

"Now, my plan for you is this," he said. "You shall dress and lie out in the sun on your balcony. And, after you've had dinner, you shall go for a sleigh drive, and walk a little on your way back. Then balcony again, till it's dark."

"But mayn't I skate?" asked Archie, who didn't really want to.

"No, not just yet. We'll have you skating before long, but not at present. The more you do as you're told, the sooner you'll skate."

During the next week, but so gradually that at no moment was it a discovery, it dawned on Archie that he was ill, and that his illness dated from the time when his mouth bled. The knowledge did not in the least depress him, because with it came the absolute certainty in his own mind that he was going to get quite well again. For the most part he did not feel ill, though there was often an uncomfortable period towards evening when he felt sometimes hot and sometimes cold, and one moment would want another coat on, and soon would have liked to throw off all the clothes he had. These odd feelings were accompanied by a sort of extra vividness in his perceptions: he felt tingling and alert, and the lights seemed brighter than their wont. But when this had been more marked than usual in the evening, he always felt very tired next day, and more than once he did not get up at all but had his bed pulled out on to the balcony. Then, as the weeks passed on, there was less of this, and before long he was allowed to tie his toboggan to the back of the sleigh, and be towed up-hill through the pine-wood that climbed the slopes behind the village. That was a delightful experience; on each side stood the snowy trees frosted like a Christmas cake, now almost meeting above the narrow track, and then standing away from it again, so that the deluge of sun poured down as into a pool, while from in front came the jingle of the horse's bells, and from below him the squeak of his runners. Then they came out again on to the ski-ing slopes, where visitors to Grives played the entrancing game of seeing, apparently, who could fall down most often in the most complicated manner. Where the slope was steepest there was erected a sort of platform, so that the runner, flying down the slope above, was shot into the air, touching ground again yards below. Or, on other mornings, when things went well, and there had been no hot-and-cold period the evening before, he tobogganed down the slope below the house to the edge of the skating-rink and sat there in the snow, with everything round frozen hard, yet feeling perfectly warm, so potent were the beams of this ineffable sun through the thin, dry air. Jeannie was learning to skate and progressed, in wobbling half-circles, and shrilly announced that this and no other was the outside edge. Or four of the experts in a railed-off and hallowed place at the end of the huge rink would put down an orange, and proceed to weave a mystic dance in obedience to the shouted orders of one of them. At one moment all four would be swiftly converging on a back-edge to their orange, and, just at the moment when a complicated collision seemed imminent, would somehow change their direction, and, lo, all four were sailing outwards and forwards again in big, sweeping curves. Then there were the hoarse, angry cries of the curlers to listen to, and the pleasant sight of the stone sliding swiftly down the ice and butting, with a hollow chunk, into any other that stood in its way. And then a slow sliding stone would come down, and people swept violently in front of it to encourage it not to lie down and die, which for the most part it did. But always too soon, his mother or Blessington would come to tell him that it was time to go home again and he would tie his toboggan to the back of the sleigh, and be pulled up-hill to the house. That was a tiresome moment, and Archie found himself wondering, with a pang of jealousy, why, when so many were hale and hearty round him, it should be just he who was obliged to go and lie down on the roofed balcony, instead of skating or curling. But even when he had set-backs, and had to lie all day on the balcony, he never faltered in his belief that he was going to get well.

Here then, in brief, were the outward aspects of Archie's life at Grives, new and attractive and full of sun and dry, powdery snow. He took no active part in the activities, and was but an observer, but all the time there were inward aspects of his life, which no one shared with him, and which no one ever observed. He was always on the alert, even on those mornings of tiredness after he had had a rise of temperature the evening before, for the development of a certain thing, the existence of which came to him only in hints and whispers. But the thing itself was always there, though he had no control over its manifestations. He could no more bring it into the exterior life of the senses, he could no more see or hear it or produce any evidence of it, as he willed, than he could make the sun pierce and scatter the clouds, which for a whole week in January alternately rained and snowed on to Grives. All he could do was to wait for it, and he waited in a perpetual serene excitement. It came always when he was alone: he got to think of solitude, in this present stage, as an essential for its manifestation. And, as the weeks went on, he associated it more and more with the balcony on which he lay for the greater part of the day. It, the thing he waited for, and was completely silent about even when he had intimate good-night talks with his mother, was no other than "Martin" (whoever Martin might be) whose presence had come into his mind with such unexpected vividness when first he saw the chalet. Never was the idea of "Martin" absent from his mind: it might lurk concealed behind the excitement of trailing after the sleigh, or of watching the skaters on the ice, but at all times it was ready to enfilade him. And, among all the diversions of the snow and the ice and the sun, he had an inward eye turned towards this inscrutable "Martin"—no winged nester in the sand-cliffs, but somebody, somebody…

Lessons in a mild way had begun again before this wretched rainy and snowy week, and Miss Bampton sent out from home the most entrancing and topical copies. "Hot outside-edge for lunch," was one, in allusion to the news of Jeannie's skating; "Cold inside-edge for dinner" was another. Whatever the weather was, Archie was out of doors all day, and Jeannie, during lesson-time, used to sit out on his balcony and do her more advanced tasks, which, with his, were taken in to Lady Davidstow for correction. More often his mother used to sit on the balcony, too, but during this damp, abominable week she suffered from a heavy cold, and the lessons were brought to her by Jeannie. And on this particular morning, Jeannie had finished her French translation first, and so went in to her mother to have it corrected, leaving Archie to finish the last three lines of his copy.

Ever since his first entry into the house, there had been for him nothing more than the perception of Martin's presence. With the patience of a child who wants something, a thing only equalled by the patience of a cat watching a mouse-hole, he had never taken his inward eye off this. He was always ready for it. As Jeannie went in with her completed French lesson, he laid down his pen, and looked for a moment at the streaming icicles on the eaves of his shelter, and listened with a sense of depression to the drip of the melted water that formed grey pits in the whiteness of the snow below. Because there was a thaw, the air felt colder than when there were twenty degrees of frost, and the blanket on his couch was studded with condensed moisture. "It is warmer," thought Archie to himself, "so it ought to *be* warmer. But it's colder."

At this moment he felt a sudden thrill in his right wrist, and thought that a melted drop had fallen on it. But he saw there was no drop there, and wondered at this sensation of touch. Then he saw his fingers begin to twitch, and instantly recognized the sensation he had felt once before. He swept his incomplete copy off his pad of blotting-paper, and took his pen up again. Surely he could write on his blotting-paper.

At first the meaningless scribbles appeared, made more grotesque and senseless by the running of the ink.

There was a pencil on the table by him, and he took that up instead of the pen, while his hand twitched and jerked to be at its task again. The day before he had pinched his finger in the hinge of a slamming window, and he saw the moon-shaped blot of blood below the nail quivering as his fingers starved to hold an instrument of writing again. Then his hand settled down, like a hovering bird on to a bough, as he picked up the pencil.

For a little while the scribbles went on: then, watching the marks on the blotting-paper just as an excited spectator watches the action of a play, he saw words coming. His brain did not know what they were till they appeared on the paper.

"Archie, Archie," said the pencil, "I want to talk to you. I can't always, but sometimes I can. Dear Archie, try to be ready when I get through. Lovely to talk to you. Can't to mother."

An incontrollable excitement seized the boy. "Oh, who is it?" he said aloud. "Is it Martin?"

He felt the twitching die away in his fingers, and presently he was left sitting there, his copy on the floor and the scrawl on the blotting-paper. But he had, somewhere inside him, a sense of extraordinary satisfaction. Something or somebody had "got through," whatever that meant. The words in pencil on his blotting-paper had "got through." And he turned it over

hastily, and picked up the unfinished copy, as the door-
handle into his room rattled, and Jeannie came out on to
the balcony again with her corrected French exercise.

Several days of this chilly dripping weather, with the
foehn wind from the south went by, and when that
ceased, and the wind veered to the north, blowing high
over Grives, and raising feathers of snowdust on the
peaks to the north, while the sheltered valley basked in
calm and sunlight again, there were eventful days of
carting the snow from the rinks before any further
development took place in Archie's secret life. This
carting of the snow was splendid fun, for, when a hand-
sleigh of it was piled high, Archie would squat on the
front of it (thereby adding considerably to the weight)
and in a shrill voice direct the men who pushed it to
right or left, in order to reach the steep bank down
which they discharged their burden. When they were
come to the edge of it, some large, strong man lifted
Archie off his perch, and waited with him, while the
sleigh was pushed to the very brink, and its burden
overturned in a jolly lumpy avalanche that poured down
the built-up bank of the rink. Then Archie mounted his
throne again and was pulled back to where the men with
spades loaded up again... When the sleigh seemed to be
sufficiently full he called out "Stop," and made the
return journey to the side of the rink. This was all
tremendously grand, and he had an idea that the clearing
of the rink could never have taken place without him.
Certainly his sleigh worked much faster than any other,
for, in his honour, those who pushed always ran to

discharge their burden at top speed, instead of going slowly like the others.

"Oh, that was a pace," he would say as somebody lifted him off. "Look, mummy, they're going to turn it over."

The rink then was clear again (thanks to Archie's great exertions) before his secret life made any step forward. But one afternoon, when he had been watching the skating from his balcony, something further occurred. He was alone, for his mother had gone down with Jeannie to the rink, and Blessington had gone shopping, and there was a bell by him, by means of which he could summon Madame Seiler if he wanted anything. But he had no thoughts of summoning Madame Seiler; he was extremely content to lie in the sun, and watch the rink sometimes, and sometimes to read a fascinating book called *The Rose and the Ring*, which his mother had given him. There were absurd pictures of Prince Bulbo, an enormously fat young gentleman, whom Archie did not wish to resemble, but was rather afraid of resembling, since Dr. Dobie at his last visit had told him he was getting fat...

It was all very peaceful and happy, and he had lost interest in Jeannie's falls and even in Prince Bulbo's executions, and was staring placidly at a very bright spot of glistening snow which caught the sun at the edge of the rink, when lines of shadow began to pass over the field of his vision, exactly as they used to pass over the green-lit ceiling of his night-nursery at home. This was interesting: he did not feel in the least sleepy, but very wide awake, and was conscious of sinking down through this lovely luminous air, with the bright spot of light getting every moment higher above him, when he suddenly heard his name called.

"Archie, Archie," said the voice, which was close to him, and wonderfully friendly. And at the same moment he felt on the back of his hand the touch of another hand that was smooth and young and somehow familiar, though he had never felt it before.

He tried not to disturb the impression. There was some sort of spell on him, light as a gossamer-web, which the slightest movement, physical or mental, on his part, might break.

"Yes, I'm Archie," he said.

But, the moment he spoke, he knew that he had spoken somehow in the wrong way. Another part of him, not his lips and their voluntary movements, should have answered. He ought to have thought the answer with that part of him that saw the lines of shadow passing across the bright steel surface of the rink below, that felt himself sinking down and down beneath the bright spot opposite... He could not have explained, but he knew it was so, and instantly there was he back on his balcony again with *The Rose and the Ring* in his hand, and Jeannie on the rink. Madame Seiler clattering dishes in the kitchen, and himself all alone, lying in the sunshine. He knew that something inside him had been tremendously happy when his name was called and his hand touched in that intimate manner, and, now that the touch and the voice were gone, he felt something akin to what he felt when he was feverish, and Blessington had said "good-night" and left him. But then, he always knew that Blessington had only gone into the next room, and could be summoned. And he could not summon him who had called "Archie" to him. He had not the least doubt that it was Martin who had called, that it was Martin's hand that had been laid on his. But who was this dear person called "Martin," and where was Martin? Secure in the knowledge that it was Martin who had come to him, and touched him and called to him, he put down his book, and shut his eyes so that his feeling of being alone should be intensified.

"Martin," he whispered. "Oh, Martin!"

He lay there tense and excited, sure that Martin would come again. Then in a dim, child-like manner, not formulating anything to himself, but only feeling his way, he knew he had called wrong. He must call differently, if he hoped to have any reply, call from inside. But, the more earnestly he attempted to "call from inside," the further he got away from that "inside" mood, which he knew, but could not recapture.

"Oh, what rot!" he said at length, and picked up *The Rose and the Ring* again to ascertain whether Bulbo was really going to be executed on this second occasion when he piled his table on his bed and his chair on his table, and his hat-box on his chair, and peeped out of the window from his horrid cell, to see whether it was eight o'clock yet...

Every day, in this return of frost and sunshine, Archie felt stronger, and soon the desire to skate took firm hold of him. Oddly enough, the pleasant Dr. Dobie began to agree with him, and within a day or two of the time when Archie's desire to skate became a pressing need, Dr. Dobie sanctioned it, and Archie had a humiliating hour or two. He had seen Jeannie lean outwards, and announce the outside edge, he had seen Jeannie lean a little inwards and proclaim the inside edge and round she went in curves that Archie could not but envy. He had only got to lean outwards and inwards like that, and surely he was master of his curves. But he found that his curves were master of him, and tumbled him down instead, or would have done so if a kind Swiss on skates had not always been on hand to prevent any disaster of this kind. But then Jeannie had learned, so it seemed to Archie, by falling down, and he resented the hand that saved him from falling.

"Do let me fall down," he said. "I can't learn unless I fall down."

"Better not fall down, sir," said this amiable young man. "I hold you; you learn best so."

"But Jeannie didn't," said Archie.

"No; but she is a girl," whispered his Swiss.

"Oh, ought girls to fall down and not boys?" asked Archie, rather interested in this new difference between the sexes.

* * * * *

Archie was allowed, by the end of January, to skate for half an hour before lunch with his Swiss hovering over him like a friendly eagle, to have lunch with Jeannie seated side by side on a toboggan at the edge of the rink, and skate for half an hour again afterwards at the end of which time a second eagle appeared in the person of Blessington or his mother, and carried him off to the sleigh. Right on through half February lasted the golden frosty weather; then came a great snowfall, and with that the frost broke. The snow degenerated into rain, the wind veered again into the slack south, and the roofs dripped and the trees tossed their white burdens from them. But, as the snow melted, wonderful things happened in the earth at the summons of the suns of spring, for gentians pushed their lengthening stems up through the thinning crust, and put forth their star-like flowers, deep as the blue of night and brilliant as the blue of day. The call of the spring, though yet the snow-wreaths lingered, pierced through them, and the listening grasses and bulbs pricked up their little green ears above the soil. Wonderful as last spring had been, the first that

Archie had ever consciously noticed, this Alpine Primavera was twice as magical, for winter was caught in her very arms, and warmed to life again. Morning by morning the pine-woods steamed like the hot flank of a horse, and when the mists cleared nature's great colour-box had been busy again with fresh greens, and more vivid reds on the tree-trunks, and weak, pale snowdrops and mountain crocuses shone like silver and gold in the sheltered hollows. A more tender blue took the place of the crystallized skies of winter, and for the barren, brilliant light of the January sun was exchanged a fruitful and caressing luminousness that flooded the world instead of merely looking down upon it. Soon from the lower slopes the snow was quite vanished, and instead of the tinkle of sleigh-bells there came from the pastures the deeper note from the bells of feeding cattle, which all winter long had been penned up in chalets, eating the dry cakes of last year's harvest of grass.

Archie had been lying in his balcony one morning writing an account of these things to Miss Bampton. His mother had gone back to England to take Jeannie home, but would be back at the end of the week, and in the absence of an instructor Archie's task was to write a long letter daily to somebody at home. This he enjoyed doing, for the search for words in which to express himself had begun to interest him, and he had just written: "If you listen very hard, you can almost hear the grass and the flowers fizzing. Is it the sap? It's like fizzing anyhow. That's what I mean."

As he paused at the end of his third page, he felt something in his hand that also reminded him of fizzing. There was that queer thrill and twitching in his fingers, which he recognized at once, and words, not searched for by him, but coming from some other source, began to trace themselves on the blank fourth page. To-day there were no preliminary scrawls, the firm, upright handwriting was coherent from the first.

"Archie, I've got through again," it wrote. "Isn't it fun? If you want a test ("Test?" thought Archie, "what's that?") you'll find a circle cut on the bark of the pine opposite the front-door. Dig in the earth just below it. There's a box and some things in it. I hid them."

A wave of conscious excitement came over the boy, and instantly his hand stopped writing.

"Oh, bother; it's stopped," he said to himself. "I wish I hadn't interrupted it."

But he had interrupted it, and, since he could not get back into that particular quiescence which, he had begun to see, always accompanied these manifestations, he could at least do what the writing suggested, and, slipping off his couch, he tip-toed downstairs in order not to let Blessington hear his exit.

There were two pine-trees, either of which might have been described as opposite the front-door, and he searched in vain round the first of these for any sign of the circle cut on the bark. Then, coming to the other, he at once saw, with a sudden beating of his heart, a rough circle cut in the bark just opposite his eyes. A grey ring of lichen had grown into it, making it so conspicuous that he wondered he had never noticed it before. Next moment he was down on his knees, grubbing up the loose earth directly below it, with the eager, absolute certainty of success. The earth came away very easily, and his hole was not yet a foot deep when he saw something white and shining at the bottom of it, and presently he drew out a small, round tin box, like that which stood on the table in his father's study, and held tobacco. He hastily filled the earth into his excavation again, and, undetected, tip-toed back to his balcony.

For a while the lid resisted his efforts to open it, but soon he got it loose and looked inside. On the top lay a folded piece of paper; below there was a stick of chocolate in lead paper, a pencil, a match-box, and a photograph of a boy about nine years old whom Archie instantly knew to be like himself. Then he opened the piece of folded paper, and saw words written on it in a hand he knew quite well:

"This is Martin Morris's," was the inscription, "and belongs to him alone, and not anybody else at all ever."

Archie read this, looked at the photograph again, and a flood of light poured in on his mind. It was no wonder that he had felt that Martin was friendly and affectionate, that Martin wanted to talk to him, that

Martin told him of the *cache* he had made, for to whom should he tell it but to his brother?

Yes: Martin was here, for Martin had written to him, had called him... And then, in a moment, more light flashed on him. Certainly Martin was alive, but he was not alive in the sense that his mother was alive or Blessington. In that sense Martin was dead. There was nothing in the least shocking or terrifying in the discovery, and it burst upon him as the sense of spring had done. It was just a natural thing, wonderfully beautiful, to find out for certain, as he felt he had found out, that there was close to him, always perhaps, and certainly at times, this presence of the brother whom he had never seen, but who in some way, not more inexplicable than the appearance of the blue gentians pricking up through the snow, could occasionally speak to him, calling him by name, or using his hand to write with.

A few days afterwards Lady Davidstow arrived back from England, and on the first evening of her return, after dusk had fallen, Archie was sitting on the floor against her knee in front of the one open fire-place in the house, where pine-logs fizzed and smouldered and burst into flame, and glowed into a core of heat. Sometimes, for that pleasant hour before bed-time, she read to him, but to-night there had been no reading, for she had been telling him of the week she had passed at home. They had moved up to London while she was there, and London was miry and foggy and cold.

"Altogether disgusting, dear," she said. "You don't want to go there, do you?"

"Not an atom," said Archie firmly. "I like this place better than any I have ever been in."

"I'm so glad, Archie. I was afraid you would dislike it after the frost went."

Archie was staring dreamily at the fire, and suddenly he knew that Martin was here, and he looked quickly round wondering if, by any new and lovely miracle, he should see the boy whose face was now familiar to him from the photograph. But there was nothing visible; only the firelight leaped on the wooden walls.

"What is it, Archie?" asked his mother.

Suddenly Archie felt that he could preserve his secret no longer. As on the day in church when he wanted his mother to share with him the pleasure of that glorious comedian, the man with the wagging beard, so now he wanted her to share with him the secret joy of Martin's presence.

"Mummy, I want to tell you about Martin," he said. "You know whom I mean: Martin, my brother."

"Archie, who has been telling you about Martin?" she asked.

Archie laughed.

"Why, Martin, of course. It's too lovely. Once he called me out loud, and he writes for me. He's written for me three times, once at home and twice here. I knew he was particularly here, the moment we got here. And last time he told me about what he had hidden under the pine-tree, and I found it. Don't you want to see it? I hid it away in the paper in my portmanteau. Oh, and what is a test? He said it was a test."

"A test? A test is a proof."

Archie laughed again.

"That makes sense," he said. "Now shall I show you the test? I kept it all together with what he wrote to me about it first."

He came back in a moment with his precious possession.

"Look, that's what he wrote on the paper of my letter to Miss Bampton," he said. "He said there was a circle cut on the pine-tree, and I found it, and I dug as he told me, and found this. Look! Isn't it lovely, and that's Martin's photograph, isn't it?"

It was impossible to question the validity of this evidence, and, indeed, Lady Davidstow had no desire to do so. For herself, she believed implicitly in the fact of life everlasting, without which the whole creation of God, with its pains and its agonies and its yearning and its love, becomes the cruellest of all sorry jests concocted by the omnipotent power of a mind infinitely brutal and cynical, who tortures the puppets He has created with unutterable anguish, or ravishes their souls with a joy as meaningless as dreams. Well she remembered Martin's cutting the circle on the pine-tree, but what its significance was he had never told her. But now, five years after his death, he had told it, she could not doubt, to the brother who had no normal remembrance of him. There they were, the little pathetic tokens of his childish secrecy, a pencil, a piece of chocolate, a photograph, and, above all, the well-formed, upright handwriting identical with that of the message traced on the last page of Archie's unsent letter. How it happened, what was the strange mechanism that fashioned by material means this mysterious communication between the living and the dead she had no idea, but of its having happened she had no doubt.

She turned these relics over, she kissed the handwriting so long buried, and tears of tender amazement rose in her eyes.

"Oh Archie, my darling," she said. "You lucky boy!"

"Aren't I?" said Archie. "But does Martin never write to you?"

"No, dear; I suppose he cannot."

"And why is he so particularly here?" demanded Archie.

She paused a moment.

"He died here," she said.

"In this house?" asked he. "Which room?"

"Blessington's."

Archie gave a great sigh.

"Oh, mummy, do let me have that room instead of mine!" he said.

BOOK II

CHAPTER V

Archie was precariously perched on the side of his little Una-rigged, red-sailed boat, looking with dancing blue eyes at the rocky coast all smothered in billows and sunlit spray some quarter of a mile ahead, and wondering if he would be able to make the harbour of Silorno on this tack. He wondered also what was the best thing to do if he could not. There seemed to be two alternatives, the one to beat out to sea again and come in on another tack, the other to run before the wind to the head of the bay, away to the right, where he knew there was a sandy beach, tumble himself out as best he might, and, he was afraid, see his beloved *Amphitrite* being pounded to bits by the rollers; for, with all his optimism, he could not picture himself hauling her up out of harm's way. But even this seemed preferable to the other alternative, for to beat out again in such a sea seemed really a challenge to the elements to swamp him, in which case he was like to lose the *Amphitrite* and his own life as well.

The wind was blowing with all the violence of a summer Italian gale straight down the bay from the open sea. A high wall of rock against which the breakers smashed themselves, and would smash anything else that rode them, was in front of him; then came the narrow opening into Silorno harbour for which he was making, after which the rocks, on the top of which ran the road to Santa Margharita, continued right up to the head of the bay. It had been rough when he started to sail there, in order to get some cigarettes, which now were stowed away in his coat which he had wrapped round them and placed where it would receive as small a share as possible of the spray that from time to time fell in a solid sheet into the boat. That seemed almost the most important thing of all, to keep the cigarettes dry, for it would be too futile to have taken all this trouble, and so greatly have ventured himself and his *Amphitrite*, if at the end the cigarettes should prove to be a mash of tobacco and salt water, for they were only in a cardboard box. And next in importance came the need of demonstrating to his mother and Harry and Helena and Jessie that he had been perfectly wise and prudent in sailing across to Santa Margharita, in spite of their land-lubber fears, in a freshening gale and a lumpy sea, in order to get these Egyptian cigarettes instead of the despised Italian brand. He made no doubt that the whole party of them were at this moment watching him through glasses from the terraced garden of the Castello that sat perched at the top of the steep, olive-clothed hill in front of him, and he spared a second to wave a hand in their direction in case they were there. But he did it in a rather hurried manner, for he wanted that hand to be ready to loosen the sheet in case any more wind was on its way to him, and the other hand must retain its hold on the tiller.

Archie was clad in a jersey stained and whitened with salt-water, and the rest of his attire consisted of grey flannel trousers. His coat was defending to its last dry stitch the trophy of cigarettes; his shoes he had put under his coat, for it was just as well to keep them dry, while, if by any chance he had to swim, they would be of no use to him either dry or wet. The sleeves of his jersey rolled up nearly to his shoulder, disclosed slim, strong arms, incredibly browned with a month of sea-bathing, and his sockless feet were of the same fine tan of constant exposure. His hair, thick and dripping from the spray, had for the present lost its tawny curliness, and he had to throw back his head from time to time, in order to keep it out of his eyes. And in his mind there was the same wildness of out-of-doors rapture that characterized the youth of his supple body: he could have laughed with pleasure at the mere fact of this doubtful battle between himself and the wind-maddened sea. But all the time in some secret chamber of his brain there sat, so to speak, a steadfast and keen observer, who was making notes with all his might, and pushing them down into the cool caves of memory, to be brought forth (in case Archie came safely to land) from their cold storage, and fitted with words which should reproduce the exultation of wind and sun and sea. And in a chamber more secret yet, a chamber not in his brain but in his heart, sat the knowledge that among the others his second cousin, Helena Vautier, in particular was surely looking at him from the terraced garden high above the cliff. She should see (and, for that matter, so should her sister Jessie) how to handle a boat. She had been strong in her dissuasion of his starting at all, and that, if Archie was quite honest with himself, was one of the principal reasons why he had insisted on doing so. She had mentioned casually the other day that there was nothing in the world she liked better than the careless "go-to-the-deuce" attitude towards danger which to her represented manliness, and Archie had been only too delighted to give her this vigorous exhibition of it. But it tremendously pleased him that, on his announcement of his intention to go across the bay, she should have so strenuously dissuaded him. To his mind that conveyed the impression that she liked him as much as she liked exhibitions of manliness.

He was already opposite the opening into the harbour and still several hundred yards distant, and for the time all the attention of the observer who some day was going to put this experience into words, and of the other observer who knew that Helena was watching him, was diverted to the job that engaged his more superficial self. But that part of him, intent and eager though it was on the hazard that lay before it, sang and shouted with glee at the fact that he was alone out here on the sea. For this very sane and healthy personage, Archie Morris, might almost be described as an aqua-maniac, so intense was his passion for that gladdest and most glorious creature of God. He did not want to be a sailor, for a sailor inhabited an impregnable fort which, though surrounded by sea, was still impenetrably removed from it, and defied it by means of colossal cylinders and pounding pistons and steel sides. Best of all was to be swimming in the sea, but not far removed from that was to coax and wheedle the sea through the medium of a big sail and a tiny boat: being alone with the sea, as with all lovers, was necessary to the full realization of passion. A river was a fair substitute for the sea or a lake; but there had to be a quantity of water. He loved to dive, and open his eyes under water, so as to see the sun shining through it. That was a very early passion, dating from the time when he had stepped out of a boat in his anxiety about a pike that was on the end of his line...

Then, for a moment, all other considerations were subordinated to keen physical activity. The wind was sweeping him across the mouth of the harbour, and he had either to put about at once to avoid being taken onto the rocks at its northern end, or, risking being swamped, put his helm even harder a-port, and tighten his sheet. With his habit of swift decision, he determined to go for it, and, throwing his leg across the tiller, he pulled on his sheet with both hands. The spray from the waves that broke themselves on the rocks fell solid and drenched him, but next moment, with but a yard or two to spare, he skimmed by them into the broadening harbour. There the promontory on which the Castello stood came between him and the wind, his sail flapped idly, and in dead calm he picked up his sculls to row the *Amphitrite* to her anchorage. But, before he took them up, he laughed aloud.

"Gosh, what sport!" he said.

* * * * *

The anchorage of the *Amphitrite* lay in a bay not far from the entrance to the harbour, screened by the steep-climbing olive groves belonging to this Castello of Silorno which Archie's mother had taken for the months of May and June: Silorno itself, that incredibly picturesque huddle of pink and yellow walls, of campaniles, and lacemakers, who, with bright coloured kerchiefs over their comely heads, plied their wooden bobbins all day in the shade of its narrow streets, rose, roof over roof, at the head of the harbour. A big cobbled piazza sloped down to the quay wall where sailors chatted and dozed in the shadow all day, putting to sea for their night-fishing by the light of flares about the time of sunset. The village was impenetrable to wheeled traffic, for the road along the bay came to an end at its outskirts, and thereafter became a narrow cobbled track, built in steps where the steepness of its streets demanded. Round the town rose an amphitheatre of hills broken only by the low saddle, where the final promontory on which the Castello stood swam out seawards in three wooded humps of hills. And, sitting here, you could observe on days like these the breakers crashing on the reefs to the right, where the seas rolled in from the open Mediterranean, while the land-locked harbour, into which Archie had just brought his boat, lay smooth as a mirror at your feet towards the left. Straight in front ran the ascending path that passed below the Castello to the head of the promontory, where enlightened Italian enterprise was building an execrable and totally useless lighthouse to supplant the little Madonna chapel that had stood there for centuries.

Archie took down his sail, anchored the *Amphitrite*, and punted himself across in a small boat to the landing-stage at the foot of the hill on which the Castello stood. Here the trees stood untroubled by the gale that poured high over them from the south, though on the other side of the harbour the wind roared in the olives, and turned their green to the grey of the underleaf, and the great surges beat and burst on the rocks he had narrowly avoided. But here that tumultuous stir was unfelt, and the resinous smell of pines and the clean odour of the eucalyptus-trees hung in the warm and sheltered air. Out of that denser shade he passed into the belt of olives that grew higher on the slope, mixed with angled and contorted fig-trees, where the fruit was already beginning to swell and ripen. Above rose the great grey bastion of the retaining fortress wall, tufted with stone-crop and valerian that was rooted in the crevices, and above that again was spread the umbrella of the stone-pine that grew at the corner of the garden. The path he followed wound round the base of this wall and passed below its easterly side, where he came into the blast of the warm south wind again that swept along the face of the Castello, and made the cypresses bend and buckle like fishing-rods which feel the jerk and pull of some hooked giant of the waters. The hillside here plunged very precipitously downwards to the bay three hundred feet below, wrinkled with waves, and feathered with foam, and, lover of the sea though he was, he felt content to observe that tumult of windy water. Not a sail was visible right across to the farther shore of the gulf, and to-night there would be no illumination of the fishing-boats that in calm weather rode out there, twinkling and populous as a town. But he stood looking at the sea a moment before he turned into the narrow stone passage that led to the gate of the house, as a man may look with love on his horse that, unruly and obstreperous, has yet carried him so gallantly.

A girl came up the cobbled way from the town just as he turned in. She had on a very simple linen dress that the wind blew close to her body, and a flapping linen sunbonnet, tied below her chin, to prevent the wind capturing it. She was tall and slight, moved easily, as with a boyish carelessness; a very pleasant face, also boyish and quite plain, peered from under her flapping bonnet. Her hands were noticeable: they were large but extremely well shaped, and the fingers showed both perception and efficiency. It may be remarked that Archie had never noticed her hands at all.

"Hullo, Jess," said he. "I'm just back. Lord, I've had such a ripping afternoon. And the cigarettes are quite dry. Where have you been?"

"Just down into Silorno. Cousin Marion wanted a telegram sent about their sleeping-berths to-morrow."

Archie frowned. He had noticed that Jessie was often sent on errands. People who can absolutely be relied on usually are.

"I should have thought my mother might have sent Pasqualino," he observed.

The girl laughed.

"Oh, she wanted to, but I said I would go instead. You see, Cousin Marion and Helena were getting in what might be called rather a state about you. I tried to infect them with my own calm, but they wouldn't catch it. So I thought a little walk would be pleasant."

"Oh, was Helena frightened?" asked Archie rather greedily.

"Yes. So was Cousin Marion. I wasn't."

"Then you were beastly unsympathetic. I had an awful shave getting into the harbour," remarked Archie.

"But you knew what you were about, and I didn't, nor did Helena. So I preferred to have confidence in you and go for a walk, rather than observe you in what looked remarkably like danger."

Archie had walked up from the landing-stage with his shoes and his coat under his arm. The coat was too wet to put on, so he dusted his feet with it, and resumed his shoes.

"Oh, a ripping afternoon," he said again.

The sound of the clanging gate into the Castello was heard out in the garden, and as they walked up the dim stone-flagged passage that led out into it, another girl came running in. She, like her sister, was tall and slight, but there the resemblance altogether ended. A delicate, small-featured face, entirely feminine, gleamed below yellow hair; her eyes, set rather wide apart, giving her an adorably childish look, opened very widely below their dark eyelashes. Beside her, Jessie looked somewhat like a well-bred plough-boy.

"Oh, Archie!" she cried. "How horribly rash of you! Your mother and I have had a terrible half-hour."

"I bring you cigarettes to soothe your disordered nerves," said Archie sententiously. "I am happy to say that they are dry, though I am not."

Jessie had walked on, with that pleasant expression on her face that might or might not be a smile, and the two were left alone for a moment.

"As if I cared about the cigarettes," she said.

"You did this morning. But you weren't really anxious, were you?"

"Indeed I was. You were naughty to sail back in this gale. Do be good now and change your clothes at once. I will bring you some fresh tea into the garden. Cousin Marion and I have had tea. We drank cup after cup to fortify ourselves, and looked over the wall at your boat between each sip. Then we trembled and had another sip. Before you got past that horrid rock, we had drained the teapot and broken our chairs with our tremblings."

The strict veracity of this entertaining summary did not of course concern Archie; it was sufficient that it had Helena's light and picturesque touch. It made a tableau that caused him to smile to himself as he changed his shirt, that was now stiffening with salt, and put on a pair of socks over his tanned feet. All this he did hurriedly, for it was the last evening, so he told himself, that they would all be together, by which he really meant that it was the last evening on which Helena would be here, since to-morrow, at break of dawn, she and his mother would start for England, leaving Jessie, Harry Travers, and himself to follow after another fortnight. When, a week before, that scheme had been suggested, it seemed to Archie the most admirable of plans, since, though his mother and Helena would be gone, he would secure another fortnight of intercourse with his beloved sea instead of inhabiting that smoky cave known as London. But since then Helena had begun to dawn on him, though as yet it would be an exaggeration to say that he was in love with her. But she was dawning, her light illuminated the sky above the horizon, and, if the plan was to be suggested again to him in his present attitude of attracted expectancy, it is probable that he would have voted for London and Helena, rather than an extension of his days at the Castello.

The scheme had originally been Helena's, and, like all her plans, had been exceedingly well thought out, before it was produced in the guise of an impulse, prompted by kindliness and thought for others. It was, when edited as an impulse, of the simplest and most considerate sort. The hot weather did not really suit Cousin Marion, so why should not Cousin Marion go back to England with herself, Helena, as travelling companion? Of course Silorno was the most delicious place, and she would be ever so sorry to go, but certainly Cousin Marion felt the heat, and, though she was far too unselfish to suggest breaking up the party, she would be glad to go northwards earlier than the end of June, when her two months' tenancy expired.

Helena had produced this plan to Archie one morning as they sat after breakfast under the stone-pine.

"But my mother would not in the least mind going home alone, if she preferred to go before the end of June," he said.

Helena shook her head.

"Oh, I know she would say she didn't mind," she said, "or she would stop on in spite of her headaches sooner than break up the party—"

"Has she been having headaches?" asked Archie.

"Yes, but you mustn't know that. She told me not to tell any one," said Helena, with complete self-possession. "Promise, Archie."

"All right."

Helena felt quite safe now.

"So she must go back sooner than at the end of June," she continued, "and clearly I am the right person to go with her, for she hates travelling alone."

"Oh, we'll all go then," said Archie.

"It isn't the least necessary. Jessie or I must go with her, for she certainly wouldn't hear of your going, and Jessie is enjoying this so much that I couldn't bear that she should have her days here cut short. So it's for me to go."

"That's awfully good of you," said he, only as yet half convinced.

"It isn't the least. It's a necessity, though you are so kind as to make a virtue of it. And then there's this as well. Cousin Marion would never consent to go, if she thought it was for her sake that I was going with her. So you must go to her, and say you think that it's me whom the heat doesn't suit, and you will see if she doesn't say at once that she will go back with me. And the real reason for her going will be our secret, just yours and mine."

Archie looked at her for a moment in silence, and the silence was one of unspoken admiration. Somehow this kindly thoughtful plan kindled his appreciation of her beauty: her beauty took on a tenderer and more touching look. Before now, it had vaguely occurred to him that, of the two sisters, it was Jessie who most gave up her own way to serve the ways of others; but this secret of Helena's made him feel that he had done her an injustice.

"But I don't want you to give up your time here if you enjoy it," he said.

"Ah, don't make me tell a fib, and say that I don't enjoy it," she said. "I will if you press me. I'll say it bores me frightfully, sooner than give up my plan."

"Well, I think it's wonderfully kind of you," he said. "Now I'm to tell my mother that you are feeling the heat, and see what she says. Is that it?"

"Yes, just that," said Helena.

Archie had strolled indoors to put this plan to the test, and before he returned a quarter of an hour later with his mother Helena had approved of her own ingenuity very warmly. She had, if her scheme succeeded, secured for herself an additional fortnight of the London season, for she and Jessie were, for the present, going to make their home with their cousins and she was already satisfied that her unselfishness had made a considerable impression on Archie. This was the most important thing: hitherto she felt she had failed to make her mark, so to speak. He was on excellent friendly terms with her, just as he was with Jessie, but she wanted (or at any rate wished for) something more than that. It was not that she wanted him to flirt with her; she had much more serious ends in view. She wanted (and here was her perspicacity) to dazzle his eyes by means of touching his heart, for she guessed, with clear-sighted vision, that he was the kind of young man who, if he did not mean everything, would mean nothing, and she believed that she could not entangle his affection by mere superficial appeals. And, indeed, she was not a flirt herself; she was poor, and clever, and attractive, and she proposed to use her cleverness and attraction in the legitimate pursuit of securing a husband who was not poor. That Archie was now Lord Davidstow, and at his father's death would be Lord Tintagel, was in his favour, and to make an impression on him, and then to go self-sacrificingly away, seemed to her a very promising manoeuvre. She was not in the least afraid of leaving Jessie with him, for, with her habitual adroitness, she had conveyed to her sister, by little sighs, glances, and words that seemed to escape from her lips unawares, what her design (yet without making it appear a design) on Archie was. She had but allowed her feelings, all unconsciously, to betray themselves, as when she said "Darling, wouldn't it be lovely to be Archie's sister, instead of only cousin?" That put it quite plainly enough, and she felt sure that Jessie understood. And, in addition to this impregnable safeguard of Jessie's loyalty, she was satisfied that Jessie's friendliness with Archie was of the most unsentimental character. Indeed, to speak of her sense of security with regard to Jessie would be a labouring of the point: she was so secure that her security scarcely struck her, any more than the security of a house consciously strikes its inhabitant.

* * * * *

The week that had passed between the acceptance of her plan and this, the last night of her stay at Silorno, confirmed the soundness of her strategy. Archie's frank friendliness towards herself had undergone a subtle change, while his relations with her sister remained precisely on the same calm tableland of comradeship. But below his comradeship with herself, like the sun glowing faintly through a mist without heat at present, but with penetration of light, she knew that there was growing an emotional brightness. It was with light and with a nameless quickening that his eye dwelt on her, and now as they sat in the deep dusk of the garden, illumined only by the stars that twinkled like minute golden oranges in the boughs of the stone-pine, she knew that he was looking at the pale wraith of her face, which was all the starlight left her with, in a manner that was not yet a week old. It was so dark, here in the deep shade, that she saw nothing of his sun-tanned face beyond a featureless oval, but when, from time to time, he drew on his cigarette, it leaped into distinctness. There was emotion there, or, at any rate, the stuff from which emotion is made; there was need, not yet wholly conscious of itself, but waiting, like buried treasure, to be released.

And on her side, also, something was astir behind her calculated plan. She felt sorry, until the wisdom of her project laid its calming hand upon her again, that she was being so unselfish as to accompany Cousin Marion back to town. It would have been extraordinarily pleasant to sit here many times more with Archie, and both watch and take part in the growth of the situation of which the seed had been deliberately planted by herself. It was but a weak little spike as yet, but undeniably there was the potentiality of growth in it.

Suddenly his face leapt into light, as he struck a match, and the gain of a fortnight's London season seemed to her insignificant. And the success of her plan, the wisdom of which she still endorsed, was but a frigid triumph, for she felt to a degree yet unknown to her his personal charm.

"Oh, Archie, I wish I wasn't going away," she said. "It has been a nice time. I wish—no, I suppose that's selfish of me."

"I want to know what is selfish of you," said he.

"Do you? Well, as it's our last evening you shall. I wish I thought you would miss me more."

He moved just a shade closer to her.

"Oh, I shall miss you quite enough," he said.

She laughed.

"I don't think you will," she said. "You'll have your bathing and your boating and your writing. I expect you will have a very jolly time."

He seemed to think over this.

"Yes, I shall have all those things," he said. "And I like them. Why shouldn't I? But—no, like you, I won't say that."

"But I did," she remarked.

"Well, I will too. I shall miss you much more than I should have missed you if you had gone away a week ago."

She, too, hesitated a moment. Then very coolly she replied:

"Thank you very much."

There was calculation in that: she had thought over her polite, chilly manner swiftly but carefully. And she had calculated rightly. He chucked away the cigarette he had only just lit.

"Helena, have I offended you?" he asked. "Why do you speak like that?"

Again she traversed a second's swift thought.

"Of course you haven't offended me," she said lightly. "You'll have to try harder than that if you want to offend me. My dear, do try again. Try to make me feel hurt."

Archie was a little excited. There was some small intimate contest going on, that affected him physically, with secret delight, just as he was affected in his limbs by some cross-current to the direction of his swimming, or in his brain by the tussle for the word he wanted when he was writing. He was sparring with something dear to him.

"Try to hurt me," she said softly.

"Very well," said he. "I'm glad you're going away to-morrow. Will that do?"

She laughed again.

"It would do excellently well if you meant it," she said. "But you don't mean it."

"You're very hard to please," said he.

"Not in the least. If you want to please me, say that you'll be very glad to see me again in a few weeks."

"I certainly shall, but I shan't say it. You know it quite well enough without my assurance."

She leaned forward a little.

"But say it all the same, Archie," she said. "Say it quite out loud."

Archie threw back his head and shouted at the stone-pine.

"I shall be very glad to see you again in—what was it?—in a few weeks," he cried.

"Ah, that is nice of you. No, I'm not sure that it's nice, because you've brought Jessie and Mr. Harry out into the garden."

That seemed to be the case, for undeniably the two moved out into the bright square of light cast from the lit passage within. Archie got up swiftly and suddenly, with a bubble of laughter.

"Oh, let's be like the garden scene in *Faust*," he whispered. "Don't you know, when the two couples wander about? Ah, they've seen us: they don't do that in well-conducted opera."

This was true enough, for immediately Helena's name was called by her sister. She gave a little sigh.

"Yes, darling," she said.

"Cousin Marion thinks it's time you went to bed," said Jessie. "And is Archie there too? She wants to see him."

Archie and Helena exchanged a quick glance in the darkness. They knew it, rather than saw it: Helena, at any rate, was quite certain of it.

"I must go in then," he said. "Your fault for making me shout."

Helena recollected a revue that she and Archie had seen together.

"The woman pays," she said in a histrionic falsetto, and without further word ran into the house, feeling very well satisfied with herself. She was sure that she had made herself a little enigmatical to him, had roused his curiosity. Decidedly he wanted to know more...

* * * * *

Archie always slept in a hammock slung between the stone-pine and the acacia in the garden, for though that year which he had spent at Grives, with which our history of his childhood closed, seemed to have eradicated the deadly seeds, he was still recommended to pass as much of his time as possible out of doors. The fourteen years that had elapsed since then had given him six feet of robust height, and there seemed now but little danger of the hereditary foe again beleaguering him. He had spent five years at Eton, and now had just finished his course at Cambridge, where he had contrived to combine classics and rowing in a thoroughly satisfactory manner, distinguishing himself in each. Even as he seemed to have outgrown his physical weakness, so too he had outgrown, to all appearance, those strange abnormal experiences which had been his in childhood, his power of automatic writing and the inexplicable communications from his dead brother. Certainly since his fourteenth year there had been no more of them; it was as if they had belonged entirely to the years when he trailed the clouds of glory that hang about childhood. But even now, in the normal vigour of his young manhood, they did not seem to him to be in the least unreal; indeed, they were to him, in spite of their fantastic and unusual nature, the most substantial treasures in his store-house of memory. The difference was that now they were sealed up: some key had been turned on them in his interior life, and they were inaccessible to him. But never for a moment did he doubt that they were there: out of reach they might be, but he still possessed them, and, though he made no effort to unlock the door, he believed that the key to them was neither lost nor broken, but, rusted, maybe, with unuse, still existed within him. Some day, he felt sure, the impulse would come to him, either from without or within, to search for it, and he knew precisely where, with every prospect of finding, he would look for it. For he still had the power of letting himself lapse into that trance-condition in which he sank into a depth of sunlit waters, and in that mysterious abyss he knew he could find the key to the sealed treasures. It was long since he had penetrated there, but he knew his way.

* * * * *

To-night, as he lay in his hammock, he felt no wish or inclination to sleep, but lay with eyes open looking into the sombre dark of the pine above his head, where the stars twinkled at the edge of the needles of the foliage. The gale that had raged that afternoon had blown itself out: not a breath of breeze sighed in the pine, and of the fierceness of those uproarious hours there was nothing left but the ever-diminishing thunder of the waves three hundred feet below. From horizon to zenith the sky was bare and kirtled with stars, and to the east over the hills across the bay, the dove-colour that precedes the rising of the moon was soaking through the heavens. A faint odour from the thicket of tobacco-plants that grew at the foot of his hammock were spreading through the air, ineffably fragrant, and the dew brought with it the smell of damp and fruitful earth.

Archie lay quite still, content to rest without sleep; he was sure that he would go to sleep soon, imperceptibly to himself, and he waited quite tranquilly for the soft tide to engulf him, letting his memory hover now and then over his adventures of the afternoon, but always bringing it back to the half-hour he had sat with Helena, close to where he now lay. He had, as sleep approached, the vague sense of sinking into some quiet depth; but his mind was too tranquilly disposed to do more than register this impression, and then, quite suddenly, without the transition state of drowsiness, he went fast asleep. He had noticed just before that the moon had risen.

He slept long and dreamlessly, and then began to dream with extraordinary vividness. He dreamed that he had not gone to sleep at all, but still lay in his hammock, in the shade of the pine, while the garden outside was full of the white blaze of the moonlight and ebony clear-cut shadows. The thunder of the surf had quite died away, the tobacco-plants still gave out their odour, and the stars, a little quenched by the moon, had faded in the boughs of the pine. And then he perceived (but with no sense of strangeness) that there was something new in the garden, for, close to the door into the house, was standing a white marble statue. This brought his legs over the side of his hammock, and he got up to go and look at it, and then remembered, so he thought, all about it. It was the statue of Helena, which she had told him was a gift from her to him, and it did not seem at all unnatural that it should have been brought out and put in the garden. But, as he had not seen it yet, he walked now across to it, and found an admirable and lovely figure. It was clad in a long Greek chiton, low at the throat and reaching nearly to her feet, which were sandalled. One hand was advanced to him with a beckoning gesture; the other, with its exquisite arm bare to the shoulder, hung by her side. The statue was life-size, for, as it stood on its low marble plinth, the face was just on a level with his. Exquisite in its fidelity and its beauty was that small head on its slender neck, and it endorsed the message of her beckoning hand. The lips, uncurled in a half-smile, mysteriously invited him; the body, too, was a little inclined forward towards him; next moment, surely, she would step down from her pedestal, and, like Galatea, shake off the semblance of stone, and declare herself his.

Standing there, entranced and strangely excited, Archie drank in the amazing loveliness of the figure. White and flawless, without speck or stain, the snow of the Parian quarries gleamed in the moonlight. And then he saw that, just where the neck flowed, with the strength and tenderness of a river, into the shoulders, there was a small dark spot, and, taking a step nearer, he put out his hand to flick it away. But it did not come away: it was as if some little excrescence had stuck to the marble, and, making a second attempt, he felt that it was soft, and that it grew a little longer. It moved, too; it wriggled like the head of a worm, and then, with a faint feeling of disgust, he saw that it was indeed the head of a worm protruding from the marble, just as a worm comes up through earth. Even as he looked, there came another such speck near the mouth; this also grew and wriggled, then came another on the arm which was put forward to welcome him.

Archie stood there, transfixed no longer by admiration and wonder, but by an ever-growing sense of horror. Everywhere, from face and hair and hand, and from the folds of the lovely Greek drapery there started out those loathsome reptiles. Some nightmare of catalepsy invaded him; he could not move, he could not call out, he could not turn away his eyes, but he had to watch until where lately this masterpiece of lovely limbs had stood, there was a column, as high as himself, of wriggling corruption, bred apparently from within. Then, horror adding itself to horror, this portent of decay began to move slowly towards him.

Still he could not move, but at last, when it was not more than a foot or two from him, he found his voice, and could scream for help. He could just hear himself shouting, but no help came. Already he could feel the touch of those horrible things, and with a supreme effort he managed to move his head away from that myriad loathsome touch, and lo! he was seated upright in his hammock, and the moon was low in the west, and over the eastern hills was the light that preceded day. His face streamed with the agony of the nightmare.

He sat still a little while, drinking in reassurance from the miracle of the tranquil dawn, and wondering at the suddenness with which he had gone to sleep, so that his disquieting dream had seemed the uninterrupted continuation of his consciousness. And, as his fright faded, there faded also the memory of what his dream had been: there had been something about a statue, something about worms, something connected with Helena. Even as he thought about it, it continued to recede from him, and before he dozed off again, the whole thing had slipped out of his memory, and when, an hour later, he got up to accompany the travellers on their early start, as far as the station, there was nothing whatever left of it. He knew only that he had awoke in a state of inexplicable terror, arising from some dream which had vanished from his memory like a mist at dawn.

The three left behind adjusted themselves, as friends can do, to their narrowed circle, and moved sensibly closer to each other. They all had their tasks to sweeten the enjoyment of their leisure, for to Jessie fell the Martha-cares of the house, which she transacted by the aid of an Italian dictionary with the cook Assunta; to Harry Travers, now a junior don at Cambridge, the preparation of a course of history lectures next term; to Archie the incessant practice in the endless and elusive art of writing prose. The love of expressing what he loved in words was no less than a passion with him, and it is almost needless to add that the sea was his inspiring theme. He certainly had the prime essential of devotion both to his subject and to the technique of his art, and these little essays, called *Idylls of the Sea*, promised, if ever he could persuade himself to finish them, to be a really exquisite piece of work. They were the simplest sketches of fishers and ships and the like, but to satisfy him, the sea had to sound in every line of them, even as it sounded in the ears of those about whom he wrote. Just now he was trying to recapture all that had made the ecstasy to him of that risky voyage homewards across the bay a few days before, and to fire his words with that thrill which he never quite despaired of communicating.

As a rule, their day arranged itself very regularly: early breakfast was succeeded by a couple of hours of task, and a couple more were spent in bathing, no affair of hurried undressing, of chilly immersion and a huddling on of clothes, but of long baskings on the shore, and a mile-long ploughing, for Archie at least, out into the bay or along the coast and round beyond the furthest promontory. Much though he liked the companionship of the others, he was never sorry when first Jessie, and then Harry turned shorewards again, for the companionship of the sea was closest to him when he was alone. He would burrow his way through it on the sidestroke, buried in the foam of his progress, and, when exhausted and breathless, turn on to his back to be cradled and rocked by it, secure in its enveloping presence, even as in the days of childhood he would lie happy and serene in the knowledge that Blessington was close by him. Or he would dive deep and see through "the fallen day" the dazzle of the sun of the surface far above him, and then swim up again, and, after the greenness and the paleness below, find a red and glowing firmament. But best of all was it to swim out very far from land, and then just exist with arms and legs spread wide, encompassed and surrounded by mere sea. He did not want to think about anything at all, or to belabour his brain with strivings to cast into words the sea-sense; that would come afterwards, when with gnawed pencil and erased sentences he sat in the garden; but he only opened himself out to it, and drank it in through eye and ear and skin and widespread limbs... And all this, even when physically he most realized this sea-sense, was but a symbol, and the more vivid the physical consciousness of the sea became, the dimmer it also became in the light of what it stood for. For even as the sea, eternally incorruptible, received into itself, without stain, all that the putrefying land with its ordure and sewers poured into it, so round human life, with its sores and its decay, there lay an immense and eternal incorruption, which purified all life as it passed into it, and turned it into something pellucid and immortal. Dying would be like that, dying was no more than being poured into this jubilant ocean, and becoming part of its clean, exuberant life...

But Archie had no intention of dying just yet, and indeed these metaphysical speculations only reached him like the sound of chimes blown across the water, while far clearer was Harry's voice, calling from the beach, "Archie, it's after twelve"; and thereupon Archie would turn on his chest and swim back to land, with a frill of foam encircling his sunburnt throat and a wake of bubbles following the strokes of his strong legs. Thereafter he would cast himself onto the beach with a straw hat tipped over his eyes, and his sun-tanned legs and arms spread star-fish fashion, and lie there drinking in the sun, while Harry and Jessie reviled him for causing lunch, for which they hungered, to be again half an hour behind the scheduled time. And Archie, lighting a cigarette, turned on his elbow and called them greedy hogs for thinking about lunch, when it was possible to lie in the sun, and swim in the sea. Then, as likely as not, he would himself be aware of a celestial appetite, and step into a pair of flannel trousers and a sea-stained shirt, and in turn revile their tardiness in climbing the olived terraces that lay between them and the Castello.

They lunched in the garden, in a strip of shade outside the house, and thereafter, without any pretence at all about the matter, Harry and Jessie went to their rooms for an honest Italian siesta, with no excuse of lying on beds and reading, but with the avowed object of lying on beds and sleeping. But this two hours' swimming and basking and communion with the sea, instead of making Archie sleepy, gave him his most productive hours of work, and wide-eyed and eager he would sit with jotted notes and scribbling-paper round him, read over the last few pages of his current story, and correct and erase and rewrite with an unquenchable optimism. There would be moments of despair, moments of wrestling with a recalcitrant sentence, when he walked about in the blaze of the sun, and bit his pencil till his teeth cracked through into the lead, moments of triumph when the impalpable sensation he wished to record seemed to surrender itself to the embrace of verbs and adjectives. Up till tea-time, when the others shuffled (or so he termed it) out of the house after their slumbers, he tasted the glories and the travail of creation, or, it might be, the pangs of fruitless labour; but he knew, at any rate, the joys of ecstatic mental activity.

On one such day, some weeks after his mother and Helena had gone back to England, he felt himself fit to burst with all that he had stored within him, ready for expression. As they drank their coffee he had employed himself in sharpening a couple of pencils (for the work of transcription into ink came later in the day), so as not to interrupt, by any physical intrusion, the flow of all he knew was ready to be crystallized into words. Sometimes the least distraction broke some kind of thread when he was in communication with the sea... It may be added that no one was ever less pompous about his aspirations.

To-day Harry observed the sharpening of the pencils, and commented.

"So a masterpiece is signalled, Archie," he said.

Archie blew the lead-dust from his finger.

"Quite right, old boy," he said. "Lord! I'm full of great thoughts. Do go to bed, and then I'll begin."

Jessie joined in.

"Archie, do let me hold your pencils for you," she said, "like Dora in *David Copperfield*. I shall feel as if I was doing something."

Archie laughed.

"You would be," he remarked. "You would be making an uncommon nuisance of yourself."

"You are polite."

"No, I'm not, I'm rude. I'm being rude on purpose. I want you to be offended and go away. I want Harry to go away too. I want you both to lie on your beds and snore like hogs."

"I was thinking of getting a book and reading out here," said Jessie. "I feel it's unsociable to leave you alone."

"When you've finished being funny," remarked Archie, "you may go to bed. You may get down at once. Say your grace and get down. You, too, Master Harry. Oh, Harry, do you remember how you used to come to tea in the nursery and Blessington made us behave properly till tea was over?"

"Then did you behave improperly?" asked Jessie.

"I don't think we did really. Once we went into the shrubbery and changed clothes. At least I put on yours, but you couldn't put on mine because they were too small. That's what Browning calls 'Time's Revenges.' I couldn't put on yours now, could I? The Italian authorities would prosecute me for indecency. Lord! what a little fellow you are, Harry! Time for a little fellow to go to bed. Oh, don't rag; I never said you weren't strong. Yes, Jessie, you're strong too, and it's like a girl to pull my hair. Ah, do shut up."

Archie had reasonable cause for complaint. Jessie had suddenly come behind him, and taken a great handful of touzled hair into her grasp, so that Archie's head was held immovable, while Harry tickled his ribs. You can do nothing with your arms if your head is held quite still. Presently the wicked ceased from troubling, and Archie was left alone. But after Jessie had gone to her room she stood still a moment before making herself comfortable for her nap, and then she laid across her nose and mouth the outspread hand that had grasped Archie's hair. In her fingers there remained some faint odour of warm sea-salt, and, as by a separate memory of their own, there remained in them the sense of their closing over that brown, bright, springy handful.

CHAPTER VI

Archie thought no more either of his tickled ribs or his outraged hair when his friends had definitely removed themselves, and with a sigh of delight he took up a sharpened pencil and a block of scribbling paper. He had grasped something, he thought, this morning, that must instantly be committed to words, before he even read over his last page or two, for his hand starved and itched to be writing. There was an odd trembling in his fingers, and his conscious brain was full of what he wanted to say. But when he put his pencil on to the block, and concentrated his mind on that liquid message of the sea that had reached him to-day, he found that his hand had nothing to write. His brain was full of what he wanted to write, but his hand disowned the controlling impulse. Again and once again he cast the thought in his brain into reasonable language, but there his hand still stayed, as if some signal was against it. Simply it would not proceed.

Archie had known similar obstacles before, though they had never been so strong as this. Probably the thought was not yet clarified enough, and for that the usual remedy was a stroll about the garden, a look at the sea from the parapetted wall. He tried this, returning again with a conviction that now he would be able to give words to the impression that was so strong in his conscious brain, and, as he took up his pencil again, again his hand seemed to be yearning to write. There was that coral-lipped anemone at the edge of the water, there was a shoal of little fishes which, as they turned, became a sheet of dazzling silver, ... all that was ready for the hand that twitched in expectancy. But again his hand would have nothing to say to that: the brain-signal showed itself to an uncomprehending instrument.

Suddenly, and with distaste, Archie perceived what was happening, and, divorcing from his mind the message that his brain was tingling to convey, he let his mere hand, untroubled by a fighting consciousness, do what it chose. It was no longer in his own control: something, somebody else possessed it. But it was with conscious reluctance that he resigned this mechanism to the controlling agent who was not himself. He watched with absolute detachment the words that came on his paper in a firm, upright handwriting quite unlike his own.

"Archie, you have had a warning," his hand wrote. "Now you must manage for yourself. I shall watch, but I mayn't do more. You have got to do your best and your highest. That's the root of probation. But I am always your most loving brother. When you were a child I could reach you... (Then followed some meaningless scribbles). But it's Martin."

The pencil gave a great dash across the paper, and instantly Archie knew that his hand had returned to its normal allegiance. At once the sea-thoughts that had occupied him seethed and roared in his brain, and his hand was straining to put them down. He tore off the involuntary message from his block, and, laying it aside, plunged with all the force of his conscious self into this ecstasy of conveying, with black marks on white paper, all that had obsessed him this morning as he swam out to sea, and lay between sun and water, the happiest of earthly animals, and the nearest to the key of the symbol. Then, after a half-hour of pure interpretation, that was finished too, and he lay back in his chair and picked up the Martin-message again. It seemed a nonsensical affair when he so regarded it. What was his warning, after all? What did that mean? He had had no warning of any sort. But it was strange that, after all those years of silence, Martin should come to guide him again, though at the self-same time he told him not to look for further guidance.

Archie put the paper with its well-remembered, upright handwriting back on the table again, lay back in his long chair, drowsy, and fatigued after his spell of fiery writing. Almost at once sleep began to invade him; the outline of the stone-pine, etched against the sky, grew blurred as his eyelids fluttered and closed. And then, without pause or transition, he saw a white statue standing close to him, on the neck of which there wriggled the tail of a worm, protruding from the fair white surface, and instantly his forgotten dream leaped into his mind, with a pang of horror. That was what his dream had been: there had been a statue standing just there, white in the moonlight, and even as he worshipped and adored it with love and boundless admiration, those foul symbols of decay had wreathed about it. Next moment he plucked himself from his dozing, and there was no statue there at all, but the far more comfortable figure of Jessie, standing in its place, with laughter in her eye.

"Oh, that's what you do, Archie," she said, "when you pretend to come out into the garden to work, and despise Harry and me for sleeping."

Archie jumped up from his chair and brandished in her face the pages of his consciously written manuscript. The leaf on which the message from Martin was written still lay apart from those on the table.

"I may have closed my eyes for one second," he said. "But I've written all that since lunch. Oh, it's got the sea in it, Jessie; I really believe there's the sea there. I'll read it you this evening, if you'll apologize for saying that I go to sleep instead of writing."

She picked up the other leaf.

"Yes, I apologize," she said, "though you were asleep when I came out. But I want to hear what you've written, so I apologize for having thought so. And there's this other page as well."

Archie took it from her.

"That doesn't belong," he said. "That—"

He paused a moment.

"Do you remember what I told you about the messages I used to have from Martin when I was a child?" he asked.

Jessie nodded.

"Yes; and they have ceased altogether for years, haven't they?" she said quickly.

"Until to-day. Just now, half an hour ago, I had another. But I can't make anything out of it. He tells me that I've had a warning. I don't know what it means."

Jessie felt all the habitual contempt of the thoroughly normal and healthy mind for anything akin to psychical experiences. All ghosts, in her view, were to be classed under the headings of rats or lobster-salad; all such things as table-tappings and the doings of mediums under the heading of trickery. But, knowing what she did of Archie's childish experiences, she could not put them down as trickery, and so was unable exactly to despise them as fraudulent. For that very reason she rather feared them; they made her feel uncomfortable.

She glanced at the paper he held out to her, but without taking it.

"Oh, Archie I distrust all that," she said. "I was really very glad when you told me that for all these years you had had no communication from him. Please don't have any more."

He laughed. They had talked about this before.

"But you don't understand," he said. "It has nothing to do with my wanting or not; it just comes. This afternoon I couldn't help writing any more than—than one can help sneezing."

"You can if you rub your nose the wrong way," said Jessie flippantly.

"No amount of rubbing my nose either the right way or the wrong way would have the slightest effect," said Archie. "The thing is imperative: if Martin wants me to write, I must write. But he says here that he's not going to guide me; I must look after myself. I'm sorry for that."

"I'm not," said Jessie quickly. "There's something strange and uncanny about it. I'm not sure that I think it's right even."

She paused a moment.

"Archie, do you really believe that it is the spirit of Martin that makes you write?" she said. "Are you sure—"

He interrupted her.

"I know what you mean," he said. "It's what the Roman Catholics teach, that any communication of the sort, given that it is genuine, and not some mere mediumistic trick, is not less than converse with some evil being impersonating, masquerading as the spirit from whom the communication apparently comes. Do you mean that?"

Jessie frowned, fingering the edge of the table.

"Yes, I suppose I do," she said. "I think the whole thing is dangerous; I don't think it's a thing to meddle with."

"But I don't meddle with it," said Archie. "It meddles with me. Besides, did you ever hear of such an unwarranted assumption? Mightn't I almost as well say that a letter which reaches me from my mother doesn't really come from her, but from some evil creature impersonating her? It seems simpler to suppose that it comes from her, that her signature is genuine, just as I believe Martin's to be. Do you really think that when I was a poor little consumptive chap at Grives I was really possessed by an evil spirit? Isn't that rather too horrible an imagining? A nice state the next world must be in, if that sort of thing is allowed! I don't for a moment think it is. Can you reconcile with the idea of supreme Love governing and creating all life, the notion that there, behind the scenes, there are evil and awful beings who can get leave to communicate with a child, as I was, pretending to be the spirit of the brother I never knew? Does it sound likely?"

Jessie paused a moment again. She hated the subject, she hated the idea of Archie's being concerned in these dim avenues to the unseen. She had, for herself, a perfectly unreasoning and childlike faith that there was this world, and the next world, and that God reigned supreme over both. But somehow it offended this instinctive attitude that the next world, and those who had gone there, should be mixed up with this world. They were not dead; she did not think they had ceased to exist; but they had done with this world, and it was something like a profanity to meddle with them. But then Archie had not meddled, as he most truly said: they seemed to have meddled with him. Their meddling had stopped altogether for a dozen years, and here on this half-sheet of paper was the evidence that something of the sort had begun again.

"I thought you had dropped all interest in it," she said. "I thought it was all finished, like a childish fairy-story, like the Abracadabra legend Cousin Marion told me about. Oh, there's tea; shall we have tea?"

Pasqualino had spread their table underneath the stone-pine, and she hailed this as a possible dismissal of the whole affair. She did not want to talk any more about it, and, if below her silence there should lurk a fear, she preferred to cover it up, not examine it. Archie got up.

"Certainly let us have tea," he said. "Perhaps your mind will be clearer after tea. I'm not going to quit the question, Jessie. The historian is at his histories, and we shall be alone, you and I, and I want to talk it out. Something has happened, you see, this afternoon. Martin—or somebody—has written again. You were quite right to imagine that for me the whole thing was finished, had become an Abracadabra-myth as you said. As far as normal life goes, I thought it had too. But I always knew that it might come back. And it has come back without my asking for it, though it—he—says he's going to leave me alone. But, after all, he says, 'You've got to do your best and your highest.' Now I ask you, as a reasonable female, does that look like a message from a devil? No, it's Martin all right, bless him. But let's have tea."

They moved across into the shadow of the pine, where the table sparkled with the specks of stray sunshine that filtered through the boughs. And Jessie, sane and normal, held on to those evidences of the kindly ordinary human life, as an anchor to prevent her drifting out into perilous seas. But to Archie no seas were perilous: they might engulf his body and drown him, and, as it seemed to him, they might engulf his spirit, but they were not perilous in his view. They were just the sea, the great encompassing presence...

"Archie, you are so odd," she said, knowing that he meant to have the subject talked out, and that his will dominated hers, "You spend the day bathing and sailing and writing; you eat and you sleep, and then suddenly you spring a surprise upon me, and show me a letter you have had from Martin. Which is you, the surprise or the Archie that I know?"

Archie's mouth was extraordinarily full of rusk and cherry-jam. He politely disposed of them before replying.

"But they're both me," he said. "Of course we have all two existences."

"Dual personality?" she asked.

"Dual fiddlesticks. What I mean is that in everybody there is the conscious self and the subconscious self, but they do not make a dual personality, but one personality. Most people—you, for instance, or Harry, or my mother—transact everything through the conscious personality. For all practical purposes your subconscious self doesn't exist. But in some, and I'm one of them— the subconscious self is accessible. I can reach it if I want. I can make it act. It is the essential life which we all of us contain, and, as such, it is that part of ourselves with which the essential life of those who have quitted this unessential life can communicate. Martin doesn't communicate with that part of me which directs and controls my conversation with you. He speaks to my subconscious self, and, by some rather unusual arrangement, my subconscious life can speak to my conscious life and convey what he says to my hand, or, as once happened, when at Grives I heard him call me, to my ear. I am a medium in fact, though that would usually suggest something charlatanish. I can bring my subconscious life to the surface; sometimes, as when Martin speaks to it, it comes to the surface of its own accord, with strong compulsion over my conscious self."

He paused a moment.

"It's all very odd," he said. "Until this afternoon, my subconscious self had lain quite quiet for years. Now suddenly it asserts itself and produces that page of writing, because Martin talked to it, and told it to make my hand write. What other explanation is there, unless indeed you imagine that I have merely perpetrated a silly hoax? But I swear to you that something outside myself made me write. Baldly stated, it was Martin who spoke to my subconscious self, and my subconscious self said to my conscious self, 'Take a pencil and write.' I know that is so."

Once again Jessie had to anchor herself against this current running out to sea. There was Archie sitting opposite her, large and brown and hungry, talking of things which were altogether fantastic, unless they were dangerous. And somehow, they were not either fantastic or dangerous to him; they were as ordinary as the cherry-jam which he was so profusely eating. She had suddenly come on a great undiscovered tract of country, dubious and full of dangers.

"I dislike it all," she said. "I'm too ordinary, I suppose, my—my subconscious self doesn't act, you would say. But what proof is there that there is such a thing as the subconscious self? Why should I suppose that there is anything of the sort? I have no reason to suppose it. It is all nonsense."

Archie laughed.

"My dear Jessie," he said, "you are arguing not with me but with yourself. You have an uneasy conviction that I am right."

"Not a bit," she said. "I want a proof."

Archie rubbed his hand over his head.

"I wonder how I can give it you most easily," he said. "Of course there are lots of ways, though it is quite a long time since I have practised any of them."

He thought for a moment.

"Well, here's one," he said. "The subconscious self— to talk more nonsense, as you say—is practically unlimited by the material laws of the world. It is a sort of X-ray, a sort of wireless... I can set my subconscious self to work, and I will, to prove its existence to you."

His voice sank a little, and Jessie saw that his eyes were fixed on a bright speck of sunlight that gleamed on the table-cloth. A sudden ridiculous terror seized her.

"Don't, Archie," she said. "It's such nonsense."

"It isn't nonsense," said he quietly, "and you mustn't be such a baby. There's nothing to be frightened at."

As he spoke he took his eyes off the bright speck at which he had been staring, and looked at her with his blue, dancing glance.

"What are you going to do?" she said.

"Whatever you like. Let me look at that bright spot there, while you sit quiet, for two minutes, and I'll tell you anything you choose. Think of something, anything will do, and I'll tell you what you're thinking about."

"Oh, just thought-reading," said she.

"*Just* thought-reading! But what is thought-reading? If you can remember what you thought about when you went up to your bedroom to sleep after lunch to-day, for instance, I'll tell you that. Or, there is Harry writing his history lecture for next term at this moment. I'll tell you the words he is writing. At least I think I shall be able to. But I'm out of practice. I have not cultivated the particular mood for years. But I had it when I was a child, and I expect I can get back into it."

Jessie felt an extreme curiosity about this. She had, even as Archie had said, an uneasy conviction that he was right, and for her peace of mind she longed to have that conviction shattered. In her reasonable self she did not believe that Archie could possibly tell her what Harry was writing, but behind that reasonable self sat something unreasonable which wanted to be convinced that this was all nonsense.

"But you won't have a fit or anything, will you?" she asked.

"No. Pour boiling tea over me if I do, and I shall come to myself."

"But what are you going to do?"

"I'm going to look at something bright. That spot of sun on the table-cloth will do. Then I shall just submerge, like a submarine, and tell you what Harry is writing at this moment, if that is the test you select. What fun it all is! I haven't done it, as I said, for ever so long. Oh, take a bit of paper, and write down what I say. I don't suppose I shall be able to remember it."

Again his voice sank, as he fixed his eyes on the bright spot he had indicated, and Jessie, watching him, pencil and paper in hand, saw an extraordinary change come over his face. For a few seconds it got troubled, and his eyes stared painfully, while his breath came quickly in and out of his nostrils. Then he grew quite quiet again, his mouth smiled, and he spoke very slowly as if the words were dictated by a writer.

"It is hopeless to try to comprehend in the whole," he said, "the splendour of that unique age. We can only think of it in fragments. One afternoon there was a new play by Sophocles; another day Pericles made the funeral oration for the fallen; on another the great Propylaea to the Acropolis were finished, Socrates talked in the market-place, or supped with Alcibiades. In the space of a few years all those things happened, and as yet more than twenty centuries have failed to grasp their full significance. And in this, my last lecture to you—"

Archie rubbed his eyes and sat up.

"He has finished for the present," he said.

There was a stir in the room just above them, where they sat in the garden, and Harry looked out.

"Any tea left?" he said.

Archie looked up.

"Hullo, Harry," he said. "I thought you were going to finish your lecture and not appear till dinner."

"I was, but I think I'll finish it up to-morrow."

"Bring it down and read us as far as you've got," said Archie. "Jessie won't mind."

"All right. It got a little purplish at the end, and that's why I stopped. I hate purples."

He moved away from the window, and Archie spoke to Jessie. "Did I say anything?" he asked.

"Yes; I've got it all down."

Archie jumped up.

"Now you'll see," he said. "You won't sauce me again in—in the wicious pride of your youth, as Mr. Venus remarked. I'm sure I got through that time."

* * * * *

It was the knowledge that he had indeed "got through" that Jessie took up to bed with her that night. Word for word Harry had read out at the end of his lecture precisely the sentences that Archie, in that queer dreamy state, had dictated to her, just before Harry had looked out of the window and asked if there was any tea left. There was no room for doubt: even as Archie had said, some piece of his mind had been able to divine exactly what Harry was writing at that moment. In his conscious state he could not know what that was, but according to his own account certain people, of whom he was one, were able to direct not only their conscious selves but also the subconscious self that lay below. It, so he asserted, was practically unfettered by material laws: it could perceive what was happening at a distance, at a spot invisible to it, and it could penetrate as by some X-ray process into other minds. For its free action (in his case at any rate) the conscious self had to be obliterated; by looking at that bright spot on the table-cloth he had been able to put it to sleep, to hypnotize it, thus allowing the subconscious self to pass the portals where normally the conscious self kept guard, and to do its errand.

So far there was nothing to disquiet her or make her uncomfortable. It was, as she had said, "just thought-reading," an example of a purely natural law, which, however dimly understood, was fully admitted by scientific investigators. No one, except the most hide-bound of pedants, questioned the existence of the subconscious self, and, if here was an example of an abnormal development of it, still there was nothing to fight shy of. She had asked for a proof of its powers, and undeniably she had got it...

But Archie had gone far beyond that in his exposition of the powers of the subconscious self, and it was this which caused her a very vivid disquiet. Through the subconscious self, in those who had the gift of releasing it, of allowing its activities, could come, so he believed, communications from the individual consciousnesses which had passed out of the material world. Even as the subconscious self could get into touch with the thoughts of living people (as she had seen for herself that afternoon), so also could it get into touch with the thoughts of the dead. It was thus, so Archie announced, that when he was a mere child, and knew nothing whatever of conscious and subconscious selves, Martin, the brother whom he had never heard of, used his hand to write with, as if it was his own, and with it wrote in the handwriting which had been his. Jessie fully believed in the survival of personality; to her the so-called dead had but passed on to a further and higher plane of existence; but there was to her something inexplicably repugnant in the notion that they could come back, and speak or write to those who still lived on this plane of existence.

Jessie lingered late by her window, overlooking the bay, trying to disentangle and lay bare the roots of her repugnance. It was late; below in the garden she could perceive the grey lines of Archie's hammock swung between the acacia and the pine, and Archie lying there like a chrysalis. He was just like that, she thought; most of the world were only caterpillars, eating their way through the allotted span of their years, but Archie was a stage more advanced than anybody she had ever known. This world and the next were one to him, not by any spiritual insight, but from that instinctive conviction that there was really no difference between the living and the so-called dead. It was not by any enlightenment, through any stress of prayer and aspiration that he had arrived at that. He had been gifted with it as a child; he was a medium, who by some special gift could talk to a brother, who had died long years ago, with just the same naturalness as he talked to her. If he died to-night, he would find nothing strange about it: he would but burst his chrysalis, hang for a moment, weak and fluttering, and then expand his wings. But to most people death was an awful affair. They were caterpillars; they had to learn the intermediate stage, which he was already familiar with. And yet the fact that he was a stage more advanced coupled with it a sort of helplessness for him. There he lay in his cocoon; any evil thing might attack him...

Jessie shook herself, mind and body; she was being fantastic in her fears and her misgivings, and with set purpose she forced herself to drink in, be penetrated by the assured serenity of the material world that lay spread before her. Above wheeled the stars in the silent sky, and on the silent sea shone the constellations from the fishing-boats. The trees stood motionless in the holy summer-hushed night beneath, while, though all seemed to sleep, the great renewing forces of the world were ripening the olives and enriching the twisted buds that would flower in fresh harvest of azure on the Morning Glory when the sun warmed them. There was nothing to disturb her; she could let her soul lie open to the night and think out the cause for her disquietude.

She hated the idea of commerce between the living and the dead; there was the root of it. The strangeness of the idea made it seem unnatural. Yet where, if she examined it more closely, was the unnaturalness? Why should not loving souls, who had passed that tiny rivulet called Death into the fuller life beyond, be allowed to call from the other side to those they loved? Was there not something exquisite, something supremely tender in the thought that Martin, who had been but little more than a child when he died in that Swiss chalet, should tell Archie about the cache he had made under the pine-tree? It was a childish communication, it brought no message of consolation or encouragement; but it was just what Martin, had he been alive on this side of Death, might have told Archie. Besides, who knew that he did not give that as a test, as a proof of his identity, for surely nothing could have been devised so convincing? And if God willed that the dead should be able, under certain circumstances, to speak from the sunlit beyond to those who still moved among material shadows, who was she, Jessie, to question so wonderful an ordinance? And if he could speak like that to a young and innocent child, why should he not continue to speak to his brother when he grew up?

She looked elsewhere for the grounds of her repugnance, and for a moment thought she had found them. For she had once been to a seance, at the house of a professional medium, and that afternoon still was vivid and degrading in her memory. They had all sat round a table in a darkened room while the medium went into trance, and instantly ridiculous knockings and melodies from a musical-box began to resound in the gloom. These were supposed to be played by spirits called Durward and Felisy, who, for some absolutely unconjecturable reason, liked spending the afternoon in these puerile idiocies. Meantime, the medium breathed heavily, which was the only evidence that he was in trance at all, and after a while said, "Here's the dear Cardinal," in a husky voice, and his niece, who sat next him, informed the circle that this was Cardinal Newman, who, like Durward and Felisy, could find nothing better to do on the other side than attend these awful sittings, for he always came when you paid your guinea to the medium and sat in the dark. To encourage him they lifted up their voices, at the suggestion of the medium's niece, and sang "Lead, kindly Light," which gratified him so much that he joined in singing the second verse and sang his own hymn to the tune given in *Hymns Ancient and Modern*. Then, when the hymn was over, he made some moral reflections and blessed them in Latin. Then there came materializations; the head and shoulders of Durward appeared in the middle of the table. He was dressed in white, and had a large black beard, and round his ear the wire with which the beard was attached to his face was clearly visible. During this the circle was warned to keep their hands touching all round the table, for, if any one made a break, the consequences to the medium might be very serious, since the spirit had built itself up from material derived from the medium and the "electric fluid" contributed by the sitters. So, if the electric fluid was withdrawn the material would not be able to get back into the medium, who would completely collapse and possibly die, though whether Durward would thereupon again become a visible and permanent dweller on this planet was not explained. By this time Jessie had been so convinced of the wicked and profane fraudulence of all these proceedings that she furtively withdrew one of her hands, and thus cut off the electric fluid altogether. But Durward didn't mind a bit, but continued to tell them about the joys of Paradise, which, according to his account, must have been like the Crystal Palace erected in the middle of the Botanical Gardens. And when he had regaled them enough he withdrew in the direction where the medium sat, took off his beard, and became Felisy with a veil and an alto voice. Surely all this was enough to make one despair and contemn the whole idea of intercourse with spirits...

But Jessie suddenly became aware of a basic illogicality in her position. It was not intercourse with spirits she despised, but those despicable swindlers who, with the aid of false beards and musical-boxes, pretended that they could materialize and cause communication with spirits. She did not deride the memory of that afternoon because the spirits of Cardinal Newman and Durward and Felisy had moved among them, but because they hadn't. It was no use accounting for her repugnance towards genuine intercourse with spirits by her repugnance towards quacks and charlatans. The whole history of spiritualism teemed with these undesirable gentry and these faked phenomena, but they had no more connection with Archie and his communications from his brother than had a forged bank-note with the credit of the Bank of England. She found she did believe that the knowledge, say, of the cache beneath the pine-tree came to Archie from other than normal human sources. It was known to no living being in the world, so far as she could tell, and if she looked for an explanation she must search for it in the supposition that the knowledge came to him from a living intelligence beyond the veil. She intensely disliked being forced to that conclusion, and now she knew why. It was for the reason she had suggested to him this afternoon.

These things came from those regions, those conditions of existence into which people passed when they died. But in those regions there existed not only the souls of the dead who lived in an environment and under conditions at which we could not ever so faintly conjecture, but other spirits, some good, some evil. Every good impulse that came into the hearts of men, came from over there; so, too, did every evil impulse that would blight, if it could, the garden of God. And who knew whether the man who by that strange faculty which Archie possessed of opening the doors of his subliminal self, through which, as he averred, these messages came, might not open them to other and evil things? If possession by an evil spirit was a psychical possibility (and certainly it was not more fantastically strange than such phenomena as Archie could produce) would it not be thus, and in no other way, that the evil possession would enter? Yet in childhood Archie had, in ignorance and in white defencelessness, opened more than once the door of his soul, and no harm surely had come to him. Was she being unreasonable, full of fear where no fear was, twittering with groundless and superstitious fancies?

There was yet another side to the question. If the spirits of the dead could indeed return, and speak of what they knew, was it not worth while running some risk on the chance of the wonders they might tell of the existence which now was theirs? Whatever else might be of interest in human life, supreme over all was any hint or fragment of information about the timeless and everlasting day that lay beyond the dawnings and settings of the sun. Nay, more: if to any one was given this wonderful gift by means of which voices could reach him from beyond the veil, was it not his duty to use this endowment for the enlightenment and consolation of those who mourned and who sat in darkness? God would never have bestowed so spiritual a gift on any, if He did not mean it to be used. The Christian Faith taught that the dead were alive in a wider sense than ever they had been on earth; why then should it be forbidden, to those who had this amazing gift, to speak with them, to learn about their life? The Roman Church had fulminated its anathemas on Galileo, a thing scarcely credible to a more enlightened age; it was more than possible that its pronouncements against this intercourse with the dead was but one instance the more of a similar cowardice and narrowness. Who could doubt that a man of science three hundred years ago would have been burned as a dabbler in diabolism and witchcraft, if he had exhibited a manifestation of wireless telegraphy or an X-ray photograph? But nowadays there was not a living being who did not rank such as the discoveries of a natural law. The sorcery of one age was the science of the next.

Jessie propounded this to herself, and her reason could not find a flaw in it. But something that sat behind her reason—superstition it might be, or instinct, or spiritual perception—refused to accept the conclusion. Like a child afraid of the dark, it trembled and hung back, and no amount of logical assurance from its nurse, no amount of demonstration that the room when dark contained only the familiar things which the light made manifest, could reassure it. It didn't like the dark; nothing could persuade it that danger did not lurk in blackness...

Well, it was no use going over all the ground again, she knew it thoroughly now. Reason made no headway against instinct, or instinct against reason, and she swept the matter from her mind, and tried to calm a certain intimate agitation that trembled there, by letting her eyes pour into her soul the superb serenity of the Italian night. The moon had risen and spread across the bay a silver path to the edge of the world, and in the sky the wheeling innumerable worlds kept sentinel over the earth. Never had she looked on a stillness more peaceful and more steadfast. Not a breeze stirred in the cypresses, but in the thickets of ilex below the Love that moved the sun and the other stars thrilled in the hearts of innumerable nightingales. That Love permeated everywhere; the world was soaked in its peace...

And just then, over the hills to the north, there flickered a flash of lightning from some storm very far away. Long afterwards, and scarcely audible, came a muffled murmur of thunder.

* * * * *

Jessie came downstairs next morning before either of the two young men were astir, and indeed, on going into the garden, she found Archie still serenely slumbering in his hammock in spite of the sun that filtered through the pine-tree on to his brown face and curly head. But perhaps some intangible shaft from her pierced down into the gulfs of sleep, for immediately he sat up, flushed with slumber like a child, but fresh and bright-eyed from his night in the open air.

"Hullo, Jess," he said. "You down already? I suppose I'd better get up. Is it shocking for a young lady to see a young gentleman's bare feet and his pyjamas? If so, you must shut your eyes. Now you're going to see them. Don't scream."

"I shall," said Jessie. "You always wear patent leather boots and a fur-coat when we bathe."

"Yes, that is so. But bear it for once. Lord, what a morning!"

He threw off his blanket and dangled his legs over the side of the hammock, and instantly lit a cigarette.

"Archie, why do you smoke before breakfast?" she asked.

"Because it makes me feel so jolly dizzy. Ah, you can't guess how good a cigarette tastes when you have had nothing but your tongue and your teeth in your mouth for eight or nine hours. Hullo! Here's the post. English papers? Who cares for what happens in England? No letters for me, two for Harry, and one for you. Goodbye; I shan't wash much because I shall bathe all the morning."

Jessie's letter proved to be from Helena, and its contents instantly absorbed her whole attention. Colonel Vautier, her father and Lady Tintagel's first cousin, had gone out to Egypt over some government irrigation work, and, instead of coming back in June, would be detained out there till September. In consequence, Lady Tintagel hoped that the two girls would live with her instead of going back to their father's house till his return. Helena's comment on this was enthusiastic, and also very characteristic.

"Darling Jessie," she said, after the statement of this proposal, "I do hope you'll say 'yes.' Cousin Marion encloses a note for you, so you'll see how much she wants us to, and Uncle Jack—I've begun to call him Uncle Jack, though he isn't an uncle at all—gave quite a pleased sort of grunt when it was mentioned, which means that he approves. So don't be independent, and say you would sooner go back to Oakland Crescent, because I've simply set my heart on stopping here. It's horrible at home in the summer with the sun blazing into those little tiny rooms and the smell of greens flooding the house. And it really would be a kindness to Cousin Marion; she says so herself, as you'll find when you read her note. And besides, there's another reason which I know you can guess. In fact, I think it's our duty to come, and when duty takes the form of anything so pleasant as this, there really is not the slightest reason for neglecting it. And, as I'm the youngest, I feel that you should do as I want. Besides, it's the greatest fun here. There are no end of dances and parties and dinners, and there are horses to ride and motor-cars. I'm having the loveliest tune, so it will be very selfish of you if you want to go home. But I know you will say 'yes.'"

A charming enclosure from Lady Tintagel accompanied this:

"I so much hope that you and Helena will stop with us. You must think of it as a great kindness to me, for it will be the utmost comfort to me, now that both my girls are married, to have you two with me for the rest of the season. I spoke to Archie about it while we were at Silorno, so ask him whether he approves or not. I hope all goes well with you. Is Archie quite black yet from bathing? Send me a line as soon as you have thought it over. Helena is having the greatest success in town; every one thinks her charming, and admires her enormously."

Jessie read this over as she waited for Archie to rejoin her at breakfast. There was every reason for accepting so cordial an invitation, and it would give pleasure to Helena, to Cousin Marion, and apparently also to Archie. She knew she would have to consent: there was no cause that could be spoken about which she could possibly adduce for refusing. A week ago that cause did not exist, but now she wondered how she could bear to see Helena and Archie in the close companionship which this would imply, and watch his feeling for her expanding from the bud into the flower. If she had thought that Helena loved him it would all be different. But she felt certain that Helena did not. There, for her, was the poignancy of it...

In a manner that she could not explain, Jessie knew that she knew the tokens by which love betrays its existence. She, barely yet twenty-two, had somewhere stored in her soul the language of love, which it speaks even when it thinks it is dumb—talking in its sleep, it may be. She had seen in the last week of Helena's sojourn here that Archie talked to her like that. "There was neither speech nor language": he said nothing of which the words betrayed his dawning passion, but his love spoke in his silence, even as the rosy clouds high above the earth herald the dawn. It was her own knowledge that enlightened her: she too knew the silent language, and knew that Archie conversed in it, though no word came, when he talked to Helena. Something kindled behind his eye, some secret alertness possessed him... But there was the defencelessness and the blindness of love, for when Helena answered him she but pretended to talk the same tongue, and Jessie, knowing it, knew that she spoke a mere paltry gibberish. It sounded the same, or it looked the same; but it was nonsense, it was not authentic. Yet Archie never talked in the secret tongue to Jessie; and, in consequence, she had never answered him in it. To-day it seemed her native tongue when she talked to him, and all she said must needs be translated out of that into the language of those who were friends, dear friends, but no more than friends.

All this was instantaneous: she seemed to read it between the lines of Helena's letter. She recalled, too, between the lines, the tokens that she knew. Archie would look at Harry, as they sat at dinner, then at his mother, then at her, in order that in due time he might look at Helena. And when he spoke to any of them they never got more than one ear and an inattentive mind from him. The other ear and the attention were always with Helena. Helena knew that quite well: no woman or girl could fail to know it, and, by way of response, she had made this Scythian retreat to England. No doubt that was clever of her, but in Jessie's opinion clever people are found out even sooner than stupid ones. The only inexplicable folk are the wise, and wisdom has very little to do with cleverness. Wisdom is perhaps the cleverness of the soul, that looks down with pity on the manoeuvres of the mind.

Archie made his absurd entry. He had a dressing-gown on, perhaps some sort of abbreviated bathing-dress, and canvas-shoes.

"I didn't dress," he said, "for where's the use of dressing if you are going to undress again almost immediately?"

"Aren't you going to work this morning?" asked Jessie.

"No. This one day, as Mr. Wordsworth said, we'll give to idleness. I'm going to bathe all the morning instead of half the morning. I want a holiday. I think I'm overworked. What's happening in that foolish England, if you've read the papers?"

"I haven't," said she.

Suddenly his face changed; he began to talk the secret language, which Jessie understood and Helena counterfeited.

"And what other news?" he asked. "You had a letter from somebody."

Jessie pretended not to understand what she knew so well.

"Yes, I did have a letter," she said, determined that Archie should be more direct than this.

"From Helena or mother?" he said carelessly. "I haven't heard from either of them, except that telegram to say they had got home safely."

He was talking the secret language still; the very carelessness of his tone betrayed it.

"I heard from them both," she said. "The letter was from Helena, and there was an enclosure from Cousin Marion."

Archie said nothing in answer to this, but it seemed to the girl that his silence was just as eloquent in the language without words. Eventually he remarked that Harry was very late, and Jessie knew that he had beaten her. He always did, just because he had nothing, with regard to her, at stake.

"Archie, I want to talk to you about what they have written to me," she said.

"Talk away," said Archie. "I say, what good little fishes!"

Jessie was not proposing to yield like that. If he, in the code of the secret language, professed an indifference to what he was longing to hear, she would be indifferent too.

To Archie's intense irritation she continued to talk about little fishes, in a tone of great interest, till Harry's entrance. She agreed they were very good; probably they were fresh sardines caught last night by the fishers. Or were they... and she could not remember the Italian name of the other little fish which were so like sardines.

Archie's serene brow clouded, and he but grunted a greeting to Harry. And next moment her heart smote her. She knew how easily Archie could put the sun out for her without meaning to do it, but she had, out of a sort of piqued femininity, intentionally done the same for him. She felt as if she had spoiled a child's pleasure. He was so like a child, but lovers were made of child-stuff. He got up almost immediately, and, full of a tender penitence, she followed him.

One behind the other they went out into the garden, where Archie, in a superb unconsciousness of her presence, became instantly absorbed in the despised English papers.

"Archie!" she said.

He rustled with his paper.

"Oh, er—what?" he answered.

"I wanted to talk to you about Helena's letter," she said, "only you would talk about sardines. Put that paper down; I can't talk through the paper."

She noticed that he kept his finger on a paragraph, and she would have betted her last shilling that he had no idea what that paragraph was about. And, though a moment before she had been penitent, now she stiffened herself and determined that he should meet her more gracefully than that.

"I'm sorry; I'm interrupting you," she said. "I'll tell you some other time."

Archie suddenly threw the paper into the air.

"Oh, aren't we behaving like idiots?" he said. "At heart I am, and so are you really. But I'll confess: I'm just longing to know what Helena writes about. But aren't you an idiot, too? I shall like it enormously if you say you are."

"I am an idiot, too," said the girl. "And Cousin Marion wants Helena and me to live with her till father comes home. She told me to ask you if you approved."

He leaned forward to her.

"Ah, do, Jessie," he said. "I hope you will. I can't see why you shouldn't. Can you?"

She looked straight into the eager blue eyes that were so close to hers. For her there was a wealth of frankness and friendliness, but the light in them was not for her, and she knew it.

"Helena wants to," she said.

"Does that mean that you don't?" he asked. "I'm sorry if that is so."

She got up.

"No, it doesn't mean that a bit," she said. "It's delightful of you and Cousin Marion to want us. Of course we'll come."

Archie rose too.

"That's perfectly ripping of you," he said. "We shall be a jolly party, we four."

Quite suddenly a pause fell, very awkwardly, very constrainedly.

"You see, my father doesn't appear much," he said at length. "That's what I meant. He is very often in the country, and—well, we don't see him much."

Archie soon took himself off to the sea, armed with paper and pencils, for, with four hours in front of him, there would be much basking to be done between his bathes. Already another of those sea-sketches was beginning to take shape in his mind, and he found that there was no hour so fruitful in inspiration as when, after a swim, he returned to this empty, sandy beach, and lay spread out to the sun to be dried and browned and made eager for another dip. So, to-day, after the first swim, he lay for a while on his back with his arms across his face to shield his eyes from the glare, and opened his brain, so to speak, to let the sea-thoughts invade it. They came swarming in at his invitation, and presently he turned over and propped himself on his elbow and began to catch them and pin them to his paper. The rim of the sea, with its weed-fringed rocks, its diaper of moving light in the shallow water, the shoals of little fishes, almost invisible one moment, the next, as they turned, becoming a shield of silver flakes, were all ready to be hammered into sentences; and yet the hammer paused...

Somehow at the back of his mind was a topic that inhibited his hand, or would not allow the connection between hand and brain to be made, and he thought he knew what this was, for only this morning he had heard that Helena was to be an inmate of their house in London. Yet it did not seem to be that which was preventing him, and he wondered whether it was the thought of his father and his habitual intoxication, which was always like a black background at home, and which just for a moment had popped out into his conversation with Jessie, that hindered him. But that again did not seem a sufficient cause for his inability to start the mechanism which translated thought into language.

And then he became aware that his fingers itched and ached to write with a compelling force which he knew well. And yet only yesterday Martin had said that he should not come to him again. But the quality of the force seemed unmistakable, and presently he yielded to that which he really had not the power to resist and wrote as his hand bade him write.

There were but a few sentences scribbled, and then his pencil, as usually happened when the message was complete, gave a dash. He had no notion what he had written, and when it was finished he read it through.

"Archie, I have come through this once more," it said, "to repeat that you have been warned. But I can't get through again.—MARTIN."

So here again was this inexplicable mention of a warning, and Archie's conscious mind was blank with regard to any such warning. But the repetition of it did not long occupy him, for immediately he found that the inhibition between his brain and his hand was gone, and sentence after sentence of his sea-sketch flowed through his fingers. By degrees, but not till a couple of his pages were full, did the inspiration exhaust itself, and then he lay back on the sand again full of the ecstasy that always accompanies the completion of a piece of work that has been done as the creator meant to do it. Bad or good, it has fulfilled his intention.

His brain brooded over that for a little, and then slipped back to the incident that had preceded it. He could make nothing at all of it, and, determining to dismiss it from his mind, and speak of it to nobody, he tore up the sheet that contained the message, buried the fragments in the sand, and lay back again roasting himself in the sun. Soon that delectable warmth would increase on his bare limbs, till they cried out for the cool embraces of the sea again, and he would fling himself into it. But just for a little longer he would stew and stupefy himself in the sun and with half-closed eyes watch the vibration of the hot air over the beach and listen to the hiss of the ripples. Except for them the morning was extremely quiet, the sun poured down over his outspread limbs, the sea waited for him. And, as he lay there and dozed, the memory of his evil dream went across his brain like a flash, and vanished again.

* * * * *

Already the Italian days were beginning to draw to their sunny end; they were numbered and could be easily counted. Both Archie and Jessie counted them when they woke in the morning, and in the evening both said to themselves, "Another day gone." But their reflections on this diminishing tale and the colour of their emotions were absolutely opposed, for while they both intensely enjoyed these Italian hours, Jessie counted them with the grudging sense of a school-boy who enumerates the remaining days of his holiday; but to Archie they were the days of term-time which still (though enjoyable) must be got through before the holidays began. Never before had he contemplated a stay in town with eagerness; but now, as he thought of her who would be living with them, he had never been so expectantly enamoured of London.

At the close of their last day the divine serenity of June weather was troubled, and, as evening drew on, the clouds, which for a few hours past had been weaving wisps and streamers over the sky, grew to a thick curtain that stretched from horizon to horizon. It was of opaque grey, but here and there in it were lines and patches of much darker texture, as if it had been rent, and had been darned again with a blacker thread. Instead of the coolness which succeeded sunset, the heat, clear no longer, but impure like the air of a closed room, got ever sultrier, and, for the refreshment of the evening breeze from the sea, there was exchanged a stifling stagnation. All life had gone out of the atmosphere: it was as if some immense Othello was smothering the world. The air was heavy and charged with electricity, but as yet no remote winking of lightning nor rumble of thunder showed that there was relief coming.

They had dined out in the garden, where the candles burned unwaveringly in the stillness, and afterwards had strolled to the far angle of the supporting wall of the fortress, where, if anywhere, they might find some hint of movement in this intolerable calm. But no breath visited them even there, and the very bamboos that grew at the corner of the garden-bed were as motionless as if they had been made of lead.

Archie mopped his streaming forehead.

"If it interests anybody," he remarked, "I may say that I am going to die. I can't bear it any longer. I think I shall die in about half an hour."

Jessie fanned herself. That did not do a particle of good, it only seemed to make her hotter, as when you stir the water in a hot bath. But she tried to interest herself in Archie's approaching decease.

"And are we to take your corpse back to England to-morrow?" she asked.

"Just as you like. I shall have no more use for it. Lord, and I haven't finished packing yet. Fancy having to pack in this heat."

"You needn't, surely, if you're going to die."

"I must. My immortal manuscript would be lost in the general confusion caused by my death. Or shall I go to bed? It can't be hotter in my hammock than here. Yes, I shall get into my pyjamas, go to bed, and do my packing in the morning."

He trailed off into the house, and presently appeared again attired for bed and strolled across to them.

"Well, I'll *wish* you a good-night," he said, "but I very much doubt whether you'll get it. You needn't do the same to me, for I know I shan't, and your wishes would be hollow."

He moved away again towards the stone-pine where his hammock was hung, a pale tall ghost of a figure against the blackness.

Then, quite suddenly, some panic impulse seized Jessie, the result perhaps of her overstrung nerves and the overcharged atmosphere, and she sprang up, not knowing why.

"Wait a moment, Archie," she cried. "Don't go— something is going to happen."

Even as she spoke the whole world seemed enveloped in fire, and the core of the fire, a white-hot line, plunged downwards into the stone-pine, which was rent from top to bottom. Absolute blackness filled with the deafening roar of the thunder and deluging rain succeeded, and they rushed towards the shelter of the house.

For a moment they all three stood there recovering their balance from that tremendous crash and convulsion. Then Archie, with his soaked silk clinging close to his shoulders and legs, turned to Jessie.

"I wonder why you called out to me," he said. "What made you do it? You saved my life, I expect."

Jessie laughed; little as she was given to hysteria that laugh was half-way towards uncontrollable tears.

"Why, I didn't want you to die in half an hour," she said lightly.

* * * * *

But she remembered that moment when it came for her to save Archie's life indeed. Some inexplicable signal from love had flashed upon her that night, and should flash upon her again.

CHAPTER VII

Helena was having breakfast by the open window of her bedroom in her cousin's house. It was not yet nine in the morning, and, though she had been dancing till three o'clock, she had already had her bath, and was feeling as fresh as if she had had eight instead of hardly more than four hours in bed. Outside the square was still empty of passengers, and the pale primrose-coloured sunshine of a London June shone on a wet roadway and rain-refreshed trees, for a shower had fallen not long ago, and through the open window there came in the delicious smell of damp earth. But she gave little heed to that or to the breakfast she was eating with so admirable an appetite, for her brain, cool and alert in this early hour, was very busy over her own concerns. Soon she would have to go down to Cousin Marion and see if she could be of any use to her, for it was quite worth while doing jobs for Cousin Marion, as she always paid kindnesses back with a royal generosity. And she must get some flowers to give a welcoming air to Archie's room, who with Jessie was expected back to-day. That also would not be a waste of the time she might have spent more directly on herself. She would get some for Jessie, too, for she had the character of unselfish thoughtfulness to keep up. It would be unnecessary to pay for them, for she could get them at the shop where Cousin Marion dealt.

Helena had enjoyed the most entrancing fortnight, during which time she had occasionally thought of Silorno, and had oftener talked of it to Cousin Marion, for she had that valuable social gift of appearing to talk with keen attention of one thing while she was thinking about something quite different. She could easily interject "Dear Archie, it will be nice to have him back," or "Darling Jessie wrote me such a delicious letter: she is enjoying herself!" and if Cousin Marion expressed a wish to see the letter, it was equally easy to say that she had torn it up. Meantime her brain would be busy with recollections of the day before, as they bore on her plans for the day to come. They might go off on to tangents for brief spaces, but her well-ordered and singly-purposed mind was never long in recalling them to their main topic.

Helena had made something of a sensation during these last weeks. She was not beautiful, but she was quite enchantingly pretty, and her mind had the qualities which might rightly be supposed to underlie that delicious face and inform those slim, graceful limbs. Nothing seemed to mar her good-nature and her superb gift of enjoying herself. It was worth while being agreeable to everybody, and if her lot happened for an hour or two a day to be cast with elderly bores, she was indefatigable in her attention to them at the time, and in telling their friends afterwards how immensely she had enjoyed talking to them. It paid to do that sort of thing, provided that it was done with a gaiety that made it appear genuine and spontaneous: if your appreciation came bubbling out of you, no one suspected you of design, and she seemed the most designless, delicious girl in London, for it is next to impossible to see through an object that dazzles you. To crown all these gifts, she had the intensest power of enjoying herself, and there is not another key that unlocks so many doors. In this whirl and mill-race of entertainment which characterized the last gay summer that London would see for long, there was no time to make friends, but only to take the scalps of enthusiastic acquaintances. That perhaps was lucky for her.

But Helena, as she finished her breakfast, recalled her mind from these shining experiences, except in so far as they bore on the theme that insistently occupied her. There was no doubt, especially after that quiet talk in the paved garden outside the ball-room last night, that Bertie Harlow was dazzled, according to plan. Heaven only knew when he had last been to a ball, for he was close on forty (Helena had naturally looked him up in a Peerage, since she liked to know about her friends), and she felt pretty certain that he had danced with no one but her. You could perhaps hardly call his share of the performance dancing; he had "stepped a measure," and twice trodden on her toe; but, after all, it did not matter whether your husband danced or not, since naturally, when those relations had been arrived at, he would not dance with you. Many women no doubt, when they were married, would think it an advantage that their husbands did not dance, since then they would not dance with anybody else. But it was not in Helena's nature prospectively to grudge him such amusements, should he desire them, when once she had got him. But she had to get him first, and to do that she had to keep him dazzled. He must not get accustomed to her.

Helena had a very strong belief in the desirability of simplifying life. This did not in the least imply that she thought there was anything attractive in the simple life: her simplification amounted to this, that she formulated exactly what she wanted, and then without deflection of aim did the very best with her efficient armoury of weapons to get it; while the second clause in the simplification of life was to find out what irritated or bored you, and with all your power eliminate it from your existence. If you could not get what you wanted without getting something that bored you, it was merely necessary to ascertain how the balance between these conflicting interests lay. As practically applied to the case in hand, she was aware that Lord Harlow bored her, though not badly, and that his nose irritated her. That she would almost certainly get used to, while on the other side of the scale were quantities of things she liked. She liked immense wealth, position, and the liberty she would undoubtedly enjoy if she married this amiable man, whom so many had tried to capture. That in itself was an incentive to her pride, and, without being a snob, she saw no objection to being a Marchioness.

But here the simplification ended, and a complication intruded itself. It was not so long ago that she had sat under the stone-pine with Archie, and seen his face glow in the darkness as he drew on his cigarette. In point of attractiveness there was naturally no comparison between her cousin and this amiable middle-aged man; but, owing to the impossibility of even the most limited polyandry, it was clearly no use to think of marrying them both, and all that was left was to choose between them, supposing, as she most sincerely did, that it was, or soon would be, for her to choose. Certainly she was not in love with Archie, if she took as an example of that the ridiculous symptoms exhibited by Daisy Hollinger, who by some strange freak was in love with Lord Harlow. Helena had behaved very wisely over that, for she had instantly seen the advantage of becoming great friends, in her sense of the word, with poor Daisy, who poured out to her a farrago of amorous imbecility, and Helena was sure that she was not in love with Archie like that. Anything so insane seemed incomprehensible to her (and was).

But Archie was a dear—she had quite wished he would kiss her that night, of course in a cousinly fashion, which she would have scorned to be offended with, whereas she did not in the least look forward to the moment when Lord Harlow would kiss her. Apart from that, the simplification of life came in again, and against Archie there were certain items which it would be imprudent to disregard. His father was a drunkard, and Archie himself had been consumptive as a child. Consumption ran in families, for Archie's brother had died of it; and so perhaps did drunkenness, though she did Archie the justice of trying and failing to remember that she had ever seen him drink wine at all. These were serious objections in a husband.

There was another, perhaps not less serious. She knew from Cousin Marion that Uncle Jack had lately lost a great deal of money; there was even the question of shutting up or letting the London house next winter. Of course, if she married Archie, they could not spend the winter down at Lacebury, or live with poor Uncle Jack; but London, as wife of an impoverished son, would be very different from London as the wife of a very wealthy man who, so to speak, was nobody's son. Finally, there were certain stories that Cousin Marion had told her about queer messages and communications that had come to Archie, while he was still a child, from his dead brother. That seemed to Helena's practical mind pure nonsense, and yet she had been pleased to hear that, since he was but young in his teens, these rather uncomfortable phenomena had ceased. She felt that she did not believe in them; but, though they had no real existence, she disliked the thought of them. And, though it was so long since there had been any repetition of them, they might (though they were all nonsense) crop up again. She had no belief in ghosts, but she would not willingly have slept in a haunted room. The dead were dead, whereas she was very much alive.

Well, it was time to dress and go down to Cousin Marion. This long, frank meditation (for she was always frank with herself, which perhaps was the reason that she had so little of that commodity to spare for other people) had helped considerably to clear her mind and provoke simplification. And, like a good housewife who will permit no waste of what can possibly be used, she thought she would have a very useful function for Archie to perform when he arrived that evening.

She found Lady Tintagel busy with her morning's post. There was a quantity of invitations, most of which, owing to press of others, had to be declined, and Helena having marked each of those with an "Accept" or "Refuse," laid them aside to answer. There was one, where the Russian dancers were to perform, which she very much regretted having to say "no" to, since that evening was already filled, and wondered if by any contrivance it would be possible to manage it. A glance at Lady Tintagel's engagement book showed her that the prohibiting acceptance was for a dinner and concert at Lady Awcock's, where all that was stately and Victorian spent evenings of unparalleled dreariness. Helena had already produced the most favourable impression on Lady Awcock by listening to her practically endless dissertations on political society forty years ago, and she thought she could manage it.

"And shall I enter all the invitation you accept in your engagement-book, Cousin Marion?" she asked.

"Yes, my dear, will you? That's really all I have for you this morning. What will you do with yourself?"

Helena gathered up cards and engagement-book.

"I think I shall stop at home," she said. "You often do want something more, you know, and I hate not being here to do it for you."

"Nothing of the sort. There's the motor for you if you want to go and see anybody."

Helena considered.

"Oh, I should like to do one thing," she said. "It won't take long. May I get some flowers for Archie's room and Jessie's? Flowers do look so cool and refreshing when you've been a day and a night in the train."

"Of course you may. It was nice of you to think of that. But then you do think of rather nice things for other people."

"Oh, shut up, Cousin Marion," laughed the girl.

* * * * *

Helena retired to the table in the window with her materials and proceeded to execute a very neat and simple piece of work. The entries in Lady Tintagel's engagement-book were only made in pencil, and she erased the inconvenient Lady Awcock's name from the evening some fortnight ahead and wrote in its place that of the giver of the Russian party, to whom instead of a refusal she sent a line, in her cousin's name, of grateful acceptance. Then she wrote a charming little letter of penitence to Lady Awcock, abasing herself and at the same time pitying herself. She had done the stupidest thing; for she had accepted Lady Awcock's invitation on an evening when they were already engaged. The letter proceeded: "I can't tell you how disappointed I am, dear Lady Awcock, for I was so looking forward to another talk with you, and to hear more of those interesting things you told me; but perhaps, if I have not disgusted you beyond forgiveness, you would ask me again some day. And would you be wonderfully kind and not tell Lady Tintagel what a stupid thing I have done, for she lets me keep her engagement-book for her, and if she knew, I am afraid she would never trust me again."

This last touch thoroughly pleased Helena; it was confiding and childlike. For the rest she relied on Cousin Marion not happening to remember that they had once accepted an invitation to Lady Awcock's, and, even if she did have some impression of it, her engagement-book, with no such entry appearing in it, would show her that her memory had played her false. But probably Cousin Marion would remember nothing whatever about it; indeed, in the multiplicity of engagement, it seemed to Helena that the risk she ran was negligible.

Helena found time to go to Victoria to meet the travellers that afternoon, and to reflect, as she waited for the boat-train to come in, that she in her cool pink blouse and her skirt of Poiret stuff would certainly present a very refreshing contrast to poor Jessie in dishevelled and dusty travelling-clothes. She did not in the least want Jessie to look bedraggled except in so far as she herself would gain by the contrast, for she was good-natured enough not to want any one to be at a disadvantage as long as that did not add to her own advantage. Jessie was a dreadfully bad sailor, too; but it was quite enough that she should have travelled for a night and a day, without hoping that she had had a bad crossing. Helena merely wanted to appear fresh and brilliant herself. At length the train came in, and, though she quite distinctly saw Archie step out, she continued searching for him with her eyes in the crowd, until he made his way up to her.

"Ah, my dear," she said, "how lovely to see you! And don't be cross with me for coming to meet you if it bores you to be met at the station. But I did want to welcome you. And where's Jessie? There she is! Jessie darling, what fun!"

Archie did not look as if he was at all bored to be met at the station.

"That's perfectly ripping of you," he said. "I am glad you came. We've been baked and boiled all the way from Silorno. And the crossing! I thought it was always calm in the summer."

"Archie, don't allude to it," said Jessie.

Helena took her sister's arm.

"Darling Jessie, I am so sorry," she said. "Archie's a wretch for mentioning it. Now you go straight to the motor and sit there quietly. Archie and I will see to your luggage."

If Archie, as is probable, drew the contrast he was intended to draw between the sisters, Helena on her side drew another between him and Lord Harlow. There he stood, looking eagerly at her as they waited the emergence of their trunks, face and neck and hands so tanned by the sun that every one else looked ill and anaemic by him. He was tall and lithe and slender, with the quick movements of some wild animal, and in his brown face his blue eyes shone like transparent turquoises. He seemed an incarnation of sun and sea and wholesome virility, and, as the thought of the rather heavy Kalmuck face of Lord Harlow, and staid aspect suitable to his forty years, she almost wondered whether, in her estimate made this morning, she had allowed enough for personal charm. But there had been other factors as well, and who knew whether below this engaging exterior there were not planted the seeds of tragic outcome? But it was certainly pleasant to reflect that his exuberance of young manhood would, she made no doubt, be all hers if she made up her mind to want it. In any case, was there another girl in London who had so attractive a second string to her bow?

Archie had, on the appearance of one of their pieces of luggage, insinuated himself into the crowd and Helena was left outside, when a sight odd to see at a station attracted her attention. Beyond, the platform lay empty, and out of some porter's shed there, there bounded a big tabby cat with a mouse in its mouth. Its tail switched, its eyes gleamed with the joy of the successful hunter; but it did not prepare to eat the mouse immediately. It trotted a little farther off, lay down, and, depositing its prey, dabbed at it softly with velvet paws and sheathed claws. It even let it run a few inches away from it, and then gently shepherded it back again. Once it let it seem to escape altogether, gave it a start of at least a couple of yards, while it watched it with quivering shoulders, and then playfully bounded in the air, and reminded it that it was not its own master. Then there came a dismal little squeak as from a slate-pencil; the poor mouse's troubles were over, and a pleased cat blinked in the sun and licked its lips.

Helena followed this gruesome little drama with an interest that surprised and even rather shocked her. She was altogether on the side of the cat; the cat, according to its lights, was not being cruel, it was merely doing the natural thing with a mouse. It happened to like teasing its prey, letting it think that it had escaped, sheathing the claws that had caught it, and playing with it. There was nothing horrible about it: the cat was doing as nature intended it to do. She was rather sorry for the mouse, but that is what came of being a mouse... And there was Archie, triumphant, with a porter and his rescued luggage. Archie had a way with officials: he smiled at them in a confident, friendly way, and they always did what he wanted and never searched his traps.

* * * * *

There was a dance somewhere that night, but Helena, letting the fact be reluctantly dragged out of her that there was such a thing, only said how nice it would be to go to bed early.

"Are you tired, dear?" asked Lady Tintagel.

Helena made a little deprecating face, the face of the prettiest little martyr in the cause of truth ever beheld.

"No, I can't exactly say I am," she said. "I think—I think I was speaking on behalf of Archie and Jessie."

"But I'm not tired either," said he. "Let's go to somebody's dance. I can't dance an atom, but Helena shall teach me. There's nothing like practice in public. What dance is it, by the way?"

"Oh, that's all right," said she. "It's your Uncle and Aunt Toby. But, Archie, I'm sure you're tired."

"But I'm not, I tell you. It's whether you want to go."

Lady Tintagel struck in.

"If you all go on being so unselfish," she said, "you will never settle anything. Try to be selfish for one moment Helena; it won't hurt. Do you want to go?"

"Enormously," said she, with a sign of resignation.

"And you, Archie?"

"Dying for it. Let's call a taxi."

"And you, Jessie?"

"I should hate it," said Jessie very confidently.

The matter, of course, was settled on those lines, and Helena was duly credited with having wanted to go enormously, but with having done her utmost to efface herself for the sake of others. This was precisely the end she had in view all along, and now, having had the dance, so to speak, forced on her, she was quite free to enjoy herself. She had produced precisely the impression she wanted on Archie and his mother, and, though it was likely that Jessie, with her long familiarity with such manoeuvres, was not equally unenlightened, she knew, by corresponding familiarity, Jessie's loyalty. She gave a little butterfly kiss to Cousin Marion, and a murmur of delighted thanks, and went to her sister to finish up this very complete little picture.

"Darling Jessie," she said, "go to bed soon and sleep well. I shall tiptoe in, in the morning, and, if you're still asleep, I shall tell them not to wake you till you ring. May I do that, Cousin Marion?"

Jessie understood all this perfectly well, and her mouth had that curve in it that might or might not be a smile.

"Good-night," she said. "Have a nice dance, and teach Archie well."

To speak of luck is often nothing more than another mode of expressing the success that usually attends foresight; chance favours the wise calculation. Helena last night had dropped the most casual hint to Lord Harlow that she was probably going to this dance to-night, but she was satisfied that he had been attending, and was not unprepared to see him there. Even if she had not been able to come, she suspected that he would do so, and her absence would have been delightfully explained to him afterwards. But there he was, not dancing, but standing about near the door of the ball-room, and quite obviously interested in arrivals. Undoubtedly he saw the brilliant entry of herself and Archie, but she contrived to put a few of the crowd between herself and him as she passed near him, and for the present gave him no more than a glance and a smile, a downdropt eye, and then one glance again, and passed with Archie into the ball-room. There an ordinary old-fashioned waltz was in progress, and not one of those anaemic strollings about which were becoming popular, and she slid off with her radiant partner on to a floor not overfull. She had a moment's misgiving when she remembered that Archie had said he couldn't dance, for it would vex her to appear in the clutch of a bungler; but, after all, Archie could hardly be awkward if he tried. Immediately all her fears vanished, for they had hardly gone up the short side of the room before she knew that if any one was the bungler it was she. She might have guessed, from seeing him walk and move, that he could dance; what she could not have guessed was that anybody could dance like this. They floated, they glided; it was the floor surely that moved under them; it was the wind of that swinging, voluptuous tune that wafted them on as in some clear eddy of sunlit water.

"But, my dear, you said you couldn't dance," she exclaimed.

"Oh, this sort of thing," said he. "I meant the steppings and crawlings of the new style."

Helena was too content to talk; her whole being glowed with the satisfaction of this flowing movement. The floor got ever emptier: lines of expectant fox-trotters and bunny-huggers stood round the wall, but none of them objected to watching for a little longer the entrancing couple who now had the floor almost to themselves. Couple after couple dropped off and stood looking, and to Helena's gleaming eyes they passed in streaks of black and white and many-coloured hues as she and Archie moved ever more freely and largely over the untenanted space. She could just see the faces of friends as she passed, and knew that Lord Harlow had come in and was standing by the door. There was no question of luck in that; he was but doing what she knew he was obliged to do. Then the web of sound that poured out of the gallery grew more brightly coloured as it quickened to its close, and still Archie and she moved without effort as if they were part of it and of each other. And then the whole fabric of that divine dream of melody and motion was shattered, for the dance was over.

Archie had not spoken either since he intimated that he had alluded to steppings and crawlings, and now he paused for a moment in the middle of the room, breathing just a little quickly and bewildered as with some dazzling light. Ever since he had put his arm round the girl and taken her hand in his, he had had that sense of sinking into sunlit waters, where he arrived at his true and naked self. Now he had swum up again, and he was clothed in black coat and white shirt, and Helena was standing a step apart from him, and every one else at the edge of the room was very far away. Instantly a mingling of wild consternation and triumph seized him.

"Oh, Helena, were we doing that all by ourselves?" he said. "How frightful! Let's get out of it. But wasn't it divine? May we do it again soon? Or will they have nothing but crawlings?"

It appeared that crawlings were to be the next item, and Archie noticed that in the crowd that now came about them again a particular man had his eye on them, and was unmistakably burrowing towards them.

"Yes, Archie; of course we will," said the girl. "Go and see your aunt, and ask if we may have another waltz ever so soon. Oh, here's Lord Harlow; I want to introduce you."

This was done, and Lord Harlow turned to Helena again.

"I feel as if I had been present at some Bacchic festival," he said in a very precise voice. "But you should have vine-leaves in your hair, and er—your partner a tunic and a thyrsus. I feel myself as prosaic as a Bradshaw. But may I be your Bradshaw?"

Helena looked from one to the other; if she had had a tail she would certainly have been switching it.

"Ah, do," she said. "A Bradshaw is quite indispensable. Archie, go and get a thyrsus—will a poker do, Lord Harlow?—and persuade Mrs. Morris to have another waltz before long."

Now that the sheer animal exhilaration of that adorable waltz, which quite precluded talking, was over, it seemed perfectly suitable, as she plodded along the weary way of the fox-trot, to talk again, and in answer to Lord Harlow, who had not caught Archie's name, she said:

"Yes, Lord Davidstow. Surely I told you about him" (she knew that she had purposely not done so). "He is Lady Tintagel's son, with whom I am staying."

Lord Harlow quietly assimilated this as he turned slowly round.

"And does he do other things as well as he dances?" he asked.

"I think he does," said she, "though I never really thought about it. When people are such dears as Archie, one doesn't consider what they do. They just are."

"He certainly is. He appears very much alive."

"Yes, he's madly alive."

She gave him a swift glance, and, guessing she had gone far enough on that tack, she put about.

"I think it's possible to be too much alive," she said. "It's like a hot-water bottle that is too hot: it burns you. But you can't help being carried off your feet by it—I don't mean the hot-water bottle."

He paused a moment for the purpose of phrasing.

"I must weight you with a Bradshaw," he said. "That will keep you to earth. We can't spare you."

Helena laughed.

"You say things *too* neatly," she said. "What a delicious notion! What have you done all day?"

"I have waited for this evening."

"And I hope it doesn't disappoint you now that it has come," she said.

"It is up to my highest expectations just now," said he.

Suddenly it flashed into Helena's mind that this was the temperature of his wooing. He was engaged in that now: those neat and proper sentences, turned as on a lathe, were the expression of it, they and the mild pleased glances that he gave her; and yet, discreet and veiled as it all was, she divined that, according to his nature and his years, it was love that inspired it. She found it quite easy to adjust herself to that level, and if his kiss (when the time came for that) was of the same respectful and finished quality, she could deal with that too. But she wondered how Archie would make love... It was necessary to fox-trot a little longer, and, while trotting, trot also conversationally, and with intention she let herself press a little more against his arm.

"Oh, I am glad of that," she said lightly. "It is such a dreadful pity when people are disappointed. But I think I would sooner anticipate something nice and fail to get it, than not anticipate at all. Can you imagine not looking forward to the delicious things you want?"

"Do you want very much?" he asked.

"Yes, everything. And I want it not only for myself but for everybody."

She made the mental note that he was very shy, for he had nothing in response to this, except that his shirt creaked. But that suited her very well; she did not want him to follow this up, just yet.

Meantime the sedate marchings and retreats and occasional revolution of the fox-trot went decorously on. The room was very full, and, when there was nowhere to march to, they stopped where they were and marked time and rocked a little to and fro. Then perhaps a narrow lane opened in front of them, and they waddled down it, brushing shoulders against the hedges. She had seen Archie go to Mrs. Morris, after which he had appeared for a moment in the gallery where the band was, and now he was back again, standing near the door and watching her. She gave him little glances from time to time, elevated her eyebrows as if in deprecation of this unexhilarating performance, or smiled at him, guessing that he had arranged for another waltz.

At last the end came, the fox-trotters ceased to clutch each other, and walked away with about as much Terpsichorean fervour as they had been dancing with. Dull though the last twenty minutes had been from that standpoint, Helena felt quite satisfied with it, while motion—or perhaps emotion—had made her partner hot; he gently wiped his forehead with a very fine cambric handkerchief.

"Perfectly delicious," he said. "I should have liked that to go on for ever. And how long shall I have to wait before it begins again?"

Archie had sidled through the crowd up to them.

"Helena, we're going to have another waltz at once," he cried. "Don't let us waste any of it."

She laid her hand on his arm.

"We?" she said. "Are you quite certain?"

"May I say 'we' also?" asked Lord Harlow.

She turned towards him, but her hand still rested on Archie, and he felt the slight pressure from her fingertips.

"Oh, I was only teasing my cousin," she said. "I had promised him another waltz. But, later, may I borrow my Bradshaw again?"

The band struck up, setting her a-tingle for the repetition of what had gone before.

"Oh, Archie, come on," she cried. "*Au revoir*, Bradshaw."

Alert for movement, with the heady tune of the waltz already mounting into them like wine, they stepped off on to the floor. It was like stepping on to some moving platform; it and the tune, without any conscious effort of their own, seemed to carry them away. But Archie had one question to ask before he abandoned himself.

"Bradshaw?" he said. "I thought you told me his name was Harlow."

She gave a little bubble of laughter.

"Oh, that was only a joke," she said. "He told me that you and I were like a Bacchic festival, and he felt as prosy as a Bradshaw in consequence."

"But what does it matter to him what we are like?" asked he.

"Well, it was a compliment; he meant it nicely," said she. "Don't let us talk; it rather spoils it."

* * * * *

Helena reviewed those manoeuvres when she got home that night, and she congratulated herself on the neatness and efficiency of her dispositions. She felt sure that she had stirred up a livelier ferment in Lord Harlow, and had also managed to inspire him with a vague distrust and jealousy of her intimacy with Archie. She suspected that he was a little sluggish in his emotions, and this would serve admirably as a stimulant. She quite realized that she had not yet brought him up to the point of proposing to her, for his inured bachelor habits would want a good deal of breaking; but it was clear to her that she had made a crack in them, and that the judicious use of Archie might be profitably used to widen that crack. Under the influence merely of her charms, he might hold together for a long time yet, and she wanted him, if she could have it entirely her own way, to propose to her about the end of the season. The effect of Archie constantly with her would be cumulative: it was not a wedge that would cause him to fly into splinters forthwith; it would just widen the crack, prevent it closing again, and then widen it a little more.

And meanwhile it was extremely pleasant always to have this wedge in her hand, to hammer from time to time, as it suited her main plan, and at others to stroke and play with. She was not in love with Archie, but it made her purr to see that he was certainly falling in love with her, to dab him with sheathed claws, to wish that he had those material advantages which had made her choose the elder man. It clearly served her purpose to use him, and the using of him gave her pleasure. But the pleasure was secondary—it was the assistance he gave her in breaking up Lord Harlow that was of primary importance.

* * * * *

Archie brought all his gaiety and charm to bear on his love-making. Falling in love did not appear to him, at this stage, anything but the most exhilarating, almost hilarious experience. The flirtation that Helena seemed to be having with Lord Harlow amused him enormously; not for a moment did he believe that Helena meant anything. Lord Harlow was not the only man on whom Helena exercised the perfectly legitimate attraction of her extreme prettiness and her enthusiastic child-like enjoyment.

"Oh, every one is so kind and so awfully nice," she said to him one day as they returned from an early morning ride. "I love them all by the handful."

"Including the Bradshaw?" asked he.

"Yes, certainly including the Bradshaw. Don't you like him? He likes you so much."

Archie considered this.

"I don't know if I like him or not," he said. "I don't think I ever thought about it. He doesn't matter. But you matter awfully to him. Did you know that you are the most outrageous flirt, Helena?"

"Archie, how horrid of you!" said she. "Just because I like people, and to a certain extent they like me. Why should I be cross and unpleasant to people, as if it was wicked to like them?"

"Well, if you'll give me long odds I will bet you that the Bradshaw asks you to—to be his 'ABC' before the end of the season," said Archie.

"My dear, what nonsense!" said she, with a sudden thrill of pleasure. "What can have put that into your head?"

"I can see it. That's the way a man like the Bradshaw looks at a girl when his—his affections are engaged. He looks as if a very dear aunt was dead. He has *amour triste*."

That certainly hit off a type of gaze to which Helena felt that she had been subjected, and she laughed.

"Well, I'll give you five to one in half-crowns," she said.

"Don't. Some day I shall have twelve and sixpence."

They turned and cantered back along the soft track. The dew of night had not yet vanished from the grass, and the geometric looking plane-leaves, the rhododendrons, and the flower-beds were still varnished with moisture, and, early though it was, riders and foot-passengers were plentiful. Probably the day would be hot, for the heat haze, purplish-brown in the distance, was beginning to form in the air, softly veiling the further view. Presently they dropped again into a walking-pace, and Helena, whose mind had been busy on Archie's description of a certain sort of love-lorn look, spoke of a subject suggested by it.

"How do you think Jessie is?" she asked.

"That's exactly what my mother asked me last night," said he. "She's rather silent and preoccupied, isn't she?"

"That struck me," said the girl. "I thought perhaps she wasn't very well, but she told me there was nothing the matter. Darling Jessie is so reserved. She never tells me anything. Certainly she looks well: do you think she has anything on her mind?"

"I don't see what she could have. But it's odd that it has struck all of us."

Helena sighed and shook her head with a pretty, unreproachful air.

"I sometimes wish that Jessie would make more of a friend of me," she said. "I try so hard to get close to her, but all the time I feel she is keeping me at arm's length. It would be lovely to have a sister who would admit me to her own, own self. But I always have to tap, so to speak, at Jessie's door, and she so often says she won't open it."

"Was she always like that?" asked Archie, seeing that Helena's eyes were dim and bright.

"Yes, but lately I think it has been worse. I wish Jessie would let me in. However, I am always waiting, and I think Jessie knows that. It is no use pressing for confidence, is it? One can only wait."

This picture, so simply and pathetically conveyed by Helena of herself waiting, a little dim-eyed, for Jessie to admit her, was very convincing, and Archie wondered at the contrast between the two sisters, the one so childlike in her confidence that all the world was her friend, the other holding herself rather detached, rather aloof, without that welcoming charm of manner that surely was the expression of an adorable mind. It was not wholly the light of his dawning love that invested the sketch with such tender colouring, for there was a great finish and consistency in Helena's presentation of herself which might have deceived the most neutral and heart-whole of observers.

Such was the first impression: then suddenly some instinct that lay below the surface surged up in rebellion against it, and washed the tender colouring out. It told him that the impression was a false one, that Jessie, so far from being callous and self-centred, as was the suggestion conveyed by Helena's words, was of faithful and golden heart. And then, looking idly over the crowd that was growing thick on the broad gravel walk, he suddenly caught sight of Jessie herself looking at them. She was some little distance behind the rails that separated the ride from the path, and she instantly looked away, spoke to a girl who was with her, and strolled on. But Archie felt quite sure that she had seen them.

He turned to Helena.

"Surely that is Jessie," he said to her, pointing with his whip.

Helena had seen her also, and she smiled rather sadly, rather wistfully.

"Yes," she said. "But she doesn't want us, Archie."

And at that the instinct which had spoken to him so emphatically a moment before sank out of hearing again, and the colour returned to Helena's deft little sketch.

CHAPTER VIII

It was four o'clock on an afternoon of mid-July, and the westering sun had begun to blaze into the drawing-room windows of Colonel Vautier's house in Oakland Crescent. It was pleasant enough there in the winter, for the room, being small, was easily heated; but in the summer, with even greater ease it grew oven-like, and Helena, sitting by the open window for the sake of any air that might possibly wander into the dusty crescent, was obliged to pull down the blinds. She had tried sitting in her father's study, but that had an infection of stray cigar-smoke about it which she did not want to catch, and the dining-room and her own bedroom, since they faced the same way as the drawing-room, presented no counter-attractions. So, reluctantly, she was compelled to sit here, while Jessie, with a book in her hand, sat at the other end of the room. Jessie had a slight attack of hay-fever, and from time to time indulged in a fit of sneezing. It seemed to Helena that she was being very inconsiderate: it was always possible to stifle a sneeze. But Jessie never thought about other people. Helena, by way of waiting patiently at Jessie's door (according to the tender image she had fashioned for Archie's benefit) had just expressed this opinion slightly veiled, and she was pleased to see that at this moment Jessie left the room. A sound of sneezing from outside indicated that at last her sister had grasped how exceedingly unpleasant her hay-fever was for other people. Then there came the sound of ascending steps, and she guessed that Jessie had gone to her bedroom. The floors were wretchedly thin and ill-constructed; you could, from any room in the house, hear movements from any other room, especially since Colonel Vautier and Jessie had such solid, resounding steps when they went anywhere.

Left to herself, Helena cleared her decks, and enumerated her cause of complaint against Providence, who ought to have been so kind to an innocent, loving little soul. In the first place, her father had finished his irrigation business in Egypt unexpectedly soon, and instead of arriving in London not before September, had come two months earlier than the most pessimistic daughter could have expected. The news of his approaching arrival had provoked a perfect conspiracy against Helena's comfort and her plans, for every one, including Cousin Marion, who had been so insistent on the girls' staying with her till he got home, had taken it for granted that they would at once rejoin him. Surely it would have been sufficient for Jessie to go (and she did Jessie the justice of allowing that she was perfectly ready to do so), leaving Helena to help Cousin Marion in the answering of her letters in the morning for some half-hour, in the entertaining of her numerous guests, and in accompanying her to any of those pleasant gaieties which swarmed about that desirable house. But instead, Cousin Marion had been quite unaware, to all appearance, of the hints Helena had subtly suggested, and Archie had been equally uncomprehending. When she had said, "This house seems so much more like my home than any other," he had certainly glowed with pleasure, but had not thought it was meant to have any application with regard to her going back to Oakland Crescent. No one had taken her hints; it had occurred to nobody how suitable it was that Jessie should go to look after her father, and Helena remain to look after her cousin. But since her hints were not taken, Helena, like the excellent tactician she was, had retreated in preference to standing her ground and suffering defeat. She had to retreat, and she retreated with exactly the proper mixture of regret at leaving Grosvenor Square and of joy at her father's premature return. And when his taxi cab drew up palpitating at the door, it was she who ran down the three concrete steps from the front-door and across the awful little dusty yard called the front garden, with its cinder path that circulated round one laurel-bush, and flung herself into his arms, and helped the parlour-maid to carry in his bag, while Jessie waited in the narrow entrance that reeked of the ascending fumes of dinner, for the parlour-maid, as usual, had left open the door at the head of the kitchen stairs.

There was a grudge against Providence even deeper than this unnecessary transplanting of herself to Oakland Crescent, when she might so comfortably have flourished in Grosvenor Square, Archie had dined with them two nights ago, before taking her on to a dance, and in the interval that followed dinner, when her father and Archie remained downstairs, she had a painful scene with Jessie. Jessie, according to Helena's public version, had misunderstood her in the cruellest manner, but she knew that her real complaint here was not that her sister had cruelly misunderstood her, but had, in fact, cruelly understood her, which was more intolerable than any misunderstanding could have been. She could have borne a misunderstanding very patiently, but to be understood was of the nature of an exposure, of a kind scarcely decent, and impossible to forget.

It had begun so stupidly, so innocuously. She had but left a few orchids on her dressing-table, and Jessie, who naturally was not going to the dance, but was remaining at home to keep her father company, most kindly offered to get them for her. She came down again so ominously silent that Helena had asked her what the trouble was, and it appeared that Jessie had seen on the dressing-table the card of Lord Harlow with a safety-pin attached to it.

"Yes, darling, why not?" Helena had said. "He sent me those lovely orchids—thank you so much for getting them. He is going to be there to-night, and as he sent expressly for them from Harlow, naturally I shall wear them. It would be rude not to, don't you think?"

Jessie did not reply, and Helena repeated her question. For answer, Jessie had said in that soft rich voice which was the only thing that Helena envied her:

"You revolt me."

Helena became quite cool and collected. She might represent herself as being tearful and pathetic at the thought of Jessie's unkindness, but that attitude was useless with Jessie alone, and she never adopted it.

"Oh! May I ask why I revolt you?" she asked.

"Certainly, although you know already. Archie is in love with you."

Helena adopted the phrases of affection. She did so simply to irritate her sister.

"Darling, how delicious you are!" she said. "But mayn't I wear a flower from Tom, Dick, or Harry for that reason? I don't grant the reason for a moment; but, even if I did, what then? Besides, Archie hasn't given me any flowers, and one must have flowers at a dance."

But Jessie refused to be irritated. Helena's speech seemed to have exactly the opposite effect on her: she became gentle and apologetic.

"I'm sorry I said that you revolted me," she said. "It was thoughtless and stupid. But, O Helena, you are so thoughtless too. Do forgive me for questioning you, but—but are you intending to marry Lord Harlow if he asks you? If so, do make it clear to Archie, before things get worse, that you have no thought of him. You like him, don't you? You might save his suffering."

This was the understanding, not the misunderstanding, that was so cruel. But Helena was quite capable of being cruel too. She smelled her orchids, and pinned them into her gown. Simultaneously she heard feet on the stairs, and Archie's resonant laugh. She got up.

"I might almost think you were jealous of Archie's affection for me, darling," she said, in her most suave tones.

Before the door opened she saw Jessie's face flame with colour, and laughed to herself at the defencelessness of love. Next moment Archie launched himself into the room.

"Hullo! What fine orchids!" he said. "Who sent you them, Helena? I bet you the Bradshaw did. What a thing it is to have opulent admirers! I wish I had got some."

But since that evening, now nearly a week ago, Jessie had not spoken to Helena except when mere manners in the presence of other people required it. That was a tiresome, uncomfortable situation. In a big house it would not have mattered much, for they could easily have sat in different rooms; but here it made an awkwardness in the narrow existence. But Helena had the consolation of knowing that she had not merely knocked at Jessie's door, but had battered it in. The secret chamber stood open to her, and the shrine in it was revealed before unpitying eyes.

Here, then, were two grievances against the world, that might have taxed the patience of Job, and certainly super-taxed the patience of Helena. On the top of these, Ossa on Pelion, was perched an anxiety that had begun seriously to trouble her, for already it was the middle of July and Lord Harlow had as yet said nothing which suggested that he was going to propose to her. She knew that she charmed and captivated him, who had never looked seriously at a girl twice (nor at poor Daisy once); but he was undeniably a long time making up his mind, and Helena, though accustomed to repose the greatest confidence in herself, did not feel sure that she would prove equal to defeating the long-standing habit of celibacy. Even the continuous use of Archie in the capacity of a wedge seemed to make no impression, and she was beginning to be desperately afraid that the wedge would turn in her hand, and ask her to marry him before Lord Harlow succumbed. This would be a very awkward situation; most inauspicious developments might follow, for it would be tragic if she accepted Archie, and Lord Harlow proposed immediately afterwards, while, if she refused Archie, it would be a crown of tragedy if Lord Harlow did not propose at all. She had determined, in fact, if Archie proposed first, to ask him to wait for his answer.

A little breeze was stirring now, and Helena pulled up the blind to let it and the sun enter together, rather than endure this stifling stagnancy any longer, and gazed with the profoundest disgust at the mean outlook. The house stood in the centre of a small curve of three-storied buildings; in front was its little square of cindery walk with the one laurel in the middle, and a row of iron palings with a gate that would not shut which separated it from the road. On the other side of that was a small demilune of a garden, which gave the place the title of Crescent, and beyond that a straight row of houses all exactly alike. A milkman was going his rounds with alto cries, and slovenly cooks and parlour-maids came out of area gates with milk-jugs in their hands. A lean and mournful cat, with dirty, dishevelled fur, as unlike as possible to the sleek, smart mouser she had seen at the station, sat on a gate-post, blinking in the sun, and every now and then uttering a faint protest against existence generally. Helena could have found it in her heart to mew in answer.

The hot afternoon wore itself away, and presently the parlour-maid came in to lay a table for tea. This entailed a great many comings-in and a great many goings-out, and she usually left the door open, so that there oozed its way up the stairs a mixed smell of cigars and incipient cooking. The cigar smell came from the little back room adjoining the dining-room where Colonel Vautier, with tropical habits, spent the hour after tiffin (it seemed that he could not say "lunch") in dozings and smokings. Meantime the parlour-maid came in and out, now with a large brass tea-tray, to place on the table, now with plates and cups and saucers to put on it. She breathed strongly through her nose, and wore a white apron with white braces over her sloping shoulders.

From outside, during these trying moments, there came the sound of a motor-horn, and immediately afterwards the soft crunch of gravel below a motor's wheels. From where she sat, Helena could look out of the window, and from her torpid discontent she leaped with a bound into a state of alert expectancy. She hazarded, so to speak, all the small change she had in her pocket. For a moment she put her slim fingers in front of her eyes and thought intensely. Then she spoke to the parlour-maid.

"Take a tray of tea to Colonel Vautier in his study," she said, "and say that I have got a headache and told you to bring his tea to him there. Tell Miss Jessie"— Helena paused a moment—"tell her that a friend of mine has come to see me, and that I want to talk to him privately here. That's all: now open the door, and say that I am in."

Helena rushed to the looking-glass above the fire-place, and disarranged her hair a little. She took a book at random out of the shelves, and sat down with it. She heard a little stir in the hall below, and had a moment of agony in thinking that her father's door had opened. Then the stairs creaked under ascending footsteps, and her visitor was announced.

"Who?" she said, as the parlour-maid spoke his name, and then he entered.

She rose from her chair, with a smile that was almost incredulous.

"But how lovely of you!" she said. "I am delighted. What a business you must have had to find your way to our dear little slum."

Her hopes rose high: he looked like a man who had made up his mind. He was clearly nervous, but it was the nervousness of a man who has definitely sat down in the dentist's chair, and has resolved to get rid of that aching. He sat down in the chair Helena indicated, and looked round the room. It really was rather pretty. Helena had the knack of projecting her graceful self into any room she much used. Archie had sent a hamper of roses only this morning.

"Slum?" he said. "I should like to live in this slum."

Helena looked at him gravely.

"Well, there is a spare room," she said, "which we can let you. You won't mind a gurgling cistern next door, will you? But wasn't it lovely? Daddy came home a whole month earlier than I had expected, so I flew back here to be with him. Cousin Marion wanted me to stop with her, and let Jessie come back. It was sweet of her to want me, but how could I remain when Daddy was here? Tea?"

She gave him his cup, and continued her careful prattle.

"So of course I flew here," she said. "Sometimes I rather wish that a fairy-prince would descend, and pick up the house, and put it somewhere where there weren't quite so many barrel-organs; but one gets accustomed to everything. I think Daddy and Jessie must be out. They planned going out together, I know, and I haven't seen either of them since lunch. They are such dears! They are so much to each other! Sometimes I should get a little bit jealous of each of them, if I allowed myself to. Ah! do have one of those little cakes. They are made in the house; you probably smelled them as you came upstairs. How lucky I asked the cook to make some to-day. Sometimes she is cross, and won't; but to-day she was kind. Did she have a brain-wave, do you think, and know that you were coming?"

He ate one of the little cakes which really came from the pastry-cook's just round the corner, and while his mouth was full, Helena proceeded with her talented conversation. She was working at full horse-power, she wanted to dazzle without intermission.

"I daresay all the people who were so friendly will find their way here in time," she said, "but will you pity me, just in a superficial way, sometimes during August? Darling daddy has so much to do at the Colonial Office, or the Irrigation Office, or whatever it is, that he will have to be here all August."

"But he won't keep you in London?" asked he.

Helena laughed.

"Certainly he won't, for I shall keep myself," she said. "I shall try to persuade Jessie to go down to Lacebury with Cousin Marion, and I think I shall succeed. And where will you be? Up in Scotland, I suppose."

He put down the end of the cigarette which Helena had given him. He was less likely, if he was smoking, to smell the faint odour of cigar that had mounted the stairs. But, as a matter of fact, he would not have noticed the smell of burned feathers just then.

He turned to her quickly.

"I shall be—wherever you will permit me to be," he said. "But, wherever that is, mayn't we be together? I want never to be away from you any more. I want nothing else in the world but that."

Helena raised dewy eyes to him.

"Do you mean...?" she began. "Do you mean...?"

"Yes. And I want your answer."

"That is, 'yes,' too," she said.

She had an almost irresistible desire to burst into peals of laughter, but it was not so difficult to transform that into an aspect of radiant happiness. He kissed her, and she could feel his hands laid on her shoulders, trembling. And, out of sheer gratitude, she found herself able to respond quite passably, for the innate respectability of passion touched her. He had paid her the sincerest compliment that a man can pay a girl, in expressing his desire to have her always with him, to be the father of her children, to renounce such freedom as had been his, and to take in exchange for it a devoted slavery. And, since it was exactly that which she had set her purpose to accomplish, it was no wonder that she was content.

But, as soon as he had left her, without translating into the sphere of practical arrangements the when and how of their mutual pledge, Helena, after one tip-toe dance round the drawing-room, sat down again and was instantly immersed in those considerations. He would have liked to dine with them that night, but Archie was coming, and so, before he called again next morning, it was necessary to indulge in careful thought so as to produce a spontaneous suggestion next day. On her face she wore the happiness of child-like smiles, and throughout her meditations that never faded. Occasionally it was as if the sun was withdrawn behind some fleece of a summer cloud, but, if there had been a machine for the registration of her internal sunshine, there would scarcely have been a break in the record of serene hours.

Archie occupied her first; she was sorry for Archie, because the blow that this would be to him glanced back on to her. She had long ago made up her mind not to marry him if she could succeed in the quest now accomplished, but she regretted that now she would never see his eyes glow as he blurted out—she knew he would blurt it out, and probably kiss her with that light, rough eagerness which was so characteristic of him—the tale of his love. Not so many weeks ago, at Silorno, she had determined to marry him, but that was before the wider horizon opened to her. If he had proposed to her then she would certainly have accepted him, but she felt, though so much finer a future had now dawned on her, a sort of grudge against him for not having done so. That made the thought of telling him not unpleasant to her; there was an excitement in the thought of seeing his blank face—would it be blank? She thought so—when he heard her news. Perhaps the sight of how much it hurt him would hurt her also, but that pain would somehow enfold a rapture, for it would be clear how much he wanted her. But why had he not kissed her, when they sat on that last evening in the dark garden at Silorno? All might have been different then. Never till this afternoon had a man kissed her, and that kiss had struck her as being a little prim and proper. Archie would not and could not have been prim, he would have been quick and impulsive; there would have been something romantic about it, for with him she could have supplied that gleam of romance herself.

There had been fleecy clouds during this part of her meditation, and they gathered again, ever so light, as she thought of Cousin Marion and Jessie. Everybody was so clever nowadays, and she was afraid that Cousin Marion had seen that Archie was in love with her, even as Jessie had done. It would be tiresome if they behaved censoriously about it, and replied frigidly to congratulations, and made cold faces at the wedding. But she thought she could get round Cousin Marion, who, from experience, she knew was very easily convinced, but Jessie was more clear-sighted… And then, with a sense of refreshment, she remembered how Jessie had betrayed herself not so many days ago. Thereat the sun came out quite serenely again, and remained out when she thought of her father. He loved shooting, and Helena determined that he should enjoy quantities of shooting. He loved all sorts of the nice things that money made so easily procurable, comfort and good cigars and riding and bathrooms attached to bedrooms. Certainly there should be a delicious room for him in all her houses; she would name it "daddy's room." The filial sentimentality of this quite overcame her, and she murmured "darling daddy," and felt just as if she had sacrificed herself for him and made this marriage in order to secure him a comfortable old age. Bertie and he would get on excellently together: they could talk about tiger-shooting, and temples, and exotic affairs—for Bertie was a great traveller, and, if he wanted to travel again, she had no intention of being an apron-stringing wife. Marriage became a sacrilege rather than a sacrament if it was an affair of watch-dogs on the leash, ready to follow up trails. And again she softly applauded the nobility of her sentiments.

There was a faint stir and rattle of crockery in the room below, which implied that the parlour-maid was removing her father's tea. Helena knew all the noises of the house, down to the gurgling sound of tooth-cleaning that came from her father's bedroom, which showed that he was nearly dressed, and now, correctly interpreting the chink of plate and tea-cup, she was certain of finding him in his study with his after-tea cigar. Very likely Jessie had gone there too; for she often took the evening paper in to her father and read him the news, and Helena hoped that this was the case to-day. She could let Jessie know the event of the afternoon with less embarrassment if there was somebody else present. She could tell her father about it much more easily than she could tell Jessie alone. She would sit close to him, and whisper and hide her head... her sense of drama would make it all quite simple.

She fastened one of the cream-coloured roses that Archie had brought her into the front of her dress and went down to her father's room. It was a stale little apartment, dry and brown and smoked like a kippered herring, furnished chiefly with books and files and decorated with the produce of oriental bazaars, spears and shells and things suggestive of mummies. He was in a big basket chair close to the window, and in the window-seat, as she had hoped, sat Jessie, with the evening paper.

Helena had not forgotten that she had sent a message to him that she had a headache, and to Jessie that a friend had come to see her with a wish for a private conversation. She made these little plans quickly perhaps but always coolly, and remembered them afterwards. Sometimes a little delicate adjustment was necessary, but she seldom got caught out...

"Darling daddy," she said, "may I pay you a little visit? Or are you and Jessie engrossed in something I shan't understand?"

"No, come in, dear," said he. "How's the headache?"

She hovered for a moment like some bright bird, and then perched herself on the arm of his chair, between him and her sister.

"It's quite gone, ever so many thanks," she said. "I think I must have had a little snooze just before tea, which took it away. And then, as I told Jessie, somebody came here especially to have a little talk to me. Daddy, how delicious your cigar smells!"

"And who was you visitor?" he asked.

"Lord Harlow," said she very softly, and paused.

Jessie had put down her paper, and Helena could feel that she was listening in tense expectation. She did not look round, but firmly laid her hand on Jessie's clasping it. The other she tucked into her father's arm, and leaned her head against his shoulder.

"Daddy, I had a long talk to him," she said, "and he is coming here again to-morrow morning. At least, he did the talking, and I only spoke when he had said what he had come to say. Oh, my dear, I am so happy, so awfully, awfully happy."

Helena felt that she had done that quite beautifully. If she had thought about it for ever so long, she could not have improved on it. A few boisterous ejaculations from her father followed, and, finding that Jessie had disengaged her hand, she completed the circle round her father's arm. Then presently she rose, with smiling and suffused face, just kissed him, and left the room.

"Well, I'm sure that's the best bit of news I've heard for a long time," he said. "Certainly he is a good deal older than she, but there's no harm in that. I was twenty years older than your mother, Jessie. And what do you think of it all?"

"I think Helena will be very happy," said Jessie.

"So do I, and I'm sure she deserves to be. If she's as kind and loving to her husband as she has been to her father, we shan't hear any complaints. Dear me! What a bit of news!"

He was silent a moment.

"How we old folk get out of touch with young people!" he said. "If I had been told to guess who it was who would ask Helena to be his wife, I should have said it was Archie. Didn't you think that Archie was very fond of her?"

Mixed with Jessie's misery for Archie's sake, and with her bitter contempt for her sister, was a pity for Helena, as deep as the sea, that she could be what she was. She could wear the roses Archie had sent her, and not be burned alive by them...

"I never though that Helena really cared for him," she said quietly.

"No? Well, you were more clear-sighted than I. But I fancy Marion thought so too. He's dining with us to-night, isn't he? Or will Helena put him off? And are we to say anything to him about it?"

"I expect Helena will tell us what she wishes," said Jessie.

He laughed.

"No doubt she will. She—what's the phrase?—she pulls the strings in this piece, doesn't she? Bless me, it's after six o'clock. We might go across the bridge and have a stoll in Battersea Park. I expect Helena will like to be left alone. Yes; what is it?"

The parlour-maid had come in, with the request that Colonel Vautier would go to see Helena for a minute now, or some time before dinner. Accordingly he went upstairs, in high good humour, stumbling on the carpet-rods.

"Oh, daddy, how sweet of you to come to me at once!" she said. "Archie's dining here to-night, and I think I will tell him my news myself. He's such a dear; it would hurt him to hear it from anybody else."

Colonel Vautier felt that he had perhaps not been so wrong after all.

"Yes, my dear, that is kind and thoughtful of you," he said.

"So I'll tell him as soon as he gets here," said she. "Will you and Jessie be very kind and let me have two minutes with him?"

Helena's eyes wandered away a minute, and returned rather dewy to her father's face.

"Perhaps you would tell Jessie for me," she said.

She opened her eyes very wide, in a sort of childlike bewilderment.

"I wonder why Jessie is so cold to me," she said. "I must have vexed her somehow without meaning it. I feel sad about it. She did not say one word when I told you and her my news; she did not kiss me…"

"Jessie is never very demonstrative," said her father, intending to speak to Jessie about this.

"No; perhaps that's all. Thank you ever so much, daddy."

She watched them going out together, and thought what a pity it was that some people were so frank as to say that others revolted them, even though they apologized afterwards. It never paid to be coarse and rude like that…

Helena, according to her plan, was in the drawing-room among his roses when Archie arrived.

"It was delicious of you to send them," she said. "And I've got—something for you."

"Hurrah!" said Archie. "What is it?"

She had put a half sovereign and a half-crown on the corner of the mantel-piece, and handed it to him.

"A tip?" he said.

"No; a bet. I am poor but honest."

He looked at the money.

"Twelve and six?" he said. "When did you bet me twelve-and-six?"

Helena came a step closer to him. Even in the middle of London there was something of sea-wind and open spaces about Archie.

"Oh, you stupid boy!" she said. "How many half-crowns is that?"

Suddenly Archie remembered the wager he had made with her one morning in the Park, that Lord Harlow would propose to her before the end of the season. He pocketed the money with a shout of laughter.

"Ha! I knew I should win," he said, "but it wasn't nice of me to laugh. I take back the laugh. Poor old Bradshaw! Did he mind much?"

Helena looked at him, still standing close to him, smiling and in silence. She really found him most attractive at that moment, and she wondered with how changed a face he would presently look at her.

"Yes, he proposed to me this afternoon," she said, still smiling, and still looking at him.

"Well, poor old Bradshaw!" said Archie once more. But he did not say it with quite the same confidence.

She laid her hand, that soft hand with sheathed claws, on his arm.

"Archie, aren't you going to wish me happiness?" she asked.

The lines of his laughter still lingered on his handsome mouth, but now they were merely stamped there and meant nothing.

"Wish you happiness?" he rapped out in a hard snappish voice.

"Yes; isn't it usual between friends?"

"Do you mean you've accepted him?" he asked.

"Yes, my dear. Haven't I told you?"

"Is it a joke?" he asked. "Shall I laugh?"

Helena moved a little away from him, and rang the bell. Archie looked so strange. She had expected something far more moving and dramatic than this wooden immobility.

"Tell Colonel Vautier and Miss Jessie that Lord Davidstow has come," she said to the parlour-maid.

Archie said nothing till the door had closed again. He felt that he was made of wood, that everything was made of wood, he and Helena and the roses he had sent, and the Persian rug on which he stood. And when he spoke, it was as if a machine in his mouth said the words which had nothing whatever to do with him.

"I congratulate you," he said. "I hope you will be very happy."

Colonel Vautier entered; he had been to the cellar to get out a bottle of champagne in which to drink the health of Helena and the man she had chosen.

"Good evening, my dear Archie," he said. "I know Helena has told you her news."

Archie shook hands, and then his eyes went back to Helena again. She had never looked more entrancingly pretty, but she was made of wood. And then Jessie came in; they were all there, and dinner was ready, and down they went. In this wooden world, everything went on in precisely the same way as it had done when people were made of flesh and blood. Some cunning mechanical contrivance enabled them to talk and smile and eat: food tasted the same and so did the champagne in which presently they drank Helena's health. It was the same prickly, bubbly stuff, with a little sting in it, that he so seldom drank. But it unfroze the surface of the stricture that bound him, as when the first stir of a thawing wind moistens the surface of ice. He began to feel again, to be conscious that somewhere within him was a deep well of the waters of pain. But anything was better than that cataleptic insensibility, which was like being unconscious, and, all the time, knowing that he was unconscious.

They were not going out that night, and after dinner they sat down to a rubber of bridge, in which as usual Helena took Archie as a partner, because she always insisted that she could form some idea of the principles on which he played, whereas the other two but wandered in a starless and Cimmerian gloom when mated with him. But Helena claimed that her spiritual affinity with Archie enabled her to perceive that, when he declared hearts, he wished her to understand that he hadn't got any, and that she would do well to declare something different. "Bridge, properly understood," Archie had enunciated once, "is a form of poker: you must bewilder and terrify your adversary. And then the fun begins, and you get fined." What added to the hilarity was the concentrated seriousness which Jessie and her partner brought to bear on the game, and the miser's greed and avaricious eye with which Jessie was popularly supposed to see her score mounting. All these jokes, these squibs of light-hearted nonsense, were there to-night, but there was nothing behind them. It was as if they were spoken from habit; a frigid rehearsal of some pithless drama was going on; they were tinsel flowers stuck into arid and seedless ground, and sprang no longer from the warm earth.

The sense of wooden unreality soon began to close in again on Archie, with that utter absence of feeling which was so far more terrible than any feeling could be, that soulless insensitiveness as of a live consciousness that knew it was dead, and he rose from the table after Helena had delivered him from the consequence of some outrageous declaration, and went across to a side-table where were placed syphons and spirits. But now, instead of pouring himself out a glass of soda-water, he half filled his tumbler with whisky, and but added a cream of bubble on the top of it. Immediately almost his sense of touch with life returned; there stole back into himself and the figures of Colonel Vautier and Jessie the perception of their several identities, and into Helena the love with which he had endowed her. But that, and all that it implied, was better than feeling nothing at all. He knew, too, that when Jessie spoke to him, or looked at him, her voice and her eyes held for him a supreme and infinite sympathy. He could not reach it, but he knew it was there. Perhaps when he got used to those new conditions of nightmare existence, he could make it accessible, get into touch with it. At present he scarcely wanted it; he wanted nothing so long as this perception of life still ran in his brain, except Helena. He thought that she rather pitied him too, but it was not her pity he wanted, for it was she who had brought her pity on himself.

They played two or three rubbers; Jessie's miserly greed was assuaged by precisely the sum that Archie had won from Helena, and Colonel Vautier, after seeing him out, went back to his study to indulge himself in the cigar which was not permitted in the drawing-room, and the two sisters were left there. Helena's brain had long been busy, beneath the habitual jests of their game, over her future relations with Jessie, and she had come to the conclusion that the sooner they talked the matter out the better. She found that it affected her comfort to be practically not on speaking terms with her sister, and, since she had no shrinking from what might be a painful interview for others, she had made up her mind to ascertain exactly how Jessie meant to behave to her in the few weeks for which they would be in close daily and hourly contact, for Lord Harlow had expressed his mind very clearly about an early date for their wedding, and Helena entirely agreed with him.

Jessie, on her part, could scarcely manage to think about her sister at all. With Archie in front of her all evening she had barely been conscious of anything but his bitter and miserable disillusionment, his awakening from the dream that had become so real to him. She was still seated at the card-table, and with that need for trivial employment which so often accompanies emotional crises, she was building a house with the cards they had been using, devoting apparently her whole faculties to its breathless construction. The strong, beautiful hands which Archie had never noticed hovered over it, alighting with their building materials, putting each card delicately and firmly in place, and her grave face watched the ascending stories, as if Babylon the Great was rising again for the marvel of mankind. Then Helena sat down by her, and, leaning her arm on the table, caused a vibration that demolished Babylon from garret to cellar.

"Oh, Jessie, I'm so sorry," she said, and she was; the fall of an ingenious card-house was the sort of thing that provoked her pity.

Jessie swept the cards together and seemed about to get up.

"It doesn't matter," she said. "It is bed-time, isn't it?"

Helena put her head wistfully on one side.

"Aren't you being horribly unkind to me?" she said. She did not suppose it was much use playing on the pathetic stop, that made, as a general rule, so insincere a bleating in her sister's ears, but it was worth trying.

"I don't think there is any use in talking, Helena," she said. "If I am unkind, if I can't bear what you have done, it is because I simply can't help it."

Helena fingered the debris of the card-house with those more delicate fingers that could caress and claw so exquisitely. Essentially, she cared not one atom what Jessie thought of her, but she wanted not to be uncomfortable for the next few weeks.

"Ah, that is it?" she added. "You are satisfied to hate and detest me because you can't help it. That seems to you a final and unanswerable excuse. But nobody else may do anything because she can't help it."

"But you could have helped what you have done," said Jessie. "You made Archie think you cared for him. You let him fall in love with you on that assumption."

"He let himself fall in love with me," said Helena. "That was not my fault. Besides…"

She was silent a moment, weaving delicate spider-threads in her mind. She really wanted to propitiate Jessie just now, otherwise she would certainly have reminded her that she, anyhow, had allowed herself to fall in love with Archie, though she would not say that that was Archie's fault. It would have been amusing to suggest that, but it did not seem to tend towards reconciliation. She bent her graceful head a little lower over the fallen card-house. It had collapsed with tragic suddenness, even as Archie had collapsed.

"Besides," she went on, "it was open to Archie to propose to me. He did not. We were several weeks together at Silorno. And then I came to London and met Bertie. Was it my fault that I fell in love with him? I think you are horribly unkind to me."

Jessie came a step nearer.

"Are you in love with him?" she asked. "If you tell me you are in love with him…"

"Do you think I should marry him if I was not?" asked Helena, looking the picture of limpid, childlike innocence.

Jessie made no reply. She could not say that she believed Helena was in love with him, though she was assuredly going to marry him. She could not tell a lie of that essential kind; merely the words would not come.

"If I have wronged you in any way, Helena," she said at length, "I am most sincerely sorry for it. I ask your forgiveness unconditionally."

Helena rose, wreathed in tender smiles and liquid eyes.

"Darling, you have my forgiveness with all my heart," she said. "And may I ask you one thing? Will you try to feel a little more kindly towards me? If you only knew how your unkindness hurts me."

* * * * *

But Jessie, lying awake that night, striving, with all the sincerity that permeated her from skin to marrow, to make the effort that Helena had asked of her, made no headway at all. She utterly distrusted and disbelieved her. And somewhere, lying beneath the darkness of the windless night, was Archie, for whose happiness she would have given her heart's last blood. But all of it would not help him one atom while he, in the perverse dispensations of destiny, wanted only what he could not get, Helena's love. He could not get it because it did not exist. She did not love; the faculty had been denied her.

* * * * *

Suddenly she felt frightened about Archie. He had sunk somewhere out of reach this evening; a lid had shut down on him. Once or twice it had seemed to lift for a moment, and she remembered what made it lift.

BOOK III

CHAPTER IX

Late one afternoon about a week after, Archie was sitting with his old nurse, Blessington, in the room that had once been his day-nursery. He had left London the day after Helena had so honourably paid him the five half-crowns he had won from her, and since then he had been living here alone with his father. This evening, his mother and Jessie were coming down from town, his mother to remain here till she went up to London again for Helena's wedding which had been fixed for the end of the first week in August, while Jessie was but coming for a long week-end. Helena remained in town, where she was very busy shopping, and unpacking the lovely presents which Lord Harlow sent or brought to her, morning, noon, and night. They were really delightful presents, and the material of them was large precious stones, exquisitely set.

Archie had long made it a habit, when he was at home, to pay a visit to his old nurse before he went to dress for dinner. She had become housekeeper after the fledging of the family, and now, half-way through the decade of her seventies, did little more, when Archie was away, than sit white-haired and stately with her sewing or her knitting, and feel that she was very busy. But when Archie came home she would burst into violent activities, and constitute herself his nurse again, to whom he was always "Master Archie," and quite a little boy still. It mattered not one rap to her that he had his own valet, none other indeed than William, who in days gone by had fished him out of the lake, and received a gold watch and chain for the rescue, for Blessington was always in and out of his room, taking coats and trousers away to have buttons more securely adjusted, and loading her work-basket with piles of his socks and underclothing in which her eyes, still needle-sharp for all her seventy-five years, had detected holes that required darning. This habit of hers sometimes drove William nearly mad, for Blessington would take away all Archie's washing when it came back from the laundry, in order to inspect it thoroughly, and when his distracted valet wanted clean clothes, and applied to her for them, she would often entirely forget that she had taken them, and firmly deny the appropriation. Then William would craftily manage to get her to open her cupboard door, and lo, there was all Archie's clean linen. And Blessington would exclaim, "Eh, I must have taken it, and it went out of my head." Or she would abstract his sponge from the bathroom in order to put a stitch into it, and Archie, sitting in his bath, would find nothing to wash himself with. But Blessington was a sacred and a beloved institution, and as long as she was happy (which she most undoubtedly was when Archie was there to look after and inconvenience) no one minded these magpie-annexations of portable property.

* * * * *

Of all hours in the day Blessington loved best this evening visit of Archie's, when he sat among the tokens of his childhood, the play-table which now scarcely reached up to his knees, the little arm-chair, with its bar of wood strung through the arms so as to imprison and guard the sitter, the box of oak-bricks with which he used to build houses of amazing architecture, the depleted regiments of lead-soldiers which still stood on the mantel-shelf. Her great delight was to recall to him the days of his childhood, his naughtiness, the scrapes he got into, the whole patchwork of memories that retained still such lively and beloved colouring. And for him, too, during this last week, there had been in these talks a way of escape from this nightmare of his present experience; it was he himself, after all, who had put the coals on his mother's hearthrug, had fished for pike with William, had attended, in rapturous trepidation, the advents of Abracadabra. These days seemed much further off from him than they did from her, for a bitter impassable water lay between them and him, while for her they had only receded a little further into the placid and sunny distance of her days. But, when he talked them over with her, he could recapture a dreamlike illusion of getting back into a life of which the most alarming feature was the presence of his father. Over everything else there hung enchantment.

He was sitting now in Blessington's rocking-chair, having tried without success to squeeze himself into the imprisoning seat of his childhood, and she was recalling the awful episode of the burnt rug.

"Eh, whatever possessed you to go and do it," she said, "I can't understand to this day, Master Archie. I'm speaking of when you set fire to your mamma's rug."

"Tell me about that," said Archie.

"Well, it was on an afternoon when you had a cold, and your mamma had allowed you to sit in her room while she went out driving. And what must you do but empty all the fire from the hearth on to her rug. You nearly got a whipping for that from your papa!"

Archie remembered that moment quite well, and how he had stood in his father's study, frightened but defiant, and refusing to say he was sorry when he was not. Then his mother had come in and had pointed to a bottle on the table, and told his father that he ought to learn his lesson first before he gave Archie one... That had puzzled him at the time, though it was clear enough now. His father still had that lesson to learn, and Archie, during this last week, had begun to understand a little why his father had not yet learned it, if learning it implied the giving up of all that battles stood for.

He recalled himself with a jerk: he wanted to get back into the enchanted land which Blessington's reminiscences outlined for him.

"Yes, that hearthrug," he said. "That was a bad business, wasn't it, Blessington? What do you think put it into my head to empty the fire on to it?"

"Bless the boy, I don't know," said Blessington. "It was just mischief."

"Yes, but what's mischief?" asked Archie.

Blessington was a simple and direct theologian.

"Well, I shouldn't wonder if it's doing what Sapum wants you to do," said she, Sapum being her equivalent for the arch-enemy.

"I shouldn't wonder either," said Archie. "But it's rather beastly of Sapum to take possession of a very small boy with a bad cold in the head."

"Eh, he takes possession of us all, if we let him," observed Blessington. "But that was the naughtiest thing you ever did, dear. I wouldn't lay it up to you now."

"Was I good as a rule?" asked he.

"Yes, Master Archie, for a boy you were," said Blessington. "Boys are more trouble than girls, as is natural and proper."

"But doesn't Sapum enter into girls, too?" asked he, with another thought in his mind.

"Yes, to be sure, but not so violent-like. And when after that you were took ill, and we all went out to—eh, what's the name of that place in Switzerland—I must say you were wonderfully good. It was as if some angel took possession of you, not one of Sapum's flibertigibbits. You were no trouble at all; and see how quick you got well."

Archie rocked himself backwards and forwards for a minute in silence.

"I wish I could remember Martin," he said at length. "Tell me something about Martin."

"Eh, dear lamb!" said she. "Couldn't he be naughty too, when the fit took him! But then he got ill, and many's the time when I've longed for him to be naughty again, and he hadn't the spirit for it. He didn't want to die, and right up to the end he thought he'd get better. You papa never loved any one like he loved him, and nobody could help loving him. He was like a April morning, dear—sunshine one minute and squalls the next. And there was months, Master Archie, when we thought you would follow him."

Blessington grew a little tearful, with the sweet, easy tears of old-age over this, and Archie changed the subject.

"And Abracadabra, now?" he asked. "What evenings those birthdays evenings were, weren't they? I wish Abracadabra came still, bringing all we wanted. What would you choose, Blessington?"

Blessington beamed again.

"Eh, I know what I'd choose," she said. "I'd choose a nice young lady to come here, and you and she take a fancy to each other, dear. That's what I'd choose. Isn't there some nice young lady, Master Archie?"

Archie stopped his rocking for a moment, and a bitter word was on the end of his tongue. Then he smiled back at his nurse's radiant face.

"I'm going to marry you, Blessington," he said, "when you're old enough. Don't you go flirting with anybody else now."

Blessington gave a little cackle of soft, toothless laughter.

"Well, I never," she said. "Who ever heard such a thing?"

"Well, you've heard of it now," said he. "Blessington, I believe there's somebody else after you. I say, did you ever have any lovers once upon a time?"

Blessington looked solemn again.

"Well, there was your papa's game-keeper once," she said, "who made a silly of himself, as if I'd got nothing better to do than go and marry him. I didn't suffer any of his nonsense... And there's the sound of the motor. That'll be your mamma and Miss Jessie coming. There's a nice young lady now!"

"Do you like her better than Miss Helena?" asked Archie.

Blessington nodded her head very emphatically.

"Not that I say she isn't a nice young lady, too," she said mysteriously.

"What's the matter with her then?" asked Archie.

Blessington looked the incarnation of discretion.

"I say nothing," she said. "But there's some as are artful, and some as are not. Now, my dear, you must go and see your mamma, or she'll be wondering where you are."

"I'm with my young woman," said Archie.

"There! Get along with you," said Blessington. "Eh, Master Archie, I love a talk over old times with you."

* * * * *

Archie went reluctantly away to greet his mother and Jessie, for these talks with Blessington had become to him a sort of oasis in this weary wilderness of scorching sand through which he had to travel all day and for many hours of the night. She was the comforter of the troubles of his earliest childhood; it was she who had always been by him if some nightmare snatched him from sleep, or if the dark developed terrors, and that habit of calling on her for aid, established among the mists of dawning consciousness he found still alive as an instinct, when there came on him now the maturer woes of love and manhood. Throughout his school life and his three years at Cambridge, he had never quite let go of Blessington's hand, which had been the first to direct and sustain his tottering attempts at locomotion. Now, too, she was the only member of his immediate circle who did not know of his trouble, and it was an unutterable relief to feel that he was not being pitied and sympathized with by somebody. For, though there is nothing in the world better than sympathy and pity, no sufferer smarting from a recent wound wants to live exclusively in such surroundings. Pity and sympathy, though they heal, yet touch the wound, and he never got over the impression when he was with his mother, for instance, that his wound was being dressed… Jessie did not force that on him so much, yet with her he was always being reminded of the fact that she was Helena's sister. But with Blessington he could go back into the sunlight of the past: talk with her, and another occupation, temporary, he told himself, to tide him over those days, enabled him to get away to some extent, from himself.

He met his mother in the hall, and instantly those anxious eyes of love, which, for all his affection for her, he found irritating, were on him. She was at his wound again, taking off the bandages, seeing how it was getting on…

"And how are you, darling?" she said, looking at him with the tenderness that got on his nerves.

Archie kissed her.

"I am quite well, thanks," he said. "I have just been having a talk with Blessington."

"My dear, how she would like that!" said Lady Tintagel with eager cordiality. "That was thoughtful of you."

Archie jerked himself away from her: though his mother said nothing direct, he felt that pity filled her mind. He was in its presence, and longed to get away from it. All the time another distinct piece of his mind wanted to hear about Helena. But he could not ask any question about her.

"How are you, Archie?" said Jessie quietly.

Archie's exasperation suddenly flared up.

"I have just told my mother I am very well," he said. "I am still very well, thank you."

Jessie laughed; she managed better than Lady Tintagel.

"In that case, come and have a game of golf-croquet with me," she said. "There's time before we need dress, isn't there? I do want some air so badly after town."

Archie glanced at the clock; he usually went to his father's study about this time, when they celebrated the approaching advent of dinner with a cocktail or two. That was the beginning of the tolerable part of the day: there was plenty of wine at dinner, and afterwards a succession of whiskies and sodas, and to be alive became quite a bearable condition again. On that first evening when Helena had told him her news and paid her half-crowns he had found that alcohol broke down his sense of being stunned, of being made of wood. Now he drank for another reason: by drink he got rid of the misery of normal consciousness and emerged into some sort of life again. It stimulated his brain, he could by its means escape for a little from that one perpetual thought of Helena that went round in his head like a stick in a backwater, and get into the current again. Sometimes he would go to his room, taking a whisky and soda with him, and wrestle with the sea-sketches he had so enthusiastically worked at at Silorno. By degrees the liquid in his glass ebbed, and his pile of cigarette-ends mounted, and he would go back for fresh supplies. But, while these hours lasted, he lived, and what to-morrow should bring he did not in the least care. He could escape for a few hours now, and that was sufficient. Also, when he went to bed, he could sleep heavily and dreamlessly.

There was still time for a game with Jessie, before going in to his father; Jessie would take longer to dress for dinner than he, and there would be a few minutes to spare after she went upstairs. But, even as they were strolling across the lawn to get the croquet-balls from their box, she a little ahead of him as he nursed a match for his cigarette, he looked up, and there in front of him might have been Helena. The two were of the same height and build, they moved like each other. It was Jessie, of course, but just for a second, while his match burned up in the hollow of his hand, it was not she at all...

He threw the match away.

"Get the balls out, will you?" he said. "I've left my cigarette-case in my father's room."

He ran back to the house, and went in through the garden door of his father's study. Lord Tintagel was sitting in the big leather arm-chair, with his feet up on another, and a glass beside him.

"Just come for a cocktail, father," said Archie. "Hullo, they're not here yet. It doesn't matter; I'll take a glass of whisky and soda."

"By all means; take what you like," said the other drowsily. "You mother's come, hasn't she?"

"Yes, mother and Jessie," said Archie, pouring himself out some whisky. The soda-water was nearly exhausted, but the dregs of it gurgled pleasantly over the spirit. He drank it in a couple of gulps.

"What are you going to do now?" asked his father.

"Only have a game with Jessie."

"All right. Call in here when it's time to go up and dress. There'll be a cocktail for you then. Infernal lazy fellows the servants are not to bring them in earlier. Chuck me over the evening paper, will you?"

The evening remission from deadness and dulness and misery had begun for Archie. He played his game with Jessie, drank his cocktail, and by the end of dinner had risen to such naturalness of good spirits again, that his mother commended herself for the wisdom of her plan that he should leave London and seek a change of mind in a change of scene. He had done some writing since he had been here; he seemed pleased with the way it was going, and she talked hopefully to Jessie when they held a rather protracted sitting in the drawing-room before the two men joined them. Perhaps they had both overrated the strength of Archie's attachment: certainly to-night he did not appear like a boy who had so lately suffered an overwhelming disappointment in his affections.

"And Blessington says he has been just as delightful and affectionate to her as usual," said Lady Tintagel. "He goes and talks to her every evening as he always did. I think you must have been wrong, dear Jessie, when you thought he was so mortally hurt."

Jessie did not reply at once: she felt sure that she, with the insight of that love which is more comprehending than any mother's love, was somehow right about that point. It was not the mere lapse of a week that had restored Archie. Besides, Blessington did not know about his troubles. She could easily conjecture what a relief he might find in that. She knew that she would feel the same in his place; she could understand how much easier it was to behave normally with those who did not know than with those who did. Yet Archie's father knew, and all through dinner she had seen how friendly and intimate the two had become. Archie used to be constrained and awkward with his father, while his father used to be rather contemptuous of him. But this evening there had been none of that on either side, and now they lingered together a long time over their talk and their cigarettes. It was as if some bond of sympathy was springing up between them. But she shrank from admitting the explanation to herself: it might be that a man, who had been so bitterly disappointed about a girl, found something in another man that suited his mood. Women would remind him of a woman...

There was a shout of laughter in the hall outside, and Archie came in, followed by his father. He did not communicate the grounds for his merriment, but, looking a little flushed, very handsome, and very content, sat down on the sofa by his mother.

"Well, mother darling?" he said.

Instantly her love yearned forth to him.

"My dear, it is good to hear you laugh," she said. "What have you and your father been talking about?"

The sense of being watched, the love that irritated did not trouble Archie now. The sunny hours would stretch unclouded until he fell into bed. He laughed again, looking across to his father.

"I say, father," he said, "shall I tell her, or would she think it not quite…?"

"Just as you like," said Lord Tintagel.

The door into the garden, already ajar, swung gently open, admitting a breath of cool night-air into the room. It stirred in Jessie's hair as it passed her, and moved across to Archie, making the flowers in a vase near him vibrate. And for just that moment some impulse from the untainted tranquillity stirred in his soul, and his overheated, stimulated brain drank it thirstily in. His own laughter, and the subject of his laughter, the whole contents of the last hour or two, seemed stale and stuffy. The air of them was thick with the fumes of wine, with the fancies and images that it evoked, smoke-wreaths that hung heavy in the atmosphere, swirling and turning like dancers and melting into other shapes. But for that moment when the night-air came in from the crystal-clear dusk outside, that liquid tabernacle of sapphire in the holy night, where stars sang together and nightingales burned, the hot fumes dispersed, and he drew in long, tranquillizing breaths. This physical impression had, too, its psychical counterpart, for even as the air that stirred in Jessie's hair brought a coolness and a refreshment to him, so from the girl herself there seemed to stream into it a current of something wholesome and human and unfevered, unvexed by desire, and untouched by bitterness...

"It's rather hot in here," he said. "Will you come for a stroll, Jessie?"

They went out together... The heavens were full of stars, and a slip of a moon was near to its setting. Over the beds below the windows there hovered the fainter fragrance of sleeping flowers that stood with hanging heads and leaves that glimmered with the falling dew. Beyond lay the dimmed mirror of the lake, and beside it rose the dark mass of the wood in which the nightingales were singing. The scene seemed prepared for some human love-duet, when lovers fancy that nature is arranging her most sensuous effects for their benefit, though in reality she is but pursuing the path ordained for her by the wheeling seasons, and predicted by barometers and apparatus that is concerned only with heat and movements of the moon. And, of lovers, there was one of each pair absent, as the two walked quietly towards the wood of the nightingales; for Jessie there was no eager mate, and for Archie none… Two hungry souls, both longing, both unsatisfied, went forth on that twilit pilgrimage. Spring still stirred in them, and there burned above them the everlasting choir of the stars. But that helped in no way: had they been lovers, an autumn squall or a winter snow-storm would have served their purpose just as well.

Archie chattered for a little while, comparing the moon to a clipped finger-nail, the dimmed mirror of the lake to a frozen rink in Switzerland, with all the hollowness of superficial talk, when the tongue speaks from habit, which is as lightly rooted as the seed on stony ground. Heart-whole, he had often chattered like that, and Jessie had sunned herself and responded to those silly things; but now she knew, as well as he, that the babble was no more than blown sea-foam. It made her heart ache that he should talk it to her, for, though she made no claim on his love, it was miserable that he could not recognize how true a friend it was who was by his side in this song-haunted darkness. She knew—none better—that he had no love to give her, but her love that was so disciplined to go hungry without crying out, starved for a word from him that should fly the flag of friendship, noblest of all ensigns that are not of royal emblazonment.

They had come to the edge of the lake, and a moorhen steered its water-logged flight across the surface. And then Archie's foolish chatter died, and he was silent as he watched the rayed ripple of water. The wash died away in the reeds, and chuckled on the bank, and at last he spoke.

"Why did Helena treat me like that?" he said. "It wasn't fair on me. Why did she encourage me? She might so easily have shown me that she didn't care. She knew: don't tell me she didn't know! Do answer me. Didn't she know? All the time that we were in town together she knew. And she let me go on. She was waiting to see if she could catch the Bradshaw. If she couldn't, perhaps she would have taken me. Was it so? You ought to know: you're her sister."

His voice had risen from the first reproach of his speech to a fury of indignation.

"Did she love me or didn't she?" he cried. "Do tell me if you know."

His passion had found combustible material in her: she flamed with it.

"Helena doesn't love anybody," she said. "Oh, Archie, poor Helena!"

"Poor Helena!" said he. "Why 'poor'? Surely it's far more comfortable to love nobody. Oh, don't remind me of that stupid rot about it being better to have loved and lost. Anyhow, a worse thing is to have loved and not found. That's what has happened to me, and she made me think I had found. She meant to make me think that. Damned well she succeeded, too. And, if you're right about her not loving anybody, do you mean that she doesn't love the Bradshaw?"

Archie had closed a grip on her arm: now she shook his hand off, though loving to have it there.

"I can't answer you that," she said. "And I oughtn't to have said that Helena loves nobody. I withdraw that entirely."

"The saying of it, you mean," said he. "You don't withdraw your belief in it."

"I don't know the truth of it. What I said was only my opinion, and I withdraw it. I oughtn't to have said it."

"But you keep your opinion?" asked he.

"You shouldn't ask me that. I have withdrawn what I said. Please accept that."

In this high noon of stars she could see his face very clearly. It was not angry any longer: it was just empty, as if there was no one there behind the eyes and the mouth. It was a face empty, swept, and garnished, ready for any occupant who might take possession. The sweet, clean water of his nature must have run out on to desert sands; the cistern of the body into which it had so swiftly and boyishly bubbled all these years was empty. Just for one second that impression lasted, inscrutably frightening her, with some nightmare touch.

"Archie," she cried, "are *you* there? Is it you?" She heard a dreary little laugh for answer.

"Oh, I suppose so," he said. "I answer to my name, don't I?"

She longed, with a force of passion quite new to her, to be able to reach him in some way, to let her love be coined into the commoner metal of friendship, if only that could get to him, and give him the sense that he had something in his pocket worth having, even though it was not gold. She would have gleefully melted all her love into a currency that could have enriched him, for he did not want her love, and she had no other use for it except to help him in some way. And, as if to answer her yearning, he took her arm again, not angrily now, but with the quiet pressure of a man with a sympathetic friend.

"You're a good pal, Jessie," he said. "I'm awfully grateful to you. You won't play me false with your friendship, will you?"

"No, my dear," said she, stumbling a little on the words. "I'm—I'm not like that. The more you count on me the better I shall be pleased. I'm stupid at saying things, but, oh Archie, if a friend is any use to you, you've got one. And let me say, just once, how sorry I am for all this miserable business."

"Thanks, Jessie," said he.

They had turned back towards the house, and Jessie, unconscious of anything else except Archie, saw that they were already half across the lawn that lay dripping with dew. Her thin satin shoes were soaked, and the hem of her dress trailed on the grass. But she regarded that no more than she would have regarded it had she been walking in the dark with her lover.

Then Archie spoke again—there was no more emotion in his voice than if he had been speaking through a telephone.

"Do keep on trying to be friends with me, Jessie," he said. "I'm nothing at all just now; I'm dead, but will you watch by the corpse? It likes to know you are there. There's no complaint if you go away, but when sometimes you have nothing to do, you might just sit with it."

"Archie, dear, don't talk such nonsense," she said.

"I daresay it is nonsense, but it seems to me sense. I don't feel as if I was anybody... I can imagine what a house feels like that has been happily lived in for years, when the family goes away, and leaves it empty. There's a board up 'To let, unfurnished,' and the windows get dirty, and the knocker and door-handle, which were so well rubbed and polished, get dull. There used to be curtains in the windows, and in the evening passers-by in the street could see chinks of light from within, and perhaps hear sounds of laughter. But now there are no curtains, and the pictures have gone from the walls, leaving oblong marks where they used to hang. And the spirit of the house stares mournfully out, thinking of the days when there was laughter and love within its walls. Haven't you ever seen a house like that? They're common enough."

She pressed the hand that lay loose in the crook of her elbow.

"Oh, Archie, you give me such a heartache," she said.

"Well, I won't again. But if you think me wanting in affection to mother, or you, or anybody, just remember that I'm an empty house for the present. I daresay somebody will take me again."

Jessie felt that this was a truer Archie than he who had stopped so long in the dining-room and come in afterwards with a shout of laughter over something that he would not recount. But by now their stroll had taken them close to the long grey front of the house, and for the present Archie had no more to say, and was evidently meaning to go indoors again. Upstairs all was dark, but below, the five windows of the drawing-room, uncurtained and open, cast oblongs of light on to the gravel, and next to them the two windows of Lord Tintagel's study were lit. Even as they stepped from the grass on to the walk, and their footsteps became audible again, his figure, silhouetted against the light, appeared there, and the window-sash rattled as he opened it wider.

"Is that you, Archie?" he called. "Come in and see me before you go upstairs."

"All right, father," said he, "we're just coming in."

Jessie heard a fresh vigour in his quickened voice, and in the light from the windows she could see that his face was alert again. And it was with a sense of certainty that she guessed what had given him this sudden animation. Perhaps it was only the knowledge of his father's habits that informed her, perhaps it was a brain-wave passing from him to her that told her that inside his father's room were the things for which he craved, the cool hiss of bubbling water on to the ice that swam in the spirits...

"You're not going to sit up long, are you?" she said.

"Oh, I don't know. My father and I often have a talk in the evening. And sometimes I do some writing before I go to bed. It's quite a good time for writing when every one has gone to bed and the house is quiet."

"You always used to say at Silorno that you wrote best in the morning."

"Yes, but that was at Silorno, where I could lie on the beach, and go for a swim at intervals. Lord! What jolly days they were! It's a pity they are all dead."

They went through the French window into the drawing-room, and found that Lady Tintagel had already gone upstairs. Archie stood by Jessie, shifting from one foot to the other, in evident impatience at her lingering.

"Well, you'll be wanting to go to bed," he said. "I daresay you'll go in and have a talk with my mother. And, do you know, my father's waiting for me; I think I'll join him. I shall soon come upstairs, I expect. I feel rather like writing to-night."

"I'm glad you're going on with that," she said. "That's something left, isn't it? The house isn't quite empty, Archie."

He laughed.

"No, I can trace my name in the dust on the window-panes," he said. "But I'll go to my father. Good-night, Jessie."

* * * * *

Lord Tintagel, rather unusually, was deep in the evening paper when Archie entered. Archie noticed, with some surprise, that his glass still stood untouched on the tray.

"Rather nasty news," he said, not looking up. "Give me my drink, Archie, there's a good fellow. Plenty of ice and not much soda."

"And what's the news?" asked Archie.

"Well, it looks as if there might really be trouble brewing. Servia has appealed to Russia against the Austrian ultimatum. I wonder if Germany can really be at the bottom of it all. And the city takes a gloomy view of it. All Russian securities are heavily down."

"Does that affect you?" asked Archie, bringing him his drink.

"Yes, I've got a big account open in them. I wonder if I had better sell. Of course there won't be war; we're always having these scares, and they always come to nothing. But if dealers are anxious, prices may fall a good bit yet, and I should find it difficult to pay my differences."

Archie poured himself out his first tumbler. He held it in his hand a moment, not tasting it, now that he had got it. Delay, when the delay was voluntary, would but add deliciousness to the moment when his mouth and throat would feel that cold sting...

"I don't understand," he said, watching the bubbles stream up from the sides and bottom of his glass.

His father threw down the paper.

"It's as simple as heads and tails," he said. "I've bought a quantity of Russian mining shares, without paying for them, in the hope that they will go up. If they do, I shall sell at the higher price and pocket the difference. But if they go down I shall have to pay the difference at the next account. If the shares are each worth L8 now, and at the next account are only standing at L6, I shall have to pay L2 on each share. If I like, I can telegraph to my broker to sell now, while they're at L8. I shall have a loss because I bought them at L9, but I shall no longer be running any risks. But it's thirsty work talking. Just fill my glass again."

"But then, if the scare dies down again, I suppose your shares will go up," said Archie.

His father laughed.

"Sound business head you've got, Archie," he said. "You've got the hang of it; it's just heads and tails. Never you speculate: it's a rotten business. I've got into the habit now, but I recommend you not to take to it. It's easy enough to take to it, but it's the devil to break it. Same with other things. Make a habit of virtue, and you'll never go to the deuce."

He watched Archie a moment, who with head thrown back, and young, strong throat throbbing as he swallowed, was reaping the rewards of his delay in drinking. And when, with brightened eyes, he put his glass down, he stood there like some modern incarnation of Dionysus, his face pure Greek from the low-growing brown curls to the straight nose and the short round chin. With a cloak over his shoulders in exchange for his dress-clothes, with sandals for his patent leather shoes, and a wine-cup for his tall glass, he might have stepped straight from some temple-frieze, and his father wondered how any girl in her senses could have chosen the precise, pedantic man whom she was soon going to marry, when Archie was but waiting, as she must have known, for his moment. He, poor fellow, was often a very dreary and dispirited boy all day; but in the evening he came to himself again, and was what he used to be. And yet, though it seemed to Lord Tintagel a cruel thing to wish to deprive him of the few hours of the joy of living that were his during the day, he was smitten, with the easy and vague remorse of a man only half-sober, to see the effect that alcohol had on Archie, who, all his life till now, had scarcely tasted it. But he remembered when he himself had been at that stage; he remembered also his father giving him just such a warning as he now proposed to give Archie. He wished he had taken notice of it, and he hoped that Archie would.

That evening, thirty years ago, he recalled now with extreme distinctness. The scene had taken place in this very room, and his father, already half-tipsy, as his habit was, had warned him of the dangers of drink, and he remembered how laughable and grotesque such a warning had seemed coming from lips that had lost all precision of utterance. But he told himself that he was not going to commit any such absurdity: he was perfectly sober, indeed it seemed very likely that it had never entered Archie's head to think of him as a drunkard. Sometimes he stumbled a little going upstairs at night, sometimes he had an impression that his pronunciation was not quite distinct; but he never became incapable, as he could remember his father becoming, and being carried off to bed by two perspiring footmen.

He put down his second glass without tasting it.

"There's something I want to speak to you about, Archie," he said, "and you mustn't be vexed with me, because I'm only doing what I believe to be my duty. You won't be vexed, will you?"

Archie looked at him in surprise.

"No, I don't suppose I shall, father," he said. "What is it?"

His father got up and stood by his chair quite steadily, for he leaned back against the high chimney-piece.

"Well, I want to you be careful about that stuff," he said, pointing to the bottle. "That's one of the habits I was speaking about, which they say is so easy to keep clear of, but so hard to break. You drink rather freely, you know, whereas a few months ago you never touched wine or spirits. It's an awful snare—you may get badly entangled in it before you know you are caught at all."

Archie kept his lucid eyes fixed on his father's, and not a tremor of his beautiful mouth betrayed his inward laughter, his derisive merriment at this solemn adjuration delivered by a man who spoke very carefully for fear of his words all running into each other like the impress of ink on blotting-paper. It really was ludicrously funny, and the immortal Mr. Stiggins came into his mind.

"I hope you don't think a whisky and soda after dinner is dangerous, father," he said. "You usually have one yourself, you know."

He moved across to the table as he spoke, and handed his father the drink he had mixed for him but a few moments before. Lord Tintagel, quite missing the irony of the act, began sipping it as he talked.

"No, of course not, my dear boy," he said. "I'm not a faddist who thinks there's a microbe of delirium tremens in every glass of wine. But—though you may never have heard it—your grandfather was a man who habitually took too much, and it's strange how that sort of failing runs in families."

Archie's mouth broadened into a smile.

"Skipping a generation now and then," he said gravely.

His father turned sharply on him.

"Eh? What?" he asked.

He looked hard at Archie for a moment—as hard, that is, as his rather wandering power of focus allowed him—and suddenly beheld himself with Archie's eyes, even as, thirty years ago, he had beheld his father when he spoke to him on precisely the same theme. He put down his glass, and a wave of shame as he saw himself as Archie saw him, went over him.

"I know: this doesn't come very well from me, Archie," he said. "It's ridiculous, isn't it? But I meant well."

He looked at the boy with a pathetic, deprecating glance.

"If I make an effort, will you make one, too?" he asked. "I've gone far along that road, and I should be sorry to see you following me. I should indeed. Just now I know you're unhappy, and a bottle of wine makes things more tolerable, doesn't it?"

Archie, in his empty, exasperated heart felt a sort of pity for his father, which was based on scorn. Something inside Lord Tintagel was probably serious and sincere, and yet it was what he had drunk that stimulated his scruples for Archie. He was in a mellow, kindly, moralizing stage in his cups that Archie had often noticed before. Certainly he himself did not want to become like that, but he felt that he was not within measurable distance of the need of making any resolution on the subject, so far was he from needing the exercise of his will. Just at present, even as his father had said, he was unhappy, and his unhappiness melted in the sunshine of drink. He did not care for it in itself; he but took it, so he told himself, like medicine because his mind was ailing.

"Well, let us talk about it to-morrow," he said. "We'll make some rule, shall we, father? And don't imagine for a moment that I am vexed with you. But I shall go upstairs now, I think. I've got some writing I want to do."

He hesitated a moment.

"I'll just take a night-cap with me," he said. "Good-night, father."

"Good-night, my dear boy; God bless you! We'll have a talk to-morrow."

Archie took the glass he had filled out into the hall, and waited there a moment, and the pity faded from his mind, leaving only contempt. It was just the maudlin mood that had prompted his father to be so ridiculous, and talk about resolutions. Certainly resolutions would do him no harm, and the keeping of them would undoubtedly do him good, for, instead of the firm, masterful man whom Archie had known as the rather prodigious denizen of that formidable room, there sat there now a weak, entangled creature. Archie could hardly believe that, in years not so long past, he had been afraid of his father: now his whole force, that dominating, intangible quality, had vanished. Occasionally he still flew into fits of anger that alarmed nobody, but that was all that was left of his power.

Archie sat for a few minutes on the hall-table, instead of going upstairs, for he meant, with a certain object in view, to go back to his father's room, on some trivial errand, and, as he waited, the big clock ticked him back into boyhood. There was the fire-place by which Abracadabra sat on the last of her appearances; there the screen behind which, as he had subsequently ascertained, William had hidden with a trumpet and the servants' dinner-bell, there the side-door into the gardens through which, pleasingly excited, he had hurried with the box for coffin of the dead bird which the cat had killed... A hundred memories crowded about him, and not one, save where Blessington was concerned, held any romance or tenderness for him. They were as meaningless as pictures taken out from the empty house and leaning against the railings in the street: in the house itself, his bitter, lonely spirit, there was nothing left but the places where once they hung.

He went back to his father's room, crossing the hall with light foot, and turning the handle of the door with swiftness and silence. There was his father by the table, filling his glass again. It was just that which Archie wished to verify.

"I only came back for a book," he said. "Good-night again."

CHAPTER X

Archie went straight up to his room: his brimming glass was difficult to carry quite steadily, and he reduced its contents half-way upstairs. William had orders always to put whisky and soda in his room in case he wanted to sit up and write; but sometimes William forgot, or, at any rate, did not obey, and Archie wondered if the man did it on purpose, with perhaps the same excellent intentions as those which flowered so decorously in his father's mind. But to-night all was as it should be, and, as it was very hot, Archie undressed and put on his pyjamas before settling down to work. Writing, the absorbing joy of creation, the delicate etching of sentences that bit into the plate, still possessed him when he had taken the requisite evening dose.

But to-night, though he had got his material ready, his hand could not accomplish the fashioning of it, and he got up and walked with bare feet, once or twice up and down the room, wondering why he could not link up his thoughts to his power of expression. He was nearly at the end of one of those sea-stories, which he had begun at Silorno, and he knew exactly what he meant to say. The brain-centre that dictated was charged, and sufficiently stimulated, and yet he could get nothing on to paper that was worth putting there, though he was ready to write, and wanted to write.

He had not drunk too much and made himself fuddled; he had not drunk too little, and left the bitter weeds of daily consciousness uncovered, like rocks at low tide.

He sat and thought, wrote and impatiently erased again, and at last put down his pen. Perhaps even this, the only living interest that just now existed for him, was being taken from him also, and was following down the channel which had emptied itself into Helena. She had taken from him everything else that meant life: it would be like her consistency to take that also, and leave him nude and empty. It was not that she wanted the gift which she—in his vague, excited thought—seemed to be robbing him of; it was only that she and the memory of how she had treated him was a vampire to his blood. She had sucked him empty, drained him dry of happiness, of joy of life, of human interests. More than that, his love, the best thing which he had to give her, and for which she had no use, she now seemed to have treated with some devilish alchemy, so that it turned bitter; hate, like some oozy scum, rose from the depths of it, and covered its crystal with poisonous growth.

This would never do; the rocks at low tide had become uncovered, and, while he slipped and stumbled among them, bruising himself at every step with the thought of Helena, he could never get that abstraction and detachment which he knew were the necessary conditions of his writing. And all power of achieving that seemed taken from him; he felt himself an impotent atom, unable to order the workings of his own brain, defenceless against any thoughts that might assault him.

The house was perfectly quiet; the stillness of the midsummer night had flowed into its open windows and drowned it deep in that profound tranquillity that was yet tense with the energy of the spinning world and the far-flung orbits of the myriad stars. The moon had long since sunk, but the galaxy of uncounted worlds flared on their courses, driven onwards by the inexhaustible eternity of creative forces that ran through the stars, even as it ran through the humblest herb that put forth its unnoticed blossom on the wayside. But Archie, in this bitter stagnation that paralysed him, seemed to himself to have no part in life: all that current of energy that bubbled through the world, with its impulses of good and evil, love and hate, seemed to have been cut off from him. He neither loved nor hated any more. There was the nightmare of this death in life: at any price, and under whatever inspiration, he longed to be in the current again. Tonight even drink had failed him.

He had walked across to the window, and came back to his chair at the table where was spread the sheet of paper covered with the scrawlings and erasures which were all the last two hours had to show. And at this precise moment, as he looked at them in a dull despair, and idea flashed across the blank field of his brain. Perhaps there might still be some spark of life, of individuality latent without him, which he could reach by that surrender of his conscious self which had been familiar to him in his childhood. There, just in front of him, below his shaded lamp, lay his cigarette-case, with one bright point of light on it, and, lying back in his chair with half-closed eyes he gazed at this in order to produce that hypnotic condition in which the subconscious self comes to the surface.

Almost at once the mysterious spell began to act. Across the field of his vision there began to pass waves of light and shadow, moving upwards with a regular motion, while through them like a buoy moored in a rough sea there remained steadfast that bright speck on his cigarette-case, now for a moment submerged in a wave of shadow, but appearing again. Upwards and upwards moved the waves, and then it seemed that it was they which were stationary, while he himself was sinking down through them, as through crystal-clear waters, looking up at the sunny surface which rose ever higher and more remote above him. As he sank into this dim, delicious world, the sensation of being alive again and in touch with living intelligences grew momently more vivid. It was the very seat and hearth of life that in him before had been cold and numbed; now, though surface perceptions were gradually withdrawn, his essential being tingled with the rapture of returning vitality.

Once or twice during this descent his ears, through which there poured the roar of rushing waters, had been startled as by some surface perception of the sound of loud rappings somewhere in the room; but they had not disturbed his steadfast gaze at the point of light; and once again he had heard a voice faintly familiar near him that said "I am coming." But he was far too intent on his progress to let the interruption break in upon it, and indeed those sounds seemed to be less an interruption than a confirmation to his surface-senses of what was happening to him... And then he knew, as he sank down to rest at last on the bottom of that unsounded sea, who it was who was filling him with the sense of life again, for, echoing not only in his ears, but somewhere in his soul, he heard the same voice, which he now clearly recognized, and which had spoken to him years ago at Grives, say, "Archie, I am here."

* * * * *

Archie was conscious on two separate planes of consciousness. All round him and high above him were the gleams and aqueous shadows of the subconscious world, but here and there those seemed to be pierced, and through them, as through rents of mist, he had glimpses of the material plane. He could see, for instance, part of the sheet of paper in front of him, and he could see the far corner of his table. And by it, very faint and unfocusable, part of it in the mists of the subconscious world, part in the harder outlines of reality, there was standing the figure of a young man. How it was dressed he could not see, or did not care to notice, but when for a moment the mist cleared off its face, he recognized the strong likeness to himself, even as he had recognized the likeness to himself in the photograph which he had found in the cache. But here was no photograph: instead, mysteriously translated into outlines and features visible to mortal eyes, was the semblance of Martin himself. It wavered and flickered, like the blown flame of a candle, but it was there, standing at the corner of his table. And, as it spoke, he saw the mouth move and the throat throb.

"I have managed to come back, Archie," he said, "because you were in such trouble, and because you didn't understand the warning you had. Do you understand now?"

The whole explanation flashed on him.

"The dream?" he said. "The white statue of Helena and the worms?"

"Surely. It was odd you didn't understand. You only loved the white statue. You loathed what came out of it, just as you loathe what has come out of the white statue since."

Archie leaned forward, peering into the mist that at this moment quite enveloped the figure.

"But I love her, too, Martin," he cried. "I long for her."

Out of the mist came the unseen voice:

"You long for what she looks like," it said. "You hate what she is."

"That may be. But the whole thing makes me utterly miserable."

Table and figure, the white paper and the tray with syphon and whisky became suddenly visible.

"You must learn not to be miserable," said that compassionate mouth. "Be very patient, Archie. You think you are stumbling through absolute darkness, but in reality, you are flooded with light. I can't see the darkness which you feel is so impenetrable: I only see you walking towards the ineffable radiance, always moving towards it. Occupy yourself, and try to grow indifferent to that part of Helena which you hate. Cling to love always. Just cling to love. Never hate; some time you may get to love what you hated."

The voice sank lower.

"The power is failing," it said. "I am losing touch with you."

"Oh, don't go," said Archie. "Martin, stop with me. Talk to me. I want to say so much to you."

He reached out his hand, and for a moment, out of the sunlit mists that had gathered again he felt, perfectly clearly, the touch of fingers that pressed his. But they died away into nothing as he clasped them, and the voice faded to the faintest whisper.

"I will come again, dear Archie," it said. "It is easiest at night."

* * * * *

The lines of shadow and light that undulated before his eyes grew thinner and more transparent, and he could see the drawn-back window-curtains and the black square of the night through them. The bright point at which he had been looking withdrew on to the surface of his cigarette-case, and slowly the whole room emerged into its normal appearance. Archie became suddenly conscious of a profound physical fatigue, and, leaving all thought and reflection till to-morrow, put out his light and stepped into bed. But instead of the empty desolation that had made a wilderness round him, waters of healing had broken out in his soul, and the desert blossomed...

Archie slept that night the clean out-door sleep which he had been used to at Silorno, and woke next morning, not with the crapulous drowsiness that now usually accompanied his wakings, but with the alert refreshment that slumber in the open air gave him. He sprang into full possession of his faculties and complete memory of what he had experienced the night before. He was quite aware that any scientific interpreter (science being best defined as the habit of denying what passes the limits of materialistic explanation) would have said that, tired with the effort to write, he had fallen asleep over his table and dreamed. But he knew better than that: the experience with its audible and visible phenomena, was not a dream, nor did it ever so faintly resemble one. A dream at best was a fantastic unreality; what he had experienced at his writing-table last night was based upon the firm foundations of reality itself. It was no hash-up of his own conscious or subconscious reflections, no extract distilled from his own mind. It came from without and entered into him, and, unlike most of the communications that purported to reach the minds of sensitives from the world that lay beyond the perception of their normal senses, there was guidance and help in it. Often, if not invariably, these messages from beyond were trivial and nugatory; it was a just criticism to say that the senders of them did not appear possessed of much worth the trouble of sending. But Martin's visit had not been concerned with trifles like that: he had sympathized, as a brother might, with Archie's trouble; he had explained, so that Archie could not longer doubt, the manner of the warning he had received before but not understood; he had spoken of Archie as being wrapped, according to his own sensations, in impenetrable darkness, though, to one who looked from beyond, he was ever moving towards the ineffable radiance. It was the same discarnate intelligence that, when he was a child, had conveyed to him the knowledge of that cache under the pine-tree, which was unknown to any living being (as men count living) and that could not have been conveyed to him through any telepathic channel except one that had its source and spring not in this world. And now, from the same source, had come this message from one who saw through the gross darkness of Archie's emptiness and bitter heart, and had promised to be with him again. Archie had no doubt whatever, as he got up with an alertness that had not been his for weeks, of the genuineness of the communication. It linked on with Martin's previous visits, and the glimpses he had received of the materialized form of his visitor confirmed exactly the recognition, years before, of the photograph he had found in the cache which Martin had told him of. And the Power in whose hands were all things had compassionated his trouble and had allowed, in pity for his need, the gateless barrier to be again unbarred, and a spirit, individual and recognized, to pass to and fro between him and the realms of the light invisible.

It was just when his soul despaired that this happened; when he felt himself denuded of all that he had loved, empty, and cast out from life itself. Just in that hour had Martin been permitted to come back to him...

He found his mother and Jessie at breakfast when he went down; his father, as usual, had not appeared, and again, as last night when he came out of the dining-room after a prolonged sitting, he felt kindly and affectionate. But this was not from the sottish satisfaction of wine: the light came from that subtle window in his soul, from which once more the shutters had been thrown back. The moment Jessie saw him she felt the quality of that change; he was like the Archie of Silorno again.

"Good morning, mother darling," he said, kissing her. "Good morning, Jessie. How bright and early we all are! And has everybody slept as serenely as I?"

"You didn't sleep very long, Archie, did you?" asked the girl, whose room was next his. "I heard you hammering at something after I had gone to bed, and I awoke once and heard you talking to somebody."

Archie, at the side-table helping himself to sausage, paused a moment. He made up his mind that for the present, anyhow, he preferred that Jessie should not know about the return of Martin. Perhaps he would tell her quietly when alone…

"Hammering?" he said. "Yes, there was a despatch-case, and I couldn't find the key. So I whacked it open. About talking—yes, I was writing last night, and I believe I read it aloud to myself before I went to bed. I never know what a thing is like unless I read it aloud."

"Oh, do read it aloud to me," said the girl.

"When it's in order: it wasn't quite in order when I read it over. But I was sleepy and went to bed."

Jessie said no more, but for some reason this account left her unsatisfied. The hammering had not sounded quite like the forcing of the lock of a despatch-case; it had been like sharp blows on wood, and for a moment she had thought that Archie was tapping loudly on the door that separated their rooms. It had stopped, and began again a little later. As for the talking, it had sounded precisely like two voices; one undeniably Archie's, the other low and indistinct.

Archie changed the subject the moment he had given this explanation, and made some very surprising observations.

"Helena is married on the 10th of August, isn't she?" he asked. "I must get her a wedding present. And I shall come to her wedding. That will convey my good wishes in the usual manner, won't it? I want to assure her of them."

Both of the women looked at him in the intensest surprise. To Lady Tintagel he had never mentioned Helena's name since the day she had accepted Lord Harlow, while to Jessie, only last night, he had loaded her with the bitterest reproaches, and had spoken of the abject despair and emptiness which had come upon him in consequence of what she had done. And he looked at each of them in turn with that vivid, brilliant glance which had been so characteristic of him.

"Yes, I make a public recantation," he said. "It suddenly dawned on me last night that I have been behaving just about as stupidly as a man can behave. I've said nothing to you, mother, but Jessie knows. I want her to try to forget what, for instance, I said to her last night. I can do better than that, and at any rate I propose to try.

All the time that I haven't been mad with resentment I've been dead. Well, I hereupon announce the resurrection of Archibald. That's all I've got to say on the subject."

* * * * *

At that moment, swift as an arrow's flight, and certain as an intuition, there came to Jessie the odd idea that it was not Archie who was speaking at all. It might be his lips and tongue that fashioned the audible syllables, but it was not he in the sense that it had been he down by the lake last night. Savage and bitter as he had been there, he was authentic; now, all that he said, despite the absolute naturalness of his manner, seemed to ring false. She could not account for this impression in the least. It was not the suddenness of the change in his attitude, though that surprised her: it was some remoter quality, which her brain could not analyse. Something more intimate to herself than her brain had perceived it, and mere thought, mere reason, were blind to it.

Archie did not accompany his mother and Jessie to church that morning, but waited for Lord Tintagel's appearance, and the discussion of the good resolutions which were to be so beneficial to each of them. He sat in his father's study, and, having to wait some time before he made a shaky and disastrous entrance, thought over, in connection with the events of last night, what he himself had said that morning at breakfast. That surely was the gist of Martin's message to him: he must try to grow indifferent to that part of Helena which he hated; he must learn not to be miserable, to grasp the fact that the darkness in which he seemed to walk appeared to Martin no darkness at all, but a flood of light from the ineffable radiance. It was in the glow of that revelation that he had spoken at breakfast, trusting in the truth of it, and yet, as he sat now, waiting for his father, he knew he did not feel the truth of it. But, in obedience to Martin, that was how he had to behave. He must behave like that—this was what Martin meant—until he felt the soul within him grow up, like some cellar-sown plant, into the light. Hopefully and bravely had he announced his intention, but now, when in cooler mood he scrutinized it, he began to feel how tremendous was the task set him, how firmly rooted was that passionate resentment which must be alchemized into love. It had been true—Martin saw that so well—that it was the white statue, the fair form he had loved, and loved still with no less ardour than before. That, it seemed, according to his interpretation, Archie must keep: it was the other that must be transformed. But it would have been an easier task, he thought, to let his love slide into indifference, then raise his hate to the same level. But that was not the King's road, the Royal Banners did not flame along such mean-souled ways as these. He must cling to such love for Helena as he had, and transform the hate. But, first and foremost, cling to the love...

It was thus that he stated to himself the message that Martin seemed to have brought him last night, and, stated thus, it was a spiritual aspiration of high

endeavour, and it did not occur to him how, stated ever
so little differently, and yet following the lines of the
communication, it assumed a diabolical aspect. The love
which he had for Helena was a carnal love, that sprang
from desire for her enchanting prettiness; that love he
was to cling to, not sacrifice an iota of it. The hate that
he felt for her, arising from her falseness, her
encouragement of him for just so long as she was
uncertain whether she could capture a man who was
nothing to her, but whose position and wealth she
coveted, Archie was to transform into indifference; he
was to get over it. But, though it was hate, it had a
spiritual quality, for it was hatred of what was mean and
base, whereas his love for her had no spiritual quality: it
was no more than lust, and to that under the name of
love he was to cling... Here, then, was another
interpretation of the words he had heard last night, and,
according to it, it would have been fitter to attribute the
message to some intelligence far other than the innocent
soul of the brother who had so mysteriously
communicated with him in childlike ways. But that
interpretation (and here was the subtlety of it) never
entered Archie's head at all. A message of apparent
consolation and hope had come to him when he was
feeling the full blast of his bitterness, the wind that blew
from the empty desert of his heart and his stagnant
brain. He had called for help from the everlasting and
unseen Cosmos that encompasses the little blind half-
world of material existence, and from it, somewhere
from it, a light had shone into his dark soul, no mere
flicker, or so it seemed this morning, like that spurious

sunshine which he and his father basked in together, but rays from a more potent luminary.

Till now Archie, with the ordinary impulse of a disappointed man, had tried to banish from his mind (with certain exterior aids) the picture of the face and the form that he loved. But now he not only need not, but he must not, do that any longer: he had to cling to love. And while he waited for his father he kept recalling certain poignant moments in the growth of Helena's bewitchment of him. One was the night when they sat together for the last time in the dark garden at Silorno, and he wondered whether the suggestion of a cousinly kiss would disturb her. What had kept him back was the knowledge that it would not be quite a cousinly kiss on his part... Then there was the moment when he had caught sight of her on the platform at Charing Cross: she had come to meet his train on his arrival from abroad... Best of all, perhaps, for there his passion had most been fed with the fuel of her touch, had been the dance at his aunt's that same night, when the rhythm of the waltz and the melodious command of the music had welded their two young bodies into one. It was not "he and she" who had danced: it was just one perfect and complete individual. Here, on this quiet Sunday morning, the thought of that made him tingle and throb. It was that sort of memory which Martin told him he must keep alive... It was his resentment, his anger, that must die, not that. Helena had chosen somebody else, but he must long for her still.

Lord Tintagel appeared, unusually white and shaky, and, as lunch-time was approaching, he rang for the apparatus of cocktails.

"I sat up late last night, Archie," he said, "bothering myself over those Russian shares. It's really of you and your mother I am thinking. It won't be long before all the mines in Russia will matter nothing to me, for a few feet of earth will be all I shall require. But, before I went to bed, I came to the conclusion that I was wrong to worry. I think the scare will soon pass, and the shares recover. Indeed, I think the wisest thing would be not to sell, and cut my loss, but to buy more, at the lower price. I shall telegraph to my broker to-morrow. But I got into no end of a perplexity about it, and I feel all to bits this morning."

He mixed himself a cocktail with a shaking hand, and shuffled back to his chair.

"Help yourself, Archie," he said. "Let me see, we were going to have a talk about something this morning. What was it? That worry about my Russians has put everything out of my head."

Once again, as last night, it struck Archie as immensely comical that this white-faced, shaky man, who was his father, should be pulling himself together with a strong cocktail in order to discuss the virtues of temperance, and make the necessary resolutions whereby to acquire them. He felt neither pity nor sympathy with him, nor yet disgust; it was only the humour of the situation, the farcical absurdity of it, that appealed to him.

"We were going to make good resolutions not to drink quite so much," he said.

Lord Tintagel finished his cocktail and put the glass down.

"To be sure; that was it," he said. "It's time we took ourselves in hand. Your grandfather gave me a warning, and I wish to God I had taken it. But we'll help each other—eh, Archie? That will make it easier for both of us."

"I don't care a toss whether I take alcohol or not," said Archie. "As you remarked last night, father, I hardly touched it till a month ago."

Lord Tintagel laughed.

"But you've shown remarkable aptitude for it since," he said. "You found no difficulty at all in getting the hang of the thing."

Faintly, like a lost echo, there entered into Archie's mind the inherent horror of such an interview between father and son. But it was drowned by the inward laughter with which the scene inspired him, and his spirit, whatever it was that watched the play, looked on as from some curtained box, where, unseen, it could giggle at unseemliness, at some uncensored farce. Last night the same thing had amused him, but then he was in that contented oblivion of his troubles which alcohol lent him, whereas now it was morning and the time when he was least likely to take any but the most bitter and savage view of a situation. But all morning he had been possessed by the sunny lightness of heart with which Martin's communication of last night had inspired him. He must be patient, disperse and blow away by the great winds of love the hatred and intolerance that had been obscuring his soul. And surely it was not only for Helena that he must feel that nobler impulse: all that touched his daily life must be treated with the same manly tenderness. Nothing must shock him, nothing must irritate him, for such emotions were narrow and limited, incompatible with the oceanic quality of love. All this seemed directly inspired by Martin, who had brought him the first ray of true illumination. And yet, while he sunned himself in the light, there was something that apparently belonged to his bitter, his disappointed self that cried out for recognition, insisting that these dreams of love and tolerance were of a fibre infinitely coarser than its own rebellious attitude. It strove and cried, and the smooth edification of Martin's voice silenced it again.

The suggested compact between father and son soon framed itself into a treaty. There was to be nothing faddish or unreasonable about it: wine should circulate in its accustomed manner at dinner; but here, once and for all, was the end of trays brought to Lord Tintagel's study. A glass or two of claret should be allowed at lunch, but the cocktails and the whiskies in the evening were to be closed from henceforth. And the arrangement entered into appeared to be of a quality that sacrificed the desire of each for the sake of the other, or so at least it passed in their minds. Archie stifled the snigger of his inward laughter, and thought how clear was his duty to save his father, even at this late day, from falling wholly into the pit he had digged, while to his father the compact represented itself as an effort to save Archie from the path he had begun to tread. But, even as they agreed on their abstemious proceedings, there occurred to the minds of both of them a vague, luminous thought, like the flash of summer lightning far away which might move nearer…

Once again Archie was seized with the ironic mockery that all the time had quaked like a quick-sand below his seriousness.

"I haven't had my cocktail yet, father." he said. "I'll drink success to our scheme. You've had yours, you know. Our plan dates from now, when I've had mine. After that—no more."

His father's eyes followed him as he mixed the gin and vermouth.

"Well, upon my word, Archie," he said, "you ought to ask me to have a drink with you."

Archie somehow clung to the fact that his father had had a cocktail and that he had not.

"Have another by all means," he said, "and I'll have two. But do be fair, father."

And once again the horrible sordidness of these proceedings struck, as it seemed, his worse self, that part of himself that had all those weeks been uninspired by Martin. Martin was all love and tolerance: he gave no directions on such infinitesimal subjects as cocktails or whiskies. He, outside the material plane, was concerned only with the motive, the spiritual aspiration, with love and all its ineffable indulgences.

* * * * *

Jessie was leaving for town early next morning, and once again, as twenty-four hours ago, she and Archie strolled out after dinner into the dusk. But to-night, his father and he had followed the two ladies almost immediately into the drawing-room, and the two younger folk had left their elders playing a game of piquet together. That was quite unlike the usual procedure after dinner, for Lord Tintagel generally dozed for a little in his chair, and then retired to his study. But to-night he showed no inclination either to doze or to go away, and it was by his suggestion that the card-table had been brought out. He seemed to Jessie rather restless and irritable, and had said that it was impossible to play cards with chattering going on. That had been the immediate cause of her stroll with Archie. The remark had been addressed very pointedly to Archie and also very rudely. But Archie, checking his hot word in reply, almost without an effort, had apologized for the distraction, quietly and sufficiently.

"Awfully sorry, father," he had said. "I didn't mean to disturb you. Come out for a stroll, Jessie."

So there they were in the dusk again, and again Archie took Jessie's arm.

"Father's rather jumpy to-night," he said. "But I think he wanted to get rid of us: he may wish to talk to my mother. So it was best to leave them, wasn't it?"

Jessie's heart swelled. She knew from last night all that Archie was suffering, but the whole day he had been like this—gentle, considerate, infinitely sensitive to others, incapable of taking offence.

"Yes, much best," she said. "You know, Archie, you do behave nicely."

He knew what she meant. He knew how easy it would have been to make some provocative rejoinder to his father. But simply, he had not wanted to. Martin, and Martin's counsel, was still like sunlight within him.

"Oh, bosh," he said. "The gentle answer is so much easier than any other. I should have had to pump up indignation. But he was rather rude, wasn't he? Isn't it lucky that one doesn't feel like that?"

Archie drew in a long breath of the vigorous night-air. To himself it seemed that he drew in a long breath of the inspiration that had come to him last night.

"Jessie, I'm going to save father," he said. "We had an awfully nice talk this morning, and it was so pathetic. He has been a heavy drinker for years, you know. His father was so before him. So one mustn't think it is his fault, any more than it was my fault that I had consumption when I was little. It isn't a vice, it's a disease. Well, I've made a compact with him. I found that he had got it into his head—God knows how—that I—I know you'll laugh—was beginning to take to that beastly muck too. So I saw my opportunity. He's fond of me, you know; he really is, and it had seriously occurred to him that I was getting the habit. So I took advantage of that. I said I wouldn't have any more whiskies and cocktails if he wouldn't. We made a bargain about it. Without swagger, it was rather a good piece of work, don't you think?"

Jessie knew exactly what she honestly felt, and what she honestly felt she could not possibly say. For though it was a good bargain on Archie's part, the virtue of it would affect not only Lord Tintagel, but Archie himself. But the knowledge of this added to the sincerity of her reply.

"Oh, Archie," she said, "that was brilliant of you. Do you—do you think your father will keep to it?"

"He can't help it," said Archie triumphantly. "I'm going to be down here, except when I go up to town for Helena's wedding, and I'm always in and out of his room. I should know if he doesn't keep to it."

He paused, thinking out further checks on his father.

"There's William, too," he said. "William's devoted to me, simply, as far as I can tell, because he saved my life when I was a tiny kid. If I ask William to tell me whether my father gets drinks through him quietly when I'm not there, I'm sure he will let me know. How would that be?"

Jessie had an uncomfortable moment. The idea of getting a servant to report to Archie on his father's proceedings was as repugnant to her as, she thought, it must be to Archie. Possibly his main motive, that of taking care of his father, was so dominant in him that he did not pause to consider the legitimacy of any means. But, somehow, it was very unlike Archie to have conceived so backstairs an idea.

"Oh, I wouldn't quite do that," she said. "You wouldn't either, Archie."

"I don't see why not. The cure is more important than the means."

Jessie suddenly felt a sort of bewilderment. It could scarcely have been Archie who said that, according to her knowledge of Archie.

"But surely that's impossible," she said. "What would you feel if you found your father had been setting William to spy and report on you?"

Archie's voice suddenly rose.

"Oh, what nonsense!" he said. "You speak as if I was going to break my bargain with my father. I never heard such nonsense."

Once again the sense of bewilderment came over Jessie. That wasn't like Archie…

"I don't imply anything of the kind," she said. "But I do feel that it's impossible for you to get William to have an eye on your father, and report to you. And I'm almost certain that you really agree with me."

Archie considered this, and then laughed.

"I suppose I do," he said. "But the ardour of the newly born missionary was hot within me. Are missionaries born or made, by the way? Anyhow, I'm a missionary now. Nobody could have guessed that I was going to be a missionary."

Their stroll to-night was only up and down the broad gravel walk in front of the windows. It was very hot and all the drawing-room windows were open, so also were those of Lord Tintagel's study and the windowed door that led into the garden. As they passed this Archie saw a footman bring in a tray on which were set the usual evening liquids, and he guessed that his father had forgotten or had omitted to say that the syphon and some ice was all that would be needed. He thought for a moment, intently and swiftly.

"Jessie, they've brought in that beastly whisky again," he said. "I must tell them to take it away: my father mustn't see it. Just go down opposite the drawing-room windows, will you, and make sure my father is still playing cards, while I take the bottle away. Make me a sign."

Archie waited outside till this was given, and then went into his father's room. The man had gone away, and he took up the whisky-bottle with the intention of putting it back in the dining-room. But, even as his fingers closed on it, without warning, his desire for drink swooped down on him like the coming of a summer storm. He half filled a glass with the spirit, poured soda-water on the top and gulped it down. That was what he wanted, and then, with a swift cunning, he rinsed out the glass with soda-water, drank that also, and, filling it half up again with water, put it on the table by the chair where he usually sat. Then there was the bottle to dispose of, and he went out into the hall to take it to the dining-room. But, even as he crossed the foot of the stairs, another notion irresistibly possessed him, and up he went three steps at a time, and concealed it behind some clothes in his chest of drawers. He had discovered an excellent reason for doing that, for, if he left it in the dining-room, his father might find it there. It was much safer in his room. Then, tingling and content, and feeling that Martin would approve (indeed it seemed that he had prompted) this missionary enterprise, he rejoined Jessie again, his eyes sparkling, his mouth gay and quivering.

"I've done it," he said. "I thought at first of taking the bottle to the dining-room, but my father might have found it there."

"What did you do with it?" asked Jessie.

Archie took no time to consider.

"I rang the bell and told James to take it away again to the pantry," he said.

"That was clever of you, Archie."

"I know that. They're still playing cards, aren't they? Let's have one more turn, then. Jessie, I wish you weren't going away to-morrow."

"I must. I promised my father to get back. And Helena wants me."

"Oh well, that settles it," said Archie. "Helena must have all she wants. That is part of Helena, isn't it?"

For a moment Jessie thought that he was speaking with the bitterest irony, but immediately afterwards she withdrew that, for it struck her that Archie was, in some inexplicable way, perfectly sincere: there was the unmistakable ring of truth in his voice; he meant what he said. And, as if to endorse that, he went on:

"We all do what Helena wants: you, I, the Bradshaw, all of us. She wants to be loved, isn't that it? and to want to be loved is a royal command; all proper people must obey. I have been a rebel you know, and,—oh Jessie, how awfully ashamed I am! I let myself hate Helena; I encouraged myself to hate her. But I've returned to my allegiance, thank God."

She turned an enquiring face to him.

"Archie, dear," she said, "I am so thankful that you are so changed. You're utterly different from what you have been. Last night you were bitter and terrible: you made my heart ache. But all to-day you've been absolutely your old self again. And it's so immense and so sudden. Can't you tell me at all what caused it? I should love to know, if you feel like telling me."

He took her arm again.

"I'll tell you one thing," he said. "You did me a lot of good last night when you made me realize your friendship. That helped; I do believe that helped."

Jessie could not quite accept this, though it warmed her heart that Archie thought of that.

"But you always knew my friendship," she said.

"I know I did. But I appreciated it most when I felt absolutely empty. There's something more than that, though…"

He paused.

"Ah, do tell me," said Jessie.

He could not make up his mind on the instant, for he knew Jessie's repugnance to the whole idea of those supernatural communications. But he felt warm and alert and expansive; besides, her friendship, which he truly valued, yearned for his confidence, which is the meat and drink of friendship. Sometimes it was necessary to deceive your friends; it had been necessary for him to deceive her about the disposal of the whisky-bottle; but, though she might not approve, he could at least tell her what had made sunshine all day for him, and what was making it now.

"It's this," he said. "Martin came to me last night. I talked to him; I saw him. It has put me right: he has made me see things quite differently. He told me to be patient, to cling to love always, to let my hate be turned into love. I can't express to you at all what a difference that made to me. I felt he knew; he could see, as he said, that the darkness in which I thought I walked was not darkness at all. I know you have no sympathy with his coming to me: it seems to you either nonsense or something very dangerous. But I know you have sympathy with the result of it."

Suddenly his explanation of the voices she had heard last night occurred to him.

"When you told me this morning that you had heard talking in my room," he said, "I did not mean to tell you about Martin, and so I invented something—oh yes, that I had been reading aloud what I had written, to account for it. It wasn't true, but I had to tell some fib. And did you really hear conversation going on? That's awfully interesting."

"I thought I did," said she. "And there was knocking or hammering. Did you invent something about that too?"

"Oh yes," said Archie. "But I don't really know what the knocking was. As I was going off into trance, I heard loud knocking of some sort, but I didn't let it disturb the oncoming of the trance. It deepened, and then Martin came, and I talked with him and saw him."

"Oh Archie, how do you know it was he?" she cried, wildly enough, hardly knowing what she meant, but speaking from the dictate of some nightmare that screamed and struggled in her mind.

"Why, of course it was he," said Archie. "I recognized him, superficially, that is to say, from my knowledge of my own face, just as I recognized the photograph in the cache at Grives from its likeness to me. But I know it was he in some far more essential and inward manner. It *was* Martin."

"Will he come again?" asked the girl.

"I hope so, many times. Indeed, he promised to. I needed him, he got permission to come to me in my need. Is he not ministering to it? Haven't you seen the immense change in me?"

Undeniably she had seen that, and for a moment a little pang of human disappointment came over her.

"I'm afraid, then, the knowledge of my friendship hasn't had much to do with it," she said.

"Jessie, don't think I undervalue that," said Archie, speaking quite frankly and sincerely. "I thank you for it tremendously; I love to know it is there. I may count on it always, mayn't I?"

They still stood a moment under the star-swarming sky, sundered by the night from all other presences.

"I needn't assure you of that," she said. "And, Archie, I may be utterly wrong in what I feel about Martin's communications to you. Who knows what conditions exist for the souls of those we have loved, and whom we neither of us believe have died with the decay of the perishable body? But, my dear, do be careful. If in some miraculous way you have been given access which is denied to almost all mankind, do use it only in truth and love and reverence."

"You're frightened about it," said Archie.

"I know I am. If Martin can come to you, why should not other spirits? Other spirits, intelligences terrible and devilish, might deceive you into thinking that they were he. You remember at Silorno he said he couldn't come again."

"I know; but I wasn't in sore need then," said he.

They had again come opposite Lord Tintagel's study, and, even as they passed, Archie saw him with his finger on the bell. Instantly he guessed that he was ringing to know why the whisky had not been brought. The footman would come and say that he had brought it...

Archie felt an exhilarated acuteness of brain: the situation had only to be put before him for him to see the answer to it. In his presence, remembering the contract of the morning, his father could not ask for the whisky.

"Come in and say good-night to my father, Jess," he said.

They entered together and immediately afterwards the footman came in from the hall-door. Lord Tintagel looked at him, then back at Archie, who was watching.

"It's nothing, James," he said. "I rang for something, but it doesn't matter."

The man left the room and immediately afterwards Jessie said good-night and went also. Archie turned to his father with a broad, kindly smile.

"Father, I believe I'm a great thought-reader," he said. "I believe I can tell you what you rang for."

His father's grim face relaxed.

"You young devil," he said.

Archie laughed.

"I've guessed right, then," he said. "You surely don't want to drink success to our contract again."

"But I don't know why James didn't bring the whisky as usual," said he. "I—I forgot to tell him not to."

"But I didn't," said Archie.

"I see. Well, a bargain's a bargain. Only now there doesn't seem to be any particular reason for not going to bed."

Archie yawned rather elaborately, and went to the table where, earlier in the evening, he had put down his glass half filled with soda. He drank it, sniffing to see if there was any taint of spirit about it. But he had rinsed it thoroughly.

"I came in during my stroll with Jessie and took some soda," he said. "Not a bad drink, but I think it makes one sleepy. I shall go to bed, too."

* * * * *

Jessie left early next morning, expecting to be gone before anybody else made an appearance. But, just as she got into the motor, Archie, rosy and suffused with sleep, like a child that has lain still and grown all night, came flying downstairs in dressing-gown and pyjamas.

"Had to come down and say good-bye, Jessie," he said. "Do come back; come down for next Sunday, and we'll go up together for Helena's wedding. Promise!"

Jessie looked at that "morning face" which glowed with the exuberance of boyish health and happiness. She herself had slept very badly, dozing for a little and then being awakened by the sound of talking next door, and of peremptory resounding tappings. And here was Archie, radiant and fresh and revitalized, and her love glowed at the thought that he wanted her, even though it was but friendship that he sought and friendship that he had to offer.

"Yes, Archie, I should love to come," she said.

"That's ripping. I say, shall I drive with you to the station just as I am? Why shouldn't I? Pyjamas and dressing-gown are perfectly decent if William will fetch me my slippers, which I seem to have forgotten, unless he lends me his boots."

"Your bath's ready, my lord," said William with a broad grin.

"Well, perhaps I'll have it then. Good-bye, Jess. Come early on Saturday."

CHAPTER XI

Archie was lying on the turf in front of the enclosed bathing-place where the stream debouched into the lake. There was a good stretch of deep water free from weeds, and for the last half-hour he had been swimming and diving in it. Now, with hair drying back into its crisp curls under the hot sun, he lay on the short warm turf, with his chin supported on his hands, in an ecstasy of animal content. At this edge of the water the bank was made firm and solid with wooden boarding that went down into deep water, but across the estuary of the stream, broadening out into the lake, the shallow margin was fringed with bulrushes and loosestrife. A strip of low-lying meadow land behind was pink with campion and ragged-robin and starred with meadow-sweet, the scent of which mingled with the undefinable cool smell of running water. A bed of gravel made the bottom of the stream, and through the sunlit water the pebbles gleamed like topazes through some liquid veil.

Never before had Archie been so permeated with the sense of the amazing loveliness of the world, and of the ineffable joy of living and of being part of it. He had wrestled with the swiftness of the stream as it narrowed, had clung to rocks and tree-roots below the surface, letting the current comb over and around and almost through him, then, letting go of his anchorage, had been floated down into the lake again with arms and legs outspread, and now, lying close-pressed to the turf with wet chest and dripping shoulders, he seemed to be part of the triumph of the summer, and of the immortal youth of the world. Surely there was no further heaven than this possible, namely, to be young and to desire and to have desire gratified, and whet the appetite for more. There was no clearer duty in the day than to be bathed in the bliss of life, to suck out the last drop of sweetness from the world which had been created for the joy of men and the glory of God. There was no such thing as evil; evil was but the label attached by the sour-minded to the impulses and acts for which they had not sufficient vitality... And it was Martin who had taught him all this.

Archie had come back home this morning after a day and a couple of nights in town. He had bought Helena her wedding present, he had taken his completed manuscript to his publishers, he had dined and danced and supped, and filled the hours of day and night with the extravagant excesses in which up till now he had never indulged. Some innate fastidiousness or morality had led him to look on the looser pleasures of youth with disdain or disgust; now he smiled indulgently at himself for his narrow priggishness. How utterly wrong he had been to think that such things stained or soiled a boy; they had but caused him to realize himself and intensified existence for him. They were the exercise of the faculties and possibilities with which God had endowed him, and which were not meant to rust in disuse. It was right for him "richly to enjoy," as Martin had said: it was a crime against love and life to starve on a meatless diet... Above all, he had seen Helena again, had confessed and recanted the bitterness he had felt towards her, and she had forgiven him, and welcomed him back "with blessings on the falling out, that all the more endears," as the prim little poem said.

Archie laughed quietly to himself and said aloud:

"When we fall out with those we love,
And kiss again with tears."

"But there weren't many tears," he added.

He understood Helena now. She wanted, so sensibly, to make herself quite comfortable for this journey through life. If Marquises with millions desired her to go shares with them, naturally she consented. But to do that was not the least the same as taking vows and going into a nunnery. It was the nunnery that she was coming out of. Of course, just for the present Archie understood he would not see her, for she and the Bradshaw were going a yachting tour in the Norwegian fjords. But they would be back again before the end of September. So much and no more had her voice told him, but her eyes said much more intimate things, though naturally she did not express them, and when he asked if he might kiss her (that cousinly kiss which she had wanted at Silorno) her lips agreed with what her eyes said. She had never been so adorably pretty, and she had never been so demurely clever. She had said nothing which a girl who was to become another man's wife in a few days should not say, and yet Archie felt that he understood perfectly all the things she did not say. Most brilliant perhaps of all was her warning, "I shall tell the Bradshaw that I allowed you to kiss me," she cried. "But I'm not frightened: he is such a dear."

Gone, then, were all Archie's troubles and bitternesses on this point. He had love to cling to, and he scarcely felt jealous of the Bradshaw. For, if things had been the other way about, and Helena had been engaged to him, would she have allowed the Bradshaw to kiss her? He knew very well that she would not.

Archie turned over on to his back, and lay with arms and legs spread out to the sun, warming himself as with the memory of that expedition to London. But he had not in the least wished to postpone his return, since the joy of life lay so largely in its contrasts, and after thirty-six hours of that fiery furnace there had come a temporary satiety, and he wanted to lie and sleep like a gorged tiger. Soon he would awake and be hungry again, but it was part of the joy of life to be satisfied and doze, and stretch out tranquil limbs. And, lying there, his ribs began to twitch again into laughter as he thought of the contract he had made with his father last Sunday. Archie had entered into it, with the view of encouraging and helping his father to rid himself of the chain that was riveted so closely round him, and he was delighted to do it, if his father derived support for his abstinence in the thought that he was helping Archie. But Archie need not abstain, so long as his father thought he was doing so, and only just now he had filled with water and sunk in the weeds several empty bottles that he had brought out in his towels from his bedroom. He knew perfectly well that he was in no danger of becoming a slave to the habit, it had served him as medicine to mitigate his misery with regard to Helena, and, now that that was quite removed, it helped him to get into communication with Martin. Of that he felt convinced. Once or twice he had tried to do so without drinking, and had failed; but alcohol seemed to drug the surface-consciousness and clear the way of access, and it was for that he used it now. It was more that it cleared the access than that it drugged him, for he found that it produced not the least effect in the way of making his head hazy or his movements wavering: it only seemed to sweep clean those mysterious channels through which communication came. The power of communicating he could not possibly give up: all happiness and joy of life sprang from it; therefore he could not possibly give up that which facilitated it. But he performed the purpose of the contract by keeping his indulgences secret from his father, and once again Archie's ribs, with their smoothly swelling muscles under his brown skin, throbbed with amusement as he pictured his father's heroic struggle with himself. Occasionally Archie had doubts whether that struggle was quite consistently successful, for once or twice Lord Tintagel had shown signs of evening content and serenity, followed by morning shakiness, which indicated that he had made some temporary armistice. Archie thought that perhaps he would lay some trap for his father, or make some quiet detective investigations to satisfy himself on this point. But beyond doubt his father was putting up quite a good fight on behalf of a non-existent cause. His will was to abstain, and, if occasionally he failed, it was unchristian to judge failure hardly. Besides, Archie only conjectured that sometimes his father's resolution was unequal to the strain imposed on it; he did not know.

* * * * *

All this week Archie's sense of comradeship and brotherliness with Martin had marvellously increased. There was nothing priggish or puritanical about Martin, nor anything namby-pamby that suggested wings and halos and hymns. He was intensely human, and sympathized completely with the fact of Archie's being a glorious young animal, bursting with exuberant health. That seemed quite clear, for when this morning, sometime about four o'clock, Archie had gently let himself into the house in Grosvenor Square a little ashamed and weary, and went up to his bedroom, he became instantly aware that Martin was waiting for him. There was no need for him to light his electric lamps, for dawn was already breaking, and, drawing his curtains apart, he threw off his clothes, so as to let the delicious chill of morning refresh his skin, and sat down for a moment in front of his dressing-table and looked fixedly at a bright point of light on the bevel of his looking-glass. Almost immediately the waves of light and shadow began to pass before his eyes, and the room was full of vivid, peremptory tappings. Then he was aware that there appeared in the reflected image of himself a strange luminous focus over his left breast and a little wisp of mist, like a puff of escaping steam, began to come from it. This grew and collected in wavering masses of weaving lines, formless at first, but then arranging themselves into definite shapes, and he saw, with a thrill of excitement and wonder, that out of them there was being built up the image of Martin, which had issued out of himself. Soon it was complete, and Archie in the glass beheld Martin's face leaning lovingly over his shoulder, and Martin's arm bare like his own, and, warm and solid to the touch, was thrown round his neck.

"Archie, I've been with you all night," he said. "I love to see you and feel you realize yourself. Throw yourself into life: live to the uttermost, and have no thought for the morrow. There is nothing in the world but love and joy. Cling to them, press close to them, lose yourself in them…"

Martin's smile was compassionate no longer: it was a sunbeam of radiant happiness, and that happiness, so it seemed to Archie, had its source in sympathy with and love for him.

"Don't ever think you are yielding to base impulses," he went on, "provided only you are happy. Happiness is the seal and witness of what is right for you: it is the mark of God's approval. Evil is always painful and repugnant; that is the seal and witness of it. The fruit of the spirit is love, joy, peace; and aren't you more at peace, more full of joy now that you have resolved to put hate out of your heart? Isn't it sweeter to kiss Helena than to curse her?"

* * * * *

Suddenly, like the stroke of a black wing, there passed through Archie an impulse of sheer abhorrence. All that Martin said sounded divinely comforting and uplifting, but did there not lurk in it the whole gospel of Satanism? And, as that thought crossed his mind, he saw an expression of the tenderest reproach dim for a moment the brightness of his brother's eyes, and the mouth drooped.

"But you are tired now," said he, "and your trust in me is a little weakened. Sleep well: it is dawn already."

The apparition faded, or rather it appeared to be withdrawn again into himself, and, emerging from the light trance, Archie was conscious only of an overpowering but delicious fatigue, the fatigue of utter satisfaction. He had had a glorious thirty-six hours, and, as Martin said, he was tired. And Martin approved.

He slept the deep, recuperative sleep of youth for four or five hours, and awoke hungry and eager, and clear-eyed. He left town immediately after breakfast, motored himself down home with William holding on to the side of the car as he slowed round corners and came straight out to his beloved bathing-place. It was bliss to be alive.

* * * * *

He had not seen Jessie during his short raid on London, for really there had not been a moment to spare; besides, Jessie was coming down next day for the week-end. But she knew he had been in town, for Helena said she had seen him, and, with her usual acuteness, had told her sister that Archie was deliciously his old self again, and that they were the greatest friends. That, to Jessie's very sensible judgment and to the intuition her love gave her, was the most inexplicable of developments. Only a week ago there was no reproach bitter enough for Archie's opinion on Helena's conduct to him, no angry taunt of misery sufficient for her vilification. And then, in a moment, the whole of that bitterness had been dried up, the Marah had been sweetened. More than that, the normal joy of life had returned in full flood to him, and the cause of all this was, in his account, the fact that the spirit of Martin had shown him the true light. That Archie possessed that mysterious, and, in her view, dangerous gift of mediumistic perception she did not doubt, for there was no questioning those weird manifestations of occult power which she knew had occurred in his childhood, and she felt now that she ought only to stand in an awed wonder and thankfulness that this supernormal perception of his had, in a moment, worked in him what could be called no less than a miracle. But, though she ought to feel that, she knew that she felt nothing of the kind, and, as she travelled down next day to Lacebury, she set herself to analyse the causes of her mistrust.

They were simple enough. First of all, there was her rooted antipathy to the whole notion of spirit-communication. Instinctively it shocked her and seemed opposed to all religious faith. Beyond that, there were but a couple of the most insignificant matters that appeared to her possibly connected with her mistrust, the one that Archie had made a false, swift invention to account for the noises she had heard coming from his room, the other that he had proposed to get William to spy on his father with a view to ascertaining whether he was keeping his part of their bargain. She knew they were both tiny incidents, but the spirit that prompted them was in both cases utterly unlike Archie. She could not imagine Archie making such an invention or such a suggestion, from what she knew of him, it was outside him to do so. And if it was the influence—to call it no more than that—of Martin which prompted these things, if it was the same direction as that which had taken away all his bitterness towards Helena, what sort of influence was that? Finally, could it be right that the boy whom Helena had so cruelly led on only to disappoint should, on the eve of her marriage, suddenly become close friends with her again? There certainly he obeyed the precept of that which had spoken with him, and had promised to communicate again, and she could not but think it a dangerous, if not a diabolical counsel. But she tried to reserve her judgment; in a few minutes now she would see Archie again, and could note what change for good or ill this week had brought. Very likely she had been disquieting herself in vain, making wounds out of pin-pricks and mountains out of mole-hills.

Archie had come to meet her, and, as the train slowed down into the station, she saw him out of the carriage window. But he did not see her, for his eyes were intent on a very horrible sight. There were two tipsy women violently quarrelling, and, just as the train got in, they flew at each other, scratching and striking. The encounter lasted not more than a few seconds, for a couple of porters ran in and separated them, but Jessie had seen Archie's face alight with glee and amusement. As they were separated he frowned and shrugged his shoulders, and seemed to remonstrate with the man who had stopped their fighting. At that instant he saw her get out of her compartment, and ran to meet her, his face quite changed. But the moment before it had not been Archie's face at all: it had been the face of some beautiful and devilish creature, alert with evil excitement.

"Hullo, Jessie, there you are," he said. "It's ripping to see you. Look at those two viragos there; they flew at each other like wild beasts. It was a horrible sight."

He turned a sideways eye on her, cunning and watchful, which utterly belied the frankness of his speech, and her heart sank, and a vague, nameless terror seized her, as once again she found herself thinking that this was not Archie, who so gaily took her bag for her, and ever and again looked back to where a small crowd had collected round the two women. They had a few minutes to wait, while her luggage was brought out, and once more he sauntered back into the station, leaving her in the car. From outside she could hear hoarse screams, and, long after her trunk had been put into the car, she watched the door for Archie's exit. First one and then the other of the women were brought out to be taken to the police-station, and at last he emerged.

"Sorry to keep you waiting, Jessie," he said. "But my mother wanted some magazine from the bookstall. Now, if you aren't nervous, we'll make up for lost time."

The road lay straight and empty before them, opening out like torn linen as they raced along it. Some way ahead there were a couple of cottages by the road-side, and, as they came near them, there wandered out into the road an old and lame collie. Instantly Archie's face changed into a mask of impatient malignancy.

"Archie, take care," said Jessie, "there's a dog on the road."

"Well, that's the dog's look-out," said he. "What right has a mangy brute like that to stop us?"

He made no attempt whatever to slow down, but just at the last moment he caused the car to swerve violently, and they missed the dog by a hair's-breadth. And he turned on her a face from which all impatience and anger had vanished, and from it looked out Archie's soul in agonized struggle.

"I couldn't, I couldn't!" he said. "I didn't touch it, Jessie: it's all right."

"I thought you must run over it," said she. "Why didn't you slow down, Archie?"

That glimpse of the agonized soul utterly vanished again.

"People have got no business to keep a decrepit old beast like that," he said. "I expect the kindest thing I could do would be to turn round and put it out of its misery. Never mind. I'll do it some other day."

Jessie clung to her glimpse of the other Archie.

"No, you won't," she said. "You'll risk your life and mine, too, not to hurt it."

He laughed.

"One can't tell what one will do," he said. "I hated and loathed that dog, but I couldn't run over it, when it came to. Hope I didn't give you an awful shaking, Jessie."

After lunch Archie proposed a campaign against a certain great pike which he had seen, and, while he went to his room to change his clothes, Jessie paid a visit to Blessington. The old lady was delighted to see her, and dusted a perfectly speckless chair for her.

"And it's jolly for you, isn't it, Blessington, having Archie here so long?" said Jessie.

Blessington made no answer for a moment.

"I make no complaints," she said, "and I daresay Master Archie is very busy."

"Why, what do you mean?" asked the girl.

Blessington's wrinkled old face began to work, and she looked piteously at Jessie.

"It's a week since Master Archie set foot in my room," she said. "Why does he never come to see me now, Miss Jessie? And when I meet him about the house, he's never got a word to give me. Me, who has looked after him and loved him since he was born."

At this moment Archie's step was heard outside, and he came in.

"Oh, Blessington, I wish you wouldn't go meddling with my things," he said roughly. "William tells me you took some flannels of mine away to mend or put a button on. Where are they?"

Blessington got up without a word and went to her cupboard.

"Here they are, my lord," she said. "I have mended them."

"Well, please don't carry my clothes away again. Come on, Jessie. I'll be ready in a moment."

Blessington's hands came together with a trembling movement as Archie twitched the flannel coat away from her. But he did not even look at her, and went out of her room, banging the door.

Blessington sat down again, and began to cry quietly. "There now, you see, Miss Jessie," she said. "And that's my own Master Archie."

For a minute or so Jessie sat with her, trying vainly to comfort her, and shocked beyond expression at Archie's brutal callousness to his old nurse. And then the door opened again, and Archie looked in. Once again all his anger and impatience had died out of his face, his real soul looked from his eyes as from a prison-house, and his voice shook as he spoke.

"Go away, please, Jessie, and leave me with Blessington for a minute," he said.

And then he came across the room to her, and knelt down by her, and took her withered old hand in his, and stroked it and kissed it. So much Jessie saw before she closed the door behind her.

"Blessington, my old darling," said Archie, "I can't think why I have been so beastly to you. It wasn't me, that's all I can tell you. I always love you. Can you forgive me?"

Blessington's loyal devotion rose triumphant.

"Eh, I know how busy you've been, Master Archie," she said, "and I know what a thoughtless body I am with your things. But I'd like you to be angry with me fifty times, if you'll only come back to me at the end. There pray-a-don't kiss my hand, dear. It isn't right for you to do that."

"Where's your darling face then?" said Archie. "If you don't give me a kiss this minute, I shall know you've been flirting with father's keeper again."

Blessington gave a little squeal of laughter.

"Eh, and him dead this twenty years," she said. "And you know, my dear, that whatever you did, and asked me to give you a kiss afterwards, give it you I would, because nothing you could do would stop my loving you."

Blessington's love, Helena's love… which was real? Two things so utterly different could not both be love. And for him, too, which love was real, his love for Blessington, all ashed over save for the little spark that somehow lived below the cold cinders, or his love for Helena that blazed and scintillated? Suddenly the thought of that glowed within him, and it seemed dreadful to kiss this withered cheek. And yet the dim old eyes had never wavered in their loyalty and love for his worthless, corrupted self.

"And shall we have a talk this evening again before dinner?" he asked.

"Eh, that would be nice if you're not too busy," said she.

"All right, then. But I must run along now: Jessie's waiting."

"That'll never do to keep her waiting," said Blessington. "And if you're going on the lake, Master Archie, pray be careful and don't fall in."

* * * * *

Lady Tintagel with Jessie and Archie were going up to town on Monday to attend Helena's wedding the day after, and all through the hours of that week-end there was piling up ever higher and more menacingly the storm that so soon was to burst upon Europe in tempest of shot and shell. Before they left on Monday afternoon war was already declared between Russia and Germany, between Germany and France, the territory of Belgium was violated by the barbarian hordes who issued from the Central Empires, and Belgium had appealed to England to uphold the treaty which Germany had torn up to light the fires or war. But, as in so many English homes in these days, the inevitable still seemed the incredible, and, though from time to time they discussed the situation, life went on its normal course. Indeed, there was nothing else to be done: whether England was going to war or not, dinner-time came round as usual...

Of them all, it was on Lord Tintagel that the suspense and anxiety beat most strongly, and that because the panic on the Stock Exchanges of Europe threatened him with losses that might bring him within reach of ruin. But Lady Tintagel still clung to a baseless hope, less substantial than a mirage in the desert, that diplomacy would still avert disaster, Archie went about the customary diversions of life with more than usual enjoyment and absorption, while for Jessie there loomed in the immediate foreground a dread and a horror, which, though it concerned not warring millions, but just one individual, engrossed her entire soul.

It was as if she saw him whom she loved with all the strength of her deep and loyal heart in danger of drowning, not in material waters that could but kill the body and set free the soul, but in some awful flooding evil which threatened to submerge and swallow the very source and spiritual life of him. And, all the time, he swam and splashed about in those waters, below which lay hell itself, with the same joyful gaiety as he used to churn his way out to sea at Silorno. As by some hideous irony, the love of deep waters far from shore that all his life had possessed him, so that his physical self was at the zenith of its capacity for enjoyment when the profound gulfs were below him, and the land far off, so now evil, essential and primeval evil, had beckoned his soul out over unplumbed depths that seemed to him bright with celestial sunshine. Not yet was he doomed to sink there, though she guessed, as in a nightmare, in what deadly peril he stood, for now and again some inkling of that which menaced him reached his true self, and he turned back with shuddering and contrition from some evil prompting. All the time this betrayed itself to Jessie in things that might so reasonably have been called mere trifles. An impatient, impetuous boy, as Archie undoubtedly was, might so naturally have lost his temper with a decrepit old dog which strayed on to the path of his flying car, and made him say that it would be the kindest thing to run over it. That same boy might so naturally have felt an unedifying curiosity in two drunken women fighting together, or have reasonably been annoyed when, in a hurry to change his clothes, he found that his old nurse had taken them away. Indeed, it was the strength of his own reaction against such impulses that showed how alien he knew them to be to his real self. But her own feeling about them was the final test, for she knew it was based on the infallible intuition of her love for him. It was impossible that that should be mistaken, and it told her that it was not Archie at all who had committed these acts, which might be trifling in themselves, but, like wisps of cloud in the sky, showed which way the great winds were blowing. And on the top of these was something which Jessie could not conceive of as being a trifle, namely, Archie's complete reconciliation with her sister. She could not believe that it was a noble impulse which prompted that, and extinguished his bitter resentment against her as easily as a candle is blown out. He was right to be bitter against her, and the love, with which he seemed inspired again, was not love at all. But he believed that this desire was love, and according to his account it was the spirit of Martin which had taught him that and opened his blinded eyes. It was Martin, then, who possessed him. And that, to Jessie, was the most incredible of all. It was not, and it could not be, Martin.

She sat by her open window that Sunday night, wishing that she could think that some madness had fallen upon her, which caused her to conceive such inconceivable things. Archie's laugh still sounded in her ears, gay and boyish, as she had heard it but two minutes before she came up to bed. And she shuddered at the cause of it. Once again, she and Archie had strolled out after dinner, and, on passing the windows of his father's study, their steps noiseless on the grass, Archie had laid his hand on her arm with a gesture to command silence, and had tiptoed with her across the gravel to his father's windows. Lord Tintagel was inside, and, even as they looked, he took a bottle out of which he had been pouring something, and locked it up in a cupboard.

Archie turned a face beaming with merriment on her.

"Come in," he whispered, "to say good-night. Leave it all to me. It will be huge fun."

He waited a moment, and began talking loudly to her on some indifferent subject for a few seconds. The he said:

"Come and say good-night to my father, Jessie," and they entered together.

Lord Tintagel was seated in his chair by this time: there was just one empty glass on the tray, with a syphon, and no sign of a second one. Archie began walking up and down the room, his eyes looking swiftly and stealthily in every direction.

"Jessie and I have just come in to say good-night," he said. "We're all going up to town to-morrow. Won't you really come, father?"

"I've already said I won't," said Lord Tintagel sharply.

Archie suddenly saw what he had been looking for.

"Hullo, here's a funny thing," he said. "Here's a glass on the floor."

He picked it up, smelled it, and burst into a peal of laughter.

"Father, it's too bad of you!" he said. "There have I been keeping our bargain, while you—"

He broke off, laughing again.

"No, I'll confess," he said, "because I'm so pleased at having found you out. I've been having some quiet drinks up in my bedroom while you've been doing the same down here. What did you do with your bottles? I put mine in the lake. I say, that is funny, isn't it? But it's rather unsociable. Let's follow Germany's example, and call our treaty waste paper."

And Archie had laughed over that miserable sordid exposure, just as light-heartedly as he had laughed over the jolly innocent humours at Silorno, and, sick at heart, Jessie had left the two together with the bottle which there was no need to conceal any more.

She sat long at her window in a miserable state of horror and fear and agitation, now trying to persuade herself that she was taking these things too heavily— Helena had always told her she took things heavily— now letting her fears issue in terrible cohort and looking them in the face. It was her powerlessness to help that most tortured her, her fate of having to stand and watch while Archie pushed out ever farther, with delight and joy, on to the perilous seas. But now there was to her a reality about it all which she had never wholly felt before. Often she had told herself that she was imagining perils, but to-night, in the darkness and the quiet, she felt herself face to face with the grim, deadly facts. Spiritual and ghostly enemies were about, and next moment she had slid on to her knees. No words came: she tried just to open her heart to that light that surely shone through the evil that swarmed about her. Something, ever so faint, glimmered there, and presently she rose again with her soul fixed on that little spark shining within her. In any case, she must make every effort to help, instead of succumbing to her sense of powerlessness.

At that moment she heard light, swift footsteps on the stairs, and instantly her mind was made up, and she came out into the broad passage just as Archie was opposite her door. His face was eager and alert; there was no trace of intoxication there.

"Hullo, Jessie," he said, smiling. "Not gone to bed yet?"

She had to be wise: mere helpless prayer would avail nothing if she did not exert herself and make use of her wits and her love.

"No: I didn't feel sleepy," she said. "You don't look sleepy either. Are you going to bed?"

"No, not yet," said Archie.

Jessie came a step closer to him.

"Oh, Archie, are you going to talk to Martin?" she asked. "Mayn't I come? I should so love to, for I know all that Martin means to you. You know I did hear him talking to you before. It would be lovely if I could hear you talking together, so that I knew what he said."

Archie looked at her.

"Well, I don't know why not," he said. "But you must promise not to interrupt. Perhaps you'll neither hear nor see anything. But I don't see why you shouldn't try. It's just a seance. Come along, Jessie."

He led the way into his bedroom, and shut the door.

"I shall really rather like you to be here," he said. "I'm glad you suggested it. For now and then I go into very deep trance, and then I can't remember what exactly has happened. I only know that there has been round me an atmosphere—to call it that—in which I glow and expand. Sometimes I rather think I struggle and groan: you mustn't mind that. It's only the protest of my material earthly self. Come on: let's begin. I long for Martin to come."

Jessie felt her dread and horror of the occult surge up in her, and it required all her resolution to remain here. But the call of her love was imperative: if she was to be permitted to help Archie at all, she must learn what it was that possessed him, and find means to combat it. She had to know first what it was, penetrate, so far as her love had power, into the source of it, diagnose it, if she was to help in curing.

"What are you going to do?" she said.

"It's very simple; you'll soon see. Sit down, Jessie."

He went to the window and drew aside the curtains. He put on the table in front of where he was to sit the silver top of some toilet-bottle, and then went to the door and turned out all the electric lights at the switch-board. The moonlight outside, without shining directly into the room, made the objects in it clearly though duskily visible, and Jessie, where she sat with her back to the light, could see Archie's face and outline, when her eyes got accustomed to the dimness, quite distinctly. He sat close to her at the end of the writing-table, and just in front of him glimmered the stopper from the toilet-bottle.

"Now I'm going to look at that till I go off into trance," he said. "Watch what happens very closely, for I may go into deep trance, and promise me not to move till I come round again. I daresay you will neither hear nor see anything, but I don't know."

For some few minutes, as far as the girl could judge, they sat in silence. Once or twice Archie shifted his position slightly, and she heard his shirt-front creak a little as he breathed quietly and normally. Outside a little wind stirred, and the tassel of the blind tapped against the sill.

Then there came a change: his breathing grew louder, as if he panted for air, and now and again he moaned, and she saw his head drop forward. This moaning sound was horrible to hear, and, but for her promise, and the insistent urging of her love, she must have got up and roused him. His breath whistled between his lips as he took it in, and his face seemed to be shining with some dew of anguish, and his arms twisted and writhed as if struggling against some overmastering force. Then suddenly all sign of struggle ceased, he sat bent forward, but perfectly still, and from the table in front of him came three loud, peremptory raps, as of splitting wood. From the dusk of the room came others which she could not localize.

Archie raised his head, and, instead of leaning over the table, sank back in his chair, his arms hanging limp by his side. He began to whisper to himself, and soon Jessie caught the words.

"Martin, are you here?" he kept repeating. "Martin, are you here? Martin, Martin?"

There was more light in the room now. It came from a pale greyish efflorescence of illumination, globular in shape, that lay apparently over his left breast. It made its immediate neighbourhood quite bright: she could see the stud in his shirt with absolute distinctness. Out of it there came a little wisp of mist that floated up like a stream of smoke above his shoulders. In the air there, independently of this, there was forming another mist-like substance, and the stream that came away from Archie seemed to join this. It began to take shape: it spread upwards and downwards into the semblance of a column, its edges losing themselves in the dark. Lines began to be interwoven within it: it was as if something was forming inside it, like a chicken in an egg. It lost its vagueness of outline, plaiting and weaving itself together: there appeared an arm bare to the shoulder; above that she could see a neck, and slowly above the neck there grew a smiling, splendid face. There seemed to be a grey robe cast about the body, from which the bare arm protruded, but much of this was vague.

Jessie felt as if some awful paralysis of terror lay over her spirit. The whole room, cool and fresh with the night-air passing through the open window, reeked, to her spiritual sense, with evil and unnameable corruption. Over her conscious superficial self, the mechanism that directed her limbs and worked in her brain, she had complete control: for Archie's sake she was learning about this hellish visitor who came to him. But within, her soul cried out in a horror of uttermost darkness. Then her will took hold of that too: whatever God permitted must be faced for the sake of love.

Just then Archie spoke in an odd muffled voice.

"I'm going very deep," he said. "But, Martin, you've made me so happy all day. You've hardly left me at all. You're getting to be part of me, aren't you? Let's talk about Helena. I say, she is a devil, isn't she?"

Jessie had not known that anything could be so horrible as the smiling face that the apparition bent on him.

"But you've ceased hating her," it said. "You love her, don't you? Always cling to love!"

"I know, I adore her. I believe she loves me too." He laughed and licked his lips and his voice sank, so that Jessie could catch no word of what he said. But he spoke for a long time, laughing occasionally, and making horrible little movements with his arms as if he clasped something. Now and then he would perhaps ask a question, for in the same inaudible manner the apparition answered him, laughing sometimes in response. Once or twice in that devilish colloquy she caught a word or two of hideous and carnal import, and her sickened love nearly withered within her. But because love is immortal, and cannot perish though all the blasts of hell rage against it, it still stood firm, though scorched and beaten upon. If she let it die, she felt that she would be no better than that visible incarnation of evil that smiled and bent over Archie.

Presently that devilish whispering ceased, and she saw that the apparition was beginning to lose its clearness of outline. Slowly it began to disintegrate into the weavings of mist out of which it came, and Archie said, "Good-bye, Martin, but not for long." Some of these streamers seemed to disperse in the air, others, like an eddying water-spout, seemed to draw back into that focus of light which lay over Archie's breast. Then that too began to fade, and in the stillness and quiet she again heard the creaking of his shirt as he lay back in his chair with closed eyes. Then the struggles and moanings, the writhings of his arms began again, and again subsided, and he lay quite still. Outside the night-wind stirred and dropped.

Then Archie spoke in a tired, husky voice.

"Hullo, Jessie," he said, "it's all over. By Jove, it was ripping. But I went awfully deep. I can remember nothing after Martin came. What did he say?"

Jessie got up.

"I heard hardly anything," she said. "He spoke in whispers, and so did you."

"Did you see him?" asked Archie.

"Yes, quite clearly. But I think I'll go to bed now. You look very tired."

He had got up and turned on the electric light, and stood by the door rubbing his eyes.

"Yes, I am tired," he said, "but I'm divinely happy. Tell me to-morrow whatever you can remember. Good-night, Jess. You are a good sort."

He detained her hand for a moment.

"We're cousins, Jess," he said, "and you're an awfully good friend. Won't you give me a kiss?"

For one second she shrank from him in nameless horror. The next she put it all from her, for her shrinking, no angel of the Lord, but a weak, cowardly impulse, stood full in the path of love, and while it was there she could not reach Archie.

"Why, of course," she said, kissing him. "Good-night, Archie; sleep well."

She went to her room, and turned on all the lights. She felt as if she had been assisting at some unclean orgy, she felt tainted and defiled by the very presence of that white evil thing that had stood close to her, and whispered and laughed with Archie. As yet she had but looked on it; what lay in front of her was to grapple with it and tear it out of the tabernacle which it had begun to inhabit. As far as she could understand the situation, it was not wholly in possession as yet, for part of it, when it materialized, seemed to form itself in the air, and part only to ooze out of its victim. Through what adventures and combats her way should take her she could form no conception, but what she had gained to-night, which was worth a hundred times the sickness and horror of her soul, was the certain knowledge that some spirit of discarnate evil was making its home in her beloved. It had usurped the guise of Martin, it masqueraded as

Martin, Archie thought it was Martin. She remembered how, just a week ago, he had told her that he was like an empty house, denuded of the spirit that dwelt there, a living corpse by which he asked her to sit sometimes. At the time that had seemed to her just the figure by which he expressed the desolation of his heart; now it revealed itself as a true and literal statement. And there had begun to enter into him, as tenant of the uninhabited rooms, the horror that she had seen.

Jessie fell on her knees by her bedside, and opened her heart to the Infinite Love. It was through Its aid alone that she would be able to accomplish the rescue for which she was willing to give her life and soul.

CHAPTER XII

Archie was walking back to the house in Grosvenor Square from Oakland Crescent, on the afternoon of Helena's wedding. Owing to the acute suspense of the European situation, the plans of the newly married couple had been changed, and, instead of setting off at once in the yacht for a month in the Norwegian fjords, they had gone to a house of Lord Harlow's in Surrey to await developments in the crisis or some kind of settlement. It was still uncertain whether England would be drawn into the war, though opinion generally regarded that as inevitable, and in this case no doubt Lord Harlow, an ex-Guardsman, would rejoin his regiment. Archie's mother, after the departure of the bridal couple, had also left town for Lacebury, taking with her Jessie and Colonel Vautier for a few days' visit; but Archie had decided to stop another night in London.

There had been the usual crowds and chatterings and excitement, the front pew kept for a princess, the signing of names in the vestry, the red carpets and wedding-marches, and the whole ceremony had filled Archie with the greatest amusement. But the subsequent proceedings had not amused him so much, and Helena's departure, looking prettier than ever, with her husband, had annoyed and exasperated him. He did not like to think of them together, and, though only a couple of nights ago he and Martin had found good cause for whispers and laughter over this, it was not so diverting when it actually occurred as it had promised to be. Part of that midnight seance which he could not at first remember had found its way into his conscious mind, and he knew that had been talked about, and had ascertained, with considerable relief, that Jessie had not been able to hear it. But now there was a savage bitterness in his mind about it; Helena seemed to have played him false again. She ought to have refused to marry the Bradshaw at the last moment, and it was an ineffectual balm to know she did not care for him. Perhaps, as Jessie had once said (though withdrawing it afterwards), she cared for nobody, but now Archie believed that she cared for him. It maddened him to think that she was the Bradshaw's "ABC," and in those circumstances he had judged it better to remain in town for the night, and distract his mind and soothe his longings with the amusement and aids to forgetfulness which London was so ready to offer to a young man who was looking for adventures.

But London proved disappointing: it did not seem to be thinking of its amusements at all. Archie called to see a friend who last week had shown himself an eager and admirable companion, but, found him to-day disinclined for another night of similar diversion, for he could neither think nor talk about anything else than the imminence of war. Archie felt himself quite incapable of taking any active interest in that; it weighted nothing in the balance compared with the stern duty of seeking enjoyment and forgetting about Helena. What if England did go to war with Germany? Certainly he hoped she would not; she had made no more than a friendly understanding with her Allies—indeed they were not even Allies, they were but well-disposed nations—but, even if she did, what then? There was an English fleet, was there not, which cost an immense amount of money to render invincible; but it was invincible. Why, then, should he bother about it, since he was not a sailor? It was further supposed that Germany had an invincible army; and there you were! And if England had no army at all to speak of, it was quite clear she could no more fight Germany on land than Germany could fight her by sea. So what on earth prevented a little dinner at a restaurant and an hour at a music-hall and a little supper somewhere and anything that turned up? Something always turned up, and was usually amusing for an hour or two. But his friend thought otherwise, and kept diving out into the street to get some fresh edition of an evening paper hot from the press and crammed with fresh inventions, and Archie left this insane patriot in disgust at his excitement over so detached an affair as a European war. He tried a second friend with no better success; there was a certain excuse for him, as he was a subaltern in the Guards. But for the first friend there was none, as he was only in an office in the city.

There were still four or five hours to get through before it would be reasonable to think about dinner, after which, even if he started alone, the hours would take care of themselves very pleasantly; but he had to fill the interval somehow. There were some proofs of his book waiting for him at home, and, hoping to get interested in this first-born public child of his brain, he sat down with a view to correcting them. But he found himself reading the pages as if there was nothing intelligible printed on them. True, if he forced himself to attend, he could see that grammatical sentences succeeded each other; but they conveyed no further impression. There was a lot about the sea, but why on earth had he taken the trouble to write it? He could remember writing it; he could call up an image of himself sitting in the garden at Silorno, eagerly writing, conscientiously erasing, walking up and down in the attempt to frame a phrase that should exactly reproduce some mood of his mind. But what had inspired those strivings and despairs and exultations?

Here was the record of them, and it seemed now to be about nothing. "The rain in the night had washed the white soil into the rim of the sea, and it was clouded like absinthe." He could well remember the search for, and the finding of that particular simile. He and Harry had been into Genoa a week before, and, out of curiosity, had ordered absinthe at a cafe. The drink, *qua* drink, was mildly unpleasant, resembling aniseed, but it had been worth while having it, merely to have got that perfectly fitting simile. The effect, too, had been rather remarkable; it produced a sort of heady lightness and sense of well-being; colours seemed strangely vivid and intensified, and…

Archie got up from his meaningless proofs. It was absinthe that would help him to fill up those dull hours till dinner-time, and he remembered having seen in some little French restaurant in Soho the stuff he wanted. Very likely you could get it anywhere, but he wanted it from that particular place, for there had come in one evening, when he dined there, a most melancholy-looking person who had ordered it and sat and sipped. Somehow the man's face had made an impression on him, so unhappy was it. He remembered also his face half an hour afterwards, when he began his dinner, and no serener, more contented countenance could have been imagined... So he must have his absinthe from that restaurant; clearly they had a very good brand of it there.

As he drove out alone that evening to dine, he heard the newsvenders shouting out the English ultimatum to Germany, and saw the placards in the streets. The shouting sounded wonderfully musical, and below the roar of the street traffic was a muffled harmony as of pealing bells. The drab colours of London were shot with prismatic hues; never had the streets appeared so beautiful. There was even beauty in the fact of the outbreak of war, for England was going to war for the sake of liberty, which was a fine, a noble adventure. And how lovely the English girls and boys were, who crowded the pavements! They were like beds of exquisite flowers. For himself, he was going back to dine at the French restaurant in Soho, for that would be in the nature of supporting our new Allies. Afterwards there were the streets and the music-halls, and all the mysteries of the short summer night. Then dawn would break, rose-coloured dawn, with her finger on her lips, and sweet, silent mouth, a little ashamed of her sister, night, but sympathetic at heart. Dawn was always a little prudish, a little Quakerish.

* * * * *

The days of a divine August went by, and the line of German invasion swept forward like a tide that knows no ebb over all Belgium and North-East France. The British Expeditionary Force started, and was swept back like the flotsam on the seashore. The call came for the raising of an army, and east and west, north and south, the recruiting offices were like choked waterways, and still the flood of men, in whose hearts the fact of England had awoke, poured in. Hospitals were gorged with the returning wounded; women by the hundred and by the thousand volunteered as nurses, and went to hospitals to be trained. The whole of comfortable England, intent hitherto on its sports, its leisure, its general superiority to the rest of the world, suddenly became aware that an immense and vital danger threatened it. A chorus of objurgation arose from the brazen-throated press, each organ striving to shout the loudest, at the unpreparedness of the country, and much valuable energy was spent in headlines and recriminations. There was a shortage of guns, a shortage of ammunition, a shortage of everything which constitutes the sinews of war. The only thing of which there was not a shortage was of those who threw aside all other considerations, such as income and secure living and life itself, and gave themselves to assist, in what manner they could, the cause for which England had gone to war.

To Archie this all seemed a very hysterical and uncomfortable attack of nerves. In several ways it affected him personally, for William, than whom there was no more reliable servant, was among the first to leave his well-paid situation and present himself at a recruiting office. Archie hated that: there would be the nuisance of getting a new servant, who did not know where precisely he ought to put Archie's tooth-powder, and how to arrange his clothes. William had announced the fact too, in the suddenest of manners; he brought it out as he brought in Archie's morning tea.

"And if you can spare me at once, my lord," he said, "I had better go on Saturday."

Archie felt peculiarly devilish that morning; it rained, and the absinthe that should have arrived last night had not come.

"I think it's very inconsiderate of you, William," he said. "But I suppose you expect to get on well, and draw higher pay than you get here. So I shall have to raise your wages. All right; I'll give you a pound a month more, and don't let me hear any more about it."

He knew perfectly well that this was not William's reason, but it amused him to suggest it. He wanted to see how William would take it. The fact that he knew that the man was devoted to him made the point.

William busied himself with razors and tooth-brushes, replying nothing.

"Can't you hear what I say?" asked Archie, pouring himself out his tea.

William faced round.

"Yes, Master Archie," he said. "I heard. But I knew you didn't mean that. You know how I've served you and worked for you all these years. You would scorn to think that of me, I should say."

Archie had noticed the "Master Archie" instead of "my lord"; both William and Blessington often forgot that he was "my lord," and it always used to please him that to the sense of love he was still a young boy. And, in spite of his irritation and peevish morning temper, it touched some part of him that still loved below the corruption that was spreading over him like some jungle-growing lichen. But he had to force his way through that to reply.

"You must do as you think right, William," he said.

William had finished the arrangements of his dressing, and stood for a moment by his bedside with Archie's evening clothes bundled on to his arm.

"Yes, Master Archie," he said. "And you'll be joining up too before long, won't you? I should dearly love to be your soldier-servant, sir, if you could manage it."

All Archie's ill-humour returned at that unfortunate suggestion.

"Perhaps you had better not be impertinent," he said. "That'll do."

William's face fell.

"I had no thought of impertinence, my lord," he said. "I only thought—"

"I told you that would do," said Archie.

* * * * *

Three days afterwards William left. He came to say good-bye to Archie, who did not look up from the paper he was reading. Archie was suffering inconvenience from his departure, and this was the best way of making William feel it. But when the door had shut again, and William was gone, he felt a sudden horror of the thing that seemed to be himself, and he ran out, and called William back. All these days he had not had a word or kindly gesture for him...

"Good-bye, William," he said. "I wish you all good luck. I've treated you like a beast these last days, and I'm awfully sorry. You're the best fellow a man could have, and you must try to forget the horrid way I've behaved."

William stood with his hand in Archie's for a moment.

"You're always my Master Archie, sir," he said.

* * * * *

Well, there was an end of William: before he had got back to his paper again Archie wondered what had possessed him to throw a kind word to a dog like that, who had left him at three days' notice to join this ridiculous military conspiracy. William did not care how much he inconvenienced Archie, who had always treated him more like a subordinate friend than a servant. He had helped William in a hundred ways: had given him old clothes, had constantly asked after his mother, had left his letters about for William to read if he chose. It seemed rank treachery…

Others were treacherous too; his mother, for instance, was immediately going up to town, to take charge of the house in Grosvenor Square, which was to be turned into a hospital for wounded officers. She was to become a sort of housekeeper, so Archie figured it, and merely superintend domestic arrangements. She would have nothing to do with the nursing and the surgery, which had a certain fascination… He could picture a sort of pleasure in seeing a man's leg cut off, or in standing by while doctors pulled bandages off festering wounds. To feel well and strong while others were suffering had an intelligible interest: to witness decay and corruption and pain was a point that appealed to him now. But Lady Tintagel was going to do nothing of the sort: she was just going to be a housekeeper. It was very selfish of her; Archie would certainly want, from time to time, to go up to town and spend a night or two there, and now he would have to go to a hotel or a club, instead of profiting by the spacious privacy of his father's house. Charity begins at home; and his mother had started charity on most extraneous lines. Jessie had followed this lead, "the lead of so-called trumps," as Archie framed a private phrase. She would start by being not even a housekeeper, but a sort of kitchen-maid at the same hospital. She had an insane desire to work, to do something that cost her something, instead of engaging a kitchen-maid, and paying her wages to go to some hospital or other. There was a craze for "personal service," instead of getting other people to do work for you, if you felt work had to be done. People wanted to "do their bit," to employ an odious expression which was beginning to obtain currency. The nation was going to be mobilized; hand and heart had to serve some vague national idea. Occasionally, as on the night when war was declared, Archie saw an aesthetic beauty in the notion of upholding rights and liberties; but he had not then reckoned with the fact that personal inconvenience might result from that quixotic revolution. Quixotism was fine in theory, but it was a dream, not to be encouraged in waking hours, when far more important and realizable commodities, like whisky and absinthe, engaged the true attention.

But, whoever else was treacherous, his father at least was loyal, and showed no sign of becoming a butler or a footman, to correspond with his wife and Jessie. Occasionally some grave report concerning the German advance through Belgium used to reach his brain, and he would walk up and down his room in the evening with a martial tread, and a glance at a sword that hung above his writing-table, and wish he was younger and able to "have a go" at those invading locusts. But invariably this mood, which was always short, was succeeded by another, not bellicose but domestic.

"This damned war is going to break up home-life in England," he would say, "and I've no doubt that was what the Germans aimed at. And they're succeeding too. Look at this house: there's you mother going to leave us, and there's Helena's husband expecting every day to be sent to France, and there's Jessie leaving her father to wash up dishes. What's going to become of our English homes if that goes on?—for, mark you, they are the root of our national life. It's digging up the trees' roots to break up English homes. You and I, Archie, are the only ones who are staunch to our homes. Pass me that bottle, will you?"

"May I help myself on the way?" said Archie.

"Yes, of course, my dear boy. I say, it was a funny state of things when you and I used to have our evening drinks alone, instead of enjoying them and chatting over them together. Your man, William, too, he's gone and enlisted, hasn't he? The old bulwarks of England are going fast: the homes are being broken up, and the very servants come and go as they choose. An establishment was an establishment in the old days: it all stood and fell together, if you see what I mean. But I wish I was young enough to have a go at the Boches."

"I'm thinking of going," Archie would say, merely in order to enjoy his father's reply.

"Well, in my opinion, you'll be doing a very wrong thing, then," said Lord Tintagel. "I hope you won't seriously think of that. I tell you your duty is here, with your poor old father. When I'm gone you may do what you please, and I daresay you won't have very long to wait. But, while I'm here, I hope you'll remember that they say in church 'Honour thy father and thy mother.' You can't go behind the commandments, or the psalms, whichever it is."

But these sessions in Lord Tintagel's room of an evening, with the liquid in the decanter sinking steadily like a well in time of drought, were becoming rather tedious to Archie. Since his discovery of absinthe they had even become rather gross, and he congratulated himself on having seen the sordidness of mere swilling. That sort of thing was only fit for coarse, rough tastes; it seemed to him to lack all delicacy and aesthetic value, and he often left his father, who congratulated him on his abstemiousness after no more than a friendly glass of good fellowship, and went upstairs to his room to enjoy subtler and more refined sensations. Indeed, his chief interest in that half-hour or so in his father's room was derived from the sight of his father's heavy potations, the struggle of his maundering thoughts to emerge into language, much as a tilted half-moon struggles to pierce the flying clouds on some tempestuous night. The sight of his father's deterioration and gradual wreck somehow fascinated him; there was decay and corruption there, and those no longer aroused in him that horror with which in dream he had observed the emergence of the writhing worms from the white statue of Helena. Such things were no longer disgusting and repulsive: they claimed kinship with something in his soul that was very potent. Once Martin had alluded to that vision as a warning, and he had not taken that warning, in consequence of which he had passed an utterly miserable month after Helena's rejection of him. Now values had altogether changed: decay no longer revolted him. But, with a hypocrisy that had become characteristic of him, he told himself that the sight of his father's nightly intoxication was a lesson to himself. He must observe that degrading spectacle, and learn from it what the result of too much whisky was. And then he retired to his bedroom to think it over as he sipped the clouded aroma of his absinthe.

Jessie came down for another week-end before she took her kitchen-maid situation, and brought the news that a fresh draft of Lord Harlow's regiment was ordered to the front, and that he would leave for France within the next day or two.

Archie felt a wild desire to laugh, to skip, to show his intense appreciation of these tidings. But he remembered that Jessie was not his confidante to that extent, and checked his exuberant inclination.

"Poor Helena!" he said, with an accent of great sincerity. "She must be broken-hearted. Why, they've only been married a fortnight, if as much."

It was excellently said, and Jessie felt she would have shown herself an infidel, with regard to the general decency of the human race, if she had not accepted those words with the sincerity with which they surely must have been uttered. She resolutely put away from her all those misgivings that had assailed her when first she knew of Archie's changed attitude towards her sister.

"You have been a brick about Helena," she said. "I want to tell you that. Your forgiveness of the way she treated you seems to me beyond all praise."

"Oh, nonsense," said he lightly. "Besides, it was so dreadfully uncomfortable being always angry and miserable. Martin showed me that. But about Helena: how is she bearing it?"

It was now Jessie's turn to be obliged to cloak her meaning.

"Very calmly and bravely," she said.

"She would," said Archie enthusiastically. "One always felt there was a steel will behind all Helena's gentleness. What will she do, do you think? Would she perhaps like to come down here? There isn't much to offer her, but then London in August doesn't offer much either."

Suddenly all Jessie's mistrust stirred and erected itself. She could not believe that this scheme, which would throw Helena and Archie completely together, could be made with the apparent innocence with which it was put forward. How was it possible that Archie, who so few weeks ago was in such depths of misery and bitterness, could honourably suggest so dangerous a plan? It could not be Archie who suggested it: it came from that smiling white presence which she had seen in his room not many nights ago. And it was just that which she could not say to him.

"It's nice of you to think of that," she said.

"Not a bit: it would be nice for me, not nice of me. And besides," he added, with an amazing cynicism, "it would be my way of 'doing my bit,' which everybody is talking about, if I could make things cheerfuller for pretty women like poor Helena, whose husband has gone out to fight."

The moment he had said it he was sorry. But for the moment he had forgotten he was speaking to Jessie: the sentence had come out of his mouth as if he was but talking to himself. Also it introduced the suggestion of his own forbearance to enlist.

There was a rather awkward silence, and he felt irritated with Jessie for not changing the subject which he had so incautiously brought forward. But that was like her. She had no tact in such matters, refusing to be insincere, when insincerity was so simple a matter. His irritation grew on him, and at the same time he wanted to know what Jessie thought of his remaining inertly here, while all his contemporaries were enlisting. Why he wanted to know he did not define: the motive perhaps belonged to the time when Jessie had been so good a friend, and perhaps he knew that she was so still.

"Or do you think that I ought to behave like William, and serve my country?" he asked.

Jessie sat with eyes downcast for a moment. Then she raised them and looked him in the face, with all her affection and sincerity alight in them.

"Do you really want to know what I think, Archie?" she asked.

"Certainly I do."

"Well, I can't understand your not doing it," she said. "At the same time, I think it is a matter about which you must decide for yourself."

The sincerity of his manner equalled hers. He never spoke with more apparent frankness.

"Shall I tell you why I don't?" he said. "It's this. Do you remember one night our finding that my father was breaking the contract he made with me about drinking? Do you remember how sordid and horrible the discovery was?"

Jessie remembered quite well how Archie had laughed at it.

"I remember the evening," she said.

"Well, we've renewed our contract," said he, "and I'm the only person in the world who can keep my father to it. If I left him he would drink himself to death. Where, then, do you think my duty lies, Jessie? Isn't it clearly for me to save my father? Can there be a more obvious duty than that? Do you think I have a very delightful life down here, all alone with him? Wouldn't it be vastly easier for me to join my friends and go out alongside of them? I know my conduct lays me open to misconception, but I must be thick-skinned over that. But I hope you won't misjudge me. Besides, my father has said that he forbids me to go. Of course I could leave him; he doesn't lock me up. But I can't see how I should be right in leaving him. I'm the one anchor he has left."

He paused a moment, thinking over, with that stupendous swiftness of brain that was the result of Martin's inspiration, all he had said, and remembered his light cynicism with regard to his "bit."

"I know I rather shocked you just now," he said, "when I spoke of its being 'my bit' to console pretty women whose husbands had gone out. But sometimes one has to be flippant to conceal one's real thoughts on a serious subject, for I did not foresee then that we should talk it out. So there's the end of that jest."

So that had been a jest, not to be taken seriously. But it was a grimmer affair for Jessie not to be able to take seriously Archie's seriousness. For a moment the frankness of his manner had convinced her, but very soon her conviction collapsed like a house of cards as he went on speaking. The horribleness of the discovery of his father's drinking, for instance, when what she remembered was Archie's laughter! If he could say that, what credence could possibly be placed in the picture he had drawn of himself as his father's last hope? Or what in the image of himself as one who must silently bear cruel misconception? She could believe none of it...

Yet it was not the Archie whom she loved with all the sweetness and strength of her nature who spoke, but the Thing that was possessing him and filling his soul from the reservoir of some immense abyss of pure evil. She felt sure she did not misjudge him; true and infinitely tragic was her comprehension.

"It is entirely for you to decide, Archie," she said. "I think I fully appreciate the worth of your reasons."

Indeed, she knew not what else to say, though the bitter doubleness of her words cut her to the heart. But, if she could help Archie at all, she must at all costs retain such confidence as he gave her, must not give him the chance of quarrelling with her.

To her great relief, he seemed to accept the literal value of her words, and took her arm. And this time she felt in her soul that there was sincerity in his speech.

"You are a good friend, Jessie," he said. "Don't give me up, will you?"

"I couldn't," she said quietly.

* * * * *

They were strolling together by the edge of the lake in the hour of sunset, and Jessie, though sick at heart and tortured by the weight of her forebodings, and the tempest of fire and blood which had burst on Europe, yet tried to open her heart to the sweet spell of the tranquil evening. Somewhere behind the cloud of evil which had so suddenly taken shape in that host of barbarians who already had overrun Belgium, and which, no less, was invading the spirit of the boy she loved with the uttermost fibre of her being, there shone the eternal serenity of Omnipotent Mercy. But He dealt through human means; it was through those who had left love and home and ease behind them to perish in France that that torrent would be stayed, and through her, though in ways she could not conjecture, would come the delivery of her beloved. And in the rose-flecked sky, the leafy towers of the elms, the bosom of the lake, that Power also dwelt, no less than in the hearts that yearned for its presence and its manifestation. As in a glass darkly she beheld its reflection, which nothing could ever shatter. Of that she must never lose sight, nor cease to keep her inward eye fixed on the gleam, which some day would signal to her.

About a week later Archie was spending a delectable morning at the bathing-place. Never had there been so superb an imitation of Italian weather in England as this year, and day after day went by in unclouded brightness and strong, fresh heat. In those delightful conditions it had been perfectly easy for him to take his mind completely away from the war, and the misconceptions which he was possibly suffering under. He gave every morning but the briefest glance to the paper, for there was a tiresome uniformity about the news, and a monotonous regularity about the daily map, which marked the progress of the German line across North-East France. He gave hardly more thought to Helena, who seemed to think it more appropriate to stay in London with her father, just for the present, but had written the most characteristic of letters, saying how sweet Archie's sympathy was to her, and how acute her anxiety concerning her husband. Certainly at the moment this was the right attitude to take, and Archie really did not much care whether she was here with him or not, for he had found his way into the Paradise that forms the portico of the palace where the absinthe-drinker dwells, and not yet had he penetrated into the halls of Hell that lie beyond.

His pleasure in the fact of being alive, in the colours of morning and evening, in the touch of cool waters, in the whispering of wind among the firs, were quickened to an inconceivable degree; it was impossible to want anything except the privilege of enjoying this amazing thrill of existence. And with it there had returned to him the need of expressing himself in writing; a new aspect of the world had been revealed to him, and without struggle, but with an even-flowing pen he set himself to record it, in veiled phrases and descriptions through which, as in chinks of light seen at the edges of drawn blinds, there came hints and suggestions of the fresh world that had dawned on him. Where before it was the clear stainlessness of the sea, the purifying breath of great winds that had been his theme, now instead the satyr crouched in the bushes, the snake lay coiled in the heather. It was from the slime and mud and from among blind crawling things that the water-lily sprang, and where before the enchantment of life moved him, he felt now only the call of putrefaction and decay. The lethal side of the created world had become exquisite in his eyes, and the beauty of it was derived from its everlasting corruption, not from the eternal upspringing of life. Lust, not love, was the force that kept it young, and renewed it so that the harvest of its decay should never ceased to be reaped. His mind had become a mirror that distorted into grotesque and evil shapes every image of beauty that was reflected in it, and rejoiced in them; it seemed to him that all nature, as well as all human motive, was based upon this exquisite secret that he had discovered. But it would never do to state it with what he considered the bald realism of those ludicrous sea-pieces he had written at Silorno; he must wrap his message up in a sort of mystic subtlety so that only those who had implanted in them the true instinct should be able to fill their souls with the perfume of his flowers. Others might guess and wonder and be puzzled, and perhaps see so far as to put down his book with disgust that was still half incredulous; but only the initiated would be able to grasp wholly the message that lurked in his hints and allusions. His style, underneath this new inspiration, had developed into an instrument of marvellous beauty, and often, when he had written a page or two, he would read it out aloud to himself, in wonder at that exquisite diction, and all the time he felt that he was reading aloud to Martin, and that Martin had dictated to him.

He was employed thus on this particular morning down at the bathing-place. He had already had a long swim, and, without dressing, lay down on the short turf and got out his writing-pad, when his new servant, who had taken William's place, came down with a telegram for him. He was a very good-looking boy, quick in movement and swift to smile, and already Archie wondered how he could have regretted the departure of plain middle-aged William. Only last evening Archie, idly glancing through a field-glass, had seen the boy far off in the meadow beyond the lake in company with an extremely pretty housemaid whom he had often noticed about the passages. The two had sat there some time talking, and then Archie saw the boy look quickly round, and kiss her. He liked that immensely; that was the way youth should behave. He almost hoped that it was Thomas who had taken from his table one of those new ten-shilling notes that he had missed. He mustn't do it too often, for that would be a bore; but Archie liked to think the boy had taken it, and perhaps converted it into a decoration for the pretty housemaid. Anyhow, Thomas, with his handsome face and his kissings in the meadow, and his possible pilferings, was an attractive boy, and clearly developing along the right lines.

The boy hesitated a moment, seeing Archie dripping and naked.

"I beg your pardon, my lord," he said, "but there came a telegram for you, and I thought I had better bring it down."

"Certainly, but why beg my pardon?" said Archie. "Don't be prudish. I daresay you've got arms and legs as well as me, haven't you?"

Thomas grinned with that odd shy look that Archie had noticed before.

"Yes, my lord," he said.

"Then what is there to be ashamed of?"

Archie opened the telegram and read it, and suddenly bit his lip to prevent his laughing.

"Is there an answer, my lord?" asked the boy. "I brought a form down in case."

"Well done. Yes, there is an answer."

Archie hesitated a moment before directing the form to Helena. Then he wrote:

"Deepest sympathy with the terrible news. Command me in all ways. Your devoted Archie."

"Send that at once, will you?" he said.

When the boy had gone Archie read the telegram again, which was from Jessie, and told him that Lord Harlow had been killed at the front. Then he smothered his face in his bent elbow, and lay shaking with laughter.

CHAPTER XIII

On a September morning, some fortnight later, Archie was waiting in the drawing-room at Oakland Crescent for Helena's entry. He had seen her twice since her husband's death, and it struck him now that she always kept him waiting when she asked him to come and see her, and ascribed to that the very probable motive that she expected thereby to increase his eagerness for her coming. Certainly he wanted her to come, because he was much interested and amused in the conventional little comedy she was playing, and he looked forward to the third act, on which the curtain would presently ring up. In the interval he sat very serenely smiling to himself, and tickling the end of his nose with three white feathers that he had received in the street to-day. That always diverted him extremely; a rude young woman would come up (she was invariably square and plain, and had a knobby face like a chest of drawers) and say, "Aren't you ashimed not to be serving your country? You're a coward, you are," and then she would give him a white feather. He had quite a collection of them now; there were nine already which he carefully kept in his stud-box, and these three all in one day were a splendid haul.

He had, to occupy his mind very pleasantly, the remembrance of his previous interviews with Helena, which formed the two existing acts of the comedy. In the first she had come in, looking deliciously pretty in her deep mourning, and, with her head a little on one side, had held out both her hands to him. They had stood with hands clasped for quite a long time, and then Archie kissed her because he was rather tired of holding her hands, and because he enjoyed kissing anything so pretty. That had caused a break, and they sat down side by side, and Helena made some queer movements in her throat, which seemed to Archie to be designed to convey the impression that she was repressing her emotion. But they did not quite fulfil their design; they looked rather as if they were due to the desire to pump up rather than keep down. Then Helena gave a long sigh.

"Oh, Archie," she said, "I am utterly broken-hearted. It was so sudden, so terribly sudden. I shall never get over it. Think! We had been married only a fortnight, and next day I got a letter from him, after I knew he was dead. Such a sweet little letter, so cheerful and so loving."

Archie expected something of this sort: its conventionality, its utter insincerity, amused him enormously. And, wanting more of it, he said just the proper sort of thing to encourage her to give it him.

"Oh, my dear," he said, "but how you will love and cherish that letter! I don't suppose you were once out of his thoughts all the time he was in France."

She shook her head.

"I am sure of it," she said. "Ah, what a privilege to have been loved as I was loved by such a noble, manly heart. I must always think of that, mustn't I?"

Archie took her hand again. The touch of those soft, cool fingers gave him pleasure; so, too, did the answering pressure of them.

"Yes, indeed," he said. "And you must remember, too, that it's better to have loved and lost than never to have loved at all."

She repeated the quotation in a dreamy meditative voice.

"Yes, that is so true: it does me good to think of that," she said. "And I mustn't think of him as dead really. He is just as living as ever he was. He was so fond of you too. We often spoke of you. And his quaint, quiet humour!…"

That was the general note of the first act: it had been short, for the conversation suitable to it was necessarily limited. The second showed a great advance in scope and variety of topics. Also the *tempo* was quite changed: instead of its being *largo*, it was at least *andante con moto*.

This time, after again keeping him waiting, she had entered with a smile.

"What a comfort you are, Archie!" she said. "I have been looking forward to seeing you again. Somehow you understand me, which nobody else does. I feel all the time that neither darling Jessie, whenever I see her, which isn't often, for she is so busy, nor daddy quite understand me. I mean to be brave, and not lose courage, not lose gaiety even, and I think—I think that they both misjudge me. They expect me to be utterly broken. So I was at first, as you know so well, but I tried to take to heart what you said, and force myself not to despair. I feel I oughtn't to do that: I must take the burden of life up again with a smile."

Her hand lay open on her knee; as she said this, she turned it over towards him, making an invitation that seemed unconscious. He slipped his long brown fingers into that rosy palm. She was astonishingly like a girl he met a night or two ago.

"I must get over this awful feeling of loneliness," she said, "and you are helping me so deliciously to do so. Daddy is busy all day; I scarcely see him. Jessie is busy also. I think she enjoys washing up knives and forks and plates for soldiers, though of course that doesn't make it any less sweet of her to do it. But, anyhow, she hasn't got much time for me. I wish—no, I suppose it's wrong to wish that."

"Well, confess, then," said Archie, smiling at her.

"Yes, dear father-confessor, though I ought to say boy-confessor, for you look so young! Well, I'll confess to you. I—I'm sure you won't be shocked with me. I wish Jessie cared for me a little more. She is my sister, after all. But I daresay it's my fault. I haven't got the key to her heart. And, with Jessie and daddy so full of other affairs, I do feel lonely. But when you are here I don't. I don't know what I should have done without you, Archie. I think I might have killed myself."

This was glorious. Archie gave a splendid shudder.

"Don't talk like that," he said, in a tone of affectionate command. "You don't know how it hurts."

"Ah, I'm sorry. It was selfish of me. Do you forgive me?"

"You know I do," said he.

She had brought into the room with her a long envelope, and rather absently she took out from it an enclosure of papers.

"I got this to-day from the lawyers," she said. "It's about my darling's will, I think. I wonder if you would help me to understand it, I am so stupid at figures."

She slid a little closer to him, leaning her hand on his shoulder and looking over him as he read. The document required, as a matter of fact, very little exercise of intelligence. The house in Surrey where they had spent the week of the honeymoon was hers; and so was a very decent income of L15,000 a year, left to her without any condition whatever for her life; it was hers absolutely. The disposition of the rest of his fortune depended on whether she had a child. The details of that were not given: his lawyer only informed her what was hers.

She hid her face on the hand that rested on Archie's shoulder.

"Oh, Archie, I can never go back to that house," she said, "at least not for a long time. It would be tearing open the old wound again."

"Yes, I understand that," said he, with another pressure of his fingers. And, thinking of the L15,000 a year without conditions, he had a wild temptation to console her further by quoting—

"Let us grieve not, only find Strength in what remains behind."

But he refrained: though, apparently, there was no limit to Helena's insincerity, there might be some in her acceptance of the insincerity of others.

"Oh, you do understand me so well," she said. "And, Archie, I want to ask a horribly selfish thing of you, but I can't help it. I am all alone now, except for you. You won't go out to the war, will you? I don't think I could bear it if you did."

It was quite easy for him to promise that, but an allusion to the misconception he might incur made his acquiescence sound difficult and noble.

Since then, up to the day when he was now expecting her entry for the third act, he had thought over the whole situation with the imaginative vision which absinthe inspired. He had not the slightest doubt in his mind that Helena, according to her capacity for loving, was in love with him, and that she thought he was still in love with her. But, when he considered it all, he found he had no longer the slightest intention of marrying her, even though she had L15,000 a year for life without conditions attached. Plenty of money was no doubt a preventive of discomfort in this life, and he felt it was fine of him not to be attracted by so ignoble a bait. But no amount of money would really compensate for the inseparable companionship of Helena, with her foolishness, her apparent inability to understand that her insincerities, so far from being convincing and beautiful, were no more than the most puerile and transparent counterfeits. Certainly she aroused the ardour of his senses, but how long would that last? And, even while it lasted, how could it compare with his ardour for his absinthe-coloured dreams, and the ecstasy of his communion with the spirit that had made its home in him? She would interrupt all that; and, as a companion, she could not compare with his father. She would always be wanting to be caressed and made much of and admired and taken care of. It would soon become most horribly tedious.

There was a further reason against marrying her, which was as potent as any. He would forfeit his revenge on her, if he did that. Once, dim ages ago, it seemed, and on another plane of existence, he had loved her, and she, knowing it, had fed his devotion with smiles and glances, and at the end had chosen him whose body now decayed in some graveyard of North France, already probably desecrated by the on-swarming Germans. Now it was Archie's turn; already, he was sure, she expected to marry him, and she would learn that he had not the least intention of doing so. That delightful situation might easily be arrived at in the third act for which he was waiting now.

This time she came with flowers in her hand, and presently, as they sat side by side on the sofa talking, she put one into his button-hole. Instantly he interrupted himself in what he was saying and kissed it.

She gave him that long glance which he had once thought meant so much. It had not meant much then, from her point of view, but it meant a good deal more now. But to Archie it had passed from being a gleam of wonder to a farthing dip.

"Oh, you foolish boy!" she said.

He almost thought he heard Martin laugh.

"I don't see anything foolish about it," he said. "At least, if it's foolish, I've always been foolish."

Her lips moved, though not to speak: they just gathered themselves together, and a little tremor went down the arm that rested against his. He was perfectly certain of both those signals, and next moment he had folded her to him, and she lay less than unresisting in his arms.

Then she gently thrust him from her.

"Ah, how wrong of me," she said, "and yet perhaps it's not wrong. The dear Bradshaw would always want me to be happy. Perhaps he even thought of this when he left me so free. For this time, Archie, I shan't come to you empty-handed. But, of course, we mustn't think of all that for many months yet."

Archie, flushed and merry-eyed, looked at her with boyish surprise.

"Think of what?" he said.

"Ah, you force me to say it, do you? Of our marriage."

He was adorable in her eyes just then; she could hardly realize that so few months ago she had definitely put him from her. His warm, smooth face, his crisp, curling hair, the youthful roughness and ardour of his embrace, inflamed and ravished her.

He looked at her still inquiringly a moment, then threw back his head and laughed.

"Oh, you're delicious!" he said. "But marriage? What do you mean? A cousinly kiss, a little sympathy, a few dear little surrenders of each of us to the other: that's all I intended. Well, I must be off. Good-bye!"

Next moment, still choking with laughter, he was downstairs and out into the street. He could not resist looking up at the window, and waving a gay hand towards it. Something within him, that seemed the very essence of his being, shouted and sang with glee.

* * * * *

The house in Grosvenor Square, where his mother had become housekeeper and Jessie kitchen-maid, had at present in it only a few wounded officers from France, and during these two or three days in town Archie could still occupy his own bedroom, while his servant slept in the dressing-room adjoining. He was out very late that night, for the completeness of his revenge on Helena ran like a feeding fire through his veins, and both nourished and burned him.

Dawn had already broken when he let himself in, and went very quietly upstairs, not intending to go to bed till he had had an interview with Martin. All night he had felt as if Martin was bursting to come forth again; he was already intensely present, even though Archie had not yet sunk his conscious self and opened the door of mystic communication. That controlling spirit foamed and simmered within him; he could all but break open the door himself, and project himself without invitation. He was still just confined, but only just; it seemed that at any minute he might assert himself. But Archie, with the gourmand instinct that delays an actual fulfilment, teasing itself, while it knows the fulfilment is assured, lingered over his undressing, and planned to make himself cool and comfortable in his pyjamas, before he abandoned the fortress of his normal self. He brushed his teeth, he sponged face and neck with cold water, he arranged his chair in the window, and put on the table by his bed the moonstone stud on which he would focus his eyes, and stretched himself long and luxuriously till he heard his shoulder joints crack. Martin seemed in a great hurry to come to-night, but Martin must just wait till he was ready. And then, all of a sudden, he heard a tremendous noise of rapping. He knew that Martin had come, and an awful terror seized his soul, for Martin had come without being called.

At that precise moment his servant next door started up, wide awake, with some loud sound in his ears that seemed to come from Archie's bedroom. He tapped at his door, but, getting no answer, went in. He found

Archie lying on the floor, curled up together, like some twisted root of a tree, foaming at the mouth. He ran downstairs to get help, and brought up one of the nurses who was on duty. She instantly telephoned for a doctor, and woke Lady Tintagel.

* * * * *

All that day Archie lay in this strange seizure, apparently quite unconscious. Sometimes a paroxysm would take hold of him, and he lay with staring eyes and teeth that ground against each other, and limbs that curled into fantastic shapes. In the intervals he remained still, stiff and rigid, his eyes for the most part shut, breathing quickly, as if he had been running. Then once again the panic and the agony would grip him, and with eyes wide with terror and foaming mouth he struggled and fought against the Thing that mastered him. But each paroxysm left him weaker, and it was clear that he would not be able to stand many more of these attacks. Yet no one could wish them prolonged; it would but be merciful if the end came soon, and spared him further suffering.

Towards sunset that day Jessie was sitting by him, with orders to call the nurse next door if he showed signs of the restlessness which preceded the return of a seizure. She knew that, humanly speaking, he was dying, but her faith never faltered that he might still be saved, and that through her and her love salvation might come to him. Medical science was of no avail; it could not combat the spiritual foe that had taken him prisoner. That rescue had to be made through spiritual means, and the two-edged sword by which alone his captor could be vanquished was the bright-shining weapon of love and prayer. It was in her hand now, as she watched and waited.

He lay quite still, breathing quickly and with a shallow inspiration, but there were no signs of the restlessness for which she had to look out. But presently she observed that his eyes were no longer closed, but were open and looking steadily at the brass knob at the foot of his bed on which a sunbeam, entering through a chink at the side of the drawn window-blind made a focus of light. And, all at once, she guessed that he was looking at this with purpose, and her soul, sword in hand, crouched ready to spring. Then from the bed came Archie's voice.

"Martin," it said.

There was a dead silence, and she saw forming in the air a little in front of him a nucleus of mist. It gathered volume from a little jet as of steam that appeared to come from Archie himself. Thicker and thicker it grew; strange lines began to interlace themselves within it, and these took form. The dimness of its outline grew firm and distinct, the shape stood detached and clear, and, bending over Archie with a smile triumphant and cruel, stood the semblance she had seen once before at midnight in Archie's room. He was no longer looking at the knob at the foot of his bed, but with eyes wide open and blank with some nameless terror he gazed at the apparition.

Jessie rose and stood opposite it on the other side of his bed. Her two-edged sword was drawn now, and its bright blade gleamed in the darkness of the evil that flooded the room. And then it seemed that that incarnation of it that stood beside Archie's bed was aware, for it turned and looked her full in the face, bringing to bear on her the utmost of its hellish potency.

For one moment against that awful assault her soul cried out in panic. It had not dreamed that from all the crimes with which the world had withered and bled there could be distilled a tincture so poisonous. And then her love rallied her scattered courage, and she stood firm again. Nothing in the world but love and prayer could prevail, but nothing, if once she could fully realize that, could prevail against them. In her hand, as in the hand of all who are foes to evil, was the irresistible weapon, could she but use its power to the full…

She stood, as she knew, in the face of the deadliest peril by which any living thing, into which the breath of God has passed, can be confronted. There is no soul so strong that evil can cease to be a menace for it, and here, facing her, was the power that had already perverted all that Archie held of goodness and humanity. There it stood, one victim already its helpless prisoner, and it lusted for more. And the wordless struggle, as old as evil itself, began.

She would not give ground. Her soul laid itself open, and let the light invisible shine on it. In this struggle there were no strivings or wrestlings; she had but to stay quiet, and in just that achievement of quietness the struggle lay. Once for a moment all Hell swirled and exulted round her, for her love for Archie let itself contemplate the human and material aspect of him; the next she put all that away from her, and again stood with his soul, so to speak, in her uplifted hands, offering it to God. In the very storm-centre of this evil which shrieked and raged round her, there must be, and there was, a space where the peace that passeth understanding dwelt in serene calm. The storm might shift and envelope her again in its bellowings, but again and yet again she had to regain the centre where no blast of it could penetrate.

How long this lasted she could not tell. Her body was quite conscious of its ordinary perceptions; the blind tapped on the window, and there came from outside the stir of distant traffic. But she did not take her gaze from those awful eyes that sometimes smiled, sometimes blazed with hate. Steadily and firmly she looked at them and through them, for behind them, as behind the cloud, was the sunlight of God.

And then there came a change. It seemed that the power she fought was weakening. Its eyes shifted; they no longer looked undeviatingly at her, but glanced round for a moment, as if they looked for some way of escape. They would come back to her again with fresh assault of smiles or hate, but each time they seemed less potent. More than once they left her face altogether for a while, and were directed on Archie, as if seeking the refuge there that they knew; but, with a wordless command that they were forced to obey, she summoned them back to her again, making the spirit that directed them turn the strength of its fury on her. She gave it no rest, fixing it on herself by the strength of love and prayer.

The eyes began to grow dim; the outline of the form began to waver. The interlacing lines out of which it was woven began to unravel again, and it grew shapeless. But it was not being absorbed into Archie; there were no streams of mist between him and it, as when it had first taken substance. Already through it she could see the wall behind it, and it grew ever fainter and thinner…

There was nothing left of it now, and for the first time since the struggle began, she looked at Archie. He was lying quite still with eyes closed again. And then she saw that by her side was standing another presence. It was identical in form and shape with that which had vanished, and it bent on Archie so amazing a look of love that her soul, spent and sick with struggle, felt itself uplifted and refreshed again. And for one moment it looked at her, and it was as if Archie himself was looking at her. And then it was there no longer. She hardly knew whether her physical eyes had seen it externally, or whether it had been some spirit-vision conveyed to them from within.

There came a sound from next door, and the nurse, who was there ready to be summoned, entered.

"Has he been quite quiet?" she asked, and, without waiting for an answer, she went to the bed. She looked at Archie a moment, then felt his elbows and knees, finding them pliant again instead of being stiff and rigid, and listened to his quiet breathing.

"But there has come an extraordinary change," she said. "The seizure has passed, and yet he's alive."

She beamed at Jessie.

"Well, you are a good nurse," she said. "But I think I'll just fetch the doctor."

She went out of the room, and Archie, who had lain quite motionless with closed eyes, suddenly stirred and looked at the girl.

"Why, Jessie," he said.

She came close to the bed.

"Yes?"

"What's happened?" said he. "I've had some awful nightmare. And then you broke it up. Hasn't Martin been here too?"

"Yes, Archie, I think so," she said.

He lay in silence a moment.

"Have you saved me again, Jessie?" he said. "You did once before at—at Silorno, when the lightning struck the pine."

She could find no answer for him; not a word could she speak.

He held out his hand to her.

"Jessie!…" he said.